BLOOD BOWL

He should have stuck to fighting dragons…

DUNK HOFFNUNG is stuck in a rut. Being an adventurer is definitely not all it's cracked up to be. The pay is terrible, the conditions harsh and the only people you meet are generally monsters who are more interested in eating your flesh than sitting down and shooting the breeze…

When talent scout Slick Fullbelly spots Dunk bringing down a chimera with a spear from a hundred paces, he's sure that his search is over. Slick works for the Bad Bay Hackers, and they need a new thrower. Dunk is about to be plunged headfirst into the insane world of Blood Bowl, the fastest, meanest sport in this dark and brutal world. Dunk puts down his sword and steps off the battlefield… onto the football field.

More fantasy from the Black Library

BLOOD BOWL

Matt Forbeck

For my mother Helen Forbeck and for my father Ken Forbeck and his wife Nancy. For teaching me a sense of humour, a love of sports, and a respect for words.

Special thanks to Marc Gascoigne, Jervis Johnson, Lindsey D Le Doux Paton Priestley, and Christian Dunn. And to everyone from the Games Workshop Design Studio, winter of 1989–90. It's good to be back.

A BLACK LIBRARY PUBLICATION

First published in Great Britain in 2005 by
BL Publishing,
Games Workshop Ltd.,
Willow Road, Nottingham,
NG7 2WS, UK.

10 9 8 7 6 5 4 3 2 1

Cover illustration by Max Bertolini.

A CIP record for this book is available from the British Library.

ISBN 13: 978 184416 200 0
ISBN 10: 1 84416 200 1

Distributed in the US by Simon & Schuster
1230 Avenue of the Americas, New York, NY 10020, US.

Printed and bound in Great Britain by
Bookmarque, Surrey, UK.

See the Black Library on the Internet at
www.blacklibrary.com

Find out more about the world of Blood Bowl at
www.specialist-games.com/bloodbowl

'Hi there, sports fans, and welcome to the Blood Bowl for tonight's contest. You join us here with a capacity crowd, packed with members of every race from across the known world, all howling like banshees in anticipation of tonight's game. Oh, and yes there are some banshees... Well, kick-off is in about two pages' time, so we've just got time to go over to your commentator for tonight, Jim Johnson, for a recap on the rules of the game before battle commences. Good evening, Jim!'

'Thank you, Bob! Well, good evening and boy, are you folks in for some great sporting entertainment. First of all though, for those of you at home who are unfamiliar with the rules, here's how the game is played.

'Blood Bowl is an epic conflict between two teams of heavily armed and quite insane warriors. Players pass, throw and run with the ball, attempting to get it to the other end of the field, the end zone. Of course, the other team must try and stop them, and recover the ball for their side. If a team gets the ball over the line into the opponents' end zone it's called a touchdown; the team that scores the most touchdowns by the end of the match wins the game. Of course, it's not always as simple as that...

CHAPTER ONE

DUNK HOFFNUNG HATED his life, or what little he thought might be left of it. He hadn't always felt this way. In his youth, in Altdorf, he'd led the kind of sheltered life that only wealth and privilege could provide. As the eldest heir to the massive Hoffnung fortune, he'd lived far above the squalor of the ghettoes of his hometown. Back then, he'd been mostly and happily ignorant of the kind of existence the vast bulk of the population scratched out in the shadow of his family's towering keep.

Then everything had gone wrong.

'No one ever made a fortune without making a few enemies,' Dunk's father, Lügner, liked to say. He'd repeated it often enough that Dunk felt comfortable ignoring it. After all, he'd reached twenty-three years of age without ever having tripped over that particular dictum. Then it reached out and bloodied his nose.

So, scant months after his family's fall from grace, Dunk found himself clambering up the side of the forsaken pile of rubble called Mount Schimäre, bent on doing something to redeem his name and, by some extension on which he wasn't quite clear, that of his family.

Here in the Grey Mountains, right on the edge of the Empire and more than a hundred miles from his old life, the sky looked different, colder somehow, more distant. It was still all part of the same world though. Perhaps it was he that had changed.

Dunk was still tall, graceful and strong; the benefits of the best trainers in the arts of war and athletics that his family's gold crowns could buy. His hair was jet black, and he'd had to have it cropped short to keep it from snarling and falling into his eyes. He'd lost his fine silver combs along with everything else when his family had been run out of their home. His eyes were still the penetrating silver of a bright, full moon. They saw the same things as before, but the man behind them had changed.

Dunk's boot slipped on the gravel of the trail up to the creature's lair, snapping him out of his thoughts. Self-pity would do him no good here. No matter how much he might think he deserved death, he was determined to make the dragon at least work for it.

The people of Dörfchen had warned him against taking this path. 'Fear not, good people,' he'd told them. 'By tonight, you will no longer shiver in the shadows of the foul beast that has terrorised your hamlet for so long.'

They'd just laughed and sent him on his way. At the town's only public house, the Crooked Arrow, they'd been happy to tip a pint or three in his direction for his efforts. Old Gastwirt, the innkeeper, had even stood Dunk the price of a bottle of brandy as a sign of support. 'You can pay me for it when you return,' he'd said.

The inn's common room had fallen uncomfortably silent at those words. Gastwirt's own laugh had caught in his throat, but he'd still managed to hand Dunk the earthenware bottle with the red wax seal still intact over the cork.

Dunk had made good use of the bottle on the road to the dragon's cave. The spirits tasted like they'd been fermented in casks tainted with warpstone, the shards of coagulated Chaos that spawned the mutants that were rumoured to teem beneath the streets of the Empire's cities. Even the smell of the stuff made his head swim, but Dunk needed something to stoke the guttering fires of his courage. In that respect, the foul liquid served all too well.

Dunk hadn't realised how much he'd had to drink until the trail into the mountains had become so bad that he'd had to dismount from Pferd, his faithful stallion, a fine beast with a coat and mane as black as Dunk's hair and a cantankerous attitude to match. Only two steps out of his stirrups, the hopeful hero found the earth tilting under his feet, sending him tumbling back down the slope until he lodged in a gnarled buckthorn bush that brought him sharply to his senses.

Now, here, only steps away from the steaming mouth of the dragon's cave, Dunk's head started swimming again. His heart hammered so hard that he was amazed that it didn't knock against the inside of his armour's shimmering breastplate, announcing his presence to the creature within. His hand went to the hilt of his sword, and the earthenware bottle clanked against it, causing him to jump.

Dunk looked down at his hand as if the bottle had suddenly grown out of it. Then he pulled the cork from it again with his teeth and took one last belt for good measure. As he did, he wondered if the beast he sought could spit gouts of fire from its gullet. At that moment, Dunk felt maybe he could match that feat.

Dunk pressed the cork back into the bottle and put it down at his feet. If he survived the day, he promised himself to finish it in the victory celebration the grateful people of Dörfchen would no doubt throw for him. Otherwise, he hoped the next worthy hero who happened along might use it to toast his memory.

Finally faced with the objective of his quest, the lair of the beast whose blood he hoped to spill and thereby wash clean his sins, Dunk drew his sword and opened his mouth to speak. Though before a sound escaped his lips, he stopped cold.

Try as he might, Dunk could not think of what to do. The honourable thing, from the heroic stories on which he'd been weaned, would be to announce his presence and call the dread beast forth to impale itself on his blade. That had been what he'd intended to do once he first heard of this damnable creature, but in the clarity of the moment – such clarity as he could find with his head swimming as it was – that seemed like nothing less than sheer folly.

'Perhaps I should poke around a bit first,' Dunk said to himself, louder than he'd intended. When no winged fury came screaming out of the cave to answer his slip, he nodded to himself and crept forward as quietly as he could.

Dunk's armour clinked and clanked so much as he moved that he felt he might as well be wearing a set of cymbals, to announce him like a visitor to a foreign court. The old stories he had once been so fond of, no matter how foolish they seemed now as he peered into the darkening cave, told of the deep slumbers in which dragons waited between snacking on their yearly virgins, and he fervently hoped that at least this part of the tales might be true.

As Dunk shuffled further into the cave, he realised that he had forgotten to bring something with him to light his way. He had some torches back in his saddlebags, but those were with Pferd.

Dunk gazed behind him to the west and saw the sun dipping toward the canopy of the wide forest beyond. He knew that if he went back for a torch it would be pitch black before he could return to the cave. While the thought of putting off his destiny for another day appealed to him, he couldn't bear the thought of returning to the Crooked Arrow to spend the night. He feared that the tales the townspeople would surely repeat about the dragon would force his will from him for good and send him off to another part of the Empire in search of easier means of penance.

Instead, Dunk sheathed his sword, trotted back to the earthenware bottle, and snatched it up. Then he removed the red silk scarf he'd worn around his neck every day since young Lady Helgreta Brecher had given it to him nearly a year ago. At the time, he'd treasured the gift from his betrothed as his most valued possession. Now, his arranged marriage was nothing more than a bittersweet memory and the scarf was little more than a reminder of how far he'd fallen. It was only fitting then, that it help light the path to his redemption.

Dunk uncorked the bottle and stuffed the end of the scarf into it with the barest tinge of regret. The contrast between the finery of the scarf and the crudity of its new home struck him as appropriate, although he couldn't say how. Then he pulled his tinderbox from his pocket and struck a fire on the scarf's free end.

Carrying the makeshift light high in his left hand, Dunk drew his sword again with his right. As he entered the cave, the light from his bottle-lamp showed that the interior cavern was much larger than its mouth implied. It seemed to go back and down forever, disappearing into blackness beyond his light's reach.

The wind whistling past him like something alive, Dunk moved further into the cave. When he realised he couldn't see the walls to either side of him, he started to panic. He clink-clanked as quietly as he could over to his right until he reached the comfort of the wall there, then walked along again, hugging it close.

As Dunk crept further into the cave, the sound of the wind breathing through the cave's mouth fell behind him. He found the silence strangely comforting, although the nothingness it implied put him on edge. Where was the pile of gold and gems on which the great beast had made its bed? Or maybe that part of the stories was wrong too. But where was the beast itself?

Perhaps the dragon was out hunting, terrorizing another village elsewhere in the mountains. Could it be plotting evil ends with some fiend of Chaos in the Forest of Shadows that lay on the other side of these rough, high peaks?

It was then that Dunk tripped over the pile of bones.

He'd thought the first of them was some kind of rippling formation in the rocks, possibly formed by the heat of the dragon's fiery breath over the centuries. He'd stepped right on them, and they rolled beneath his feet like the smoothed logs on which the young Dunk once watched dwarf labourers draw battered ships out of the River Reik and into Altdorf's legendary dry-docks. He spilled forward and found himself unable to control his fall, rolling along on more and more of the brownish, flesh-stripped things until he came to a clattering halt in a heap of skeletal remains in which he could have buried a mountain bear.

Dunk thrashed about in the mound of bones for a moment, crunching them under his armoured bulk. It flashed through his head that the bones were alive, grabbing at him, trying to pull him down to share their communal grave. When he finally stopped smashing them down though, he realised the only threat they posed to him was that he might stab himself on one of the broken ends he'd created.

Throughout the fall, Dunk had managed to keep aloft his left arm and hold on to his makeshift torch. He'd dropped his blade somewhere in the process, but was pleased that he had held on to the bottle-lamp so well. He could use that to find the sword, but if he'd kept the sword instead of the light he might never have been able to find his way out of the cave.

Dunk cursed his luck as he scrambled to his feet, shards of bone falling from his armour.

'Only I could find the lair of a missing dragon,' he said. As the words left his lips, relief washed over him. He'd done his duty, faced up to his fears, and everything had come out all right. He was still alive.

Dunk wasn't sure just how he felt about that. He'd been robbed of a chance to earn fortune and glory, after all, but the thought that he'd traded that for a reprieve from all-but-certain death tempered his regret.

He brought the light closer to the bones. There had to be dozens of skeletons here, representing most of the peoples of the Old World. Many of them clearly had once belonged to humans. Others displayed the short, stout frame of dwarfs, and a few more were even smaller, either those of halflings or – the thought made Dunk shudder – children. One set of long, thin bones convinced him that the dragon must have once made a rare snack of a wood elf too. He pulled his sword from beneath its delicate ribcage.

Something grated on Dunk's nerves, and for a while he blamed it on the bones arrayed around him. He imagined the voices of all these doomed souls crying out to him for vengeance, and he grimaced at the thought that he had no idea where to find their killer.

The silence of the cave finally grabbed Dunk's attention. The noise from the wind had stopped.

Unnerved, Dunk stepped from the rattling pile of bones and made his way back towards the exit. As he drew closer, he grew concerned. The day's dying light that had streamed in through the cave's mouth wasn't where he thought it should be. Had his sense of direction become confused by his spill? He considered going back and trying to retrace his steps again when he saw the darkness shift before him.

Dunk's breath caught in his chest. He realised that one problem with wandering through a dark cave with a light was that creatures could see you long before you could see them.

The hissing noise that stabbed from the darkened region between Dunk and the exit nearly made him leap from his armour. The serpentine head that followed it, striking into the glow of his bottle-lamp's light, shocked him in a different way. The head was long and thin, mounted on a snakelike neck, but he had expected something much larger. He almost giggled in relief.

Before he could finish his thought, an angry bleat filled the cave. A goat? In here? Had the dragon been out hunting and brought back the poor beast for its evening's repast? Dunk saw the outline of the billy goat's horns stretching out on the edge of the darkness. It wasn't a fair damsel, he knew, but he could still hope to save it from joining the other bones in the back of the cave. Here, at last, was a chance for him to do someone – or rather something – some good.

Dunk's hopes for gratitude vanished like an arrow fired into the night when a deep growl reverberated throughout the cave. He snapped his head about, searching for the source of this new threat. Then the face of a lion poked into the light next to the serpent's head, on the other side from the goat.

The configuration of faces confused Dunk, and he stood stock still, staring at them as though they were a living puzzle that would somehow solve itself. And then it did.

The creature moved forward towards the would-be hero, into the makeshift lamp's light as it guttered in the face of its three breathing heads. Its leonine front paws scraped at the cave's rocky floor, as if it were sharpening the wicked claws before launching an attack. It unfurled its greasy, bat-like wings, which were wide enough to fill the cavern, brushing them against the opposing walls. Its tail, like something that should have been attached to a gargantuan scorpion, curled forward between the wings, small flashes on the tip convincing Dunk that even this appendage had eyes. As its three heads, and its tail, glared at the intrepid fool who had dared invade its home, the chimera clopped and scraped its hoofed hindquarters like a bull preparing to charge.

CHAPTER TWO

DUNK EDGED BACKWARDS as the creature came towards him, but it matched him step for step. As he moved, he spoke. 'I'm terribly sorry,' he said to the creature, hoping it might somehow be able to understand him. 'I was looking for a dragon.'

The goat-head snorted.

'You come from Dörfchen,' the snake-head hissed. It spoke the Reikspiel tongue of the Empire flawlessly, although with an oddly familiar accent that Dunk identified as hailing from distant Kislev.

The lion-head uttered a curious growl. 'You're ear-rrrly,' it said.

Dunk could have sworn the lion-head smiled. 'You… you were expecting me?' he stammered. He hefted his sword, testing its weight, just as he had before every sparring match against his trainers back in Altdorf. He'd never been in a real, to-the-death

17

fight and he hoped they'd taught him well. This time there would be no mercy, he was sure, only blood.

'Our last sssacrifissse was not ssso long ago,' said the snake-head.

'It's a booonus,' the goat-head said. 'Our reputation grooows.'

'Yessss,' the snake-head said. 'It drawsss usss fressssh victimsss.'

'Frrresh meat!' the lion-head said.

'Ah,' Dunk said. He had wondered why the villagers had been so eager to point out the location of this 'dragon's' lair to him. Old Gastwirt had even offered to draw him a map. Now it was clear. They depended on foolhardy heroes like himself to find their way up here regularly to make their regular 'sacrifices' to their local menace. In return, the creature left the hamlet alone. No wonder they'd been so friendly and free with such a total stranger.

'I'm afraid there's been a mistake,' Dunk said as his heart sunk into his boots. 'I wasn't sent up here as your next meal.'

'Explaaain!' the goat-head said. The lion-head snapped its jaws to punctuate the demand.

Dunk swallowed hard. 'The kind and dedicated people of Dörfchen,' he said, 'fear that you might be… tiring of your standard fare. They sent me up here to take your order for your upcoming repast.'

The three heads looked at each other, mystified.

Dunk continued, amazed that he could still speak and stunned at the words escaping his lips. 'Would you prefer a virgin of some sort? Or perhaps a nice little goblin? I'm told we might even be able to procure a few snotlings, or perhaps a little gnoblar to chew on?'

Three sets of eyes narrowed at Dunk. As the light from his bottle-lamp began to die, he noticed that all six orbs glowed green with the crazed light of Chaos.

'Of… of course, you can just stick with your standards.'

The lion licked its muzzle with a black, forked tongue.

'I really do recommend the snotling though,' Dunk said softly. 'It's much tastier than the hu-human.' His voice trailed off as he finished.

'Posssssibly,' the serpent-head said as it weaved hypnotically back and forth, like a snake trying to turn the tables on an unwary charmer.

'But you'rrre herrre,' the lion-head growled.

'Nooow,' the goat-head bleated. With that, the great beast slouched forward.

As the lion-head leaped out towards Dunk, he slashed at it with his blade. The never-bloodied edge cut through the creature's mane and trailed a splatter of blood in its wake. The lion-head yowled in pain and surprise, and the goat squealed in protest.

Emboldened by his success, Dunk brought his sword back for another swing. As he bought the blade forward, though, the snake-head darted out and struck the weapon from his hand. It sailed off behind him, and he heard it land clattering in the pile of what little was left of the chimera's past victims. Dunk gawked for a moment at his empty hand, sure that his bones would soon join the others.

The trio of heads loosed terrifying laughs. The cacophony startled Dunk into action. He gripped hold of the only thing he had left, the barely burning bottle-lamp, and hurled it at the creature with all his might.

The earthenware bottle smashed into the creature right where its three heads met. Its noxious contents splashed across the chimera's chest and necks, and burst into flames. The blaze blossomed against the chimera, and the three heads screamed in an unholy choir of fury and fear.

Dunk glanced back over his shoulder to where his sword had gone spinning away, but the back of the cave was shrouded in utter darkness. He'd have a better chance of finding a wishbone than his blade in that mess. Turning back towards the chimera, which was trying to beat out the flames engulfing each of the heads by banging them against each other, he realised there was only one way out of the cave: past that burning beast.

With a strength fortified by desperation, Dunk lowered his shoulder and charged directly at the monster. 'Keep low and move *through* your foe,' he heard Lehrer say, the old trainer's voice echoing in his head. 'The low man has control.'

Only this wasn't a man that Dunk faced but a beast three times his size. Still, he hoped, the same principle should apply.

The fire had blinded the chimera, and it was turning away towards the cave's entrance when Dunk barrelled into it. He caught it directly below one of its wings and knocked it sprawling into one of the cavern walls. Without stopping, he spun away from the creature, flinging himself around the beast and past it toward the twilight sky beyond.

Dunk was giddy with glee as he sprinted for the exit. If this experience had proved one thing to him, it was that he wasn't ready to die quite yet, especially if it meant becoming a twisted abomination's next meal.

As Dunk reached for freedom, though, something hard and sharp slammed into his back, its meaty tip stabbing through his armour and into the flesh beneath. Lights flashing before his eyes, Dunk tumbled forward, out of the cave, letting the force of the blow push him further from his foe.

When he finally came to a stop, Dunk scrambled to his feet and whipped about, fearful that the winged beast would come roaring out of the cave after him. From the trio of screams emanating from the flickering lights still flashing from the cavern mouth, he guessed that the beast was too busy saving its own life at the moment to finish taking his.

Dunk's left arm was numb from the shoulder down and hung limp in its socket like a piece of meat. For a moment, he feared the blow might have severed the limb, but he checked with his good hand, and it was still there. He was wondering what was wrong with it when the numbness started to fade, only to be replaced with the excruciating sensation of a thousand fire ants biting into his wounded arm. His stomach flipped about like a dying fish pulled from its cool river home and slapped down on the cruel wood of a sun-warmed dock. He bent over and retched.

Wiping the remnants of his last meal from his mouth and soaked in the stench of the Dörfchen liquor that had tasted like embalming fluid as it erupted from his gullet, Dunk realised what had been done to him. Angry and nearly blind, the chimera had lashed out at him with its two-eyed tail and stung him with its venomous barb. He had escaped its lair, but it seemed that he could not outrun the effects of its wrath.

'Never let it be said that I didn't flee with the best of them,' Dunk said to himself as he stumbled down the mountainside, wondering how he was going to be able to find his black horse as the last rays of daylight raced from the sky.

WHEN DUNK CAME TO, he found himself lying over the saddle of his horse, which was standing outside the Crooked Arrow. The night was fully dark now, although a light burned inside the place, visible through the cracks in the thick, but poorly fitted shutters that covered a window in the upper floor of the grey-plastered building.

Dunk slid from the back of Pferd and shook his head to clear the sheets of cobwebs that he felt had accumulated there. The brisk night air bit into his face and whistled through the hole in the back of his armour, poking him awake. He tested his arm and found that although it still hurt he could move it once again. The fire ants had apparently fled for a more hospitable home, one that didn't have a chimera angry at it.

Dunk tripped forward and steadied himself against the inn's scarred oaken door. It was quiet inside and dark but for the light above. It must have been late, the regulars had long since gone to bed. He knocked on the door and waited, listening.

In the room above, he heard a pair of voices, a man and a woman, arguing in hushed tones. Then the light went out.

Dunk knocked on the door again, louder this time. Only the crickets in the distance answered. He looked up and down the wide, unpaved road. The few other shops and houses that lined what could only charitably be called the centre of the hamlet were all dark too. The people who resided within them, resting easily in the shadow of the monster-infested mountain, another 'sacrifice' – Dunk, in this case – having recently been sent off to placate the neighbouring beast.

This time, Dunk banged on the door with all his might, his mailed fists making dents in the already battered, ironbound planks. 'Open up!' he shouted at the top of his lungs. 'Open up, *now*!'

He'd been trying to help these ungrateful bastards, and they'd as good as sent him to a certain death. Somebody was going to pay.

'Go away!' a voice rasped down from above. Dunk looked up to see Gastwirt leaning out through the now-open shutters, his long hair like strings of greasy white cotton and his flimsy nightshirt, which barely covered his massive gut, fluttering in the breeze. 'We're closed for the night!'

'You'll open up for me, damn you!' Dunk shouted up at the innkeeper, shaking his fist at the bewildered old man. 'After what I've been through, I've earned the right to a warm bed tonight.'

Gastwirt squinted down at Dunk and then ducked back inside for a moment. When he reappeared, he held a lantern high in one arm, and he peered down again to see who might be so bold as to make such demands. 'You!' the innkeeper said, recoiling in horror as he recognised Dunk's face. 'You're supposed to be dead!'

'And you're supposed to be an innkeeper!' Dunk shouted back at Gastwirt. 'Let me in, and give me a bed. I'm hurt!' He rubbed his shoulder as he said this, wondering just how bad it was.

Gastwirt peered down at Dunk, suspicion etched on his doughy face. 'How do I know you're not a ghost come back for your revenge on our fair town?' he asked. 'No one else has ever returned from the creature's cave alive.'

Dunk pulled off his right gauntlet and flung it at the innkeeper. The metal glove smacked Gastwirt right in his bulbous nose and then dropped back down to the ground where Dunk retrieved it.

'Could a ghost do that?' Dunk asked as the innkeeper howled in protest.

At that moment, the front door creaked open. Dunk stared into the darkness beyond, ready for a guard of some sort to spring from the shadows. He looked down and saw the small figure standing there framed in the doorway, barefooted, dressed in a grimy, once-white nightshirt and holding a small oil lamp.

For an instant, Dunk thought that the newcomer was a child with dark and curly hair, perhaps a son or grandson of Gastwirt's, who'd been roused by the arguing. Then he noticed the traces of stubble on the little person's chin and the wrinkles around his wide smile and dancing grey eyes.

'Now, son, I ask you, is that any way to make a reasonable request of your host?' the halfling said.

'Morr's icy breath!' the innkeeper cursed above. 'What are you–' He leaned further out the window until he could see the halfling waving up at him from the inn's threshold.

'Shut that door!' Gastwirt shouted before he disappeared back into the his bedchamber, slamming the shutters closed behind him as he went.

The halfling held out a hand of greeting towards Dunk and waved for him to come inside. 'I'd hurry yourself in here quickly, son, before that walrus makes his way down those stairs. He'll double bar the door for sure.'

Dunk reached back and wound Pferd's reins around the hitching post outside the inn, then slipped in past the halfling while nodding his thanks.

'I'm glad someone around here understands hospitality,' he said. He stuck out his hand at the halfling. 'I'm Dunk.'

'Slogo Fullbelly,' the halfling said, his hand almost disappearing within Dunk's much larger mitt.

'Slick, you stinking bastard!' Gastwirt howled as he slipped down the last few stairs and fell onto his rump in the back of the room.

'Slick, to my friends,' the Halfling said in a confidential tone.

The innkeeper leaped to his feet far quicker than Dunk would have guessed the man's bulk could allow. 'You've no friends here, you sawed-off con artist,' Gastwirt said, shaking a finger at Slick.

Dunk stepped between the innkeeper and the halfling before Gastwirt could wrap his thick paws around the little one. 'He did me a good turn when you refused,' he said to the innkeeper.

Gastwirt looked up at Dunk, just a hint of green haloing his face. 'I don't open the door for anyone I don't know after dark,' he said. 'Not when I've sent everyone else home.'

Dunk stepped closer and glared down into the shorter man's watery blue eyes. 'I met you earlier today.'

'And sallied off to certain death, just like all the others, sure that providence and your own sheer arrogance would let you rule the day, to kill–' The innkeeper cut himself short. 'By the gods' grace and mercy,' he said in awe, 'did you actually *kill* the beast?'

Dunk grimaced, suddenly aware of how much his shoulder still hurt. 'I made it back alive, but not unscathed.'

'Ooh,' Slick said from behind Dunk. The would-be hero turned and saw Slick standing on a nearby table, peering at his back. 'That's a mighty nasty-looking hole you have in your armour there, son,' he said.

'It's nothing...' Dunk started to say, but he couldn't bring himself to finish. 'It hurts like blazes,' he conceded.

'Allow me,' Slick said, reaching up to unfasten the buckles that held Dunk's breastplate and backplate in place.

'You can't do that here!' Gastwirt complained. 'I can't have wounded strangers stumbling into my place in the middle of the night.'

Dunk growled at the man, then reached over and snatched a long, sharp spear from where it hung over the massive mantel in the room. He shoved its wicked, barbed tip towards the innkeeper and growled again, the pain from his sudden movements tainting his wordless threat with a dose of desperation.

'I think, kind sir,' Slick said to the innkeeper gravely, 'that you'd better make friends with this man quickly if you don't wish to find yourself thrown out of your own establishment.'

Gastwirt looked up into Dunk's pained eyes. The warrior could see the thoughts whirring through the man's brain as he weighed the risks of the various avenues of action open to him. Then the innkeeper's shoulders sagged in resignation.

'All right,' said Gastwirt as he padded towards the open door and shoved it shut, then dropped two bars of solid, ironbound oak behind it. 'Let's be quick about this.' The innkeeper returned, firing up a lantern that hung from the ceiling in the centre of the room.

'Sit down, son,' Slick said to Dunk, 'and I'll have a look at that trouble of yours.'

Dunk slumped in the chair nearest the table on which the halfling still stood. He yanked his breastplate and chestplate off with one hand, but when it came to slipping out of the mail shirt, he found it hurt too much. With a wave from Slick, Gastwirt ambled over and helped the halfling pull the damaged, bloodied armour off, as well as the undershirt beneath it.

The innkeeper gasped in horror at the sight of the puncture wound in Dunk's back. Slick just clucked his tongue and ordered Gastwirt to hustle off to the kitchen and bring back a bucket of water and some clean rags. 'It's not as bad as it looks,' Slick told Dunk. 'I've seen far worse.'

'Are you a physician?'

The halfling chuckled. 'Hardly, son. I'm a Blood Bowl player's agent.'

Dunk turned and gave Slick an appraising look. 'For which team?' he asked.

'I work for my player,' Slick said. 'Negotiate his contracts, defend his honour, get him as much time on the pitch as I can, for the most pay. Some agents handle a handful of different players all at once, but I prefer to concentrate on one star player at a time. That kind of dedication to personal service makes all the difference.'

'Who's your player?'

Slick looked over to where the dying embers still glowed soft and red in the inn's fireplace. 'I've had a lot of them over the years.'

'Who is it now?'

Gastwirt burst back into the room right then, half a bucket of sloshing water in one hand and a fistful of grey, threadbare rags in the other. He set the things down on the table next to Slick, who took one of the rags and dipped it into the bucket.

As the halfling gently rubbed the wet rag around the area of Dunk's wound, cleaning the blood away, he said, 'Let's just say I'm between clients at the moment. Blood Bowl is a dangerous game.'

'I've never seen a match.' Dunk suspected that Slick was talking so much just to distract him from how much the rag stung. Either way, he was willing to go along with it.

'Really?' Gastwirt said in excited disbelief. 'If I'd lived in a big city, I'd go to the matches every week.'

'I've never much seen the point of it,' Dunk said, gritting his teeth as Slick rubbed more water into the wound. 'A bunch of grown people – or dwarfs, or elves, or orcs, or ogres or worse – chasing a football around a field? Why bother?'

'Because,' Slick said as he dried Dunk's shoulder and wrapped it with another rag, 'it pays better than thievery.' As he finished up, he patted Dunk on the shoulder and handed him back his bloodstained undershirt. 'Besides, people who go off looking to pick fights with dragons shouldn't speak ill of the career choices of others.'

'I'll take that under consideration,' Dunk said.

'You're a lucky man,' Slick said as he slid down off the table and picked up his candle from where he'd left it. 'The poison of a sting like that can be fatal.'

As the words left Slick's mouth, Dunk's head started to spin again. 'I just wish I was dead.'

'Let's get this boy a bed,' Slick said to Gastwirt.

'Right away,' the innkeeper nodded. He led Dunk to a door in the back corner of the common room. It opened onto a private quarters little larger than one of the closets in the family keep in which Dunk had grown up. A bed of straw lay scattered in the far corner. The young warrior stumbled over to it and lay down his head. He was asleep before the innkeeper shut the door.

CHAPTER THREE

DUNK AWOKE AT dawn to what sounded like a gang of angry giants tearing the roof off of the building. Still shirtless, he leapt to his feet and cast about for his sword for a moment before he remembered that he'd left it in the chimera's cave. A banging at the door brought his attention slamming back from last night to the present.

'Hey, hero!' Gastwirt said through the thin planks of the door. 'If you want to make a name for yourself, now's the time!'

As Dunk shoved on his boots and tossed on a shirt, the innkeeper threw open the door. 'No time for modesty,' Gastwirt scowled. 'Your Chaos-damned doom followed you here, and if you don't go out to meet it, it'll tear the town apart trying to find you.'

For a moment, Dunk didn't understand the man's words, but then a roaring, hissing, bleating yowl rattled the ramshackle shutters strung across the cramped room's lopsided window. The young man's eyes felt like they might spring from his head as he stared out of the window and then back at the white-faced innkeeper.

'The chimera is here?' Dunk asked, the thought gluing his feet to the rough worn floor.

'Got it in one,' Gastwirt said with a pitiless smirk. 'And it wants your head.'

'How do you know that?' the shocked Dunk asked.

The strange choir of angry voices outside changed from howls to shouts, and Dunk could make out its chorus. 'The hero!' it said. 'Bring us his head!'

Dunk glanced around him. No blade, not even a knife. He thought of running, but he knew he'd never outpace the winged beast. Pferd might be able to outrun the creature, but the last Dunk had seen of his horse it had been hitched out in front of the inn, in the open, a ripe target on which a mad monster could unleash its wrath.

The innkeeper was right. He was doomed.

Gastwirt reached out and grabbed Dunk by the shoulder, his injured one, which felt like a lance rammed through the warrior's arm. He cried out in protest and shrugged free, but the innkeeper just grabbed his other arm instead.

'Your hand put this wheel in motion,' Gastwirt snarled at Dunk. 'You placed your bet, and now it's time to pay up.'

Slick stepped in from the hallway and slipped in between the two men. 'You can't send him out there,' the halfling said. 'That beast will rip him apart.'

The innkeeper's hand let go as Dunk wrested his other arm away. Gastwirt leaned down to shout into Slick's face. 'This bastard you've befriended went out last night and enraged that carnivorous creature. If we don't give it what it wants, it'll kill us all!'

Slick nodded as he considered this for a moment. Then he turned back to Dunk and said, 'He's got a point, son. Sorry about all this, but you'd better go.'

'What?' Dunk said. As he spoke, something heavy crashed onto the inn's roof, and dust and clods of dirt cascaded down from the ceiling. 'I'm not going out to face that thing.'

Dunk turned to Gastwirt. 'You and your friends sent me off to die. You can all rot!'

Slick patted Dunk on the back of his leg. 'Come now, son, there's no reason for us *all* to die, right?' His tone sounded as if he were trying to convince Dunk to take a walk with him in the rain. 'There's no way for you to get away from that beast, so you might as well go face up to it like a man. Think of the children.'

'What children?' Dunk asked, goggling at the halfling.

Slick shrugged. 'It's a town. There have to be children here, right?' He looked to Gastwirt for some help.

'Loads of children,' the innkeeper said. 'Normally you can't walk around here without tripping over them. They're orphans, too, the whole lot of them. A pitiful bunch to be sure.'

Dunk snarled at the blatant lies. Still, he thought, there did have to be some innocents in this town, and he couldn't be the cause of their deaths.

'Fine,' he said. 'I'll go. Wish me luck, you cowards.'

Slick clapped Dunk on the back of his thigh and favoured him with a rueful smile. 'A man like you has no need for luck, son. Just go out there and face your fate.'

The chimera cried out for Dunk again. Shaking his head, the young warrior shoved past the halfling and pushed the innkeeper out of his way. He wasn't doing anyone any good stuck in this room, least of all Pferd.

As Dunk stormed into the inn's empty common room, he heard the innkeeper behind him quietly say, 'Ten crowns says that beast eats him for breakfast.'

'You, sir,' Slick said, 'have yourself a bet.'

Dunk didn't know why the halfling would be willing to wager on him. He would have bet against himself if there had been any way to collect. Still, the thought that someone – anyone – had any kind of confidence in him encouraged him.

When the building's shutters rattled again with the chimera's roar and the beating of its wings, Dunk knew, however, that confidence wouldn't get him far. 'Can you at least loan me a blade?' he called back at the innkeeper. He turned to see Gastwirt and Slick had followed him from the room, perhaps eager for the show soon to come.

The innkeeper, mindful of his bet, Dunk suspected, just shook his head. Slick, on the other hand, disappeared behind the bar that ran along the room's north wall. A moment later, something long and sharp came flying over the bar to stab into the floor near Dunk's feet.

'Every barman has one,' the halfling said as he rematerialised from behind the bar.

Dunk pulled the weapon from the floor and examined it. The sword was short, about half the length of his own blade, and it looked as if it had been used more often as a kitchen utensil than a weapon. Still, it beat using his bare hands. He hefted the thing in his hand and headed for the door.

Pferd stood there in the early morning light, straight, tall, and unperturbed. The black horse's reins remained wrapped around the hitching post. He whinnied a short greeting to Dunk but showed no signs of fear, as if the creature still whirling somewhere overhead was little more than a sparrow with a poor attitude.

Dunk remembered how he had chosen Pferd for his own. One night, a fire had broken out in his family's stables. Trapped, some of the horses had panicked and run deeper into the flames. They had all perished, but Pferd had stood his ground until the guards rescued him. He alone had survived.

'That's the horse I want, father,' the young Dunk had said the next day. 'That's a beast you can count on.' He had not once regretted making the request.

Scanning the skies above as he left the shelter of the inn, Dunk slashed out with his borrowed blade to cut loose Pferd's reins. The blade bounced off the hitching post, leaving the leather leads intact, the weapon's edge too dull to split them.

Dunk cursed as he reached out and loosed Pferd's reins with his other hand. 'Where is that thing, boy?' he asked. The horse didn't respond.

As he moved past Pferd and into the open street, Dunk used the sword to shade his eyes as he searched for the chimera among the low, dark clouds scattered by the stiff breeze that swept down from the mountains that day. He saw nothing up there, not even a lone bird. Dunk allowed himself a moment of hope that the creature had tired of hunting for him here and had flown off for other parts, but he quickly quashed it. Hope made a man lose focus, he knew, and that could be fatal.

'You'll need this, son!' Slick shouted from the doorway of the inn.

Dunk glared over at the halfling to see him wrestling with the sharp end of the massive spear that had hung over the mantel in the inn's common room, dragging the bulk of its length behind him. 'Get back in there,' Dunk ordered Slick as he dashed over and snatched the spear from him. 'That thing could snap you up without stopping to chew.'

'You're welcome!' Slick said, the sly grin never leaving his face. 'I hope you're better with a spear than you are at expressing your gratitude.'

Dunk started to come up with a snappy reply, but a loud noise from down the street saved him from having to make the effort. He whipped his head around to see the chimera pulling a holy icon from the steeple of the local temple. A man in red, priestly robes dashed out of the place, a gaggle of worshippers hot on his heels, all screeching louder than even the chimera above them. The heavy, stone icon crashed to the ground behind them as they raced up the street.

'You!' the priest said, pointing a thick finger at Dunk. The man's corpulent face was red with the exertion of having managed to dash from the church before all of his followers, despite the fact he'd been standing at the altar in front of them. His round blue eyes glared at Dunk from under bushy, white eyebrows. 'This is all your fault!'

'Sod off!' Dunk spat. He'd had enough of priests for a lifetime. He gave the gods their due, of course, but he had little time for the parasites who fed off the reputations of their chosen deities by purporting to bring their messages to the masses.

The priest's face flushed even redder, and Dunk thought, perhaps even hoped, that the man might keel over right there with a stopped heart. Instead, the priest waved his terrified congregation after him, saying, 'That's who the beast wants, dead or alive! Let's give him to it!'

As the priest charged at Dunk, the young warrior swung around the dull end of the spear and caught the holy man squarely in the chin. The priest collapsed in his robes like an item of laundry falling from a washing line. The others behind their religious leader froze in their tracks.

Dunk brought the sharp end of the spear around to bear on the handful of temple-goers staring at him. He didn't want to hurt them, but he feared they didn't share the same concern for him. The best way to end this altercation would be to stop it now. 'All right,' he snarled at those facing him, his voice dripping with menace. 'Who's next?'

'We are!' the chimera yowled in a trio of unnatural voices. Still atop the temple, it spread its bat-like wings wide and launched itself straight at Dunk, its paws and hooves ready to pummel and pound the young warrior into the dirt.

Dunk dived to the left as the creature came at him and it sailed harmlessly overhead, the tips of its claws finding no mark. It squawked in frustration as it curled back up into the open sky. The townspeople looked up after the thing, then looked at each other and scattered, each racing for a different hiding place, hoping that the chimera would choose to chase easier prey.

The priest scrambled to his feet, blood trickling from his mouth, the same colour as his robes. He glared at Dunk and yelled, 'Kill the stranger!'

It was only when the priest looked around to see who would follow him that he realised he was alone. His eyes narrowed on the tip of the spear which Dunk pointed at him, and then he too turned and fled straight back down the street.

Dunk loosed a mean laugh until he saw the chimera's winged shape swing around towards him at the end of the street. The beast rolled into position and hung in the sky for just a moment before plummeting into a dive straight down the length of the road.

Dunk's first instinct was to simply jump into a building. He noticed that Gastwirt had shut his inn's front door behind him, leaving Slick pounding desperately from the outside in an effort to get back in.

As Dunk looked about for another path of escape, he noticed that the chimera's angle of dive would take it down far short of his position. For a moment, he thought the creature had misjudged the distance or simply wanted to skim the edge of the earth and rip him from below, but then he saw its real target: the priest.

The holy man realised this at about the same time Dunk did. He turned around immediately and started sprinting back in Dunk's direction.

The priest glanced left and right madly, snapping his head all about. His parishioners had not only abandoned him, they'd locked their doors behind them. No matter where he turned, there was no help to be had.

Dunk hated to see a man cry like the priest – who wailed in desperate terror. He hefted the mighty spear that Slick had given him and took careful aim. It was heavy but well balanced. With luck, it would fly straight and true.

'No!' Slick said as he tried to crush himself into the narrow shelter offered by the frame of the inn's door. 'Don't do it, son! That priest is dead anyway! Save yourself!'

Dunk snorted to himself, not sparing a second to glance back at the halfling. His target zoomed toward him at top speed. Armed only with the spear, he was only going to get one chance at this.

Dunk cocked back his arm, his shoulder flexing against the strain. Then he stepped forward and hurled the spear with all his might.

The chimera bore down on the priest mercilessly, all three of its heads reaching for the man at once, their jaws thrown wide open to expose gaping maws, each filled with a set of vicious teeth or fangs.

The priest screamed, offering up a quick prayer for mercy from the gods.

Dunk's spear shot forth and stabbed into the snake-head, straight through its fanged mouth. It rammed up through the roof of the thing's mouth and pierced its brain from below. It kept going until the thickening shaft caught in the snake-head's skull.

At that point, the spear's momentum snapped back hard against the chimera's own, whipping the creature's middle head back and up along its serpentine neck. The creature went tumbling backward over itself, the spear pulling it along until it embedded itself in the compacted dirt of the street, pinning the creature there by its killed head.

The priest looked up from where he had fallen to his knees in the final moments of the chimera's pursuit, ready to make peace with the gods and plead for guidance into the afterlife. He saw nothing but open sky above him, and turned back to see the chimera pinned in the middle of the street like some massive insect in a particularly horrid collection.

'Praise the gods!' the priest said. 'They have saved us all! Thanks be to them in their wondrous wisdom!'

'How's that?' Dunk said.

The priest looked back to where the unarmed warrior stood in the street, naked to the waist. He tried to speak, but no words escaped his lips.

'*I* saved you,' Dunk said. Behind the priest, the chimera's remaining heads roared and bleated in fury and frustration. 'Kill you aaall!' The goat-head said as the lion-head loosed another blood-curdling cry.

The sight of the wounded beast seemed to bring the priest back to himself, and he fixed Dunk in a baleful glare. 'That creature,' he said, 'would never have bothered us if not for your interference.'

Dunk couldn't believe his ears. He shook his head as if to clear out the lies. 'You told me it was a dragon! A weak and old dragon! You sent me to my death!'

The priest snarled back at the young warrior. 'Your arrogance sent you on your path.' A cold laugh escaped him. 'You think you would have done any better against a dragon?'

Dunk gritted his teeth in frustration. 'I just saved your entire town from a menace that has plagued it for generations. The least you owe me is your thanks.'

'Really?' the priest said. 'We should thank you for destroying the balance of power in this region?'

Dunk gaped at the godly man.

'That creature you just maimed, is the most powerful in the area. While we lived in its shadow, it kept us safe from threats of all sorts: brigands, carrion, orcs, even real dragons. Now, here we are, exposed to the world around us and every horrible thing in it. You've just destroyed this town.'

Dunk fell to one knee and put his head in his hands. The man's words were madness, he knew, but they were the last thing he'd expected. He'd slain the beast, hadn't he? Where was the glory? As for fortune, the only thing he'd seen in the creature's cave had been mounds of bones. Dunk supposed that a chimera had little use for diamonds and gold.

Where had it all gone wrong?

A small hand came down on Dunk's shoulder. He turned to see Slick looking him square in the eye. At this level, the Halfling didn't look nearly so much like a child.

'That's gratitude for you, son,' Slick said. 'But it gets worse.'

Dunk shook his head at the halfling. None of this made any sense to him.

'How?' he said. He'd thought it was a rhetorical question.

Slick nodded down the street. Dunk looked up to see the townspeople poking their heads out of their homes, spotting the still-howling chimera, and then pointing their fingers at Dunk. He couldn't hear their words, but he didn't care for the tone of their voices.

'Son,' Slick said, 'don't stick around to find out.'

CHAPTER FOUR

IT WAS ALMOST dark before Dunk dismounted from Pferd and set up camp for the night. There were no other inns in this part of the Grey Mountains, not this close to the Axe Bite Pass that led through the highest peaks on its way to distant Bretonnia. It was not a safe place for lone travellers at night, but Dunk was sure that Dörfchen would have been even less hospitable.

Dunk was still stunned at how the people of that ill-fated and ungrateful town had responded to how he'd saved them from the monstrous beast that had fed upon their populace – and good-hearted strangers, it seemed – for untold years. He knew that there were bad people in the world, the near-destruction of his family in Altdorf bore stark testimony to that, he just hadn't realised *everyone* was that way.

Everyone but me, he thought. He had suspected that the citizens of Altdorf, corrupted by living in the very heart of the Empire, in the actual seat of the Emperor's power, were perhaps a special case. Those raised in such an environment could fall so easily into crime and violence, just like his younger brother Dirk.

Like many in Altdorf, though, Dunk had fancied that the people of the country, were blessed with a simpler outlook on the world, one that made them more kindly and innocent. To find out he'd been so wrong was yet another blow to his already fragile view of the world.

When Dunk heard a set of hooves clip-clopping up the mountain trail, his heart leapt into his throat. He'd been a fool to start a fire here, it seemed, but he'd been cold and hungry and too depressed about the state of the world to worry about things like brigands or worse. He hadn't seen another person since he'd left Dörfchen and so had tossed caution to the wind.

Dunk drew his long hunting knife, the only weapon he had left on him after losing his sword in the chimera's cave. He had thought about circling around town and going back for it, but the thought of the chimera freeing itself and coming home to find him in its lair once again had kept him out.

Dunk glanced around but quickly saw there was no place for him to hide. The mountain sloped away sharply from the wide trail, both up and down, but no trees grew on this rocky terrain, only a feeble bush or two, hanging on to this small strip of level ground as best it could.

Dunk stood and held his knife before him, putting the fire between him and whatever was trotting up the trail toward him. It was a moment before the rider drew close enough for Dunk to be able to pick its shape out of the surrounding darkness. It was waving at him.

'Hallo!' the rider called. Slick Fullbelly, dressed in a dark green cloak and a suit of golden-brown tweed that barely contained his eponymous gut, and riding a small, dirt-coloured pony built like a barrel. Slick smiled broadly towards the fire and the young man that stood behind it. 'I was hoping that it would be you!' He showed all his teeth.

Dunk strode around the fire, sheathing his knife as he did. The halfling was many things, but not, he hoped, a threat. He beckoned Slick to come and join him by the fire.

Slick drove his tubby pony up to the edge of the fire where it ground to a halt. He looked as though he would have had to split his legs exactly apart to fit them around the creature. The saddle sat on the pony's back like a child's cap on the head of an ogre. It seemed the only thing keeping it in place was the way the saddle was strapped tightly enough to cause the pony's fattened flesh to bulge around it on all sides. While this might have seemed cruel with another mount, the pony just took it in stride, its natural cushioning protecting it from any discomfort.

Slick slid from the pony's back as if dismounting from a boulder. Then he turned to Dunk with a grin. 'It's good to see you again, son. I was afraid you'd gotten away from me,' he said.

Dunk motioned for the halfling to sit down on a patch of ground near the fire. 'You're not after me, too, are you?' he asked. He eyed Slick warily despite himself.

The halfling laughed. 'I don't think so,' he said, a merry twinkle in his eye. 'At least not for killing Dörfchen's murderous town mascot. That thing needed to be shown the door a long time ago.'

Dunk sat down a quarter of the way around the fire from Slick. He had a bit of bacon he'd cooked up still in the pan, soaking in its own hardening grease. He offered this to the halfling without a word.

Slick took the pan and said, 'My undying thanks.' With that, he pulled a fork from the pocket of his waistcoat and set to work on the lukewarm food. He stuffed bite after bite into his mouth, seeming to take special delight in the bits to which large dollops of the coagulated fat had attached themselves.

'I've already eaten, of course,' Slick said between mouthfuls, 'but there's always room for bacon. When you're on the road like this, you never know when you might be able to eat well again, so I prefer to travel like a camel with what I need most already inside of me.'

From what Dunk could see, Slick was prepared to last through at least a month of short rations without undue suffering.

'What is it you want?' Dunk said.

The halfling stopped chewing for a moment as his eyes flew wide. When he resumed, he grinned around the fat stuffed into his cheeks. 'More suspicious already,' he said. 'I like that.

'You know I saw you yesterday in the inn. I thought about warning you about the creature in that cave, but I could see you wouldn't have any of that. You were bent on killing that 'dragon' you'd been hunting for, and little things like the truth weren't going to get in your way.'

'Hey,' Dunk started to protest.

'Oh,' said Slick, waving off the young man's concerns, 'don't think bad of yourself for it. I've seen this happen lots of times before. You're a young man, you have something to prove, you think you can make yourself into a hero. You think other people will respond to that and treat you with courtesy and respect, adoration, even love. But it just doesn't work that way, son.'

Dunk stared at the halfling, amazed. It was if Slick could see right into his heart. 'How can you be so sure?' the young hopeful asked.

'Because,' Slick said, as seriously as if announcing the death of his parents, 'I've been there.'

Dunk smiled softly in spite of himself. 'You were a hero?' he asked. 'Did you slay many dragons?'

'Now see here,' Slick said, as indignantly as he could around the fist-sized ball of lard squished in his cheek. 'It's not all about killing giant, flying lizards now, is it? Not all heroes are murderers, you know.'

Dunk's face flushed with his shame. 'I'm sorry,' he muttered.

The smile came back to Slick's greasy lips as if it had just passed behind a cloud for a moment. 'Don't fret about it, son. People make that sort of mistake about me all the time. They think just because I'm a halfling I can't make any sort of contribution to society other than keeping any plate in front of me clean.'

Dunk looked down at the pan to see that Slick had certainly polished its surface spotless. The halfling didn't miss a beat though.

'But I gave up all that hero nonsense long ago,' he said, waving his fork at Dunk before licking it clean and sticking it back into his pocket.

'Nonsense?' Dunk said. 'What's wrong with being a hero?'

Slick snorted. 'Nothing,' he said, 'if you don't mind a life filled with poverty, fear, and death. Most folks prefer the status quo, even if they're living next door to a monster that might make off with their children at any moment. Sure, it's a horrible thing, but who knows what else worse might be out there? Better the daemon you know.'

Dunk shook his head. 'I can't believe that,' he said. 'Can people really be so cynical? What about improving your lot and that of your neighbours?'

'Like you did in Dörfchen today? You saw how grateful they were about that. You're lucky you got out when you did. When Old Gastwirt told the townsfolk I'd given you that spear, they nearly lynched me on the spot. If the chimera hadn't gotten up and bitten the baker nearly in half at that point, I think they'd have had me.'

'The creature killed someone?' Dunk's heart sunk with these words. He'd hoped he'd put an end to the creature's reign of terror for good.

Slick nodded. 'He wouldn't have, of course, if they hadn't freed him.'

Dunk goggled at this. 'They did what?'

The halfling smiled as he picked a piece of bacon from between his teeth with a small sliver of steel he'd pulled from another pocket in his waistcoat. 'The fools freed him. The priest gathered together a group of men, and they went out to where the thing was staked down and pulled the spear out. They thought they could get the creature back to its cave and let it heal up so it could "protect them from the power vacuum" you were bent on creating.'

'And it repaid them by killing the baker?'

Slick sighed bitterly, the humour draining from him.

'He wasn't much of a man, a bit too slow of foot, for one, which is what did him in, but he made the best pies in the Reikland.'

After a long silence, Slick pointed his toothpick at Dunk and said, 'It makes my point, though, you see. Being a hero is a sucker's game.'

Dunk gazed upwards into the brilliant stars shining in the Old World sky. They were just the same as they'd always been for him, every day of his life, but today they seemed more distant and cold. As a child, when Lehrer had tried to explain the nature of the constellations to him, the ancient patterns had transformed themselves into creatures from the myths and legends he so loved. Now, they were just stars again.

'Now, Blood Bowl,' Slick said, stabbing with his toothpick for emphasis, '*that* is a game.'

Dunk scoffed at the mention of the blood sport. He knew all about Blood Bowl, the insane game in which two teams faced off against each other in some mad abstraction of a real battle. Instead of killing each other to the last foe, though, they had to move a ball, sometimes covered with fang-sharp spikes, past the other team's side of the field, into its 'End Zone', scoring a touchdown. The team with the most touchdowns after an hour of sometimes-murderous play won the match.

'I hate it,' Dunk said, trying to keep his voice even.

Slick's eyes grew wide and as round as his cheeks. 'Hate it? How can you hate it? It's the greatest thing to happen to sport – ever! Maybe even to civilization itself.'

Dunk nearly succeeded in stopping himself from sneering. 'Or it's the worst. It's a bunch of thugs standing toe-to-toe and beating each other merci-lessly for the enjoyment of others. The football is only a pretext for the violence. They might as well smash it flat and be honest about how the bloodshed is the only thing that keeps people coming back.'

Slick smiled with the vision that flashed in his head. 'I actually saw that happen once, in an Orland Raiders game. They were playing the Oldheim Ogres, and the ogres forgot they were in the middle of a match. The Raiders lost five players before the referees got things under control again.'

'That's horrible!' Dunk said, shuddering with revul-sion.

'Hey, son,' Slick said seriously, 'you're the one that wants to be the hero. How do you think most heroes make their names around here?' The halfling waited for a moment, but Dunk didn't answer, too aston-ished that someone would actually defend this monstrous game; and so eloquently.

'They kill things,' Slick said. 'Sometimes they kill "monsters". Other times it's their own kind. At least on the Blood Bowl pitch, there are rules.'

'That no one pays attention to,' Dunk countered. 'I've seen bar brawls with more respect for life.'

Slick smirked. 'You're confusing rules with lives. Hitting someone hard in the middle of the match isn't just legal, it's encouraged. If you can knock a foe out of the game, so much the better for you and your team.'

'But the players cheat all the time!' Dunk said. He couldn't believe he was having this conversation with a halfling here in the middle of the Grey Mountains. He'd left Altdorf behind so he could get away from such things, and now it seemed that they'd followed him into the wilderness. Perhaps he'd been wrong to head into the Reikland. Maybe the Middle Mountains would have been better.

'That's all part of the game,' Slick said. 'It's only cheating if you get caught. Then there are penalties.'

'If you haven't paid off the referees.'

Slick grinned at that. 'The other team can always try to buy the refs too. It all balances out in the end.'

'It's all about murderous greed and filthy gold.'

'And mindless violence,' Slick said. 'Don't forget the mindless violence.'

'Exactly!' Dunk said. 'It's just like, like…'

'Like real life,' the halfling finished, 'only more so. It's brilliant.'

Dunk hung his head and fell silent.

After a while, Slick spoke. In a tentative voice, he said, 'The best part about it is that you're perfect for it.'

Dunk's head snapped up. He glared at the halfling as if he'd cursed him and said, 'What are you babbling about?'

Slick grimaced, as if being forced to bring up an unpleasant topic for the sake of a good friend. 'Well, think about it. You're young, strong, and obviously trained for battle. You'd be wonderful at it.'

Dunk shook his head, perhaps more emphatically than he would have liked. 'You're talking madness.'

'Am I? I watched you fight that chimera. I saw you throw that spear straight down its gullet. You're a natural thrower if ever I've seen one. The best I've ever seen.' Slick saw the earnest doubt on Dunk's face and added, 'I swear in Nuffle's name.'

'Nuffle? The god of Blood Bowl?'

Slick nodded, 'As revealed to us in the sacred texts handed down by the first Sacred Commissioner Roze-El.'

Dunk held back a deep frown. 'That god means nothing to me.'

Slick showed a greasy grin. 'Then you're just going to have to trust me.'

'You're an agent,' Dunk said, edging his way back to where he'd been sitting by the fire. 'No one trusts an agent.'

'Not bad,' Slick snorted. 'You're not as clean-cut ignorant as you come off.'

Dunk started to say something, but the halfling cut him off.

'But then again, no one could be, right?'

Dunk held up a finger to interrupt. When he had Slick's attention, he spoke. 'Is that why you followed me here? To recruit me into playing Blood Bowl?'

The knowing smile slid from the halfling's fat face. He stared into Dunk's eyes for a moment before saying anything. Dunk suddenly felt like a particularly tasty pastry in the halfling's favourite bakery.

'I'll come clean with you, son,' Slick said. 'The answer is yes.'

He held up his hands before Dunk could protest.

'I didn't come to Dörfchen looking for you. I wasn't looking for anyone in particular, just looking for someone special, if you know what I mean. There's a team I work with that's desperate for some new blood, including a good thrower: the Bad Bay Hackers.'

'I don't recognise the name.'

'I thought you didn't follow the game.'

'I hate the game, but that doesn't mean I can get away from it.'

'Well said,' Slick nodded. 'Anyhow, these guys are from just north of Marienburg and they're a group of up and comers, just the hungry sort who require the services of someone like me.'

Dunk rocked back, holding his legs to his chest. 'How's that?' he asked. 'You don't look like much of a player.'

Slick almost choked on his laugh. 'Hardly, son. But I can find them players, fresh blood from the corners of the world they don't know much about yet. Sure, they could trade for better players, but they'd have to give up their own talent – what there is of it – for that. Better to go out and find some raw rookies and mould them into the kind of players they need.

'That's where you come in.'

'Forget it.' Dunk leaned forward and spat into the fire, which sputtered at his insult.

'But, son,' Slick said. 'It's everything you want: gold and glory. This is the way heroes are made these days.'

'I'm not interested.'

Slick nodded. 'Let me ask you a question. Do you know who Grimwold Grimbreath is?'

Dunk pouted but he played along with the halfling's game, waiting to see where it headed. 'Captain of the Dwarf Giants.'

'Hubris Rakarth?'

'The Darkside Cowboys.'

'Hugo von Irongrad?'

'The Impaler? He's with the Champions of Death.'

'Schlitz "Malty" Likker?'

'The Chaos All-Stars. What's the point of all this?'

Slick's smiled split his doughy face. 'Name me the last person to kill a dragon, in the last five years.'

Dunk opened his mouth, but nothing came out.

'The last ten?'

'There was that dragon terrorising the Border Princes, Blazebelly the Devourer.'

Slick nodded. 'But who killed him?'

Try as he might, Dunk couldn't answer.

'Gold and glory, son. If you want it, the best way is by playing Blood Bowl. And I can help.'

Dunk felt his will wavering. Slick added one more thing, softly.

'I know about the Hoffnungs, son. I know all about your family's downfall and what part you played in it.'

Dunk's breath caught in his chest. 'How?'

Slick smiled ruefully. 'I'm always on the lookout for new talent, son. Sometimes recruiting players means having leverage on them.'

'Including blackmail?' Dunk said. The thought that Slick knew of his shame and would expose it to the world drove him nearly to despair. He considered throttling the little agent right there and then, but he couldn't bring himself to do it.

'I prefer "strategic bargaining positioning",' Slick said.

Dunk felt disgusted. He hated the halfling and everything he'd said, but he hated himself even more. Hearing that Blood Bowl was the best way to make money and a name for yourself in today's world wasn't the worst part of it. *That* was the fact that Dunk had been trying to convince himself was otherwise for months. The day's events had overcome his last arguments, and the threat of public disgrace pushed him right over the top. There was for him, it seemed, only one path left.

'All right,' Dunk said to the halfling through gritted teeth. 'I'll do it. On one condition.' His stomach flipped over as he spoke. He'd hoped that he would never have to sink so low that playing Blood Bowl looked like moving up, but here he was. He'd just make the best of it. Maybe there was room for real heroes in this game too – even if he doubted it himself.

'What's that?' Slick tried to suppress his toothy joy, but failed utterly.

'Tell me who killed Blazebelly the Devourer.'

Slick shook his head sadly before he answered. 'No one, son. He killed all comers.'

CHAPTER FIVE

THE NEXT MORNING, Dunk awakened to the smell of frying bacon. He sat up to find Slick spearing fresh-cooked strips of meat and stuffing them into his mouth. The halfling waved at him as he rubbed the sleep from his eyes.

'Morning, son!' Slick said. 'You looked so peaceful there, I didn't want to wake you.'

'So you just pillaged my saddlebags instead.' Dunk shot Pferd an evil look. The horse had been trained to avoid strangers, but apparently it had decided Slick qualified as a friend. Dunk himself wasn't so sure he was ready to apply that label to the halfling.

'I prefer to think of it as "sharing",' Slick said amiably. 'After all, we're going to be spending a lot of time together.'

Dunk grunted as he got to his feet. 'I thought you were supposed to be making me rich and famous.'

Slick stabbed through three pieces of bacon and offered them to Dunk as he stepped forward. 'You expect a lot overnight,' Slick said. 'I like high aspirations. I have them for you myself.'

'Before we go too much further down this road,' Dunk said in as businesslike a fashion as he could muster, 'I have some questions.' Although Dunk's father had kept most matters of the family business from him in his youth, he had picked up some of his father's style. He knew how to handle himself in a negotiation, or so he liked to think.

'Of course, son. I'd be surprised if you didn't.'

'First, what are you paid?'

Slick smiled. 'Right! Gold before glory it is then. That's an easy one – you don't pay me a thing.'

Dunk smiled right back at the halfling, hoping he didn't look as nervous as he suddenly felt. 'You'll be my agent out of the goodness of your heart?'

'In a sense, yes,' Slick said. 'More to the point, I handle all negotiations and collections of your remuneration. When you are paid, I take a small and reasonable percentage for myself off the top and pass on the vast bulk of your earnings to you entirely untouched.'

'And how much of a percentage am I to pay you?'

Slick waved off the question. 'Son, with my experience and expertise, I'll make you so much more money than you'd make on your own that it's more like your employers end up paying me to help you.'

'Uh-huh,' Dunk said, unimpressed. 'How much?'

The halfling swallowed. 'Ten per cent.' He held up a hand. 'Before you object, I'll have you know that's entirely reasonable. Some of the other agents in the business charge up to half as much again for half the service.'

It was Dunk's turn to smile faintly. 'That's fine.' He knew from watching his father that such a percentage was customary. The only trick was making sure the halfling's fingers weren't so sticky that he took more than his share, but that was a problem for another time.

'Next: where are we going?'

'Again,' Slick smiled, 'an easy one: we're off to Magritta, where the upcoming *Spike! Magazine* Tournament is to be held at the end of the month.'

'Magritta?' Dunk's face fell. 'I thought you said the Hackers were from Bad Bay.'

'They are, and that's where I've just come from. Pegleg is desperate for new players, so I've been trailing along in their wake, looking for just the right person.' The halfling fixed Dunk in a hungry tiger's gaze. 'Lucky me.'

'Who's Pegleg?'

'Captain Pegleg Haken is the team's coach, an ex-pirate who lost both a leg and a hand at sea.'

'Sounds like a tough customer.'

'You'd have to ask the sea creature that ate those missing parts.'

'So why Magritta?'

Slick finished off the last of the bacon and started packing up. Dunk considered complaining about the meagre portion of the breakfast he'd been served, but didn't want the halfling dipping into his stores again. If they were going to Magritta, the supplies would have to last them at least until they reached Bretonnia. After that, they'd have to cross all of that nation and most of the Estalian Kingdoms too, which meant either an ocean voyage, a trip through the distant Irrana Mountains, or a long trek around them.

'The Hackers need new players, and that's where they're holding their try-outs.'

'Isn't that cutting it a bit close to the time of the tournament?' Dunk started helping Slick pack everything up.

'Welcome to the world of Blood Bowl, son. More teams lose out at tournaments from a lack of healthy players than on the pitch. They're disqualified before they face even their first opponent. You're only allowed sixteen players on a roster, but you need to be able to put at least eleven players on the field. That doesn't leave much room for error, given the injury rates in this game.'

Dunk stopped checking Pferd's saddlebags to stare at the halfling. 'Just how dangerous is this?'

Slick frowned. 'Haven't you ever seen a game?'

Dunk shook his head. 'Most of what I know comes from my little brother Dirk. He always loved Blood Bowl.'

'Well, good on him, then,' Slick said, the frown still marring his chubby cheeks. 'I don't want to lie to you, son. This is a dangerous game. People get maimed or killed all the time. It's part of the sport.'

Dunk nodded solemnly, not meeting the halfling's eyes. 'I knew I didn't like it for a reason.'

'Don' t worry about it, son. A brave lad like you can handle it. It's not any more dangerous than poking around in a chimera's lair by yourself.'

Dunk flexed his injured shoulder as he mounted Pferd. 'I wasn't too fond about how that worked out either.'

Slick scurried atop his four-legged barrel of a pony. 'Gold and glory,' he called after Dunk as he prodded its back to keep up with Pferd. 'You won't find that in a cave!'

THE TRAIL THROUGH the Grey Mountains was uneventful. As they rode down out of the range, the stark beauty of the mountains clashed with the lush green of the fertile plains beyond. Dunk stared out at it wordlessly for hours while Slick prattled on.

The halfling, it seemed, could hold forth on any subject endlessly. Slick was prepared to opine at length no matter what the topic or how little he knew about it, even in the absence of any rejoinders from Dunk.

At first it annoyed Dunk, but once he got used to it, he found he almost liked it. He'd grown up in a busy household. There was rarely a dull moment in the family's keep. Over the past months Dunk had led a solitary life, as he'd never been able to find himself the crew of stalwart companions he'd always romantically imagined would join him in pursuit of fame and fortune. The rank cowardice of others hadn't stopped him, of course, but he had missed the sound of another person's voice.

Slick supplied that in spades.

'Where to from here?' Dunk asked, cutting-off the halfling in mid-sentence. He had no idea what Slick had been babbling about anyway.

'Straight for Bordeleaux,' Slick said, pointing directly toward the setting sun. 'Right on the shore of the Great Western Ocean. Pegleg took the Hackers by sea to Magritta, sailing through the Middle Sea and down around Bretonnia and Estalia to where Magritta sits on the Southern Sea. If we hustle, we can meet the boat at Bordeleaux and hitch a ride for the rest of the journey.'

'And if we miss them?'

Slick dug his heels into his pony, sending the rotund creature cantering forward just a bit faster. 'Best not to let such issues arise,' he called back over his shoulder at Dunk.

THE DUO'S TRAIL led them through the most fertile of Bretonnia's lands, the farmland that sprawled between the River Grismerie and the River Morceaux. These were names that figured large in the legends Dunk loved. As they rode along, his mind wandered back over the exploits of Sir Leonid d'Quenelles and the brave pack of fighting souls he'd led into battle after battle.

In Dunk's youth, he'd hoped that he would one day find himself following in the footsteps of his heroes, at least metaphorically. He never imagined he'd actually follow their geographical paths.

The people of the Two Rivers Basin, as they sometimes called themselves, were friendly enough. The sight of a warrior like Dunk often put them on the defence, but Slick's charisma put them at ease soon enough. No one could possibly see the little person perched on his enormously fat steed as a threat, and anyone who travelled with such a happy creature couldn't be all bad, it seemed.

WHEN THE PAIR finally reached Bordeleaux, they'd been riding hard for over a week and had put over five hundred miles behind them. And Dunk was thoroughly sick of his travelling companion.

'Are we there yet?' Dunk asked for what must have been the hundredth time.

The testy tone of Slick's response suggested that he was ready to expand the size of his circle of friends, too. 'Not quite,' the halfling said, taking a swig from the seemingly bottomless wineskin he kept with him at all times. He'd taken every opportunity to refill it along the trail, and there had been plenty. The vineyards of Bretonnia were widely acknowledged to be among the finest in the worlds, with most of the vintners' production flowing into Bordeleaux to be shipped throughout the Old World and beyond.

'I've gotten you to the big city,' the halfling said, spreading his arms out toward the sprawl of buildings, streets, towers, and even castles that comprised Bordeleaux. 'Isn't that enough?'

Below them, the River Morceaux cut a line through the centre of the city, passing through the last of the series of locks that allowed barges and smaller ships to roam the river's upper reaches. At the last of these, the river spilled beneath the Bordeleaux Bridge. It stretched across the watery span in the shadow of the Governor's Palace and the Bordeleaux Fortress, the two largest and most magnificent structures that Dunk had seen outside of Altdorf. They stabbed into the midday sun as if to grasp that fiery orb, and the lesser buildings around them looked as if they hoped to push them to succeed in their ancient competition.

'I thought we were heading for Magritta,' Dunk said.

'There's time enough for that, son,' Slick said as he slung his wineskin into its home over his back. 'We may have a few days yet before the *Sea Chariot* arrives, possibly a week or more.'

'Or we might not,' Dunk said. 'I'd rather we got to the docks and asked after the ship before we settled in somewhere.'

'Of course,' Slick nodded, shading his eyes with his hand as he scanned the shores below. In the distance, a cluster of seagoing ships gathered on the south bank of the river, just to the west of the massive bridge. Their sails fluttered in the same easterly breeze that ruffled through Dunk's hair. 'But there's little chance they beat us here. They would have had to make – oh, burnt beef!'

Dunk stared in the same direction as Slick, craning his neck toward the docks on the river's other side. 'What's wrong?'

'They *are* here,' Slick said, grimacing. 'They must have found a tailwind straight from the Realms of Chaos.'

The halfling pointed toward the docks. 'You see that cutter there, the one with the green and gold flag?'

Dunk squinted down into the distance and spied a dark, little ship moored between a pair of frigates. It bore a single mast, rigged fore and aft, set back toward the rear of the ship. Its headsails fluttered into the wind as the sailors below hauled them into the breeze. The banner that flew from the top of the mast bore a trio of white swords forming a massive H, emphasized by a pine-green block H underlying them, all centred on a field of brightest yellow.

'It's the Hackers all right,' Dunk said, panic creeping into his voice. 'It looks like they're getting ready to set sail.'

Dunk turned to Slick to ask what they should do, but the halfling had already given his pony, which Dunk now knew was known fondly as Kegger, his heels. The round and graceless halfling bounced along atop the galloping butterball at top speed, his legs in his stirrups the only thing keeping him from flying off like a shot from a cannon.

Dunk spurred Pferd after the halfling and quickly caught up with him. 'Go – on – with – out – me!' Slick hollered, his voice jerking with every bounce on Kegger's back. 'I'll – catch – up!'

Dunk nodded and gave Pferd his head. The stallion charged forward through the congested streets of Bordeleaux, people scattering out of his way, warned by Pferd's galloping hooves and Dunk's desperate cries.

CHAPTER SIX

As DUNK REACHED the docks, he shouted for the ship to stop. He could see that the sailors had yet to cast off the mooring lines, but it would only be a matter of moments before they did.

'Ahoy, the ship!' he cried. When he saw scores of heads turn his way from dozens of ships, he changed his call. 'Ahoy, *Sea Chariot*!' he called at the top of his lungs. 'Ahoy!'

It hadn't occurred to Dunk that as much as he and Slick wanted to get to the *Sea Chariot* before it set sail, there were others who would prefer they didn't. That's why the pile of barrels that rolled in front of him was such a surprise. The large kegs of wine were waiting to be loaded onto a nearby sea barge for transport along the coast, but someone cut them loose directly into Dunk's path.

Pferd reared back and nearly threw Dunk as he tried to avoid being crushed under the heavy barrels. Somehow the young warrior managed to hold on until Pferd brought all four hooves safely back down on to the wooden docks.

'That's far enough, I think,' a voice came from the other side of the barrels.

'Do yourself a favour and forget about that ship,' called another.

A pair of mostly toothless, half-shaven faces peered over the top of the impromptu barrier and grinned at Dunk. 'A team like that's got no place for you, mate,' the uglier one said. The duo waved their longshoremen's crating hooks meaningfully.

Dunk snarled and ran Pferd back along the docks the way he'd come. When Slick spotted him, the halfling howled, 'The – other – way!'

Dunk ignored him as he spun his mount back about and spurred him on toward the barrels that blocked his way to the *Sea Chariot*. With a final burst of speed, Pferd leapt up and just cleared the top of the barrels. He would have clipped the heads of the two dockworkers, but they threw themselves to the decking as the horse bounded through the air.

Past the barrels, Dunk rode up to the *Sea Chariot*, crying, 'Hold! Hold!'

The sailors with the mooring lines in their hands looked toward the bridge for direction. There, standing just before the hatch to the captain's quarters, stood a tall, proud man. Beneath his golden tricorn hat trimmed in forest green, his long dark hair cascaded in curls onto the shoulders of his long, crimson coat, which he wore open over a ruffled white shirt and black leggings. His face might once have been handsome, in more carefree days but now it wore openly the burden of his responsibilities, marring his once-charming features. Where his right leg had once been, he now stood upon a steel-shod shaft of wood running from the knee down. A viciously shaped and sharpened hook stabbed from his left sleeve where his hand had once been. This was no doubt Captain Pegleg Haken, in what was left of his flesh.

Pegleg's eyebrows curled at the sight of the young man on the ebony horse racing towards his ship, and he stroked the end of his greasy, black goatee with his good hand. He waved his hook at the sailors at the mooring lines and said calmly, 'Belay casting off yet, dogs. Let's see how this plays out.'

Relieved, Dunk called up to Pegleg. 'My thanks. Hold but a minute more until I can find–'

Dunk turned to see the two dockworkers now accosting Slick. The halfling had tried to work Kegger around the barrier of barrels, but the pair of thugs had easily intercepted him.

'We're not letting another one get past us, mate,' Dunk heard one of them say to Slick.

'We might have to slit your throat just to make an example of you,' the other growled. 'After all, we have a reputation to uphold round these parts, don't we?'

'Back off of him,' Dunk said as he rode up behind the two men. He reined Pferd to a halt and slid from his saddle in one smooth motion, landing before the thugs as they turned to face him.

'Right,' the uglier one said, a gap-toothed grin on his face. 'Looks like this is our lucky day, don't it?'

'Got that right,' the less ugly one said, swinging his hook before him, taking cuts out of the air at every turn. 'This one's head will make a right fine trophy, won't it?'

'Run!' Slick shouted as he and Kegger scrabbled for the safety of the other side of the barrels. 'Get on the ship! I'll catch up with you in Magritta!'

'See,' the ugly one said to his friend. 'I told you this was one of them, didn't I?'

'That you did,' said the other. 'I owe you a pint.' He crept toward Dunk, his crate-hook before him and a wicked grin on his face. 'We can pay for it with what we take from his corpse, can't we?'

Dunk reached for his sword, and realised once again that it wasn't there. He'd had cause to regret this many times since leaving his blade back in the chimera's cavern but particularly now. He grabbed his hunting knife instead.

As the less-ugly thug lashed out at Dunk with his hook, the young warrior stepped inside the man's reach and grabbed his arm, causing the murderous tip of the hook to sail wide. Then Dunk slashed out with his knife and felt its glistening blade part the thug's throat, separating it from his chin.

As the first thug's life spilled from his throat, Dunk swung the dying man's now-flaccid arm wide toward his uglier friend. The errant hook slapped into the man's head, point first, embedding itself in his grimy skull. The thug's eyes rolled back up into his head as he staggered backwards and fell, nothing but the whites staring back at the young warrior who had dispatched him so easily into the afterlife.

Dunk stepped back to witness his handiwork. Both of his assailants lay dead at his feet, the blood from the first one's throat forming a rapidly spreading pool that lapped at the young warrior's scuffed boots. Neither even twitched.

A round of applause burst out from the deck of the *Sea Chariot*. Dunk looked back to see the crowd of people arrayed on the cutter baying their approval of his lethal skills.

'You, young sir,' Pegleg called out to Dunk, 'are welcome to come aboard.' He turned to his first mate, a tall, buff sailor with chocolate-coloured skin. 'Get us underway as soon as that man, the halfling, and their mounts are aboard.' With that, he entered his quarters and shut the door behind him.

Dunk glanced over at Slick, who gave him a big, grinning thumbs up. 'Wonderful work, son!' he said. 'What a great way of displaying your considerable talents. Sometimes a little showboating really pays off.'

Dunk smiled weakly as he looked down at the two corpses whose blood stained his boots. He'd never killed anyone before, he realised. All those countless hours of training, of sparring with Lehrer, with Dirk, with anyone else he could find, they'd all paid off. He just wasn't sure he liked what they'd bought.

THE FIRST MATE welcomed Dunk and Slick aboard as they led their mounts up the gangplank. 'The name is Cavre,' he said, pronouncing it 'carve'.

'Good to see you again, Fullbelly,' he said to Slick, as he shook his hand. The halfling's hand disappeared inside Cavre's massive grip. 'Who's your friend?'

'Permit me to introduce Dunk Hoffnung,' Slick said, 'a talented young player with plenty of promise. One of the best natural throwers I've ever seen.'

'That's high praise,' Cavre said as he shook Dunk's hand. Despite the man's obvious age – he was greying at the temples and his hands and arms bore many small scars – his hands were as soft and warm as a newborn's belly.

'Not *the* Cavre,' Dunk said respectfully. The tall man laughed, and it was a sound that brought a smile to the lips of all that heard it.

'I thought you didn't follow the game,' Slick said to Dunk.

'Even I've heard of one of the greatest blitzers in the game.'

Cavre blushed, his skin turning even darker. 'You flatter me, Mr. Hoffnung. I just move the ball down the field.'

'Which is more than most players can say,' Slick said.

'There's no trick to it,' Carve said. 'Just do what you're supposed to do, and do it well.'

Dunk handed Pferd's reins to a square-jawed man with short, dark hair and a black strip of a tattoo that wrapped around his head and covered his eyes. A blond-haired man with a similar tattoo took Kegger's reins and they led the mounts into the ship's hold.

'We don't normally take animals on board,' Cavre explained, 'but Mr. Fullbelly has a special arrangement with the captain.'

Slick grinned. 'See, son, the sort of crowd you fall in with can colour your fate.'

'For good or bad,' a voice growled from behind Dunk.

The young warrior turned to see a tall, broad man glowering at him. He was about Dunk's height, but broader across the shoulders. The sides of his head were shaved, but he'd grown long what was left so that it pulled back from his widow's peak to a long warrior's braid threaded through with bits of steel wire. He smiled, and Dunk saw that he'd filed each of his teeth to a dangerous point. He seemed like a walking shark.

'The name's Kur Ritternacht,' the man said as he tried to crush Dunk's hand in a vicelike grip. The young warrior gave back as good as he got, refusing to squirm in Kur's gaze.

'Never heard of you,' Dunk said. 'But then I only know of the *star* players.'

Kur released Dunk's hand, and the young warrior breathed a private sigh of relief. 'Don't worry, kid,' he said. 'I don't play for the *fans*.' His emphasis on the last word left no doubt that he considered Dunk to be a member of this lowly class, something unworthy of his attention. He turned his back on Dunk and walked away.

'Don't let him rattle you, son,' Slick said, patting Dunk on the back of his leg. 'He's just worried for his job.'

'How's that?' Dunk asked as he watched Kur shove sailors out of his way as he went to recline in a hammock set up near the ship's bow.

'He's the Hackers' starting thrower… for now.'

Dunk looked down at the halfling grinning up and him and felt a shiver run up his spine.

'Don't let him rattle you, Mr. Hoffnung,' Cavre said.

Dunk smiled at the man. 'You can call me Dunk, please.'

Cavre smiled and shook his head. 'Thanks, but no.'

'I'd feel more comfortable if you did. Only my old teacher called me Mr. Hoffnung.'

'And why is that, do you think?' Cavre asked. He raised his eyebrows and waited for the answer.

'I took it as a sign of respect,' Dunk answered, just a bit confused.

'And did you father's other employees call you Mr. Hoffnung?'

Dunk thought about that for a moment. 'No, actually, none of them. They reserved that name for my father.'

'Do you know why?'

Dunk shook his head. He had a few ideas, but he somehow knew that none of them would match up with what Cavre would tell him.

'First names are something to be shared with your peers.' Cavre smiled and then snapped a salute at Dunk before returning to his duties on the ship.

Dunk and Slick strolled over to the ship's railing so they could watch the towering buildings of Bordeleaux recede as they moved further down the river and towards the sea. The midday sun shone down on them brightly, bouncing off their red tiled roofs and piercing the smoke rising from the tall chimneys spotted throughout the town.

'Well, we're here, son,' the halfling said. 'That was the first part. Now all we have to do is complete the second.'

After a long moment, Dunk prompted Slick to continue. 'Which is?'

'To make the team, of course. Once we reach Magritta, Pegleg will set up a quick and dirty training camp and host try-outs. It'll be up to you to outshine the others. Those who do will find themselves filling out the Hackers' roster. The rest just get to go home.'

Dunk turned around and leaned his back against the railing. He scanned the people around him, many of them working the ship's rigging or helping guide it through this narrowest part of the navigable portion of the river as the *Sea Chariot* raced toward the sea. Others sat by themselves or stood gazing back at the city they'd left. A few exercised in ways that were designed more to impress the observer than condition the participant.

'How many spots are there?' Dunk asked.

'Now that's thinking,' Slick said, turning to follow Dunk's gaze. 'I like to see that in my players.'

'How many?'

'Assuming there haven't been any injuries or desertions since I left Pegleg in Bad Bay, there were twelve active players on the team. That leaves four spots to fill.'

'Who's on the team already?'

'You already met Cavre and Kur. The two men who took our mounts, those were the Waltheim brothers, Andreas and Otto. Otto's a catcher and Andreas is a blitzer. You see that woman over there?'

Dunk followed Slick's finger over to where a tall, androgynous figure swung high in the ship's rigging. The blond-haired woman swung from rope to rope, working like a spider in its web, as if she was as at home there as anywhere else in the world.

'That's Gigia Mardretti, the other catcher. Her lover is the man in the crow's nest, Cristophe Baldurson, one of the linemen.'

Dunk craned his neck back to see a small, stocky man scouting out toward the horizon and shouting orders to the bridge below.

'The man at the ship's wheel, that's Percival Smythe, a good bloke if a bit smug in his position. He's the other, other catcher.'

Slick swung his attention back toward the lower part of the ship's rigging, where men worked the sails, unfurling them into the wind where they billowed taut and tall. 'That lot there are the rest of the linemen: Kai Albrecht, Lars Engelhard, Karsten Klemmer, Henrik Karlmann. Kai and Lars have the dark hair, although Lars has thirty pounds on Kai. Karsten has the dark blond hair, and Henrik's the one with the white-blond locks.'

It struck Dunk as funny that Slick would refer to these men by the colour of their hair. They were uniformly the toughest group of people he'd ever seen. He supposed, however, that the hair was what set them apart from each other. They must have heard Slick mentioning their names, but they went about their business like trained professionals. They had no time for a hopeful rookie and his pint-sized agent.

Dunk counted up the names quickly, then glanced at Slick. 'That's only eleven,' he said to the halfling. 'You said there were twelve.'

Almost as if prompted, the hatch through which Dunk and Slick's mounts had been taken into the hold flung open, and a large humanoid creature stalked out. He stood somewhere over eight feet tall and had to have weighed in at nearly four hundred pounds. Great tusks jutted out from his lower jaw, lending a hungry look to the already monstrous face lurking below his bald and polished pate. Despite his size, his dark eyes seemed beady, set deep into his craggy face above a broken nose that featured a golden ring large enough to serve a bracelet for Dunk.

Someone in the bow of the ship screamed. A low rumble escaped the ogre's chest, and it took Dunk a moment to recognise it as laughter.

'Dunk Hoffnung,' Slick said out of the side of his mouth, never taking his eyes from the massive creature approaching them, 'meet M'Grash K'Thragsh.'

# CHAPTER SEVEN

DUNK'S BREATH CAUGHT in his chest. The ogre before him seemed like something out of a child's nightmare, so large and impossibly ugly that he could only have been excavated from the darkest fears buried in that child's mind. Its breath smelled like it had been chewing on rotting meat and gargling sour goat's milk.

Strangely, it was smiling.

Stunned, Dunk's first inclination was to reach once again for his nonexistent sword. Instead, he stuck out his hand and said, 'Well met, M'Grash.'

The ogre looked down at Dunk's hand, and thunder rumbled in his chest. He reached and took hold of the young warrior's hand with surprising gentleness. Though when he shook it, Dunk feared his arm might separate at the elbow.

'Name?' M'Grash said.

Dunk couldn't tell if the ogre was greeting him or threatening him. He had no social points of reference for this kind of meeting. In a flash, he decided to remain friendly and calm. Any other route, including leaping over the ship's railing – which he considered for a moment – seemed sure to end in a terribly painful demise.

'I am Dunkel Hoffnung, from Altdorf, the capital city of the Empire.'

A thick smile spread across the ogre's face. M'Grash's mouth was wide enough that Dunk was sure he could stuff his whole head into it. He hoped that no similar idea was passing through the ogre's mind at the moment.

'Dunkel,' M'Grash said, the name rolling around on his tongue like a side of beef, sounding suddenly all too small in that massive mouth.

'My friends call me Dunk,' the young warrior said, realizing then that M'Grash still held his hand in its massive mitt. He carefully extricated it from a grip he was sure could crush his comparatively tiny bones.

'Dunkel,' M'Grash repeated. 'You are Dunkel.'

'Um, yes,' Dunk said. 'That's fine. Call me what you like. I'd like to be your friend.'

A gurgling noise erupted from next to Dunk, and he looked down to see Slick looking as if he'd choked on his favourite kind of candy. The wide-eyed halfling gazed up at him and shook his head back and forth as he whispered, 'Oh, no, no, no, no, no.'

Before Dunk could ask what Slick was warning him against, he heard M'Grash rumble in childlike delight, 'Friend?'

Dunk snapped his head back around to look into the ogre's gleeful eyes. The young warrior knew only one thing at that moment; that he should do whatever he could to avoid disappointing M'Grash. Tentatively, carefully, he nodded, bracing himself for whatever might happen next.

'Friend!' M'Grash howled at the top of his capacious lungs. 'Friend!'

The ogre gathered up Dunk in his arms and gave him the bear hug of his life. The air rushed out of his lungs, and for a moment Dunk flashed back to an incident in the play yard of his family keep when his entire class had piled upon him during playtime. Crushed beneath so many bodies, he had wondered if he would ever be able to breathe again.

This was worse.

It only lasted for a moment more before M'Grash let go. 'Friend!' he roared again. This time, he tossed Dunk into the air and caught him in his outstretched arms. 'My friend!'

When M'Grash brought Dunk back within arm's reach, the young warrior grabbed on to the creature and embraced his massive neck with all his might. 'That's right!' he said. 'I'm your friend for life!'

'For life!' M'Grash said, returning the hug, much to Dunk's despair. As the air rushed from his lungs again, he thought to himself, at least I'm not being tossed in the air.

An instant later, Dunk found himself standing on the ship's deck again, right before the massive creature. Without moving his hands, he mentally checked through his body, searching for any broken bones or otherwise permanent damage. Other than a few possible bruises, he thought he'd live.

'My friend Dunkel!' The ogre's grin was terrifying. Dunk was afraid he'd made the creature so happy he'd keel over dead right there.

'Mr. K'Thragsh!' Cavre's voice rang out from the bridge. 'That will be enough.'

It was if a storm cloud had opened up over the ogre's head. As Dunk looked up at the creature, it seemed almost possible that he was large enough to demand his own weather. M'Grash's face fell, and his bottom lip shot out in a pout that looked like it could have beaten Dunk senseless.

'About your duties, please, Mr. K'Thragsh,' Cavre said. 'I'm pleased you've made a new friend, but we depend on your abilities to get us to sea.'

M'Grash's lip pulled at least halfway back in, and his eyes brightened. 'Bye, friend!' he said to Dunk before turning away and stomping up toward the bridge.

'By my grandmother's best buttered biscuits,' Slick said, 'I thought you'd made your last friend ever for a moment there.' He scanned Dunk over, checking for injuries. 'You need to be more careful with ogres.'

Dunk nodded, still stunned by the encounter. 'Who was that?' he said, his voice distant, as if just waking from a dream.'

'M'Grash is the Hackers' best blitzer. Pegleg found him in the forests around Middenheim. He lived with a family of loggers there who'd taken him in as an infant. Apparently the locals killed his family but couldn't bear to put the sword to a newborn.'

'But he's an ogre,' Dunk said quietly, almost ashamed of the words as they left his mouth. 'I mean, don't ogres normally eat people?'

Slick nodded. 'Most do, but M'Grash's upbringing changed that. He eats a lot, but humans, elves, halflings, and the like are not on the menu.'

Dunk shook his head to clear the cobwebs. It was as if his mind had left him during his meeting with M'Grash, keeping him from screaming out loud in absolute terror. Now it came smashing back into his brain.

'Is he dangerous?'

'Very,' Slick said. 'But he treasures his friends. Congratulations for making it on to that tiny list.'

'Really?' Dunk said, slumping against the ship's rail as the cutter found its way to deeper water. Its sails snapped briskly as it the wind pulled it to the west and the open sea beyond. 'He seemed friendly enough to have an army on his side.'

Slick smirked. 'Most folks don't respond so well to an ogre's greeting, son.'

Dunk breathed in big gulps of the salt-tinged air. He'd never been on the ocean before, and never on a sailing ship so large. The barges that crawled up and down the Talabec and the Stir as they met at Altdorf to form the mighty Reik might have been larger, but they couldn't rely on something as capricious as the wind to move them toward their goals. The whole day seemed painted with a thick coat of the surreal, and he feared life would only get stranger as the days rolled on.

'Who are those others at the bow?' Dunk asked, hoping to take his mind off what had just happened.

Slick looked over at the three men sitting together at the bow of the ship, almost in the shadow of Kur's hammock, as if he were an altar at which they worshipped. They wore their dark hair wild and greasy, and they seemed to be missing most of their teeth. They chatted with each other furtively, their eyes darting about the rest of the ship. The largest of them, a bear of a man who now seemed tiny compared to M'Grash – Dunk hoped the rest of the Blood Bowl league wasn't filled with creatures like that – glared over at Dunk and flashed him a sneer filled with golden teeth.

'Those are the other hopefuls, I suspect,' said Slick. 'Once we get to Magritta, Pegleg will hold team tryouts. Bloodweiser Beer is sponsoring the event, so they'll have plenty more give it a try once we get there. I'd guess that lot signed on back in Bordeleaux.'

'What makes you say that?' Dunk asked, still just a bit fuzzy headed.

'For one, they're Bretonnian for sure. Just listen to those mealy-mouthed accents. More importantly, though, do they remind you of anyone?'

Dunk stared at the men for a moment. The gold-toothed one spat back in his direction. Then it dawned on Dunk, as cold as a wintry dip in the Reik. 'Do all the dockworkers in Bordeleaux look so much alike?' he asked, not sure what the best answer would be.

'Only when they're brothers or cousins.' Slick shook his head. 'Blood Bowl is a deadly game, on the pitch and off. Those ruthless buggers we met on the dock didn't attack us at random. They wanted to thin out the competition for their friends here.'

'But won't there be a lot more hopefuls in Magritta?'

'I said they were ruthless, son, not smart.'

Dunk lay his head back against the railing and looked up at the open, blue sky. 'What have you gotten me in to, Slick?' he asked.

'Just settle back,' the halfling said. 'We have a long trip still ahead of us.'

DUNK AWOKE THAT night with a knife against his neck and a garlic-coated voice hissing in his ear. He knew who it was, at least within a group of three people, before he heard the words. 'You killed my brother, and now you're going to die.'

Most of the Hackers had gone below decks after sunset. Their berths were down there, as was the galley. Cavre had brought Dunk and Slick a bowl of passable stew each and handed out the same to the trio at the ship's bow. 'Recruits sleep on deck, Mr. Hoffnung,' he'd said. 'When you make the team, you'll find yourself below.'

'When?'

Cavre had just smiled and then disappeared through the hatch again.

'The agents sleep up here too?' Dunk had asked Slick.

The halfling had looked up from his bowl of stew, already over half in his belly. 'You see any other agents around here, son?'

Dunk had made a show of looking around, but he had known the answer. 'Nope.'

'Blood Bowl teams don't care much for agents. We're more what they like to call a "necessary evil".

We bring them the best talent, but we also make sure they pay the best rates for it.'

'So you're sleeping up here?'

Slick grinned as he finished up his stew and set his bowl aside. 'I wouldn't trust my neck down there.'

Now it was Dunk's neck on the line. Without thinking, he brought up his hand to grab at his attacker's knife arm. The assassin pulled back and brought his knife down at Dunk's chest instead, intending to plunge his blade deep into the young warrior's heart.

The point of the blade glanced off the breastplate under Dunk's shirt.

You think I should take it off, Dunk had asked Slick. We're on a boat after all.

Not tonight, son, Slick had said as he laid his head down on the deck and closed his eyes. Better to get the lay of the land before you let down your guard. Besides, if you get tossed overboard in the middle of the sea, you'd be better off getting dragged to the bottom before the sharks got you.

Slick had snickered at that, making Dunk think the halfling had intended it as a joke. However, when he thought of Pegleg, it didn't seem all that funny.

Dunk slid from under his attacker and let out a yell for help. He couldn't see much in the darkness. The ship sailed along under a sliver of a moon, the pilot able to pick out the coastline several miles to port, but Cavre had said the captain didn't like to attract attention at night. That sort of thing could be fatal out here, so they ran without lights instead.

The lookout in the crow's nest heard Dunk's cry and opened his hooded lantern, shining it down on the deck below, catching the young warrior in the light.

Dunk glanced back, and his assailant – one of the recruits from the bow of the ship – tackled him. Dunk slammed back an elbow and felt it smash into the man's cheek, the bone cracking from the force.

Still in the man's grip, Dunk wrenched himself about and found the man about to drive the knife down at him again. This time the attacker aimed for Dunk's eyes with a two-fisted stab straight down.

Dunk reached up with both hands and caught his attacker by the wrists, stopping the point of the knife bare inches from his hose. The man grunted with fury and strained to bring the knife down further. He was strong, maybe stronger than Dunk, and in his position he could bring all his weight to bear. Slowly, inexorably, the point of the knife drove lower and lower, glinting in the lookout's lamplight, as well as that of a beam piercing the night from the cutter's bridge.

Dunk pressed up against his attacker's arms with all his might. He tried to wriggle left and right, but the assailant held him fast with his legs. There was nowhere to go.

Dunk howled in frustration. Then suddenly the attacker was gone, hauled up into the night. The lights followed the man, and Dunk saw him thrashing about as he dangled precariously in M'Grash's grip.

The ogre held the panicked man at arm's length and roared at him. 'Don't hurt my friend!'

The terrified assassin brought his knife around to stab it into M'Grash's neck. The ogre didn't see the attack coming, and Dunk feared the killer might fell even the massive creature with a well-placed blow.

'Get rid of him, M'Grash!' he shouted.

The ogre swept his arm out and back, then hurled the assassin into the black waters beyond the ship's rail. He screamed the entire way as he arced through the night air until crashing through the waves into the deep below.

The attacker's two friends dashed forward from their spot at the bow, their rapiers drawn, and thirsty for the ogre's blood. Although he knew it was fool-hardy, Dunk pulled out his hunting knife and stood with M'Grash, ready to take on the duo if they pressed the issue.

The gold-toothed man lashed out, but Dunk leaned back, just out of reach, and the sharpened blade whizzed bloodlessly by. 'That's three lives you owe me now,' the man hissed in his Bretonnian accent.

'What in Nuffle's name is going on?' a voice shouted from behind Dunk. He glanced over his shoulder to see Cavre storming towards him and the others, four of the team's linemen behind him, each bearing a long knife. 'Stand down!' he said. 'All of you!'

M'Grash fell to his knees instantly. Even in this position, he looked down at everyone else on the ship.

The two attackers immediately started in with their lies. 'This man threatened us, and when Patric tried to defend himself, he had his pet ogre here throw him overboard!'

Off in the distance, somewhere in the water behind the ship, Dunk could hear a voice calling out for help. It was barely loud enough to hear already, but he knew the man was shouting as loudly as his lungs would let him. He started to say something, but Cavre cut him off.

'Shut your mouths, all of you!' The blitzer turned to the ogre. 'Is that what happened?'

M'Grash shook his head so violently that Dunk feared his eyes might fly from their sockets. 'Dunk in trouble. I help.'

'Their friend tried to knife me in the night. He could have killed me if M'Grash hadn't stopped him. When he tried to stab M'Grash too, he threw the man overboard.'

Cavre shaded his eyes against the light and looked up at the crow's nest. 'Is that how it happened?'

A voice Dunk recognised as Kai's called down. 'Who would you trust?' Cavre opened his mouth to respond, but Kai cut him off. 'M'Grash's pal there has it right, as far as I saw.'

Cavre glared at the gold-toothed man and his companion. 'Mr. Jacques Broussard and Mr. Luc Broussard, is it?' he said. The men nodded sullenly. 'Surrender your blades, all of them. There will be no killing here. You save that for the field.'

The men hesitated for a moment, then complied. The first only had his sword and a knife. Luc, the one with the golden teeth, removed three other blades secreted about his body and handed them to Cavre. The blitzer weighed them in his wide, soft hands for a moment, then threw them overboard.

Jacques began to protest but Cavre cut him short. 'You're lucky that's not you, Mr. Broussard. Now shut up and go back to where you were. If there's another disturbance, I'll have you thrown to the bottom of

Manann's watery kingdom, and you can search for your lost weapons there.'

The two men slunk back towards the bow of the ship without another word. The looks they shot back at Dunk felt like they might set his clothes afire. When Slick slapped him on the back of his thigh, he nearly jumped from his skin.

'That pair won't be giving you any more trouble for the rest of the trip, son,' the halfling said. 'Just leave them a wide berth.'

Dunk turned to Cavre and shook the man's hand. 'Thank you, sir, for seeing through their lies.'

The blitzer grimaced. 'I wasn't doing you any favours, Mr. Hoffnung. There may be some rivalry between those who wish to join the Hackers, but I won't permit that to spill blood on this trip. Once we get to shore, though, you're on your own.'

Dunk nodded. 'I understand.' He hesitated a moment before continuing. 'Can I ask you one more question?'

'Go ahead, Mr. Hoffnung.'

'What about the man overboard?' Dunk pointed back behind the ship, from where he could still just barely hear his attacker's forlorn cries.

Cavre's face turned even more serious now. 'For what he did, Mr. Hoffnung, I'd have had him thrown overboard. M'Grash here just saved me the trouble.'

With that, Cavre turned and led the linemen with him back down the hatch.

CHAPTER EIGHT

FIVE DAYS LATER, the ship pulled into the wide and sheltered Bay of Quietude, around which sprawled Magritta, perhaps the busiest port city in all of the Old World and certainly the busiest Dunk had ever seen. Dunk and Slick stood at the port rail as the ship slipped into the harbour and found itself a mooring at the pier. By now, the sun was high enough to splash the city with sunlight.

Guards in each of the two fortresses capping the twin horns of the bay waved down at the *Sea Chariot* as it found its way to the sheltered waters. They bellowed at the sight of the Hackers' banner, some of them starting in with a rousing chorus of 'Here we go, here we go, here we go!'

With the *Spike! Magazine* tournament about to begin, it seemed that Blood Bowl fever had infected the entire town. Dunk was just glad to get a friendly

response from the watchers in the towers. The cata-
pults and trebuchets trained toward the bay made it
clear that unwelcome guests would not enter so easily.

Other than Bordeleaux, Dunk had never been in a
seaport before, and Magritta was as different from the
Bretonnian town as Altdorf itself. The salty waters of
the bay lapped right up against the docks that lined
the edges of the city. From that buttressed border of
wood and stone, the streets wound their way up into
the hills that overlooked the water until they terminated in a tall stone wall that lined the natural ridge
encompassing the bay.

'Is it safe for us to be here?' asked Dunk, suspicious
of every new town after his reception in the previous
two.

'Very,' Cavre said over Dunk's shoulder. 'With *Spike!
Magazine* holding its tournament here, there won't be
any trouble. No one would dare, it's worth too much
to them and losing the tournament would half crip-
ple this place.'

'It's all about the crowns,' Slick said, a faraway look
in his eyes. Dunk imagined he could see the reflec-
tions of those gold coins spinning in the halfling's
pupils. 'The tournaments bring a huge number of visitors to the region with coins to toss around like
confetti. Plus, there are the sponsors: Bloodweiser
and the like. Not to mention the Cabalvision rights. I
hear the new Wolf Network – you know, Ruprect
Murdark's group – won the rights this year to bring
their camras to the field.'

'Camras?' Dunk had avoided most exposure to
Blood Bowl throughout his life. Given his brother's

passion for the game, it hadn't been easy, but he'd managed it.

'Enchanted boxes with a spirit trapped inside of them. The box is formed so the spirit has to look out through the glass lens on the front of it at all times. Back when there was an NAF–'

'A what?'

'The Nuffle Amorica Football league? The original league founded by Commissioner Roze-El back in 2409?'

'That's a hundred and fifty years ago, a bit before my time.'

'It didn't dissolve until 2489.'

'Still.' Dunk waved his hands at himself.

'Wait.' Slick narrowed his eyes at the young man. 'Just how old are you? I can never tell with humans. Never mind! Don't answer that. I'm sure I don't want to know. It'll just make me feel older than I want to be. Where was I?'

'Crowns. Camras. The NAF.'

Slick brightened. 'Right! The various broadcasting companies hire wizards to use the Cabalvision spell to broadcast whatever the spirits in the camras see. Some people pay to have these appear directly in their minds. Others prefer to watch them in their crystal balls. Some of the best pubs have dozens of them, some larger than a wagon wheel, showing all the games played around the Old World at once.'

'My family had one of those. I never knew how it worked.'

'Other people use their Daemonic Vision Renderers to keep the broadcasts around so they can play them back later. These have the games broadcast into the head of an entrapped daemon, which is ensorcelled into having to play back the games it's seen at the owner's request. Of course, most daemons have tiny brains, so they can only remember so many different games at once.'

'You're kidding,' Dunk said.

'Pegleg's got one in his cabin. That's why he never comes out during the whole trip. He locks himself in there to study the games – both ours and those of our likely opponents – picking out their weaknesses and protecting our own.'

Dunk shook his head. 'Amazing. All this over some game.'

Cavre spoke up as the ship slipped into its slot in the docks. 'It's not just *some* game, Mr. Hoffnung. It's the greatest game ever.'

SLICK WOKE UP Dunk at the crack of dawn the next morning. The Hackers had been the first Blood Bowl team to arrive in town, even though the games were due to start in only two days.

'Travelling to these games is expensive,' Slick explained as Dunk ate his breakfast and got ready for practice. 'Most teams like to cut their trips as short as possible. No other Blood Bowl games are played in the region the week before the tournament. Everyone wants to be healthy for their shot at one of the four big cups.'

'There are four of these things?'

'There are lots of these things, if by "things" you mean 'tournaments.' There's probably a Blood Bowl game going on somewhere on any given day of the year, and there are tournaments every month. The big four – the Majors – those each only happen once a year.

'Your timing couldn't be better, son, for starting out a career. The *Spike! Magazine* tournament is the first of the Majors. From there, it's the Dungeon-bowl, a series of games played in underground stadiums, but you need to be sponsored by one of the Schools of Magic to enter that, so the Hackers won't be in that this year. After that is the Chaos Cup, which is just as crazy as it sounds. It all culminates in the Blood Bowl, the greatest tournament capped by the greatest championship game of the year.'

'I thought the game was called Blood Bowl.'

'Technically, it's Nuffle Amorica Football, or just Nuffle, but most people just call it after the most important match. 'Blood Bowl' just has a much better ring to it than NAF, don't you think?'

Dunk just shook his head. 'All those games, all the blood. How does anyone survive a full season?'

'Son,' Slick said, patting Dunk on the back. 'You'd better just concentrate on surviving the tryouts.'

THE HACKERS HAD set up camp in an open area on the western shore of the bay. The tents stood on the dry part of the beach, and the gentle lapping of the waves lulled the team to sleep at night.

During the day, the team and its coaching staff assembled on a level grassy field between the beach and the great wall that ran between the city proper and the westernmost of the two fortresses that guarded the entrance to the bay. A score of hopefuls showed up for the try-outs on the first day, lured by the chance to play in one of the Majors, even for a relatively new team like the Hackers.

Slick informed Dunk that the current odds against the Hackers winning the tournament were 40 to 1 against.

'How many teams are entered?' Dunk asked

'It varies from year to year. It's somewhere in the hundreds.'

Dunk's jaw dropped.

'Son,' Slick said, 'the Majors are big. Humongous. Wait until you wander into town and see the tens of thousands of fans there. How do you think the teams can afford to pay the players so much gold?'

Dunk shook his head. 'How do they whittle so many teams down? Do some of them not have to play in the first round?'

'Sometimes I forget how little you know about the game,' Slick laughed. 'The first round doesn't have any eliminations. The teams play as many games as they like against as many opponents as they like, although you can only play the same team once. If you win, you get a point.

'At the end of the first week, the teams with the top four number of points scored enter the semi-finals. The winners of those games face off in the finals, and the winner of that game is the champion. The runner-up gets 100,000 crowns, and the team that wins first place gets 200,000 crowns and the *Spike! Magazine* trophy; a mithril spike held in the fist of a gilded gauntlet.'

Dunk whistled. 'Do the players see any of that?'

Slick raised an eyebrow at the young warrior. 'Is that a hero's first concern?'

'Isn't it a Blood Bowl player's?'

'Right you are, son!' the halfling said, slapping Dunk on the back and then looking him in the face. 'Ah, I've never been prouder.'

Dunk almost thought he saw a tear start to form in Slick's eye, but the halfling started talking again, breaking the sentimental mood. 'Some players get bonuses if their team wins a big tournament. It depends on the team and the deal that the player strikes with the team.'

The halfling's grin set Dunk's teeth on edge, as Slick hooked his thumbs into his ever-straining braces and said, 'That's where I come in.'

Dunk stood up. Having come from wealth and been sheltered by it, the topic always made him uncomfortable. He knew that he needed to make a fortune somehow to help restore his family's name and to make up for the horrible mistake he'd made to trigger his family's fall in the first place. He was going to have to get over his embarrassment at talk of money for this to work at all. While he didn't always like Slick, he was thankful that he'd found him. The halfling would give him just the kind of help he needed – or so he hoped.

'Right!' Slick said. 'It's time to report in for practice. You're going to have to look sharp. I did a bit of scouting around last night, and there's a lot more competition for those spots than we saw on the *Sea Chariot*.'

The two emerged from the shelter of their tent and trotted over to the practice field. Along the way, Dunk stopped to check on Pferd. The stallion had survived the ocean voyage well, but Dunk could tell he was anxious to stretch his legs. He'd have to take him for a ride later.

'How many?' Dunk asked.

'At least two score,' Slick answered, his tone flat and business-like.

Dunk nearly tripped over his own feet. 'More than forty?' he grimaced. 'Vying for how many spots?'

'There are four open slots.'

Dunk ran his hand through his hair. 'I didn't think there would be so many.'

'Don't worry about it, son,' Slick said. 'It doesn't matter if there are four or four hundred. You've got the talent to be the best.'

'But I don't have the first clue about what I'm doing.'

'Again,' Slick said with that grin that made Dunk shudder, 'that's where I come in. Stop for a moment, and I'll tell you what you need to know.'

Dunk nodded. 'We don't have much time.'

'It's all right,' Slick said, flipping a hand at Dunk. 'I won't get into things like throwing team-mates or avoiding chainsaws or Dwarf Death-Rollers. I'll just cover the basics.

'Blood Bowl is played on a field or "pitch" a hundred paces long by sixty wide. At each end of the pitch, there's an "end zone". The idea of the game is to take the football and get it into your opponent's end zone by any means available, and score a touchdown.

'Each game starts with a coin toss. The winner chooses to kick off the ball or receive. If the ball goes out of bounds, the fans just throw it back in, and the game keeps going. It only stops for a touchdown.

Then the team that scored kicks off to the other team, and it all starts over again.

'There are two thirty-minute halves with a twenty-minute break between. When the clock runs out, the team with the most touchdowns wins the game.'

Dunk listened intently throughout. 'That doesn't sound so hard to follow.'

'It's not,' Slick said. 'That's what makes it so popular. Even goblins can manage it. There's all sorts of fun stuff I'm leaving out, of course, like how to best cheat and how to bribe the referees but we'll have plenty of time to get to that once you make the team. The only real rule you need to remember is this: no weapons allowed.'

Dunk cocked his head at the halfling. 'I thought you said something about chainsaws and Dwarf Death-Rollers.'

Slick nodded. 'All that and more. I said they're against the rules. I didn't say you wouldn't see them.

'Blood Bowl is, at its core, an abstraction of the battles and wars that rage across these lands every day. As the saying goes, "all's fair in war".'

'That's "love and war," I think,' Dunk said.

'You don't say?' Slick said, seemingly genuinely surprised. 'I can't say I know much about love, son, but I'll teach you everything I can about this kind of war.'

◆ CHAPTER NINE

As DUNK AND Slick finally topped the rise from the beach to the level area that served as the Hackers' practice field, they saw nearly fifty hopefuls lined up along the edge of the field, waiting for Pegleg to speak to them. Slick slapped Dunk on the leg and the young warrior raced over and fell into line.

Dunk gazed along the line to check out the competition. There were humans from all walks of life and many lands around the Old World and beyond. Magritta was the crossroads of this part of the globe, and it showed in the faces of these people. There were blond-haired, axe-bearing warriors from Norsca, who wore their locks in long, complex braids under their horned helmets; olive-skinned dandies in turbans and colourful robes from Araby; even more exotic people with straight, black hair under wide, conical hats from far-off Cathay; nearly black-skinned hopefuls from the distant South Lands; and many more souls from Estalia, Tilea, Bretonnia, Kislev, and even Dunk's own home: the Empire.

Dunk noticed that all of the hopefuls were humans, not an elf, dwarf, or halfling among them, much less a goblin or an orc. In fact, of the Hackers' current players, there was only one nonhuman face among them: M'Grash. Dunk wondered how an exception to the (perhaps unspoken) rule had been made for the ogre, although he could certainly see how such a creature would be a tremendous asset to any team. Most of them were men, of course, although a few women stood out in the group, clearly ready to grind into the dirt any man who might question their abilities.

Before Dunk could think more about this, Cavre stepped up before the line and called the hopefuls to attention.

'Pardon me, kind ladies and sirs!' the dark-skinned man shouted. The chatter in the line fell silent. 'My name is Rhett Cavre. I'm not only the assistant coach here but also the starting blitzer, unless one of you thinks you're good enough to take my job.'

Nervous laughter rippled through the line at that.

'Welcome to the Hackers' boot camp, and good luck. I hope to get to know you over the next two days and maybe even play with the best of you in the tournament. As we run you through our drills and test your skills and abilities, I want you to remember the one rule we enforce above all others with the Hackers: always listen to your coach!'

Cavre turned to the side, sweeping his arms wide toward Pegleg. 'With that in mind, allow me to introduce the coach of the Bad Bay Hackers: Captain Pegleg Haken.'

Pegleg, still dressed in his captain's uniform, limped his way towards the line, step-tap, step-tap, step-tap. When he reached Cavre, he took off his sword belt and scabbarded cutlass and handed them to the star blitzer. Then, still without saying a word, he glared up and down the line, scanning the motley faces he found there. Then he drew a deep breath and spoke.

'I've never seen such a sorry lot of losers!' Pegleg growled with the voice of a drill sergeant and the attitude of a daemon. 'You stupid sods came here because you want a chance to risk your lives for a bit of glory and gold. You are idiots! Blood Bowl is a hard game for hard people. If you want to earn some money by fighting, try something safer... like joining your local *army*! At least they feed you for free there!'

Pegleg bowed his head and shook it, his black curls bouncing beneath his bright-yellow tricorn hat. 'The life expectancy of the average Blood Bowl player is measured not in seasons, but games. I'm sure that some of you have families back home that care about you, friends that wouldn't mind seeing you again while you're still breathing, maybe even a lover that hopes to hold you in her arms again.'

He looked up from under the brim of his hat. 'The best advice I can give you is to leave. Now.'

A pair of brothers from Tilea, standing next to Dunk, looked at each other and started to weep. As one, they broke from the line and raced for the beach and the safety of the streets of Magritta beyond. Five others calved off from the line and chased after the others. One of the dandies from Araby joined them, wailing the entire way.

Pegleg glared at the remaining hopefuls until the cries of the cowards faded into the distance. 'Anyone else?' he said.

Dunk felt his foot start to step forward, but he pressed it down into the soft earth instead. He hadn't come all this way to give up now. Blood Bowl couldn't be any more dangerous than fighting dragons. Or a chimera. Could it?

'Now that those weak-livered pansies are gone, we can get down to business,' Pegleg growled as he paced back and forth along the line of hopefuls. Step-tap, step-tap, step-tap. He waved his hook as he spoke, often coming within bare inches of a hopeful's face. No one dared to flinch.

'Give me fifty laps around the pitch!' Pegleg roared. 'Now!'

BY THE END of the first day of the two-day boot camp, Dunk wished he was dead. He was sure that it would hurt less. When he sat down in his tent that night, every inch of him seemed to be so sore and bruised.

'You think this is bad,' Slick said. 'Wait until you wake up tomorrow.'

The first day had been all about testing the hopefuls' raw abilities, as well as their limits. Pegleg and Cavre had run them through drill after drill: races, obstacle courses, tackling, throwing, catching, and more.

It was clear that Dunk would never be the blitzer Cavre was. He didn't have a head for tackling, and nearly half of the others were able to outrace him in a dead sprint. Perhaps he'd be best as a lineman or a catcher, although Slick was pushing him to try for thrower.

'Blitzers are often the team captains and the top-paid players,' the halfling said, 'but sadly that's not where your talents lie. Throwers are the next best.'

'Won't I just end up playing behind Kur?' Dunk asked. 'I don't think he's going anywhere soon.'

'Even the toughest players get hurt sometimes. It's inevitable. That's why they have backups. Sooner or later, those players get their chance on the pitch, often in the most important parts of the game.

'Besides, if you shoot for thrower and fall short, Pegleg can always make you a lineman instead. Aim high, son.'

'You think I can make thrower?' Dunk tried to keep the need out of his voice, but feared the halfling could hear it.

Slick patted the young warrior on the back. 'I could feed you a line of lies, son, but you'd see right through that. I'll be honest with you: I don't know. You have all the raw talent you need, but your lack of Blood Bowl skills could haunt you.'

Dunk knew what Slick meant. He'd been trained with the sword, the knife, the bow, the spear, to be a warrior, not a Blood Bowl player. While the skills needed for both overlapped, they weren't identical.

'Still,' the halfling said softly, 'I've never seen someone with an arm like yours. The way you brought down that chimera? Simply stunning.'

'It was a lucky shot,' Dunk said as he lay back on his cot.

'Then be as lucky as you can,' Slick said as sleep reached out and surrounded him like a dozen linemen and beat him unconscious.

'AWAKE, YOU ROTTERS!' Pegleg's voice shouted, waking Dunk from his dreams, seemingly only a moment after he lay down his head. 'Awake! The last of you buggers out of his tent gets cut right now!'

Dunk rolled out of his cot and stumbled out of the tent, still in the same clothes he'd been wearing yesterday. He'd been too tired to change into a nightshirt. He ran a hand over his face and another through his hair as he raced to the impromptu line forming in front of Cavre as Pegleg stormed through the camp, hollering at the top of his capacious lungs.

A dozen others joined Dunk immediately, and another few trickled in soon after, moving slowly and groaning from having to stretch their tortured muscles with such little notice.

Dunk's whole body was sore from his head to his toes, but it wasn't as bad as he'd feared. Back home, Lehrer's training program had kept him in decent shape, and the long journey to Magritta hadn't afforded him much opportunity to grow soft. Still, he'd worked himself as hard as he ever had yesterday, and he felt it.

After a full pass through the camp, Pegleg limped over to stand next to Cavre and survey the line. Of the forty or so hopefuls that had stuck around through the training yesterday, only twenty stood in the line now.

'Mr. Cavre,' Pegleg snarled. 'I told you this was a sorry lot.'

'I didn't disagree with you, captain.'

'Where are the rest of them?'

'I'll check, captain.'

'No.' Pegleg held Cavre back with his gleaming hook. 'I'll rouse them myself.'

The pirate-coach stalked through the camp, peering into the tents. Those nearest to the line were all empty, their former occupants staring back at Pegleg from the line. Dunk's tent was further back, closer to the sea.

Pegleg came to a tent and stopped. 'Wu Chen!' he shouted. 'This isn't a brothel in Cathay! Get out here.'

As the silence from the tent grew longer, Pegleg's face grew redder. With a horrible snarl, the pirate raised his hook high and brought it down, ripping through the fabric of the tent. 'I said *get out here!*' he raged. 'You *worthless*–'

Pegleg cut himself short as his hook tangled in the cloth. He tugged at it, trying to free his arm, but he only wound himself in further. With a mighty, two-handed wrench, the stakes holding down the tent gave, and Pegleg cascaded backward, the whole of the tent coming with him, entangling him in its cloth and its lines.

'Mr. Cavre!' Pegleg shouted as he fell backward, wrapped in the remains of the tent tighter than any mummy. The players, whose half of the camp lay on the other side of the bonfire in the middle of the camp, started to laugh as their leader's tent-packaged body began to roll toward the sea.

'Mr. Cavre!' Pegleg shrieked as he heard the lapping of the waves and realised the extent of his plight.

The blitzer was already on his way. 'Mr. K'Thragsh!' he shouted as he sprinted toward the captain. 'A hand if you will!'

The ogre burst out of the pack of players and dashed toward Pegleg as he rolled toward the waters of the bay, screaming, 'Mr. Cavre!'

The captain's struggles only made his situation worse. If he'd have stayed still, he probably wouldn't have continued to roll down the gentle slope toward the sea. As it was, he fought and clawed away with his hook like a cornered wildcat. At one point, he managed to tear the fabric from in front of his face. The sight of the approaching water snatched a horrifying scream from his chest, which was cut off when he rolled over on his face again.

Despite M'Grash's long-legged stride, Cavre reached the captain first and stopped him from rolling further. He stopped the man just before the high-tide mark, much to the captain's delight. However, before Pegleg could offer his thanks, M'Grash picked him up and dangled him from the end of his outstretched limb like a prize fish he'd just managed to haul to shore.

'Get me away from the water!' Pegleg bellowed. The ogre nearly dropped him in shock, but the creature managed to recover himself and carried the captain back toward the bonfire pit, still held in front of him like a newsworthy catch.

Before M'Grash got too far, Pegleg's struggles bore fruit. The tent-trap he found himself in finally gave way entirely, and he plummeted from the ogre's grasp, crashing to the ground. M'Grash blushed red as he stared at the ragged remnants of the tent, still hanging in his hand.

The players burst out in howls of laughter, which were only made worse when Pegleg tripped over his good leg as he tried to stand up. Some of the hope-fuls joined in too, although quietly. The last thing any of them needed was Pegleg mad at them.

The captain finally leapt to his peg and shook the tent's lines off of his leg. 'What are you all laughing at?' he snarled at the players. The uproar only got louder.

Pegleg stormed over to the players, his hook held out and high, ready to impale the first person he met. But before he could exact his revenge, Cavre's voice rang out.

'Captain!' he said. 'We have a problem!'

Pegleg stopped so hard, he drove his peg halfway into the beach's sand. 'It had better be good, Mr. Cavre!' he said, his face as crimson as his coat.

'It's murder, captain,' Cavre said. 'Murder!'

Even as far away as Dunk was, he could see the body lying in the spot left bare by Pegleg's destruction of the tent. It was Wu Chen's.

Pegleg rushed over to the corpse and cursed. Hold-ing the curved end of his hook against his forehead, he said something quiet and respectful over the body. As he finished, he looked up and gasped.

'Quick, Mr. Cavre,' he said, 'check the other tents.'

Dunk's stomach fell into his boots. He and the other hopefuls watched from the line in detached horror as Cavre and Pegleg went through each of the tents, pulling back their flaps one by one. One by one, they discovered a full score of dead hopefuls, each cut down in their prime.

The other players came over from their side of the camp to help. They hauled the bodies from the tents and stacked them up near the fire pit, one at a time.

Dunk tried to go down to help too, but Cavre pointed him back toward the line. 'This isn't something for the hopefuls to help with, Mr. Hoffnung,' he said.

'Why not?' Dunk asked. He'd trained with each of the victims yesterday, and he wanted to do what little he could for them.

'Tell him, Mr. Fullbelly,' Cavre said to Slick before returning to his grisly work.

The halfling took Slick by the leg and guided him back to the line. 'Think about it, son,' he said softly. 'Who stands the most to gain from all this?'

As Dunk returned to his place, he glanced up and down the line at the faces of the other hopefuls. 'We do,' he said with a grimace.

It took the Hackers the better part of an hour to pick through the place. Once all the bodies were accounted for, Pegleg looked up at the line of hopefuls. 'We don't have time for this, Mr. Cavre.'

'Aye, captain,' the blitzer said. Then he raced up to where the hopefuls still stood and said, 'You lot are with me. We have a long day ahead of us, and a few deaths never stopped a game of Blood Bowl.'

CHAPTER TEN

THAT DAY'S TRAINING was even worse than the first. This time around, Cavre fitted each of the players with a spare set of armour before practice began.

Dunk was amazed at the sophistication of the armour. Unlike the stuff he'd worn before, which was fashioned for the rigors of battle, this sort of armour was designed for the weaponless head-knocking and unarmed combat of Blood Bowl. It featured massive spaulders – Slick called them 'shoulder pads' – which were made as much for knocking down other players as for protection.

Dunk also wore a helmet that featured a wrought-iron grill over the face to protect his eyes from probing fingers, or so it seemed. Unlike traditional helmets, though, this one featured padding on the inside to protect the skull from the regular blows rained down on it by opposing players. It was painted in a loud yellow and featured the three crossed swords on a green background that comprised the Hackers' logo.

Overall, the armour fit tighter than Dunk was used to, and featured more padding underneath. It was built for speed as well as protection, to allow the wearer to run as well as survive an attack. The armour of the linemen and blitzers was just a bit heavier than that of the throwers and catchers, whose smaller shoulder pads were built so they could easily lift their arms over their heads.

The helmet, the shoulder pads, the gauntlets and even the knee and elbow pads featured sharp sets of spikes that would quickly make a mess of unprotected flesh. Their presence explained the amazing number of small dents found on most of the sets of practice armour loaned out to the hopefuls.

After getting fitted with the equipment, the hopefuls played a loose scrimmage against each other, mostly just running through a set of plays over and over again. The hopefuls lined up against each other and tried to accomplish whatever goals Cavre set for them, which ranged from successfully throwing the ball to running the ball through a phalanx of linemen. Dunk found himself in a set of thrower's armour, ready to throw the ball downfield, towards the opposing team's end zone at a moment's notice.

Dunk decided he liked being a thrower for more than just the gold and glory that Slick had mentioned. When you had the ball in the game, there wasn't much more frightening than realising that everyone on the opposing team hoped to crush you far enough into the turf that you couldn't get up without a group of helpers armed with a set of trusty shovels.

When most players had the ball, there was little they could (or at least should) do but run for the end zone and hope to find some daylight along the way. Throwers, though, could scramble around as much as they liked until they found someone downfield (closer to the end zone) to chuck the ball at. Some of the balls they worked with were spiked too, which made catching the ball a bit more of an adventure, but all of the catchers did their best, even when their efforts drew their own blood. They all wanted to make an impression, and not of the full body-in-the-turf variety.

At midday, Cavre called a break for lunch, and the hopefuls joined the team members around the fire pit for more of the team's traditional stew. This always seemed to be made of some mixture of cheese, beer, and some sort of unidentifiable meat. Dunk had already had more than his fill of the stuff aboard the *Sea Chariot*, but after a day and a half of Blood Bowl tryouts it tasted like the finest of meals ever served in his family's keep back in Altdorf.

The spirits were high among the hopefuls, although the players were more subdued. During the middle of the meal, Pegleg, who had been wandering around the camp all morning, came by and whispered something in Cavre's ear. The two men were on the other side of the fire pit, and try as he might Dunk couldn't hear a thing they said to each other. For a moment, he thought they might be looking at him, but it happened so quickly he told himself it was his imagination.

In the afternoon, the hopefuls played a full scrimmage game against the players. The professionals whipped the amateurs like orc stepchildren. Several of the hopefuls limped off the field, or were carried off, injured. Those who were left grinned openly. It left them fewer competitors for the four spots available on the team.

'You're doing great, son,' Slick said during a break in the action. 'There's really only one person you have to beat for that thrower spot.'

'I know,' Dunk said, as he tossed back a tanker of water, swished it around in his mouth, and spat it out. 'Luc,' he said, as he glared over at the Bretonnian with the golden teeth.

Luc noticed Dunk looking at him and stalked over toward the young warrior, his lip curled in a savage sneer, exposing his fake, yellow teeth. 'Give up now and leave, Imperial. I'm the Hacker's next thrower.'

'Save it for someone who hasn't seen you piss yourself in front of M'Grash,' Slick said, stepping between the two.

Luc looked down at the tubby halfling and laughed. 'Still letting others do your fighting for you?' he said to Dunk. 'On the pitch, it'll be just you and me.'

TIME IN THE scrimmage was winding down. Cavre had been swapping Luc and Dunk out for the thrower's position the whole game. Luc had made a few fine throws, but he'd also hurled three interceptions. The professionals mostly had their way with the hopefuls, as was to be expected. They were eager to take the newcomers down a peg or two, and it caused some of the amateurs to become frustrated and make even worse mistakes.

Dunk was used to this kind of pressure. Back in Altdorf, Lehrer had arranged for him to spar against only the best in the Empire, and the opponents received bonuses if they beat the young warrior. Dunk had taken many losses at the hands of Lehrer's friends, but over time he'd become a better swordsman for it.

After the professionals scored yet another touchdown, the hopefuls lined up to receive the kick-off once again. Dunk was way back with Luc, who stood on the other side of the field from him.

Cavre kept time on a stopwatch. Before the kick-off, he looked at it and said, 'This will be the last chance. The next touchdown ends the game.'

Dunk rubbed his hands together and waited for the kick. It sailed down the field, over the heads of most of the players and angled right for him. He stretched out his arms and caught it with both hands, just as Cavre had taught him.

Dunk knew exactly what he wanted to do as soon as he got the ball. The trick was finding enough time to pull it off. He looked down the field and saw the professional linemen charging straight toward him. Meanwhile, their catchers hung back to cover the amateur catchers racing for the end zone.

Dunk tucked the ball under his arm and dashed off to his left, toward where Luc was standing. 'Block for me!' he said to the Bretonnian.

'Of course,' Luc said, venom dripping from his tongue. He stepped forward to put himself between Dunk and the oncoming linemen. Then, at the last second, he dove to the side, letting the professionals past.

Dunk was not only ready for this, he'd planned for it. With the professionals charging for Luc, he'd feinted moving behind the traitor and then dashed back to the right.

The professionals weren't fooled for long though. Karsten and Henrik swerved past Luc and chased right after Dunk. The young warrior gazed downfield, hoping that one of the catchers had managed to get open. He saw a young man from Albion, Simon Sherwood, racing for the right corner of the end zone and waving his arms wildly.

Dunk heard Karsten and Henrik's boots stamping across the field behind him, growing closer with every step. It was now or never.

Dunk cocked back his arm and put everything he had into hurling the football down the field. The worst part was concentrating hard enough to ignore the sound of the two stocky linemen stormed up behind him. As he released the ball, they hit him as one, knocking him flying to the turf.

Still under the two linemen, Dunk craned his neck to the left and stared downfield. Through all of the players now charging back down toward the other end of the field, he could see the corner of the end zone he'd targeted, and Simon sprinting toward it at top speed. The only player between Simon and the ball was the terrifyingly tall M'Grash, but when he looked up to see where the ball was, he hesitated, tripped, and fell. The ball arced down out of the sky as if it were skating down a rainbow, and landed right in Simon's outstretched hands.

Pegleg let loose a blast on his referee's whistle and threw his hand and hook in the air, signalling a touchdown and the end of the game.

The amateurs went wild, shouting and screaming as if they'd just won the Blood Bowl itself. Some of them raced back, grabbed Dunk and hoisted him upon their shoulders so they could parade him around the field. The professionals stood back and watched the whole thing, smiling unabashedly at the hopefuls' joy in the game.

'Not bad, Mr. Hoffnung,' Cavre said to him as Dunk was carried past. 'Your team lost 5 to 1, but that was a fine play.'

Dunk grinned widely and glanced over at Slick. The halfling tossed him a thumbs-up.

When the celebrating died down, Cavre called out. 'Congratulations to the prospects for a game well played. You can't fault your enthusiasm.'

A round of cheers went up from the professionals, who seemed pleased to have such a solid group of hopefuls trying to join their team. They and the prospects gathered closer to Cavre to listen as he spoke.

'As you know,' the blitzer said, 'we have only four spots available on our team. I wish that we had more, but those are the rules. Those of you who don't make it, don't be discouraged. The way this game is played, there are more openings on many teams every week, and we're sure to have more by the time this tournament is over.'

The gathered crowed laughed nervously at that.

'So, as soon as Captain Haken gets here, we can get on with… ah, there he is!' Cavre pointed to his right, and the crowd assembled around him parted to let Pegleg through.

The look on the captain's face was dead serious, and the smiles left the faces of all those who saw him. He limped through the crowd and said, 'A moment of your time, Mr. Cavre.'

The blitzer excused himself, and he and the captain walked off toward the city's wall and spoke in hushed voices.

'What do you think they're on about?' Simon asked Dunk. The two had been shoved together ever since the big play.

'I don't know,' Dunk said.

'My guess,' said Milo Hoffstetter, the hulk of a man from Middenheim who'd been campaigning hard for the blitzer spot, 'is they figured out who the killer is.'

Dunk felt someone tugging at his shoulder. He looked down to see Slick trying to pull him from the crowd. 'What is it?' Dunk asked.

'I need to talk with you,' Slick said.

'What about?'

'Now, son.'

Dunk looked around and realised everyone else was watching him and Slick. He shrugged at them. 'He's not really my father, you know.'

The players all shook with laughter at that. Meanwhile, Dunk slipped away from them and after Slick.

'What is it?' he asked the halfling. He'd never seen Slick so agitated. His colour was a bit off and Dunk thought he could see him sweating, something Slick had confessed to hating so much that he would only consider it in life or death circumstances. 'They're just about to announce who made the team,' Dunk said, hoping that would cheer him up.

'That's the least of our concerns,' Slick said.

These words stunned Dunk. He'd never known the halfling to put anything above Blood Bowl. For the past few weeks, preparing Dunk to make the team had been the only thing that Slick had concerned himself with.

'You're scaring me.'

Slick looked up into Dunk's eyes, searching there for something. 'No,' he said, almost to himself. 'You didn't do it, did you? You don't have it in you.'

'What in Morr's secret names are you talking about?' Dunk's heart had just about stopped. He was so focused on Slick, he didn't hear the step-tap, step-tap, step-tap behind him until a gleaming hook fell on his shoulder.

'Mr. Hoffnung,' Pegleg said.

Dunk whirled about to face the captain. As he did, the hook sliced through the shoulder of his shirt and drew blood from his skin. 'What is it?' he asked. He saw the captain, Cavre, and everyone else in the camp all around him now, all eyes intently on him.

Pegleg reached into his long, crimson coat and drew out something bound in a white cloth. As he unwrapped it between his hand and hook, a long knife with a serrated edge appeared. It was covered with blood from end to end.

'This is the blade that killed all those hopeful souls in the dark of night,' the captain said, like a judge intoning a life sentence. 'I found it in your tent.'

 **CHAPTER ELEVEN**

THE CROWD SURGED around Dunk, and he suddenly found it hard to breathe. 'You can't be serious,' he said, trying to stay calm. 'I didn't do this! I wouldn't!'

Pegleg held the knife in his hands as if gauging its weight. 'That may well be, Mr. Hoffnung,' he said, his eyes never wavering from Dunk's. 'But this is a hard game for hard people, and some of them will do anything to get their first team contract. I've seen men do worse for gold, to be sure.'

'Pegleg,' Slick said. 'Captain. I'll vouch for this boy's character. I slept in his tent all night and didn't hear a thing.'

The captain gave the halfling a mirthless smile. 'I know you'll understand, Mr. Fullbelly, that I can't really take the word of a man's agent. Your bias here is clear.'

'But, Captain—'

Pegleg cut off Slick's words with a wave of his hook. Then he gazed at Dunk again. The young warrior thought he saw a hint of sadness in the man's eyes.

'I didn't do it,' Dunk said again. Even as the words left his lips, he could see that they were falling on deaf ears.

'Some coaches,' Pegleg said, 'would appreciate your drive. Anyone willing to kill a dozen people in cold blood could be a real asset on a Blood Bowl team.'

Dunk started to relax a bit, but then he saw Pegleg hand the bloodied blade to Cavre and begin fingering his hook.

'Others would kill you on the spot, cut you into pieces, and throw those into the sea.'

Dunk swallowed hard at that and quickly assessed the crowd. He was outnumbered nearly thirty to one, and he didn't have a weapon at hand. The Blood Bowl regulations had forbidden him from bringing even his knife onto the field.

The looks on the faces around him ranged from anger to disbelief. Two of the hopefuls, though, were grinning: Luc and Jacques. Were they just happy to see him go, or was there something more damning behind those hateful smiles?

'So,' Dunk said, summoning up every bit of courage he had and wondering if he could outrun everyone else here. He was sure that Cavre could catch him in a straight sprint, but if he kicked the blitzer in the knee before taking off he might have a chance.

'So,' he repeated again, looking straight into Pegleg's eyes, 'what do *you* plan to do with me?'

Pegleg grimaced for a moment, then waved off in the direction of the tents full of the dead. 'Those people knew what the risks were when they tried out for the team. If they didn't die in the camp here, there was a good chance they'd have never made it past their third game.'

The captain stared hard at Dunk. 'However,' he said. 'I can't have myself and every other member of this team fearing every moment for their lives. Cutthroats can't go around cutting the throats of their own kind.'

Dunk didn't like where this was heading. 'So?' he said.

'So, you're off the team.'

Most of the people in the crowd gasped. Luc and Jacques snorted out hard, mean laughs. Cavre frowned. Dunk saw tears welling up in M'Grash's eyes. Slick all but wept.

'I was never on it.' Dunk feared he was pointing out the obvious.

'You would have been,' said Pegleg, 'if not for this.'

Slick wailed openly at this, and he somehow found himself in the arms of M'Grash, who cradled the halfling in his monstrous arms like a fussing baby as he stifled his own sobs. Dunk started to say something to Pegleg. He thought that he should make some kind of a speech to punctuate a grand exit. Instead he just said, 'Fine,' turned, and left.

'IT's NOT OVER, son,' Slick said. The halfling's eyes were dry now, although the smoke in the pub, a dark, cheap place known as the Bad Water, irritated them something fierce. The place was packed wall to wall with Blood Bowl fans in town for the tournament. 'The Hackers were just our first option, not our last. Look at it this way. We got a free ride to Magritta out of them!'

The thought did little to comfort Dunk, try as he might. 'I'm not sure I'm cut out for Blood Bowl,' he said.

Slick, who was more than a little drunk at the moment, slapped a hand on his chest in shock. 'Not cut out for Blood Bowl?' he gasped. 'You, son, are the most natural talent I've ever seen in this game, maybe that the game itself has ever seen. If not for this dirty trick some scoundrel played to keep you off the team, you'd have been a definite. You'd have gotten the top starting salary, to boot.'

With that, Slick's eyes began to tear up again, and Dunk felt obliged to reach over and pat the halfling on the back. This kind gesture nearly knocked the imbalanced Slick off his extra-high barstool.

Dunk reached over to steady Slick and his stool. When he had succeeded, he noticed that someone was standing behind him and watching him. He turned to see an attractive young woman with long, auburn hair and dark black eyes that seemed to suck in everything they saw.

'Can I help you, my lady?' Dunk said in a tone that purposefully betrayed the fact that the answer to this question should only be 'no'.

'Are you Dunkel Hoffnung?' the woman said with a twinkle in her eye and a half-smile on her ruby-painted lips.

'Who's asking?' Slick said, instantly seeming sober now that he had something to take his mind off the events of the day.

'Lästiges Weibchen,' the woman said, 'on special assignment from *Spike! Magazine*.'

Slick stood up on his barstool to seem as tall as possible. It wobbled under him a bit, but he was able to right it without help from Dunk. 'You hear that, son? *Spike! Magazine* is on to you already. I told you that you were fated for great things in this game.'

'Interesting things, for sure,' Lästiges said, keeping her eyes drilled to Dunk.

'What's special about your assignment?' Dunk asked, returning the reporter's gaze without flinching.

'Have you ever heard of Dirk Heldmann?' This wasn't a question, Dunk knew.

'Who hasn't?' Slick answered. He looked over at Dunk. 'The team captain of the Reikland Reavers. They haven't had a blitzer that good since Griff Ober-wald's playing days. That's the problem with human teams,' he said to Lästiges as an aside. 'Too short-lived to ever build a real dynasty.'

'Your name,' Dunk said to the woman. ' "Weibchen." That's from Marienburg, isn't it?'

'You should know, Mr. *Hoffnung*,' Lästiges said through gritted teeth.

Dunk shook his head. 'We don't want to talk to her, Slick,' he said. 'She's nothing but trouble.'

'How *dare* you?' Lästiges said, her dark eyes flashing. 'After what your family did to mine–'

Dunk turned his back on the woman and picked up his stein of Killer Genuine Draft. 'It was business,' he said, 'and it was before my time.'

Lästiges ground out a little growl. 'Well, if you won't talk with me, I'm sure Dirk Heldmann will. *Spike! Magazine* is dying to know what the Reavers' top scorer thinks about his big brother being accused of murder.'

'Khaine's bloody teeth!' Slick said, turning to Dunk. 'Dirk Heldmann is your brother?'

Dunk slammed back what was left of his beer and turned back to talk to Slick and Lästiges, his eyes glowering at her. 'When he announced he was going to take up Blood Bowl, our parents disowned him. He changed his name before his first game.'

'Word is your family sent him off to play Blood Bowl for his own safety,' Lästiges said with a vicious grin. 'After they imploded in such a terrible mess, anyone could understand why he'd want it that way.'

Dunk considered throwing his beer at the woman, but his stein was empty. He signalled the bartender for another in case the urge struck him again.

'Nice to see the press is as fair and impartial with Blood Bowl as it is with real news,' Dunk said. 'I don't have anything to say to you.' The bartender slipped over another stein with the initials KGD chiselled on it in what were obviously supposed to be dwarf runes. It was a fairly drunk dwarf responsible for these runes, though. 'I think you should leave.'

'Really?' Lästiges said with mock surprise. 'After what's been happening with you lately, I thought you might want all the friends you can get.'

Dunk frowned. 'I've been banned from the team. What else can they do to me?'

Lästiges threw back her head and laughed. 'You see those two over there?' she asked, tossing her lustrous hair toward a far corner of the pub where two people sat, dressed in black robes. One was the shortest elf that Dunk had ever seen – thin and pale, with white-blond hair and proud, angular features – but a foot shorter than most other elves. The other was the tallest dwarf Dunk had ever seen; stocky and swarthy, with soot-black hair and a rough-hewn face, but a foot taller than most other dwarves.

In fact, the two were nearly identical in stature so that Dunk had the strange impression they were twins. Their uniform dress – dark robes sashed with red ropes and featuring a frothing Wolf embroidered across their chests – only emphasised the effect.

'Who are they?' Dunk asked, feigning indifference. As he spoke, he knew that the duo was aware he was talking about them, even if they were too far away to hear his words.

'GWs,' Slick said in what he seemed to think was a hushed whisper, although in his drunkenness it was more like a soft shout. 'Game Wizards. They work for the Cabalvision networks to keep the teams in line.' He pointed unsubtly at the wizards' uniforms. 'Those two must be here for Wolf Sports.'

'Are they the law around here?' Dunk was confused. What business was it of these people what happened in the Hackers' camp?

Lästiges giggled. On anyone else, this might have seemed cute, but with her it was clearly meant to be cruel. 'Oh, they're much worse. The Cabalvision networks make a fortune with these tournaments, and it's their job to make sure no one damages the rating with silly things like, oh, I don't know – *murdering a dozen of your fellow prospects.*'

Dunk tried to feign indifference and change the subject. 'Slick,' he said, 'do you know anywhere around here I can find myself a good blade? I feel naked without a proper sword on my hip.'

Slick pulled his attention away from the GWs slowly. 'Wha? Oh, yeah, son. We'll see what we can do about that. First thing tomorrow.'

'I've done what I can to help here,' Lästiges said merrily. 'I'd like to interview you sometime later, Dunk, maybe when you're a bit more available. Perhaps we could do you and your brother at the same time.'

Dunk stared into his stein. 'I haven't seen my brother in three years.'

'All the better,' Lästiges said. 'I just love family reunions, especially under such happy circumstances.'

Dunk gripped the handle of his stein and tried to convince himself the beer in it would be better in his belly than all over the reporter. When he looked over his shoulder to gauge the distance to his target, she was gone. He glanced at the door across the crowded room and saw her disappearing into Magritta's early dusk.

'Do I have to worry about the law in Magritta?' Dunk asked Slick.

'Ordinarily, yes,' the halfling said. 'But this is during one of the four Major Tournaments. The prince of Magritta doesn't want any major disruptions during this event. It brings a lot of crowns into the city's coffers and, by extension, into his. He's usually happy to leave things to the Game Wizards instead.'

'How much do I have to worry about them?' Dunk tried to keep his voice steady.

'Not too much, I'd say, son.'

'How's that?' Dunk shot a look at the halfling and saw him gazing toward the exit.

'They're on their way out of here right now.'

Dunk screwed up his face for a moment as he tried to figure out what was going on. He thought these Game Wizards would at least want to question him. Maybe Lästiges was leading them on to their next 'suspect' instead.

'Whew!' a voice said from behind Dunk and Slick. 'I thought those two would never leave.'

CHAPTER TWELVE

THE YOUNG WARRIOR and the halfling turned toward the voice as one. There they saw a greasy creature with wide, green eyes and a long, wide nose with a wart on each side of it. Oily wisps of colourless hair swept aimlessly over his sunburned scalp and weeping patches of acne covered his pustuled face. He extended his hand to Dunk and then to Slick, who shook it, mostly because they were too stunned by the man to think better of the gesture.

'Name's Gunther the Gobbo,' the man said. His high-pitched voice seemed to be always on the verge of breaking into a mad cackle. 'I've come to talk with your boy here. I understand he's quite a… talent.'

Dunk nodded queasily. Slick spoke up, eager as a stray dog presented with a plate of raw beef. 'You have that right. He's the best young recruit I've ever seen, and I've seen them all for the past fifty years.

Take my word for it, this kid's bound for the Hall of Fame.'

Gunther nodded excitedly. The way his head bobbed, Dunk wasn't sure it was properly attached to his neck. 'Great, great! That's just what I hear.' Then Gunther's tone lowered into a comic imitation of conspiratorial. 'I also hear you had some problems today, perhaps of your own creation.'

'I didn't kill all those people!' Dunk shouted. He'd had enough of the accusations, especially from people he'd just met.

The entire room fell silent, and all eyes snapped over to Dunk.

'Of course, you didn't, son,' Slick said awkwardly. 'It was a bloody war, and I'm sure you only killed a small percentage of them.'

The room burst into laughter, and the patrons and staff went back to their own conversations.

'Well played,' Gunther said to Slick, oozing sick admiration. 'Just the kind of person I'd like to be in business with.'

'What are you selling?' Dunk asked.

'Ha!' Gunther said. 'That's funny, kid. You must be new around here. I'm not *selling*. I'm *buying*.'

Dunk shot Slick a what's-he-talking-about look. The halfling, still standing on his barstool, put an arm around the young warrior as he spoke.

'Gunther the Gobbo here, he's one of the biggest bookmakers in the Old World. He takes bets from all comers, sets the odds, then pays the winners and collects from the losers. Best of all Gunther here has set himself up as an odds making expert on Cabalvision too.'

'I used to appear on CBS, but Wolf Sports just picked me up,' Gunther said as he flashed Dunk a smile that reminded him of the chimera.

'CBS?' Dunk asked Slick.

'Crystal Ball Service. One of the Cabalvision networks. It conjures images into crystal balls around the Old World rather than popping them into the minds of subscribers.' The halfling pointed out the large, glassy balls hanging over the bar and in various corners of the pub. They were dark and cloudy now, but Dunk suspected that was because no games were being played at the moment.

'So, kid,' Gunther said, barely catching the drool from his chin with a red velvet handkerchief that looked like it had been trapped in such service for years. 'Aren't you going to ask me what I'm buying?'

Dunk looked Gunther up and down again, then shook his head. 'No.'

The young warrior had expected the bookie's face to fall, but Gunther's grin just widened, and his handkerchief lost its battle with the drool for a moment. 'C'mon, kid, all the rookies are shy the first time they meet me. Don't you sweat it. Ask me.'

Dunk started to shake his head again, but Slick interrupted. 'Tell him,' the halfling said.

Gunther slapped Slick on the back and nearly knocked him from his barstool. Trying to right himself, the halfling lurched backward and fell neatly behind the bar.

'Oi!' the burly bartender said as he snatched Slick up and shoved him back onto his stool. The back of the halfling's green jacket was soaked with some strange mixture that smelled flammable. 'I've warned you before about trying to sneak back here for a drink!'

'You must have me mixed up with someone else,' Slick said, as politely as he could, trying to press his curly hair back into place. His voice squeaked like that of a talking mouse. 'I've never been here before.'

The bartender, a dark-haired man with a bushy moustache and a tattooed goatee glared at Slick for a moment before tossing a bar rag at him in disgust. 'Right!' he said as he went back to serving drinks to a pack of skaven – walking ratmen – at the other end of the bar. 'You half-pints all look the same to me,' he muttered.

Slick dried his hair off with the bar rag, then looked at it in disgust and tossed it back over his shoulder. 'You were saying?' he asked Gunther.

'I heard about your problems earlier today,' the bookie said. 'I can help.'

'News travels fast,' Dunk said, instantly suspicious.

'How?' asked Slick, ignoring Dunk.

Gunther leaned in towards them, and whispered low enough that only they could hear. 'I can get your boy here on the team of your choice.'

'How's that?' Dunk asked.

Slick put a hand on the young warrior's chest. 'Now, son. When someone of the Gobbo's stature offers to lend you a hand, the polite thing to do is accept.'

Gunther gave Slick an unintentionally horrible toothy grin. Things were caught in there that were rotted worse than the teeth that held them. The stench caused Dunk to reel back. He took another pull from his stein to kill the smell.

'You're a creature I can do business with,' Gunther said to Slick, and the two grinned at each other like cats about to split a wounded eagle.

'How can you deliver on a promise like that?' Dunk asked. He ignored the dirty look Slick shot him.

Gunther narrowed his eyes at Dunk. 'Let's just say that in my line of work a lot of people end up owing me favours.'

'What's the catch?' Dunk asked, returning Gunther's glare.

The bookie's face broke into a smile again. 'No catch, kid. Just a couple of friends doing each other favours.'

'We're not friends.'

'Everyone has to start somewhere, son,' Slick said. 'We haven't known each other all that long ourselves.'

'We haven't done him any favours.'

'Not yet,' said Gunther, a knowing look in his eyes, 'but someday, when I need one, you will.'

Dunk nodded. 'You fix the games you take bets on.'

Slick slapped a hand over Dunk's mouth. 'Son!' he said in a mixture of exasperation and shame. 'Don't you talk like that to our new friend.'

'*Your* new friend,' Dunk said as he pulled the halfling's tiny hand from his face.

'Any team you like,' Gunther said. 'Interested in playing for the Reavers? I can make it happen.'

'Not interested.'

Slick gasped in heartbreaking disappointment.

'Okay, kid,' Gunther said. 'Have it your way, the hard way. Those people who aren't my friends sometimes find it extra hard to win a spot on a team.'

'Is that a threat?' a voice from behind Dunk said. The young warrior had been so focused on Gunther that he hadn't heard the speaker come up behind him.

Dunk spun about on his stool, and there stood his brother Dirk. Dunk often marvelled that they had both come from the same set of parents. Where Dunk was broad and dark, Dirk was lithe and light. The younger Hoffman stood an inch or two taller than Dunk but weighed twenty pounds less. Under his straight, white-blond hair, his bright blue eyes glared straight past Dunk and down at Gunther.

'No!' Gunther said, back-pedalling a step or two. 'Of course not. I don't work that way, Dirk, you know that.'

Dirk nodded. 'I know exactly how you work, Gunther, so I'm going to warn you once: leave this man alone.'

Gunther regained some of his composure at this. 'Look here,' he said. 'The kid is an adult. He can make up his own mind.'

Dirk turned toward Dunk, finally looking him in the eye. 'Do you want anything from the Gobbo?' he asked. As he spoke, he shook his head no.

Dunk hadn't seen his brother in three years. He'd left long before the family had fallen apart, and never looked back. This had left Dunk alone to handle the Hoffnung clan's catastrophic implosion. Despite this, he found himself glad to see his brother again. He had a few more scars and looked older than the years should have made him, but it was still Dirk for sure.

Dunk shook his head in tandem with his brother. 'No,' he said.

'You heard him, Gunther,' Dirk said, turning back toward the bookie. 'Decision's made. Respect it.'

The Gobbo looked up at the two men, then flashed a wink at Slick. 'No problem, Dirk. Always happy to do a favour for you.'

'It's not a favour,' Dirk said darkly. 'It's an order.'

Gunther held up his hands in mock surrender, but he looked at Dunk before he turned to leave. 'That's okay,' he said. 'There are lots more where you came from – wherever that is.'

The three watched the Gobbo leave. Dunk watched Slick dab at his eyes with his sleeve, then turn toward Dirk and offer his hand.

'So you're Dunk's brother,' the halfling said evenly. 'I should have known.'

Dirk shook Slick's hand. 'I don't tell *all* the family secrets.'

'You didn't have to do that,' Dunk said, jerking a thumb at the door through which the Gobbo had disappeared. As he spoke, he felt his resentment toward his brother rising in his chest.

'We're brothers,' Dirk said. 'Only *I* get to abuse you, and you didn't seem to be handling it so well yourself.'

Dunk stepped off his barstool and stood nose to nose with Dirk. 'I can manage. I did just fine without you for the past three years.'

An icy smirk spread across Dirk's battle-scarred face. 'That's not what I heard from Lehrer.'

Dunk's face flushed with shame. He bowed his head to hunt for some self-control as he felt his fist clenching. Another comment like that from Dirk, and it would find itself flying toward his face all on its own.

'Aren't you going to introduce us?'

The melodious voice sounded out of place here in the Bad Water, like a morning dove singing against the background of a catfight. Dunk raised his head to see its owner, and his breath left him.

'My apologies,' Dirk said to Dunk, although the young warrior still ignored him. 'This is my team-mate, Spinne Schönheit. Spinne, this is my older brother Dunk.'

Spinne stood as tall as Dunk, although that was due to the high-heeled leather boots that stretched up to the back of her knees. Her long, strawberry blonde hair cascaded past her shoulders, where it was caught in a single, thick braid intertwined with ribbons of silver and gold. Her wide blue-grey eyes transfixed Dunk, holding him paralysed in their bright gaze. The words that fell from her wide, sensual lips each seemed so precious that Dunk wanted to hunt down each one and cage it forever.

'My pleasure,' Spinne said in a voice as smooth as a fine chocolate liqueur. 'You never mentioned you had a brother,' she said to Dirk, never taking her eyes off Dunk. 'Is it Dunk Heldmann then?'

Dunk found he could not reply.

'Hoffnung, actually,' Dirk said. 'Heldmann is my game name.'

Spinne smiled softly at this, and Dunk felt his heart would melt and run out through his boots.

'Have you come to see Dirk play?'

When Dunk didn't reply, Slick leapt into the gap. 'Actually,' he said, sticking out his hand for Spinne, 'he's here to play. I'm Slick Fullbelly, esquire, his agent.'

Spinne gave Slick her hand, and he bent over it brushing it gently with his lips. She giggled at that. Dunk had never been jealous of the halfling before, but now he ached with it.

'You?' Dirk stuck in at Dunk, his jaw gaping wide. 'Really?'

'What team are you with?' Spinne asked. Dirk stared at his brother at this, evidently interested in the answer too.

'None at the moment, I'm afraid,' Slick said with open regret. 'If you'd asked me this morning, I'd have said we'd be with the Hackers for sure, but an unfortunate event and an unjust accusation seem to have precluded that.'

'The Bad Bay Hackers?' Dirk said, still gaping at his older brother. 'I heard half their recruits were murdered this–' He cut himself off as he goggled at Dunk. 'That was… that *couldn't* have been… you?'

Spinne flashed a wide, perfect, ruby-lipped smile hungry enough to devour a dragon whole. 'I respect a man who goes for what he wants.'

'Well,' Dunk started, too stunned to be half as articulate as he wanted, 'it wasn't really like that.'

'I can't believe my ears,' Dirk said, holding his head with both hands. 'After what Lehrer told me, I thought you'd sunk as low as you could, but murdering people to get on a Blood Bowl team? That's, well, that's impossible, isn't it?'

Dunk suddenly remembered how angry he was with his brother. 'How would you know?' he asked. 'Where have you been for the past three years? Out chasing after glory and gold! Where were you when I needed you?'

Dirk's demeanour turned glacier-cold. 'I could ask the same of you, brother.'

Seeing red, Dunk smashed his stein down on the top of the bar. Beer and shards of pottery splattered everywhere. 'That's it!' he roared at his brother.

Dirk's fist flashed out and flattened Dunk's nose, sending him sprawling back along the bar and into the pack of skaven. The ratmen scattered before the much-larger man, drawing their knives as they went.

Dirk drew his blade and leapt to stand over his fallen brother, who sat covered in sawdust and the skavens' spilled cider. 'Back off!' he said to the ratmen, who chattered at him through their six-inch-long front teeth. 'No one harms him but me!'

A blade sang out from someone standing just inside the nearby doorway and slapped Dirk's sword away. The skaven skittered away, looking for some sort of hole in which to hide.

Dirk brought his blade back around to where it clashed against the newcomer's. 'What is it you want?' he snarled at the dark-skinned man.

Cavre glared steadily over their crossed swords. 'I need to talk with your brother, Mr. Heldmann,' he said to Dirk, never taking his eyes from Dunk's. 'If that's not too much to ask.'

CHAPTER THIRTEEN

DUNK HAD NEVER been in Pegleg's tent before. The coach didn't fraternize much with his players, let alone lowly prospects. It was taller and better appointed than any other tent in the Hackers' camp, floored with wooden planks that Dunk suspected had been taken from the deck of the *Sea Chariot*, perhaps directly from the captain's own quarters. A large crystal ball sat in the centre of a large, oaken desk, the surface of which was carved with letters, lines and figures Dunk could not decipher.

'I suppose you're wondering why you're here, Mr. Hoffnung,' the coach said. He sat in a chair behind the desk, and as he spoke he scratched something in the desk's top.

Dunk sat in a small folding chair opposite Pegleg. Staring up at the grim look in the ex-pirate's eyes, he had no doubt why he was here. Only the solemn vow

Cavre had given to Dirk that Dunk would not be harmed kept him from fleeing into the darkness right then and there. That, and the fact that Cavre stood directly behind him and would probably put him down at the first false move he made.

The young warrior realised that Pegleg was waiting for an answer. He shook his head. 'No, sir,' he said sullenly.

From under his brilliant yellow tricorn, Pegleg shot his first mate a concerned look. 'Cavre? Have you already informed Mr. Hoffnung of this evening's events and how they are entwined with his eventual fate?'

'Not a word, captain.'

Pegleg narrowed his eyes at Dunk. 'You are aware of the murders, then?'

Dunk nodded slowly, confused. 'That's why you cut me from the team this afternoon,' he said. 'Despite the fact I had nothing to do with them.'

A smile tickled at the edge of Pegleg's mouth. 'I see, Mr. Hoffnung. You continue to maintain your innocence then?'

Dunk nodded as if nothing could be more evident.

'Then I suppose you had nothing to do with this evening's killings either?'

Dunk froze, stunned. 'What?'

Cavre spoke. 'Sometime shortly after sundown, Andreas and Otto went to collect our newest players for a celebration. They found Mr. Sherwood and Mr. Reyes in fine condition. Sadly, the same could not be said of the Broussard brothers.'

Dunk felt the beer in his stomach start to creep its way up his gullet.

'What was wrong with them?' he asked. He forgot to supply any honorific when addressing Pegleg, but the coach ignored it.

'Why, Mr. Hoffnung, they were dead, of course.'

Using his good hand, Pegleg reached down and pulled something bundled in a crimson cloth from a drawer in his desk. He tossed it on to the desk and peeled back the fabric with his hook so deftly that Dunk suspected he could fillet a fish with its tip.

It was the same knife Pegleg had found in Dunk's tent before.

'They were killed with this.'

Dunk gasped for air. 'Don't tell me you found that in my tent again.'

'No, Mr. Hoffnung,' Pegleg said flatly. 'It was sticking out of Luc Broussard's right eye.'

Dunk's head reeled. He found it hard to focus, but he couldn't pull his eyes away from the freshly bloodied knife. He clamped down hard on his rising stomach, afraid that everything he'd put into it since that morning would come spraying onto the coach's precious floor.

Instead, out came a rousing, tent-shuddering belch.

Dunk looked up sheepishly at Pegleg and then back at Cavre, who both stared at Dunk as if he'd grown a second head. 'Um,' he said, 'excuse me?'

Cavre just shook his head at Dunk, while Pegleg seemed to be sniggering behind the hook he raised to his face.

'Well,' Pegleg said once he'd regained his composure, 'on that auspicious note, I'd like to inform you of your new status, Mr. Hoffnung.'

Dunk repressed a shiver, although whether of anger or fear he could not tell. 'You can't think I had anything to do with this,' he said.

Pegleg shook his big, tricorn hat. 'No,' he said. 'Several people placed you in the Bad Water from when you left here until Mr. Cavre brought you to me. You're off the,' he looked at the sharp, shining device in place of his missing hand, then cleared his throat, 'hook... so to speak.'

Dunk slumped back in the folding chair, astonished at the heights and depths of his day. Then he sat bolt upright again. 'What about the other killings?' he said. 'Do you still think I had something to do with those?'

Pegleg shook his head. 'We never did, Mr. Hoffnung. The attempt to frame you by placing the murder weapon in your tent was far too obvious. You may not be a great Blood Bowl player yet, but you're hardly a fool.'

'Then why did you cut me from the-? Oh.' This line of questions led Dunk to an answer he didn't particularly like.

Pegleg shook his head again. 'You're a fine player, Mr. Hoffnung, and I'd be pleased to offer you a spot on our team, but I hoped to play along with the killer long enough for me to be able to learn who he was. In all honesty, I suspected the Broussard brothers, but these most recent events seem to have taken them out of the running.'

'Unless they killed themselves out of guilt, captain,' Cavre said.

Pegleg chortled at that. 'Very good, Mr. Cavre. I'll admit I hadn't thought of that. Very good!'

Dunk stared at Pegleg, afraid that he might for a moment be serious. The captain saw the look and waved it off.

'This is all beside the point, of course. The fact is that we have two more people dead, leaving us once more short-handed on this team. Those are spots we need to fill.'

It finally dawned on Dunk why he was here. 'You want me to play for the Bad Bay Hackers?' It was a question less of curiosity than astonishment.

'Didn't I just say that, Mr. Hoffnung?' Pegleg looked over Dunk's shoulder at Cavre. 'Well, didn't I?'

'Not in so many words, captain,' the blitzer said.

Pegleg harrumphed. 'I supposed I'll have to be a bit more direct about it then. Mr. Hoffnung?' He looked Dunk straight in the eye and pointed at him with the curve of his hook. 'I'd like to offer you a position as our backup thrower. Are you interested?'

A strange mélange of emotions washed over Dunk. This was why he was here in Magritta, right? To try out for the Hackers, to launch his Blood Bowl career. At the same time, he couldn't get his father's disparaging attitude about the game out of his head. His parents had disowned his brother over playing the game, after all. That was hardly a concern these days, but it still gave Dunk pause.

'Yes!' Slick's voice shouted from outside the tent. The halfling stormed in through the closed flaps, barely disturbing them as he passed, and stabbed an index finger toward Pegleg's face. 'He'll take it!'

All eyes in the tent turned toward Slick and he suddenly realised he'd become the centre of attention. He blushed with a sheepish grin, then spoke more calmly to Pegleg. 'Assuming we can come to a mutually beneficial agreement, Captain Haken, of course.'

'Of course,' Pegleg replied, rolling his eyes.

Cavre came around from behind Dunk and walked over to a locked cabinet against the right wall. He produced a key and opened it, then extracted a large, tall bottle wrapped in woven strands of something that looked like straw to Dunk's eyes. He placed it on the table, next to the bloody knife, along with a pair of crystal glasses.

'A drink of Stoutfellow's finest to seal the deal?' Pegleg said to Slick.

'Let's start with a toast to celebrate our mutual recognition of our desire to work together,' the halfling said, 'and we can work our way up from there.'

Cavre took Dunk by the elbow and led him from the tent.

'Don't worry yourself, son,' Slick said as Cavre escorted Dunk away. 'By the time I work out your deal with this scallywag, he'll have promised us his hook and an option on his leg – the good one!'

BACK IN THE Bad Water, Cavre raised a drink to Dunk. 'Here's to the game,' he said to the rookie as they clinked their steins together. 'May you leave it better off than you found it.'

Dunk drank deeply from his KGD, then wiped his mouth and smiled at Cavre. 'Are you talking about me or the game there?' he asked.

Cavre smiled. 'The toast doesn't say, does it, Mr. Hoffnung? That's what makes it such a good toast. Congratulations.'

Dunk smiled. He hated the circumstances under which he'd come to his new position – if he even had it yet, although he trusted Slick to take care of that – but he found himself pleased to be in it. For tonight, at least, he was ready to let his ambivalence drain away so that he could enjoy the moment for the magical thing it was.

Dunk knew that thousands of people, maybe millions, would kill to be able to play Blood Bowl professionally. *And somebody did*, he thought, which gave him pause. He shoved that aside with the rest of his doubts though. He hadn't killed those people, and it seemed that Pegleg and Cavre finally believed him. That was enough for now.

Dunk let the joy of his good fortune, or fate, as the case may have been, flow over him. Doing this had to beat chasing after dragons, and it was far enough away from Altdorf that he might even be able to forget what had happened to his family back there and what he'd had to do with it. He drank deeply from his stein, then slammed it back down and ordered another.

SEVERAL STEINS LATER, the world seemed a much friendlier place to Dunk. He clapped Cavre on the back and said. 'I'm just thrilled to be able to work with you.'

Cavre smiled patiently at the rookie. 'So you keep telling me, Mr. Hoffnung.'

'We're team-mates now,' Dunk said. 'You can drop the 'mister' bit. Call me Dunk.'

Cavre shook his head. 'I work with a lot of people, Mr. Hoffnung. On a Blood Bowl team, they tend to come and go like grist on a millstone. Only a rare few do I ever call by name.'

'But I'll be the thrower,' Dunk said, the drink making him a bit more distressed by Cavre's cavalier attitude than he normally would allow. 'You're the blitzer. Those are the team's top two positions. We'll have a natural bond.'

Cavre snorted softly as he raised his stein to his lips. When he brought it down, he gazed at Dunk with his dark, brown eyes that seemed like they'd maybe seen too much over the years for their own good. 'Sometimes it works like that,' he said, 'true. But not always. I've been working with Mr. Ritternacht for two years now, and there's no such bond there.'

Dunk's heart sank. If Kur hadn't been able to inspire any kind of respect in Cavre in years of trying, what hope did Dunk have? On the other hand, Kur didn't seem like the kind of person who cared to try for such things. That lifted Dunk's spirits for a moment.

'And you're still just the back-up thrower, Mr. Hoffnung,' Cavre pointed out.

Dunk's spirits sank again. He took another belt of his KGD.

'So, sailor, what does a girl have to do around here to get a guy to buy her a drink?'

Dunk looked up to see Spinne on his other side, away from Cavre. She smiled at him, but he couldn't move his tongue, maybe *because* of that smile.

A mug full of mulled wine slid down the bar and skidded to a half in front of Spinne. Dunk looked down at it as if it had been conjured from thin air. Then he glanced back at the bartender and caught his eye. 'Put that on my tab,' he croaked out.

'It looks like you're celebrating,' Spinne said as she brought the mulled wine to her soft lips. Dunk found himself just as jealous of the mug as he had been of Slick earlier.

'Mr. Hoffnung here has just been offered a position with the Hackers,' Cavre offered from over Dunk's shoulder.

Spinne smiled. 'Congratulations!' she said, clinking her mug against Dunk's stein. He almost dropped his beer, but he managed to rally enough to join her in her toast.

'What position will you be playing?' Spinne asked.

'Thrower,' Dunk said.

'Behind Kur?'

Dunk nodded. 'For now.'

Spinne laughed. 'That's confidence for you,' she said to Cavre over Dunk's shoulder. 'Don't you find a rookie's ambitions amazing?'

'Not anymore, Spinne.'

She looked back at Dunk. 'He's just flattering me. He remembers back when I was a rookie too. I had so much to learn, didn't I?'

Dunk nodded. 'I suppose I do too.'

'More than you know, my Dunkel,' Spinne said. 'More than you know.'

'My brother used to call me that,' Dunk said. 'Do you know where he is?' He craned his neck around, suspicious that Dirk was watching him, frozen like a deer in the bright light of Spinne's attention.

'I don't have any idea,' she said. 'Is it important? Oh, you'd like to share your news with him, right?'

Dunk shook his head. The last thing he needed right now was a conversation with Dirk. He was feeling good, and he knew that would bring him crashing back down to the dirt.

'We're not together, you know,' Spinne said. 'Your brother and I. He likes to give people that impression sometimes.'

'I had that impression.' Dunk's day had just gotten even better.

'Sometimes I let people think that. You wouldn't think it would be hard to keep men away from me, would you?'

Dunk smiled, boggled by the insanity of the question. 'Is that a joke?' he asked, looking her up and down. 'I think you'd need an army – or at least a good set of linemen.'

Spinne frowned. 'I'm not some kind of princess. I'm a Blood Bowl player.'

'And one of the best around,' Carve said. Dunk turned as he heard the man's stool push back from the bar.

'I'm going to call it a night,' the blitzer said. 'I'd love to be able to help Mr. Hoffnung here celebrate his impending contract all night long, but we aren't in Magritta for pleasure.'

'Right!' Dunk said. 'I can go back with you. Is there some kind of curfew?'

'Yes,' Cavre laughed. 'But it only applies to players.'

'But…' Dunk was confused.

'Have you signed a contract yet, Mr. Hoffnung?' Cavre asked, still smiling.

'No, but I'm sure that–'

Cavre cut Dunk off with a wave of his legendary hands. 'Then your time is still your own. This is the last night that may be true for a while, Mr. Hoffnung. I suggest you enjoy it.'

With that, Cavre snapped off a quick salute and took his leave. Dunk turned back to Spinne, who seemed to be standing closer to him than before.

'Well,' he said, 'it seems I'm on my own for celebrating my good news. Would you care to join me?'

'Haven't I already?' Spinne smiled at him with dreamy eyes.

'So,' Dunk asked, 'what do you suggest a young rookie do with his last night of freedom?'

As Spinne leaned in and pressed her breathtakingly soft lips against his, she said, 'Oh, can't we think of something?'

CHAPTER FOURTEEN

THE NEXT MORNING, Dunk slunk back to the Hackers'
camp in the cold light of early dawn. His head
pounded like a dwarf jackhammer any time he bent
over, which he'd done in Spinne's room to grab his
pants before she hustled him out the door. He hadn't
bent over since, but his head was still spinning with
the events of the night before. To be cleared of murder and then to be offered a position with the
Hackers was amazing enough, but to then bed the
beautiful Spinne was too much for his brain to handle, as evidenced by the fact that it seemed ready to
spin out of his skull at a moment's notice.

'Ah!' Slick shouted as Dunk tried to sneak into his
tent. 'There you are! Cavre told me you might be out
late celebrating your last night as a civilian, but I
didn't imagine it would be *all* night. I didn't think
you had it in you.'

Dunk winced at the noise of the halfling's voice and held his ears. It conveniently allowed him to hold his head together at the same time.

'Oh,' Slick said, a bit more softly this time. 'I see you're paying the price for your pleasure last night,' he chuckled. 'Thank Nuffle you won't be playing today.'

'How's that?' Dunk said, surprised at how relieved he was by this bit of news. Then his relief morphed to concern. 'We didn't make a deal?'

Slick feigned shock at the rookie's words. 'Do you really think I would let Pegleg go to sleep last night before he made us an offer we just couldn't refuse?'

Dunk's headache eased at this. 'So we have a contract?'

Slick's grin showed all the teeth in his chubby mouth. 'It's all ready for your signing. We just need to go over to Pegleg's tent to get your ink on it.'

'How much are we talking about here?' This morning, Dunk had realised he'd spent just about every last crown he had on his celebration. Buying a round for the bar had been a lot more expensive than he'd imagined. It had cost him even more, in terms of his health, when everyone in the bar tried to return the favour to him. If Spinne hadn't taken him out of the Bad Water when she had, he might have woken up under one of the pub's tables, or maybe lying out on the docks with his head hanging over the edge of a pier.

'Seventy,' Slick said proudly.

'Seventy crowns per game?' Dunk said, nodding his approval. 'Not bad. Depending on how often we play, I might be able to send up to half that home.'

Slick snorted. 'That's not quite it.'

'Seventy per month then?' Dunk said, creasing his brow. 'That's still workable, I suppose.'

'Not per month,' Slick said, a mysterious smile still plastered across his face. 'That's per year.'

'Per year?' Dunk said, frowning now. 'I thought Blood Bowl players made real money. That's less than six crowns a month. It's liveable, but I could make more money as a ratcatcher in Altdorf. Of course, that's one of the most dangerous jobs in the Empire, shy of dragon-hunting or, I thought, playing Blood Bowl, so it doesn't pay too bad. Have you ever looked down in those sewers? I think I'd need more than–'

'Son,' Slick said. 'That's seventy *thousand* per year.'

Dunk's hangover vanished.

'You're – Slick, my head must be fuzzier than I knew. I thought you just said 'Seventy thousand crowns a year.''

The halfling nodded, his grin wider than ever, so wide he started to jump up and down to spread it further. Dunk grabbed his tiny hands and started jumping with him. The two hooted and hollered until Dunk was sure they must have woken up everyone else in the camp.

'And that's before your part of each game's take,' Slick said.

'There's more?' Dunk said, still stunned by the initial number.

'Every game a team plays comes with a purse put up by the sponsors. For non-tournament games, it's not always all that much, a few score crowns each for the winners, a little less for the losers. For any of the Four

Majors, though, it can be as much as another thousand apiece.'

'Let's go!' Dunk said, already halfway out the tent.

'Wait!' Slick said, panic nearly stealing his voice.

'What's wrong?' Dunk said.

'It's better to stay cool about these things, at least in front of your coach,' Slick said. 'You don't want them thinking they paid too much for you.'

'Right,' Dunk nodded. 'Right. Stay cool.' He found that he couldn't strip the grin from his face though. 'How am I doing?'

Slick reached up and smacked Dunk on the side of the head. His hangover came ringing back in, hungry for revenge.

'Hey!' Dunk protested, grimacing in pain.

'There,' Slick said. 'Now you look cool.'

'Thanks!' Dunk said as he aimed a fist at Slick's head, but the halfling capered out of the way.

When the pair reached Pegleg's tent, the coach called for them to come in before they even announced themselves.

'How did you know it was us, sir?' Dunk asked.

Pegleg squinted at Dunk as if perhaps regretting his decision to sign the man to a contract, no matter how much he might need him. 'It's a small camp,' he said at last. 'I heard you whooping in your tent from here. I assume Slick told you about our agreement.'

Dunk nodded.

'Excellent, Mr. Hoffnung. Then, if you're amenable to that arrangement, all we need is your signature here.' Pegleg took two pieces of parchment from the centre drawer of his desk and slipped them across the surface to Dunk. With his hook, he pushed a quill pen and a pot of the best ink from Cathay after it. 'Take your time and read it if you like.'

Dunk did. If there was one thing he'd learned from his family, it was how important it was to read something before you signed it. There were two identical copies of the contract, which was surprisingly short and simple, and the deal seemed more than fair to him.

'I thought it would be as long as a book of spells,' Dunk said, signing his name next to Captain Haken's on the bottom of both of the documents.

'They used to be,' Pegleg said, 'but we don't hire Blood Bowl players based on their intelligence. Many of them can't even read. We try to make it as easy as possible.'

Pegleg took one of the contracts back from Dunk and gave the rookie the other. He slid his contract back into the desk, then rose and offered Dunk his hand. Dunk took it and shook it firmly.

'Welcome aboard, Mr. Hoffnung,' Pegleg said. 'May you have a long and exciting career.'

'Thanks, coach!' Dunk said. He surprised himself by how much he loved calling someone that. 'I'm ready for duty. When's the next practice?'

Pegleg allowed himself a small smile. 'No practice today, Mr. Hoffnung. At noon, we have our first game of the playoffs, against the Darkside Cowboys. It's going to be a long week, with games every other day, but not for you.'

'Excuse me, coach?' Dunk said, suddenly concerned. 'Why not?'

'Regulations state that a player cannot take part in a game until twenty-four hours after he's been hired. It helps keep teams from trading ringers in and out at the last second.'

'Doesn't that happen all the time anyhow?' Slick asked. 'It's a dirty game. Why start playing clean now?'

Pegleg smirked. 'Normally I'm not so circumspect about such things, as you well know, Mr. Fullbelly. However, the murders garnered the attention of the Game Wizards, so we're not able to be so careless with the rules as we might like.' He turned to Dunk. 'You'll be eligible to play during our next game in two days. In the meantime, I have an assignment of vital importance for you that, coincidentally, will keep you from the arena today.'

'What's that, coach?' Dunk said eagerly.

'The rest of us will be in the arena,' Pegleg said. 'We need someone to guard the camp.'

OFF IN THE distance, from the stands of the Bay Water Bowl in the heart of Magritta, the crowd roared for what Dunk could only assume was another touchdown for somebody. He hoped the Hackers had scored, but he had no way to know. Pegleg had refused to activate his crystal ball for this game, insisting that Dunk patrol the camp instead. 'Otherwise, you'll be stuck in here watching the game, Mr. Hoffnung, while someone robs us blind.'

Dunk had to admit that he probably would have found it hard to pull himself away from watching the game via Cabalvision. He'd seen precious few games in his life and never watched one all the way through. Now it looked like that might not happen until his first game as a professional player, and the thought made him nervous.

To take the edge off his nerves, Dunk took to pacing around the camp with Slick. This not only helped him walk off his excess energy, but it also meant he was doing a good job at the task Pegleg had set for him.

'It's important you keep Pegleg happy,' Slick told Dunk. 'While we have a great deal with him, he can fire you at a moment's notice.'

'And then I'm out in the cold?'

'He still has to pay you for the month after you're fired, unless you take up with another team, of course. Then you're on your own.'

'But I don't want to do that. I like the Hackers.'

Slick looked up at the rookie. 'What would you do if someone offered you more money, son? A lot more?'

'Sign up with them for *next* season, or ask to be traded.'

Slick smiled wanly and shook his head at Dunk. 'That, son, is why you have me to handle the deals around here. It's not all that simple.'

Dunk glared down at the halfling. 'You can't make another deal without my say-so though, right?'

Slick nodded. 'I need your mark on the bottom of the contract, don't I?'

'Always looking out for me, right?'

'I'm not the only one,' Slick said as they strolled along. 'You might want to extend some gratitude toward your brother.'

Dunk froze in his tracks and frowned. 'For running out on our family when we needed him most?'

Slick shook his head. 'I don't know the details of all that, son. Not any more than Dirk told me, at least.'

'Dirk...?' Dunk cocked his head at Slick. 'He... he told you about my family?'

The halfling nodded sheepishly. 'You don't think I was wandering through Dörfchen on a whim? That would have been an amazing coincidence. '

Dunk stared at Slick. 'Dirk told you where to find me?' He felt like he might start to choke. His voice grew more strained as he spoke. 'He told… he told you about what happened with our family? He gave you what you needed to blackmail me into playing Blood Bowl?'

Slick put up his hands to calm the young man down. 'He was only looking out for you, son. He'd heard you'd set off to slay dragons. He was concerned for your life.'

'Blood Bowl is safer?'

Slick summoned up a wide grin. 'It pays far better.'

Dunk jammed the heels of his hands into his eyes. He wanted to throttle the halfling and then hunt Dirk down and do the same for him. His brain felt like it might burst out through his eardrums first.

Dunk pulled his hands from his face and roared at Slick in heart-rending frustration. The halfling flinched away and tumbled onto his back, raising his arms to fend off Dunk's attack.

Dunk glared down at the halfling lying there in the ground, defenceless against him. He could have gutted him with his bare hands. He could have broken his neck with a single twist, but he couldn't bring himself to do it. He threw back his head to roar again when he spied the far-off entrance to Pegleg's tent moving. He immediately fell silent and pulled Slick to his feet. 'Did you see that?' he asked the halfling.

'If you mean how you knocked me into the beach, then yes, I got that,' Slick said, spitting out a mouthful of sand.

'Someone's in Pegleg's tent.'

The halfling sat up and joined Dunk in peering around the edge of their tent. 'Are you sure?' he asked.

Dunk nodded, his anger fading away. 'I saw the flap of his tent moving, and there's no breeze in the air today.'

'Maybe Pegleg came back for something he forgot.'

'In the middle of a game?'

Dunk grimaced and drew the sword that Pegleg had given him. 'We can't have you guarding the camp with that little snotling-sticker of yours,' he'd said.

When Dunk had first pulled the blade, he'd been astonished at its sharpness and balance. It was as if it had been forged for his hand. 'It's marvellous,' he'd said to Pegleg. 'I can't thank you enough for it.'

'No,' the coach had said, 'but you can pay me. It's coming out of your first month's salary.'

'Will I have anything left?' Dunk had asked, just a bit worried.

Pegleg had narrowed his eyes at the rookie. 'Mr. Hoffnung, are you sure your agent fully explained to you the exorbitant amount of gold I'm paying you?'

The blade felt just as good now as it had before, and its heft in his hand gave Dunk a shot of confidence. 'I'm going in,' he said.

'Good on you, son,' said Slick. 'I'll stay out here to sound the alarm if you don't come out in five minutes.'

Dunk glared at Slick. 'How very brave of you.'

The halfling shrugged. 'I'm an agent, not a player.'

Dunk patted Slick on the head and then took off for Pegleg's tent at a dead sprint. When he reached the tent's door flap, he charged right through, his sword in front of him.

There, behind Pegleg's desk, stood a middle-aged man dressed entirely in robes of a dark, midnight blue, trimmed with bluish-white piping that seemed to glow against the bulk of the cloth. The man was tall and gaunt with a wispy white beard. His hair, if he had any, was covered entirely by a silver skullcap that approximated the outlines of a taut widow's peak that came to a point in the centre of his forehead. His bright green, watery eyes glared out at Dunk with a hatred the young man had rarely seen, and the man's lips trembled nervously as he spoke.

'L… leave now,' the man said, shutting the drawers of Pegleg's desk that he'd been rummaging through, 'and I will not feed your s… soul to the Blood God Khorne.'

'You're sure that's not "K… Khorne"?' Dunk said as he came at the man, his blade before him, ready to strike.

'Everyone's a c… comedian,' the man said with disgust. He turned toward the dressing screen in the back of Pegleg's tent. 'Stony, please remove this man.'

The hairs on the backs of Dunk's arms and neck stood on end as the dark-skinned creature crept around the edge of the screen. It was no taller than Dunk, except for the twisted horns curling atop its head and its wide, bat-like, claw-tipped wings that scraped against the tent's walls and ceiling as it moved forward on goat legs. It flexed its thick muscles as its full-crimson eyes, which seemed to be filled with blood, rested on Dunk, and a set of savage talons popped from the tips of its fingers.

'Yes, Zauberer,' the creature rasped, its voice like metal on stone.

'That's "master" to you, gargoyle,'' the man said menacingly. Then he pointed to Dunk. 'Kill him. Permanently. Now.'

CHAPTER FIFTEEN

DUNK LEAPT AT the daemon, his sword flashing out before him. The wizard, if that's what Zauberer was, fell back out of the way, clutching some papers in his grasp.

Dunk's sword slashed across the gargoyle's chest, biting through its thick skin and drawing blood. The sight brought a smile to the rookie's face. If the thing had been made entirely of stone, this would have been a short and fatal fight – for him. As it was, he thought he still stood a chance.

The gargoyle bellowed in pain. The closest thing Dunk had ever heard was as a child when he'd seen a man get his arm caught in a mill. The combination of the man's screams and the sound of living bone being ground to dust had set his teeth on edge in the exact same way.

The gargoyle jumped into the air on its backward-folding legs and launched itself at Dunk. It slammed into him painfully and the two went soaring back through the tent's front flap and into the open area beyond.

Caught in the gargoyle's granite grip, Dunk struggled to catch his breath. As he did, he smashed the pommel of his sword into the creature's face, drawing both blood and a sinister cackle from the thing's battered mouth. He lashed out again and his blade sliced through the edge of one of the gargoyle's grey, leathery wings.

The daemon howled in rage and shoved Dunk away from it, sending him tumbling back over himself until he came to a stop near the now-cold fire pit in the middle of the camp. When the rookie managed to recover his feet, the daemon was nowhere to be seen. The wizard, on the other hand, was sprinting along the beach, back toward the distant docks of Magritta.

His sword still in hand, Dunk burst out of the camp after the wizard. Zauberer's speed was no match for the rookie's, and soon Dunk was close enough to hear the wizard's laboured wheezing as he tried futilely to outrace him.

'Dunk!' Slick shouted from somewhere back in the camp. 'Look out! Above you!'

Dunk cursed himself for being so foolish. Of course, that's where the gargoyle had gone. He'd taken his focus off of the greater threat in this fight, and now he would pay for it, possibly with his life.

The gargoyle slammed into Dunk from behind, hard. Instead of sprawling along the wet sand of the beach, though, Dunk found himself being lifted into the air with the fervent beating of the creature's leathery wings.

The rookie wrenched himself around in the dae-mon's rough-hided arms as they climbed higher and higher into the air. Dunk looked back to see the waters of the bay growing further away by the second.

The gargoyle bared its teeth at Dunk, its face only inches from his. It was a moment before Dunk realised the creature was smiling.

Dunk smashed the creature in the face again, but it just kept smiling at him, unaffected by the blow and uncaring about the blood that it brought forth.

Dunk raised his right arm as high as he could and slashed at the creature's wings. His blade sliced straight through the top angle of one of the wings, and it collapsed instantly, unable to hold the air any longer.

This elicited a stony screech from the gargoyle as it flopped lower, struggling to keep aloft with only a single working wing. 'We are over the water,' it said in its metal-on-stone voice. 'You will kill us both!'

It was Dunk's turn to smile as he angled a blow at the creature's other wing. '*I* can swim,' he said.

The blade cut deep into the wing, and it parted like a torn sail. The gargoyle and Dunk plummeted out of the air as if struck by a boulder from one of the tre-buchets mounted on the fortresses at the tips of the bay's horns.

Dunk smashed the creature in the face again as they fell and pushed away hard. The gargoyle's arms let him loose as it began to flap them as well in a vain attempt to keep itself in the air. He kicked away from it and arced into a long, curving dive, tossing the blade clear. The last thing he needed was to impale himself on it when he hit the water.

Dunk hoped the water would be deep enough where he landed.

The rookie pierced the surface of the bay like a giant bird of prey going after a fishy meal. The waters were cool, and the shock of hitting them nearly drove the air from his lungs. He curved himself about as his momentum tried to carry him deeper, letting the water sluicing around his body bring him parallel with the bay's sandy bottom then push him back toward the surface.

When Dunk's momentum finally ran out, he kicked hard and climbed his way back to the surface as fast as he could, his arms and lungs protesting at the effort. He could see the light of the sun high overhead through the water above him. All he had to do now was reach the unfiltered light before he ran out of air.

A moment later, Dunk's head broke the surface. He nearly choked while gasping in the sweet-tasting air. His lungs filled again, he glanced about for the shore- and then made a beeline for the nearest beach.

When Dunk finally found sand beneath his feet again, he looked back at the bay behind him that had almost become his unmarked grave. The well-named Bay of Quietude was as calm as it ever was, except for the ripples his own movements threw across its surface.

'By Nuffle's horny helmet, son,' Slick said as he raced up to the rookie. 'That was amazing! I've never seen anything like it.'

'Just.' Dunk stopped for a moment to hack a few dregs of water out of his lungs. 'Just doing my job.'

Slick scratched his chin with a fat finger at that. 'I'd say this is beyond the call of duty. Perhaps we can put in for hazard pay?'

At that moment, the waters behind the pair erupted, and the gargoyle flung itself into the air again. It let loose a horrifying screech that put goose-flesh all along Dunk's waterlogged skin. Then, glaring down at Dunk with its blood-red orbs, it faded away in the light of the merciful sun.

Dunk slumped back down on the beach stripping off his wet clothes until he was barefoot and naked to the waist. 'I think the players got off easiest today,' he said. A moment later, a roar went up from the distant stadium again.

'We can but hope, son,' Slick said. 'We can but hope.'

IN DRY CLOTHES once more, Dunk, who was sore over every inch of his body from his spectacular dive, stood with Slick in Pegleg's tent. 'What do you think this Zauberer was after?' the rookie asked.

'I don't know,' Slick said, who seemed spooked to be in a tent where a daemon had recently slouched. 'And I don't care. We got rid of him, didn't we? There should be a bonus in it for us. Guard duty's supposed to be little more than busy work. It's not meant to be life threatening.'

Dunk ignored the halfling. 'He had something in his hands when he left, a sheaf of papers.'

'Contracts maybe?' Slick offered. 'Perhaps he works for another team and wants to know what Pegleg is paying his players.'

'Why would that be important?' Dunk asked.

Slick smiled, finally back on ground familiar to him. 'Lots of teams like to try to poach the best play-ers from each other. To do that properly, the more you know about your targets the easier it is. After all, it's hard for a team to outbid your current salary if they don't know what it is.'

'I suppose,' Dunk said, not entirely agreeing with the halfling. 'Wouldn't it be easier to just ask? If most players are as greedy as you imply, they'd be happy to let prospective teams know their asking price.'

Slick nodded. 'But lots of players lie about that. For one, it's a matter of pride. Everyone wants to be known as the player with the highest price tag.'

'That gives new meaning to "most valuable player".'

'For two,' Slick continued, 'players would love to get an offer that's substantially above what they're really making. With the real numbers in hand, a coach only has to offer the least amount necessary. While negotiating, it puts him in a real position of strength.'

'I'll take your word for it,' Dunk said.

Far outside the tent, the crowd in the stadium roared again.

'I hope that's good news,' Slick said. 'We could use some right now.'

'Too bad,' a gruff voice said, just before its owner entered the tent. 'Gotcha bad news right here.'

The intruder stood nearly eight feet tall and seemed nearly as broad across. He had to bend over to fit into the tent, scraping the tops of his pointed, bark-coloured ears on the canvas ceiling. His thick arms were long enough that they almost dragged to his feet. Sharp tusks rose from the bottom, lantern-shaped jaw of his savage-cut mouth, and their tips scraped raw patches on either side of his flat, upturned, almost piggish nose, which squatted just under his beady, black eyes set wide apart in his ham of a face.

'Skragger,' Slick whispered. In the silence of the tent, it sounded like a cannon's shot.

'You can't be in here,' Dunk said to the black orc.

The creature was dressed in filthy but stylish Orcidas clothing, and a thick, gold ring pierced the centre of his nose, almost daring someone to try leading him around by it. A small tuft of salt-and-pepper hair jutted from the top of his head, and Dunk was struck by the wrinkles on the creature's face. Most orcs died young. Skragger was unarmed it seemed, but so, Dunk remembered, was he.

Skragger's long, right arm reach out and smacked Dunk to the ground. It came so fast, he almost didn't see it.

'Nuff from you,' the massive orc said. 'Talk,' he said jabbing his chest with a black-nailed finger. Then he pointed at Dunk. 'Listen.'

Dunk scrambled to his feet and nodded, his cheek still stinging from where the orc had hit him.

'Dunk Hoffnung?' Skragger said, pointing at Slick. The halfling's eyes sprang wide as he squeaked and gestured toward the rookie instead.

Skragger turned toward Dunk, a satisfied smile on his horrible face. 'Dirk yer brother?'

Dunk nodded silently as he tried to scan the room. Pegleg had to have another weapon in here somewhere. He considered diving under the tent's back wall and taking his chances with outrunning the black orc. Skragger might once have been able to chase Dunk down, but it didn't seem that the years had been kind to him. Still, that would mean leaving Slick behind to the black orc's nonexistent mercies, and Dunk couldn't bring himself to risk that.

'Wuz Orcland Raiders blitzer,' Skragger said, pointing at himself now. 'My record: Most Touchdowns in a Year.' The creature pronounced the last words carefully and proudly, something the rookie wouldn't have guessed the orc was capable of.

Dunk nodded. 'Congratulations,' he said earnestly.

Another scabby orc paw snapped away from Skragger's side and slapped him to the ground.

'Don't innerupt,' Skragger growled.

The rookie nodded, silently this time, as he crawled back to his feet. Now both of his cheeks burned. At least it seemed that the black orc was more interested in talk than murder.

'Yer Dirk could break record.' Skragger frowned, exposing all of his lower row of yellowed, broken teeth. 'That can't happen.'

'Really?' Dunk said, pride in his brother unexpectedly welling in his heart. He glanced at Slick and asked, 'Dirk could do that?'

Slick nodded at Dunk from where he cowered behind Pegleg's bed. 'He's off to a great start. He almost managed it last year. He only fell five touchdowns shy.'

'*Too* close!' Skragger snarled. He aimed a blow at Slick but only succeeded in knocking a post off of Pegleg's bed, the top of which was carved in the shape of a human skull. It fell next to Slick's feet, a none-too-subtle warning as to Skragger's intent.

'Tell Dirk, back off,' the orc continued. 'Breaks *my* record, Skragger breaks him.' With that, he drew up both arms and brought them down, smashing Pegleg's thick, oaken desk in two. 'Break you too.'

Dunk looked at the splintered remains of the desk at his feet, then back up at Skragger. 'I'll let him know.'

Skragger guffawed rough and low at this. As he did, he pulled a grimy shred of parchment from the pocket of his greasy Orcidas sweatpants. From his other pocket, he pulled out a short pencil that was far too small for his massive hands. He licked the tip with a tongue as rough as sandpaper, set it to the parchment and crossed out something with a single line. Then he looked around.

'Which team?' Skragger said.

Dunk cringed as he leaned just a little over the edge of the destroyed table and said. 'I'm sorry. I don't understand.'

Skragger grimaced in anger, and Dunk braced for another smack. 'Which team owns thizzere camp?'

'Ah,' Dunk said, brightening at the ease of the question, although he didn't quite understand the motivation behind it. 'The Bad Bay Hackers.'

Skragger glared down at his list for a moment, then scowled and took out a tiny pair of wire-rimmed glasses that he perched on his nose. 'Hrm,' he said. 'Ritternacht still with ya?'

'Kur?' Dunk said, smiling. 'He's the starting thrower.'

Another slap sent Dunk reeling backwards, slipping under the back flap of the tent and tumbling into the sand. As the rookie lay there on the beach, feeling his jaw to see if it was broken, he saw the tip of a pencil appear at the top of the tent's rear flap. It tore downward in a smooth, steady move, parting the fabric neatly in two.

Skragger stepped through the new-made gap. 'That warning fer Dirk?' he said. 'Goes fer Kur too.'

With that, the black orc crossed another name off his list and then strode off toward Magritta's docks. Somewhere in the distance, a crowd roared again.

CHAPTER SIXTEEN

'As a guard, you make a wonderful thrower, Mr. Hoffnung,' Pegleg said after Dunk explained to him everything that had happened that afternoon. 'Wizards, daemons, and a black orc blitzer too?'

'I know it seems too insane to believe,' Dunk started.

'I coach a Blood Bowl team,' Pegleg said evenly as he stirred around in the remains of his desk with his hook. 'There are few things too insane for me to believe.'

Dunk hung his head. 'I'm sorry, coach,' he said. 'I did the best I could.'

Pegleg waited a moment before responding. 'It's not your fault, Mr. Hoffnung. It seems fate has it in for us today.'

'Speaking of which,' Dunk said, 'how did the game go?'

Pegleg frowned. 'We lost,' he said. 'Get out.'

'I'd like to warn my brother that his life is in danger,' Dunk said.

Pegleg rubbed the arc of his hook on his head, letting the touch of the metal cool his brow. 'Permission denied, Mr. Hoffnung. You can tell him in two days. The Reavers are next up on our dance card.'

Dunk nodded. 'What about Kur?'

'That,' Pegleg said, 'had better come from me. After the game Kur played today, though, I'd say that Skragger's record is in no danger from that quarter.'

'Okay, but–'

'Dismissed, Mr. Hoffnung.'

OVER THE NEXT two days, many of Dunk's new teammates wanted to ask him about what had happened at the camp while they'd been at the game. He told the story over and over again, keeping as best he could to the facts as he knew them. He figured that anyone on the team deserved to know what was happening with the team. After the murders during and after the tryouts, it was clear that something dangerous was happening around the team, and the incidents during the game only amplified that feeling.

'Daemons, you say?' asked M'Grash. The ogre had taken a distinct liking to Dunk, and he felt obliged to cultivate it, not least because he'd rather have M'Grash on his side than against him.

The ogre had a certain childlike, uncomplicated quality about him that Dunk admired. He was a simple creature of simple needs, and playing for the Hackers met most of them nicely. For all that, he was lonely.

'People afraid of me,' the ogre said, 'but me not bad.'

This came shortly after Dunk had witness M'Grash tear the top off a barrel of beer with his teeth. The two had settled down for a drink afterward and were now commiserating over draughts of Killer.

'Me no daemon though,' M'Grash said. 'Don't like daemons.'

Dunk smiled as he picked a splinter out of his stein. 'I can understand that. I don't like them much either.'

'Daemons kill people.' The gigantic creature shuddered, and Dunk felt a strange urge to put his arm around him and tell him it would be all right.

'Some do,' Dunk said. 'But I don't think you'd have been in any danger from this daemon, big guy. Even with his wings he wasn't half your size.'

'Little daemon?' M'Grash brightened at this.

'Compared to you,' Dunk said, raising his drink to the ogre, 'yes. Much littler.'

'Not afraid of little daemons,' M'Grash said. He rested the heel of his hand on one of Dunk's shoulders, and his fingers reached all the way to the other shoulder. 'Keep Dunkle safe from daemons.'

'I'll drink to that,' Dunk said, tapping his stein against M'Grash's half-empty barrel. And they did.

THE NIGHT BEFORE the next game, Dunk found himself sitting at the bar of the Bad Water again. He tried to tell himself that he wasn't there just hoping that Spinne would show up, but he soon admitted he was only trying to fool himself. He'd tried to stop by the Reavers' camp earlier, ostensibly to warn Dirk about the threat from Skragger, but he'd been turned away as soon as he identified himself as a member of the Hackers. Apparently visits from family were okay, but not from players on opposing teams.

Calling the Reavers' compound a 'camp' was a bit of misnomer. The place had a practice field like the one the Hackers used, but it was marked off with proper lines for the boundaries and every ten yards along the field. A host of guards patrolled the place around the clock. Of course, they didn't have much to worry about there, as the Reavers didn't sleep in tents nearby their field. Instead, they had reserved every room in the Casa Grande, the best-appointed inn in all of Magritta. Only the prince's castle had better accommodations, it was said.

The guards at the hotel had turned Dunk away too, but he'd left a message for Dirk, asking him to meet him at the Bad Water. He'd done the same for Spinne as well.

Dunk signalled for the bartender to bring him another pint of Killer. The rookie hadn't had much money to spend since he'd left his family's home many months before, and he was enjoying being able to not worry about it so much. He promised himself that he wouldn't be buying a round for the bar that night, but just before the place closed he ended up doing just that.

Dirk and Spinne never showed.

THE DAY OF Dunk's first game dawned bright and painfully early for the young man. His head felt as if M'Grash had decided to stuff it with cotton and use it for a pillow. Fortunately, as the day wore on Dunk felt better and better, and by the time the game rolled around he was ready to play.

Of course, as a new recruit and the backup thrower behind Kur Ritternacht, Dunk quickly discovered that he couldn't expect much playing time. Kur himself made this clear when he looked at Dunk after the pre-game workout and said, 'Make yourself useful, boy. Get me some water.'

Dunk looked the older thrower in the eyes, unblinking. 'I'm your backup, not your waterboy.'

Kur sneered. 'I was giving you a chance to get more exercise in another role. Something other than bench-warmer.'

Dunk raised his eyebrows at this. 'Kur,' he said, 'I'm just keeping it warm for you.'

Kur sneered as he headed into the locker room to suit up.

PEGLEG ORDERED EVERYONE to get into their full armour, even the backups like Dunk. They might not see any time on the field during the game, but they had to be ready at a moment's notice to hit the turf when needed.

The armour Dunk wore was heavy when he lifted it up, but once he had it strapped on properly it was amazingly easy to handle. The colours were just like that of the Hackers' helmet he'd worn during tryouts: green and gold.

'These are the "away team" colours, son,' Slick explained as he tried to help Dunk get the straps adjusted properly. 'Forest green shirt and bright gold pants, with all armour colour-coordinated to where it's placed. Your shoulder pads are green, for instance, while your kneepads are yellow.'

'Do we have 'home team' colours too?' Dunk asked.

Slick nodded. 'The home team is usually the highest seeded team in any particular game. "Seeds" are rankings given to the participating teams based upon who the host committee thinks are more likely to win the tournament. The other side is then the visiting team.'

'What are the Reavers seeded?' Dunk asked.

'First, although there's some argument about that. Some folks thought that honour should have gone to Khorne's Killers. With luck, we won't end up playing them. When you run up against a bunch of warpstone-tainted mutants whose only binding trait is their insane worship of a violent blood god, you can lose even if you win, if you know what I mean.'

'And what are we ranked?' Dunk asked, trying to change the subject.

'Two hundred and third.' Slick waited a moment before continuing. 'Out of about two hundred and fifty.'

'That doesn't seem good,' Dunk said. 'Are we that bad?'

'Now that you're on the team?' Slick said with forced merriment. 'Of course not.'

Dunk frowned.

'Seriously, son. We only had twelve players going into this tournament. Some people didn't even think the Hackers would survive the long journey from Bad Bay, what with Pegleg's fear of water and all.

'His what?' Slick ducked under Dunk's rotating shoulder pad. 'I thought he was a pirate.'

'Word is he was but that it ended badly. He's hated the water ever since. Given a choice, he stays dry at all times. He doesn't even drink water! Sticks entirely to burgundy wine.'

Dunk groaned. 'He doesn't even face the bay during training, does he? He always stands with his back to the water. Why would he ever travel by sea?'

Slick snorted. 'It's not that he likes to. It's just the fastest way to get to someplace like Magritta. You noticed he never came out of his cabin the entire trip.'

'I thought he was studying games on his crystal ball.'

'Oh, he does that too,' Slick said. 'It's one of the reasons he's such a great coach. He turns his weaknesses into strengths. He has to focus on those games to distract himself from his fears, and it drives him to be the best coach he can. I've never seen someone with as much of a command of the game as Pegleg.'

'I wonder what it was that turned him against the sea like that?'

'The man's missing a hand and the better part of a leg, son. Let your imagination run wild.'

Dunk fell silent for a while and let Slick work on all of the straps he was wearing. 'Do we ever play games at home?' he said, after a pause.

'You would, if the Hackers had a home stadium to play at. Like most teams, these days, they play games at stadiums owned by the cities who play host. This place, for instance,' he said, 'belongs to Magritta.'

'They don't have a home base at all? Do they just travel all year long?'

'Mostly. In between the Majors, if they can't find a game along the way, they sometimes hole up in Bad Bay. There's a field there they use for practice, although there aren't any stands. It doesn't make for much of a home field advantage, and its hard to sell tickets to it, so the Hackers spend most of their time on the road instead, pursuing the larger purses offered for games in better venues.'

'It sounds like a hard life,' Dunk said.

Slick nodded as he finished with the final strap. 'It's our life now.'

AT GAME TIME, the team lined up at the exit from the locker room, ready to race out on to the field. Pegleg stood at the ironbound oaken door and doffed his hat. It was the first time Dunk had ever seen him without it. He was amazed to see that Pegleg's long, curly hair was in fact a wig that was attached to the tricorn hat. Underneath it, he was as bald as a dragon's egg.

Just because the hair was missing, though, didn't mean Pegleg's scalp was unadorned. A tattoo of a snake wound up from under his collar and leapt onto his skull where it spread out like a hooded cobra to cover the whole of his naked pate. The eyes of the cobra were a bloody red and the fangs that pointed down toward Pegleg's shining eyes glistened with venom. Or was it sweat? Dunk couldn't tell.

The thought of venom sent his thoughts careening back to his experience with the chimera and how sick its sting had made him. He'd come a long way from that cave in the Grey Mountains in only a few weeks.

'Listen up, you scurvy dogs!' Pegleg began, shattering Dunk's reverie. 'This is our first game with our full complement of new players. That means we've finally got a chance!

'I want you to hit the Reavers with everything you've got. There is no such thing as "dirty play" in this game. The only crime is getting caught! And I've made a contribution to the Referees' Widows and Orphans Fund to guarantee the zebras won't be watching us too closely.'

The team laughed evilly at that. Dunk was a bit too horrified to say anything.

'Your first job is to get the ball into the end zone. Your second job is to stop the Reavers from doing the same. Use any means at your disposal to accomplish these lofty goals. Kick, bite, smash, punch, even *kill* if you have to. It's not necessary, of course, but if you can make sure a Reaver won't be coming back for the rest of the game, then more power to you!'

At first, Dunk's thoughts went to Dirk and Spinne. They were among his targets, his and the rest of his team's. Suddenly, he wasn't so sure about his contract anymore. Then he realised that all of the Reavers would be coming after him and the rest of his team with the same murderous abandon. Then he was absolutely positive he'd made a mistake.

Pegleg continued unabated, his voice building from simple menace to a bloodthirsty crescendo.

'Now, go out there and tear the Reavers limb from limb! Make them sorry they even woke up today! Make their mothers sorry for having them!

'GO OUT THERE AND WIN THIS THRICE-DAMNED GAME!'

The rest of the team roared in approval, and their coach threw open the door to the playing field. They charged out n single file, and as they left the tunnel from the locker room and hit the sunlit field, the crowd let loose a deafening, thunderous noise that shook the supports of the stadium until the entire ground threatened to come crumbling down into the field after the players.

'What,' Dunk asked himself as he followed the others on to what he now could only think of as the killing ground, 'have I gotten myself in to?'

# CHAPTER SEVENTEEN

IF THE NOISE from the crowd deafened Dunk from inside the locker room, it stunned him once he reached the dugout, a stone-lined pit that sat on the edge of the field, between the stadium's seats and the game's sidelines. The tunnel from the locker room came out in the middle of the dugout and stretched twenty yards in either direction, giving members of the team and staff plenty of room to move about, as well as a rat's-eye view of the action.

Dunk was glad that he had been the last through the door. When he stepped into the dugout, he stood frozen in his boots. He'd seen games on Cabalvision before but only through a crystal ball. He'd never even been in the stands for a game, and to now be here with tens of thousands of fans cheering and booing all at once overwhelmed him. He thought that perhaps dragon slaying wasn't such a bad career choice after all.

'Keep moving, son!' Slick shouted up at Dunk.

The rookie looked down at the halfling, who he could barely hear over the roaring crowd. It was like standing in the ancient market in Altdorf when the Emperor's entourage marched through. The raw emotion in the place was both humbling and moving. Although one part of Dunk wanted to turn and run, another part needed nothing more than to charge out on to that field and give the fans the kind of game they so desperately wanted.

'Keep moving!' Slick yelled again, giving Dunk a push in the back of the legs this time. 'Go find your seat!'

Dazed, Dunk gazed around the dugout. Over to the left, he spotted Guillermo Reyes, Milo Hoffstetter, Simon Sherwood and Kai Albrecht sitting on a bench. They were still in their armour, but they'd taken their helmets off to get a better look at the field. Risers lifted the bench to put them at eye-level with the players.

A thick, brick wall behind these players, with a bit of a roof slanting over them, protected them from the fans to their rear. That didn't stop the crazed spectators from throwing all manner of things down at the dugout. As Dunk walked over to join the others, dozens of steins shattered on the dugout's roof, spattering beer, ale, and some worse things all about the place. He flinched at the sound of the first few, but they soon faded into the background, suffocated by the rest of the racket.

The starting players had already raced on to the field, which seemed to be what had caused the crowd to go from simply excited to entirely insane. The two teams met in the centre of the field, on which some-one had emblazoned a beautiful blue and white crest showing a sailing ship on calm seas against a yellow field shaped like a shield.

'That's the Oliveri family crest,' Slick said from behind Dunk. 'They've ruled Magritta for over fifty years.'

The rookie turned, surprised to see the halfling there. Slick shrugged at him. 'It's the safest place I could think of. You don't think I'm going to wait in the camp after what happened during the last game?'

Dunk smiled, happy to have a familiar face around. 'What's happening out there?' he asked.

As he spoke, a voice thundered out over the stadium, louder than Dunk could have imagined. It even drowned out the roaring for a moment.

'Now, please welcome today's home team, the Reikland Reavers!'

'That's the Preternatural Announcement system,' Slick shouted into Dunk's ear over the resultant bellow from the crowd as the Reavers' starting players took the field. 'That's Bob Bifford's voice. He's been doing these games for years. Keeps bouncing back and forth between Cabalvision networks to whichever one has the contract this year.'

'Isn't he a vampire?' Dunk asked. Even he'd heard of Bob Bifford and his partner Jim Johnson, who Dunk knew was an ogre like M'Grash. 'How does he do this during the day?'

'Sun Protection Fetish,' Slick said. 'How do you think guys like Hugo "the Impaler" von Irongrad ever manage to play day games? They keep their SPF on them at all times.'

'Even at night?'

'You never know when a team wizard might conjure up some magical daylight.'

Dunk nodded at that. 'Why don't we have a team wizard?'

Slick rubbed his fingers together. 'Too much gold. Pegleg's saving his wizard budget for the semi-finals, if we make it.'

The Reavers stormed toward the centre of the field, chanting, 'Em-pe-ror! Em-pe-ror!' As Altdorf's best and brightest team, they had the favour of their nation's ruler, and they dedicated every game to him as a matter of course.

Among the Reavers, Dunk spotted Spinne and Dirk at the front of the pack. Like the other Reavers, they wore war paint on their faces, visible even under their helmets. Dunk noticed that everyone seemed to have black stripes painted under their eyes and white strips across their noses.

'What's all that for?' Dunk asked Kai, waving a hand over his face. He noticed that the lineman bore those same stripes.

Kai smiled at the rookie's naiveté. 'The black lines help keep the sun from reflecting off your face and into your eyes.'

Dunk nodded at that. 'And the white stripes?'

Kai pulled the strip off his nose and held it out for Dunk to see. It looked like a stiff, little board, but it was sticky on the side to be pressed against the nose. 'The Snot Stoppers are new. They bear a small enchantment designed to open up your sinuses so you can breathe better. It's supposed to enhance athletic ability.'

Dunk squinted at the thing as Kai put it back on his face. 'Does it work?'

Kai frowned. 'I don't know. I wear it because it helps me smell players coming at me from ten yards away. Those undead and goblin teams really stink!'

Bob Bifford's voice rang out over the PA system again. 'And heeeere we go! The teams meet in the centre of the field for the coin toss. As the captain of the visiting team, Kur Ritternacht will call it in the air.'

Dunk watched as the referee – a mean-looking, dark-skinned elf with a crimson crest of hair, dressed in a shirt with vertical black-and-white stripes – pulled out a large gold coin and spoke to Kur. 'Orcs or Eagles?' he hissed. Without waiting for an answer, he flipped the coin in the air.

'Orcs!' Kur shouted.

The coin fell to the ground and bounced high on the stony surface. When it rolled to a stop, the referee shouted out 'Orcs it is!'

Kur muttered something to the referee, who then tossed the ball to Dirk.

'The Hackers win the toss and elect to receive. The Reavers take the east end of the field and set up to receive the ball,' Bob's voice said.

'What's this made out of?' Dunk said, pointing at the field. 'I've never seen a coin bounce like that before.'

'Go ahead and touch it,' Slick said.

Dunk slipped off the bench and reached out from the dugout to lay a hand on the field. It was rough and tough like stone, but it gave and rebounded like flesh. If it had been warm, Dunk might have thought it was living. He picked at it with one of the spikes that jutted from the knuckles of his fingerless gauntlets, and a small chunk came free. When Dunk looked back at the material, though, he couldn't find where the chunk had come from. It was if the stuff had somehow managed to heal.

A stein of ale smashed against his shoulder pad, and Dunk – realizing he wasn't wearing his helmet – slipped back into the dugout before someone in the crowd developed better aim.

'It's called Astrogranite,' Slick said as Dunk took his spot on the bench again. 'Its as tough as stone, only better. Low maintenance too.'

Without warning, the crowd started to groan in a low-pitched tone. Dunk looked out to see the Reavers' kicker getting ready to boot the ball downfield. As the kicker got closer to the ball, the pitch of the crowd's inharmonious moan rose until it transformed into a screech as the kicker sent the ball sailing west.

The ball came right down toward Cavre, who caught it neatly and began dashing east, toward the Reavers' end zone. The game was on.

Dunk spent the first half of the game sitting next to the other 'scrubs', as Kai called all the players on the bench. 'Because we're the ones called in to clean things up after someone's blood has been spilled.'

'Being a backup is not so bad,' Guillermo said. 'You get to sit here on the sidelines where it's safe. You get paid the same no matter if you play or not. And you get great seats to watch the game.'

'Why did you try out for the team if you don't want to play?' Milo asked.

'My brothers bet me that I wouldn't do it,' Guillermo grinned. 'They scraped together ten crowns that said I'd wash out before the cuts. I'll do just about anything to win a bet with my brothers.'

'Including signing up to play a ridiculously dangerous game?' Simon said. The way he shivered as he spoke told Dunk that Simon was starting to regret having made the same decision himself.

'Well,' Guillermo smiled in his warm, Estalian way, 'I thought I'd just decline the offer if it came, but when Coach Pegleg sat me down to explain the terms, I just couldn't refuse.'

Dunk nodded. He knew exactly what Guillermo meant. This wasn't the career of dragon slaying he'd set out for when he left town, and he was a bit concerned how anyone from his family – well, besides Dirk, of course – would react when they saw him on the field. But the gold took the sting right out of that.

Bob's voice belted out over the crowd noise, which had finally died down a bit, although it sometimes crested like one of the monstrous waves in the Sea of Claws, on which Dunk's family had vacationed every year.

'Rhett "the Rocket" Cavre receives the ball and launches himself downfield. The Reavers' linemen charge forward to stop him, but the Hackers set up a nice line of blockers to give their star player some protection.'

'This is exactly the kind of thing the Hackers need to do to win this game,' Jim said. 'The Reavers outmatch the Hackers at just about every position, so the Hackers must play together as a team to have a prayer. Coaching will be the key here.'

'True enough, Jim, but what about the new recruits the Hackers just picked up only two days ago? Do you think they've had time to integrate with the others and gel into the kind of lean, mean, bruising machine they have to be to prevent a repeat of that gut-wrenching loss against the Darkside Cowboys?'

'Gut-*spilling*, you mean!' I haven't seen that much blood on the ground since your last family dinner!'

'Stop it, you big lug. You're making me drool!' Bob said. Dunk could hear him licking his lips.

'Oh! Cavre pitches the ball back to the Hackers' starting thrower, Ritternacht, the third-leading thrower in the league last year. Ritternacht drops back into open territory and pumps a fake. Then he sees an open man downfield and lets it rip!'

'Look at that ball sail along!' said Jim. 'It's heading right for the end zone!'

'Wait a minute! Dirk "the Hero" Heldmann has an angle on it. He leaps up and... yes! Intercepted!'

The crowd went nuts, and Dunk could barely hear the announcers as he watched the drama play out on the field.

Dirk took off with the ball, running towards the south side of the field to gather some room. Then, still charging at top speed, he hurled it straight down the field and into the end zone.

'Spinne "the Black Widow" Schönheit reaches up with those long, lovely arms of hers and hauls the ball in, dodging a last-second dive from Karsten "the Killer" Klemmer. Triple K goes wide and into the stands while Schönheit executes a victory dance in the end zone. Touchdown!'

'That's not the only thing being executed, Bob. It looks like those fans are playing wishbones with Triple K's legs!'

Dunk stood up, but he couldn't see Karsten anywhere. It was if the carnivorous crowd had swallowed him whole. From the sounds of it, they were chewing him up pretty badly.

A moment later, the crowd spat Karsten back into the end zone. Spinne pirouetted over to the injured player and spiked the ball down into his face. It stuck in his open-faced helmet, right between the top ridge and his single chin bar.

The Reavers charged back to their end of the field, leaving the Hackers to lick their wounds. A team of litter bearers raced out to collect Karsten and cart him off the field. They deposited the man in the Hackers' dugout, and Dunk could see blood trickling from a half dozen wounds in Karsten's exposed flesh.

'That took all of one minute,' Pegleg snarled, checking the green and gold pocket watch he'd pulled from his crimson coat as the game began. He'd been pacing up and down through the dugout since, watching the clock almost as much as the game. He looked over at the bench and sighed.

'It's going to be a damned long day.'

CHAPTER EIGHTEEN

FROM WHERE HE stood at the edge of the field, Pegleg looked at his bench. His gaze sliced through each of the players, evaluating them one by one.

Dunk felt Pegleg consider him for a moment and then move on, and he couldn't tell if he was relieved or disappointed. The other scrubs sat frozen stiff, afraid to attract their coach's attention with the slightest movement. Beside him, Dunk could hear Simon whispering a mantra over and over again: 'Don't pick me. Don't pick me. Don't pick me.'

Dunk looked up at Pegleg and saw the coach glaring down at him, a pitiless smile on his face. 'Mr. Hoffnung,' Pegleg said, pointing his hook at the rookie. 'You're in.'

Dunk surprised himself by leaping up and darting out of the dugout to stand next to Pegleg. 'Who am I in for, coach?' he asked.

Pegleg lowered his head and rubbed his eyes with his good hand. A low moan emanated from the other side of the dugout where an apothecary, a tall thin man wearing a grimy, once-white coat and a pair of magnifying glasses over his eyes, was working on Karsten.

'No leeches!' the lineman screamed. 'No leeches!'

'It's that or the bone drill,' the apothecary wheezed. As he spoke, he put down the slimy green things flopping about in his fists and picked up a vicious-shaped metal device. As he spun its handle, the blood-caked tip whirred and clacked. Dunk had never heard such a horrible threat.

'Leeches!' Karsten said. 'By Nuffle's dirty cleats, I'll take my chances with the leeches!'

'But Karsten's a lineman,' Dunk said. 'I'm a thrower. What about Guillermo?' The rookie looked back over his shoulder to see the new lineman drawing a finger under his throat at Dunk. He wasn't sure if Guillermo meant for him to be quiet or that the lineman wanted to kill him. Maybe both.

'You're my man, Mr. Hoffnung,' Pegleg said. 'Don't question my judgment – ever.'

'Aye, coach,' Dunk said with a snappy salute.

Pegleg glared at the rookie as if he couldn't tell if the salute was in mockery or earnest. Then he looked out at the field and said, 'No matter. Make your peace with Nuffle, Mr. Hoffnung, and welcome to your first game of Blood Bowl.'

Armed with some hurried instructions from his coach, Dunk strapped on his helmet and charged out on to the field. The crowd cheered as he raced toward his designated spot, right near the midfield line. Dunk raised his hands in the air to encourage them.

'What do you think you're doing?' Dirk said, standing opposite from Dunk across the line.

'Working the crowd!' Dunk said. 'Blood Bowl's a game that's larger than life. I'm giving them what they want.' He raised his arms again, and the cheering grew.

'Listen to them go!' Dunk said. As he spoke, he spotted Spinne standing several yards back and caught her eye. She smiled at him and blew him a kiss. He caught it in both hands and raised it into the air like a trophy before bringing it back down to stuff into his mouth. The crowed loved it.

'Do you hear what they're saying?' Dirk asked.

Dunk stopped pandering to the stands for a moment and listened carefully. It took him a moment, but he managed to pick some words out of the roar, two words that the fans kept chanting. When he realised what they were, he blanched.

'Fresh meat! Fresh meat! Fresh meat!'

Then the crowd began its collective low groan again, signifying the upcoming kick-off. As the sound grew louder and higher, Dirk beckoned Dunk with a crooked finger, saying something.

'What's that again?' Dunk asked as he leaned forward, cocking his head toward his brother.

The screaming of the crowd reached a crescendo as Dirk shouted at Dunk. 'Remember when you knocked me out of that window when we were kids?'

Dunk nodded. He'd been ashamed of that incident since the day it had happened. Dirk had fallen from the keep's east tower and nearly been killed. Only the intercession of the best apothecary in town had saved the young boy's life. It had been an accident, but the blame for it fell squarely on Dunk's shoulders.

Dirk flashed Dunk an evil grin, then lowered his shoulder and slammed his spiked pad into Dunk, knocking him flying backward to the ground. Dunk's head hit the ground, and stars zoomed past his eyes. The next thing he knew, he felt Dirk's boots stomp on his chest as the Reaver blitzer literally ran right over him.

'Now we're even!' Dirk shouted back as he charged down the field, after the ball.

Dunk crawled to his feet and shook his head. It felt like his brain was loose. The world swam around him, threatening to pitch him off its edge.

The rookie clung to what Pegleg had told him, and he started running toward the end zone.

'Your brother is going to knock you flat,' Pegleg had said.

'No he won't, coach,' Dunk had said, bouncing up and down as he surveyed the field. 'I can take him.'

Pegleg had grabbed the faceguard on Dunk's helmet and wrenched the rookie's head around until they were looking eye to eye. It had hurt, but Dunk hadn't said a word, his tongue catching in his mouth.

'You're going to let him,' Pegleg had said. 'Then you're going to get up and run for the end zone for all you're worth.'

'Which one?'

'Theirs,' Pegleg had said, pointing in the direction the rest of the Hackers were already facing.

'Got it, coach. See, I always get those mixed up, whose end zone is whose. Is yours the one you're defending or the one you're attacking. I can never–'

'Go. That. Way.' Pegleg stabbed his hook toward the Reavers' end zone to punctuate each word. Then he brought the hook around to come up under the chin trap of Dunk's helmet. The sharp tip had caught Dunk right in the fleshy part of his neck there. A single sharp jab could have shoved the hook up into Dunk's mouth so that Pegleg could lead him around by his jawbone.

'Don't disappoint me,' Pegleg had said. Although he'd only whispered, Dunk had heard him as clearly as if everyone else in the stadium had been struck dumb.

All this in mind, Dunk sprinted as hard as he could toward the Reavers' end zone, struggling to clear his head as he ran.

'This time, Kur Ritternacht fields the ball directly,' Bob's voice said. 'He gets some good blocking from the Hackers' linemen and moves the ball forward. K'Thragsh, the only nonhuman player on the field, opens up a hole for him, and he dashes through it.'

'Yes!' said Jim's voice. '"Monster" M'Grash K'Thragsh was one of the Hackers' standouts last year, and a play like that really shows you why. That's the sort of player you can build a team around – or destroy another team with!'

As Dunk ran, he heard someone else pounding after him. He glanced over his shoulder and saw Spinne racing towards him. He had the angle on her to the end zone and he knew he'd get there first. He winked at her, then looked up past her toward the sky.

There, hovering in the air like some great bird of prey, hung the football. It paused for a moment at the top of its arc, then came plummeting back to earth. As it approached, it seemed to move faster, and Dunk realised he'd have to run as fast as he could to catch it.

His eyes still on the ball, Dunk sprinted for the end zone and a date with the ball for which he could not be late. As the ball closed the last few yards toward their mutual meeting spot, he stretched out his arms as far as they could go. The ball landed hard in his fingertips, hard enough to break them, or so it felt. He grabbed at the ball as it were life itself and pulled it in hard to his chest, where he cradled it like an infant.

Dunk hit the ground and rolled hard, keeping himself wrapped around the ball, protecting it from the Astrogranite, which was not as forgiving as he'd hoped. As his momentum faded, he rolled neatly out of his tuck and to his feet. He held the ball high over his head in a moment of pure triumph, and roared along with the crowd.

'Amazing!' Bob's voice said. 'Hoffnung, the rookie phenom from Altdorf, scores a touchdown in his first minute of play!'

The moment was cut short, though, when someone hit Dunk from behind and drove him into the stands.

'Ooh!' said Jim's voice. 'Apparently Dunk's not as much of a lover as a fighter. Lady Schönheit there just made him pay so much for his score that he'll be making equal monthly instalments for the next three years!'

The fans, some of who were more frightening than the players, grabbed Dunk with their meaty paws and greasy claws and passed him bodily up toward the top of the arena. Someone ripped the ball from his hand and bit it in half with his frothing teeth; a rabid dwarf, from the look of him, with a chain that hung between his pierced ear and nose. His face and the shaved sides of his head were tattooed, except where a thin dorsal fin of hair stabbed up from the top, dyed a glaring orange.

Dunk was just happy the dwarf had gone for the football instead of his arm. He looked back down to where he'd come from and saw Spinne waving at him and blowing a good-bye kiss.

'I'll be right back!' he shouted down at her.

The fans around him burst out laughing at this and practically hurled him towards the top of the stadium. As Dunk kept moving up and up, he recalled that the edge of the stadium stood two or three stories above the ground, maybe more, and the crowd was hauling him straight toward that edge without any sign of stopping.

'Ah,' Bob's voice said, 'it looks like Magritta's infamous Dead End Zoners have decided to commemorate the rookie's amazing achievement with a trip on the Bay Water Bowl's express escalator to the afterlife.'

'No!' Dunk shouted as he flung himself about, trying to find a handhold on someone or something, anything to bring this deadly trip to a stop. He scored purchase on a snotling, but when he pulled at it, the tiny goblin simply leapt atop his chest and starting spitting in his face.

'It's sad,' Jim's voice said, his tone betraying that he felt anything but grief, 'to see such a promising career cut so short. This has to be some kind of record: first and last touchdown scored in under a minute!'

Dunk flung the snotling away, and the creature landed in a mob of fans watching him be hauled away, chanting, 'Over! Over! Over!' Someone smacked the hapless snotling into the air again, and the creature began a long circuit around the stadium, bouncing about like some kind of fleshy beach ball.

Dunk had other worries though, as he could not find a way to slow his progress toward his first and surely final attempt at flight. He thrashed about as best he could, but the fans passed him along by the spikes on his armour, holding him fast. The straps that Slick had done such a good job of tightening now trapped him inside his prickly shell, and there was no escape from it.

When Dunk reached the edge of the stadium, he flung out his arms to grab at the wall, his final chance of escaping this predicament, even if it meant brawling his way back to the field from the cheap seats on down. The fans were ready for this trick though. (It frightened Dunk to consider how many times they'd pulled this off, they executed it – and possibly him – so well.) They hoisted him high into the air and pitched him far out over the stadium's rear wall.

'Say so long to Dunk Hoffnung, you fanatics!' Bob's voice said.

'See ya!' the crowd answered as one, drowning out Dunk's screams as he fell flailing toward the ground far below.

CHAPTER NINETEEN

WHEN DUNK WOKE up, he hurt so badly he assumed he was dead. At first, he assumed the nauseating way the world rocked beneath him convinced him he'd sustained a horrible head injury. Then he smelled the tang of salt in the air, and he realised he was on a ship.

Dunk had never been below deck on the *Sea Chariot* before, but he imagined this was exactly what it would be like. He groaned as the ship crossed a particularly choppy section of sea, forcing him to feel the size and shape of his stomach in a way he never had before.

Slick was at his side in an instant. 'Nuffle's bloody balls, you're awake,' the halfling breathed. He reached out with a cool, damp cloth and laid it across Dunk's brow, which seemed to help stave off the nausea, at least for the moment. 'I thought we'd lost you for good.'

Dunk's stomach turned, and he sat up, fighting back his body's demand to vomit. Slick shoved a bucket in front of him, and Dunk clutched it like a poor man clinging to his last crown.

'Me too,' Dunk said. 'What happened?'

Slick grimaced. 'The crowd grabbed you and tossed you over the top of the stadium.'

Dunk rubbed his aching head. His hand ached too, as did his arm and every other part of his body. 'I remember that part,' he said. 'What happened after that?'

'The referee called a penalty.'

'That's good.'

'Against you.'

'What?' Dunk said. His head felt like it might explode.

'He called it excessive celebration, you jumping over the edge of the stadium like that.'

Dunk wanted to let his jaw drop, but he was sure whatever was in his stomach would come storming out after that, so he grimaced instead. 'I did not jump over that edge. I was thrown!'

Slick nodded. 'I know, son, as did everyone else in the stadium, but the fans liked the call so much it was bound to stand.'

'How could a referee make a call like that?'

Slick patted Dunk on the knee as if the rookie was a small child. 'How does any referee make a call in a gold-infested game like Blood Bowl?'

'Are you saying he was bribed?'

'Yes,' Slick nodded, 'and by both sides too. Apparently the Reavers have deeper pockets than ours, although I suppose that's no surprise.'

Dunk slumped back in his bed. 'At least I scored a touchdown.'

Slick stayed silent.

'I said, at least I scored a touchdown.'

'Yes, son, about that.'

Dunk sat up again, too agitated to think about his stomach any more. 'Don't tell me the ref negated the touchdown too.'

'He tried to.' Slick's toothy grin put Dunk's mind more at ease. 'The fans didn't like that at all though. It's one thing to buy a ref. It's another to make it so obvious.

'Also, people just loved the style you showed by rolling up into that triumphant stand. That and feeling sorry for you for being thrown over the edge of the stadium caused a bit of a riot.'

'Really?' Dunk smiled in spite of himself.

'They stormed the field and grabbed the ref. Then they sent him up after you. Sadly for him, they didn't give him the easy route.'

Dunk's jaw did drop this time. 'They sent me by the easy route?'

'You're still here, aren't you?'

Dunk rubbed his head again. 'I'm not so sure.'

'It turns out there's a series of awnings tiered below the spot where you were tossed over. You hit every one of them. Tore through most of them, but they slowed you down enough so when you hit that sausage on a stick vendor, it was not so bad.'

'Not so bad?' Dunk said softly. 'How long have I been out?'

'Three days.'

'*Three days!*' Dunk could not wrap his aching head around that concept. 'I thought you said it wasn't so bad?'

'Well, the fall wasn't so bad. The sausage vendor, though, he wasn't happy about how you destroyed his cart. He beat you senseless. It took three of our linemen to pull him off of you.'

Dunk let his head sink into his hands. So much for his great debut. Could he ever recover from this?

'Where are we now?' Dunk asked.

'The *Sea Chariot*,' Slick said. 'You're in what passes for a sickbay around here. It's mid-afternoon. Everyone else is above deck.'

'What happened to the tournament?'

'We lost, Mr. Hoffnung!' Pegleg swept into the cramped little room and glared down at the rookie. 'In no small part, the blame for that gets laid at your feet. Too busy celebrating after your first touchdown to worry about the lady Reaver coming up behind you? That was a *rookie* mistake.'

'I'm a rookie,' Dunk offered.

'That's not good enough, Mr. Hoffnung,' Pegleg said as he shoved his hook into Dunk's face. The rookie froze, afraid that the thing's vicious tip might accidentally catch his nose. 'Not *nearly* good enough. I don't pay you a ludicrous amount of money to make mistakes, rookie or otherwise. I pay you to *win games!*'

'What happened to the game?' Dunk asked, hoping to change the subject. As he spoke, though, it occurred to him that this might be the exact wrong subject to change to.

Pegleg spat on the floor. 'A tie,' he said, as if someone had just suggested he trade in his hook for a bouquet of wilted roses. 'The remaining referee called the game when he realised he'd have to face the rest of us alone. Then he fled before we could contest his ruling. Since each team had scored a touchdown, the game was declared a draw.'

'I thought the one ref had negated my touchdown.'

'The surviving ref thought better of that, son,' Slick said. 'He reinstated it.'

Dunk grinned at that. His smile vanished when he looked back up at Pegleg. 'I'm sorry, coach,' he said. 'I did my best.'

'That, Mr. Hoffnung, is exactly what I'm afraid of.' Pegleg shook his head, then turned and left.

Dunk fell back into his bed. What a rude awakening this had been. He felt like crawling up onto the deck and throwing himself overboard. At least then he wouldn't be able to mess everything up again.

'Don't feel so bad, son,' Slick said. 'Pegleg's hard on everyone.' The halfling stared at the door. 'You should feel honoured actually. He's come in here every couple hours checking on you. Considering how stuck to that crystal ball of his he usually is, I'm impressed. I've never seen him leave his cabin before if we weren't docked.'

Dunk sat back up and shook his head. 'I guess that's something.' A question struck him finally. 'Why didn't we stay in Magritta?'

'Pegleg's not a stupid man. He did the math. With two losses, it's next to impossible to make the semi-finals.'

'Then where are we going?'

'Like most teams, we're off to the next of the Majors.'

Dunk nodded. He liked the thought of a fresh start somewhere else with another chance to prove himself. 'Which one's that?' he asked.

Slick flashed Dunk a smile that made him nervous. 'We're off to see the Dungeonbowl.'

'I thought there were three months between all the Majors.'

'Roughly,' Slick said. 'You can never tell exactly when the Chaos Cup will be played, for instance.'

'Where is the Dungeonbowl then?' asked Dunk as he tried getting to his feet. The world swam under his feet as he did, but he realised now that this was the ship, not his head. 'I mean, how long will it take us to get there? Three full months?'

Slick shook his head. 'The wizards of the Colleges of Magic host the tournament every year. Each of the ten colleges sponsors a team to represent it in the games. Originally, they set this up to resolve a horrible conflict among the colleges, but they liked the game so much that they decided to keep it going. They've been playing it for more than seventy-five years now.'

'The Colleges of Magic,' Dunk asked, his head suddenly pounding harder than ever. He sat down to wrestle with his stomach again. 'So we're going to Altdorf?' Dunk wasn't ready to go home, not yet, maybe not ever.

'Oh, no,' Slick said, waving off Dunk's ignorance. 'The wizards who run the colleges are too smart to host something as dangerous as the Dungeonbowl anywhere near their main campus. It's held in Barak-Varr, the dwarf seaport that sits right where the Blood River runs down from the Worlds Edge Mountains and into the Black Gulf.'

'Sounds like a lovely place,' Dunk said. His stomach settled down as he spoke.

'It's not so bad, son, so long as you like dwarfs. Of course, most dwarfs won't go near Barak-Varr, since it's so near the sea. They think the dwarfs who choose to live there are a bit off-balance, if you know what I mean. But then, they'd have to be to come up with the complexes in which they play the game, right?'

'Who's crazier, Slick?' Dunk asked as he got to his feet again. 'The people who create the game or those who play it?'

'WE'RE NOT GOING directly to Barak-Varr, Mr. Hoffnung,' Cavre said that night as Dunk took his dinner on the deck, sitting next to the blitzer. 'Right now, we're in the Southern Sea, heading southeast. Once we round Fools Point, we'll be in the Tilean Sea, which separates Estalia from Tilea. We'll follow that coast as closely as we dare, stopping in Remas for supplies. From there, it's on to Luccini and then through the Pirates' Current into the Black Gulf.'

'How long will all this take us?'

'A good few weeks. It's not as far as the trip from Bad Bay to Magritta, but we're not in as much of a hurry. With winter coming on, most of the Blood Bowl teams have gone into hibernation until spring. The Dungeonbowl is the only major tournament held in these dark months.'

'Who's sponsoring us in the tournament?' Dunk wondered if he'd get to meet some of the powerful wizards who ran the Colleges of Magic back in Altdorf. Those were the kinds of friends that might come in handy later.

'No one,' Cavre said. 'We're not playing.'

Dunk almost dropped his spoon. 'Then why are we going there?'

Cavre smiled. Dunk realised what a great player the assistant coach must have been. After nearly fifteen years of playing Blood Bowl, he was not only still alive, he even had all his own teeth.

'We're going to watch and to learn. We just hired a quarter of our team last week, as you know, and many of the others have only a year or two under their belts.'

Cavre clicked his tongue. 'It's a rebuilding year. Not so coincidentally, Mr. Hoffnung, we have a winter training camp set up on the north coast of the Black Gulf, in one of the lands of the Border Princes. We'll train there hard until the Dungeonbowl, and when that tournament is over, we'll head back toward the Empire and hope we're in the right place when the location of the Chaos Cup is announced.'

'You don't know where it is?' Dunk asked, surprised.

'No one does. It's kept a secret until a week or two before the event. That way, no one can disrupt it.'

'Does that work?' Dunk asked, rubbing the back of his head, which was still a bit tender.

'Not really,' Cavre said. 'Most of the time the fans do more damage than any invading army ever could.'

The two fell silent for a moment, and Dunk gazed up at the stars sparkling overhead. Cavre was right about the winter. Even this far south, he could feel it getting colder. He imagined Altdorf would be covered with snow already. The thought of his home town coated with a virginal layer of white made him homesick. He remembered running snowball fights with

Dirk along the battlements of the family's keep, even though there wasn't much of a home left there to go back to.

'Have you seen Mr. K'Thragsh yet?' Cavre asked.

Dunk looked up to see the blitzer smiling at him softly. 'No. Is he all right?'

'Your "accident" shook him up a bit. He's lost a lot of team-mates over the past few years, and he thought you might be the next one. I think he's taken a real shine to you. He checked in on you more than anyone besides Mr. Fullbelly.'

Dunk snorted. 'I suppose it's better to have the ogre with you than against you. I have to say, though, I thought an ogre would be...'

'Less sensitive?'

'That's it.'

Cavre nodded. 'Mr. K'Thragsh is a special case. Years back, an Imperial army wiped out his entire village when he was just an infant. He was the only survivor.'

'That's horrible.'

'They *were* eating the people in the neighbouring village.'

'Ah. So what happened to M'Grash?'

The army's commander couldn't bear to kill an infant in cold blood. He picked up little Mr. K'Thragsh, who was probably already as big as Mr. Fullbelly, and brought him to the village. A woman who'd been widowed during an ogre attack took the baby ogre in and raised him as her own.'

'Amazing,' Dunk said. 'So, why did you ask about M'Grash?'

Cavre jerked his head toward the ship's stern. The ogre stood there, perched behind Percival Smythe, the catcher and sometimes pilot. When he caught Dunk's eye, he jumped for joy and nearly knocked Percy off the bridge. Dunk felt the ship sway with the ogre's movement.

'You'd better get over there before he capsizes the ship,' Cavre said.

Dunk put his empty bowl in the dishes bin as he walked down the deck to get the biggest hug he'd ever had in his life.

ONCE THE TEAM settled in at their winter camp, Pegleg drove them hard. 'I've never seen such a flabby and useless lot outside of Stirland!' he liked to roar at them. Slick tried to protest this slander against his people, but a wave of Pegleg's hook convinced him to let the issue lie.

Dunk took to the training as if his life depended on it. After his experience in the *Spike! Magazine* Tournament, he was sure that it did. If he didn't get better and smarter at this game, he knew it would be the death of him. Despite his initial discomfort about joining a Blood Bowl team, he wasn't ready to be murdered for it.

As the weeks wore on, Dunk found himself becoming not only a member of a team, but a family. The constant hours spent together forged the Hackers into a unit much stronger than the sum of its parts.

As with all families, though, there was some friction. Kur treated Dunk like an uppity child he felt compelled to humiliate at every turn. Dunk wasn't sure why the starting thrower disliked him so much, but he wasn't about to give in to the torture.

When, for what seemed like the fortieth time that day, Kur tripped Dunk as he raced past him while running a throwing route, Dunk leapt to his feet and belted Kur in the teeth. As soon as he did, he regretted it.

Instead of falling down, Kur just smiled at Dunk and pulled out one of his own front teeth. Then he made a fist around the tooth and pummelled Dunk with it.

Dunk's combat training had been with swords, not fists. He was faster than Kur, but he couldn't seem to get his arms up fast enough to block the taller man's hail of blows.

'Dumb kid,' Kur growled as he administered the beating like a malicious headmaster. 'If you want my job, you're going to have to *take* it from me.'

Under other circumstances, Dunk might have told Kur the truth, that he didn't really want his job, that he was content to wait on the bench and serve as a fill-in only when Kur couldn't manage it. Instead, he lashed out with his fist. His gauntlet cut the starting thrower across his forehead, splashing blood into his eyes.

Startled at how much damage he'd done, Dunk stopped, holding his fists before him to defend himself. He watched as Kur wiped the blood from his face, clearing his eyes with his fingers. Then the veteran of countless games snarled at Dunk.

'You cut my face,' he said. 'I'll cut your throat!'

Before Kur could close with Dunk to land another blow, a massive hand swept through and smacked him away. Dunk's head snapped up to see M'Grash standing between him and Kur now, growling at the veteran like a hungry lion.

'Stay away!' the ogre said to Kur, threatening him with a fist as big as Kur's head. 'Hurt Dunk, kill you.'

Kur got up slowly from where he'd been knocked to the turf. Everyone else on the team, including Pegleg had stopped to watch the fight. All eyes followed Kur, but no one spoke a word.

The veteran passer spat blood on to the ground. 'Your monster friend won't always be there for you.'

'Hold it right there, Mr. Ritternacht,' Pegleg said, cutting Kur off. 'You keep your rivalries on the field. If I hear different, then you've seen your last day on this team.'

Kur glared at Dunk, then bit his tongue and stomped off the field.

Dunk looked up at M'Grash and said, 'Thanks, big guy.'

The ogre patted him on the back. After weeks of this, Dunk was braced for it and managed to stay on his feet. 'Anything for friend,' M'Grash said. 'Anything.'

CHAPTER TWENTY

Ye Olde Trip to Araby was the kind of pub that Dunk thought he would have loved if he'd been born a dwarf. The bartender, a stubby creature, even for a dwarf, claimed that the place was the oldest known watering hole in all the dwarf kingdoms. It got its name from the fact that it was the last place dwarf warriors would stop for a drink before heading off to war against the soldiers of Araby in an effort to put an end to their jihad.

Unlike many of the other places Dunk had seen since entering the mostly subterranean city of Barak-Varr, the Trip was little more than a series of interconnected holes in walls. Most of the city featured the stunning, legendary architecture of the dwarfs, who were unparalleled in their skill with cutting and carving stone. The keepers of the Trip, however, had left the place pretty much the same over

the centuries. Each chamber was little more than a
natural cave with a levelled floor, a few torch-filled
sconces on the walls, and scattered sets of low-slung
tables and chairs. These were big enough for humans
to sit at, but they were clearly meant for dwarfs
instead.

Dunk had come here shortly after arriving in town
because he'd heard that the Reavers often met here
when they were in town. The Grey Wizards were
sponsoring Dirk and Spinne's team in the Dungeonbowl, so Dunk figured he had a good chance of
finding his brother here.

Shortly after waking up on the *Sea Chariot*, Dunk
realised that he had never warned his brother about
the murderous Skragger's threat. He promised himself he would do so at the first chance, so as soon as
the Hackers arrived in Barak-Varr, he found his way to
the Trip.

Dunk had never been in a city like this before, or in
any dwarf settlement for that matter. There were
dwarfs in Altdorf, of course, and Dunk had visited
their pubs there to sample their legendary brews, but
those places were only faint echoes of what he'd
already seen here.

The docks of Barak-Varr had been lined with ships,
many of which were fitted with paddles and mighty
engines that drove them via steam. The city itself was
carved into the faces of the cliffs that surrounded the
Blood River as it spilled into the Black Gulf. From a
distance, the cliffs looked like pock-marked cheese,
but as the *Sea Chariot* grew closer, Dunk could see
elaborate windows, doors, and balconies carved in
and around the holes. High above, a flag of royal blue

and a glittering gold axe and pick fluttered in the wind, declaring this place a home of dwarfs.

'It's the only major port the dwarfs have,' Slick had explained. 'They mostly live under mountains, and you don't get a lot of boat traffic there. They use those paddleboats to ferry goods up and down the Blood River to Everpeak, high in the Worlds Edge Mountains. That's how the people of Karaz-a-Karak get the supplies they need to survive. The rest of the world gets dwarf-made crafts and beers in exchange.'

'All the dwarfs I knew in Altdorf would spit if you mentioned the sea. Some of them wouldn't even cross the bridge over the River Reik. I'm surprised they have a port like this at all.'

'So are most of the dwarfs who don't live here. They think the dwarfs of Barak-Varr are mad. They call them "sea dwarfs", which is about as low as a dwarf can get. The ones who live here, though, they wear that title proud. They point out that there's money to be made trading goods here by the sea, and I've yet to meet a dwarf who didn't understand that kind of lure.'

A cheer from the largest of the pub's caverns went up again. This was where the Reavers were having their last dinner before the tournament started tomorrow, the bartender had said, but attendance was by invitation only. The pair of burly dwarfs flanking the doorway had kept Dunk at bay, so here he sat at the bar, nursing a delicious Gotrekugel's winter ale and waiting for Dirk to emerge. Dunk had sampled this beer in Altdorf, but it was miles better here. He wondered if it simply didn't travel well or if the Imperial dwarfs were secretly (and not nearly so masterfully) brewing it themselves.

'Hey, stranger,' a voice said from behind Dunk, 'buy a girl a drink?'

Dunk turned to see Spinne standing over him as he squatted on a short stool in front of the dwarf-sized bar. His heart melted like an icicle in a dragon's breath, and he smiled warmly at her.

Spinne reached out and caressed his cheek with her hand. 'It's good to see you again,' she said. 'After that match in Magritta, I was afraid I'd lost you.'

Dunk rubbed his head as he remembered that fall. He shuddered inwardly at the thoughts that sprang into his head.

'I never meant to hurt you,' she said. Then she caught herself. 'Well, not that badly.'

'Forget it,' Dunk said. 'Not remembering you were coming up behind me was a rookie mistake. It's my fault as much as yours.' He wasn't sure that was true, but he knew he wanted her to believe it. Then he added with a laugh, 'It won't happen again.'

'Well, well, well,' said a voice Dunk remembered far too well. He turned to see Lästiges emerge from a dark hole near the bar like some kind of a monstrous trap spider delighted to see not one but two victims come too close to her lair. 'It seems the rumours are true,' she said, innuendo dripping from her red-painted lips.

Spinne stepped back from Dunk immediately. 'There's nothing going on here,' she said, giving Dunk's cheek a playful slap. 'I'm just checking up on the health of a once and future victim.'

'That's not what my sources tell me,' Lästiges said, still gloating at her good fortune. 'I can see the headline now: "Black Widow Risks All for Rookie – and Loses Big!"'

'There's nothing wrong with what we have,' Dunk said defensively. He didn't see why Spinne would show this reporter any respect, much less fear.

'There's nothing wrong with nothing,' Spinne said, nodding in agreement. 'After all, it's common knowledge that the Reavers' contracts forbid the players from establishing relationships with members of other teams. It's a firing offence,' she said, looking right into Dunk's eyes.

Lästiges smirked at this. 'I have eyewitnesses that saw and then *heard* the two of you cavorting about during the *Spike! Magazine* tournament. I'm sure my editors would love to run a feature about this sort of thing. Sex really does sell, you know.' She looked Dunk up and down as if she could have eaten him alive, right there. 'Combine it with the violence of Blood Bowl and, oh, my!'

'I wasn't a Blood Bowl player that night,' Dunk said.

'What night?' Spinne said as she tried to surreptitiously grind her foot down on Dunk's toe. He rescued his foot and continued on.

'I didn't sign my contract until the next morning. Spinne didn't do anything wrong.'

The door to the Reavers' private room flew open. There was a roar of laughter and a tall figure stood silhouetted in the doorway.

'I hear I have family waiting out here for me,' Dirk said loudly. From his tone, Dunk could tell his brother had been drinking. A lot. 'Brother!'

Dunk rose from his stool and met Dirk halfway between the door and the bar. They embraced with a hug in which it seemed each was trying to squeeze the breath out of the other as they pounded each other on the back.

'It's good to see you again, Dunk,' Dirk said. 'Until I saw you go sailing over the top of that stadium, I don't think I realised how much I missed you.'

'Thanks,' Dunk said. 'I think.' Then he remembered what he'd come there for.

'Dirk,' he said, 'I have a warning for you from a black orc by the name of Skragger.'

'That old windbag,' Dirk said, noticing Lästiges and waving at her. 'What does he want?'

'He came and attacked me at the Hackers' camp on the opening day of the *Spike! Magazine* tournament. He said that if you broke his annual record for most touchdowns scored he'd kill you and everyone related to you.'

'Do you really think he could manage that second part? Maybe we'd be better off letting him try. Maybe he'd be the one to finally find our father again.'

Dunk frowned. 'I don't see how it would matter, if he kills us first.'

Dirk grimaced playfully at Dunk, one eye still on Lästiges. 'Don't let that old loincloth shake you, Dunk. He's harmless. I hear he does this kind of thing every year.'

'He's only killed three people so far,' Lästiges said.

Dunk glared at the reporter. '*Only* three.'

'This year.' She gazed at Dirk with her hungry eyes and drank him in. 'I'm sure a couple of young bruisers like you two could handle him.'

'He knocked me around pretty well,' Dunk said.

Dirk blushed for his brother and slapped Dunk on the back. 'I'm sure he caught you off guard.'

Dunk shrugged off Dirk's arm. 'Don't talk to me like that,' he said, letting his irritation show in his voice. 'You always do that. We're fine until I admit to a flaw, and then you're so superior.'

Dirk flashed a knowing smile at Lästiges, who giggled at it. 'I can't help what I am,' he said, grabbing Dunk's shoulders and shaking him playfully.

Dunk shoved him away. 'Don't,' he said coldly. 'I don't need any more favours from you. I know how you got Slick to do your dirty work for you. Trapping me to play this game just so you can parade yourself in front of me showing how successful you are.'

Dirk frowned. 'So it's like this again?' he said. 'That's gratitude for you. I thought maybe we were old enough to get past all that, but it's all the same, isn't it? I get myself set up in a new career, a new group of friends, and you can't stand it. You get jealous and just have to show everyone that the oldest Hoffnung is always the best.'

Dunk couldn't believe his ears, which grew redder and redder as Dirk spoke.

'You can just forget that,' Dirk said. 'This isn't the keep, and Lehrer isn't around to protect you. This is Blood Bowl. It's a killer's game, and you just don't have it in you to beat me at it.'

'He's a lover, not a fighter, I suppose,' Lästiges said, putting her hand on Spinne as she spoke, interrupting Dirk's rant. The younger brother stared at her, confused as to what she could mean. Then he saw the horrified look on Spinne's face, and the truth stabbed him in the heart.

'You didn't know?' the reporter giggled cattily. 'How tasty! Your older brother has been sleeping with your lady friend here.'

Spinne turned pale as the snow that Dunk used to play in with Dirk when they were kids. 'You thrice-damned bitch,' she breathed. Then she turned to Dirk, whose face was as red as a gargoyle's eyes. 'Please,' she said to him. 'I was going to tell you.'

Dunk stared at Spinne, trying to figure out just what was going on. He wasn't looking at his younger brother when he struck..

'You bloody bastard!' Dirk roared as his fist slammed into Dunk's face, knocking him back into the bar. 'How dare you!'

Dunk wanted to talk this over with his brother, who he loved deeply, despite the problems that had torn them and their family apart over the past few years. He wanted to sit down with him over a couple steins and figure out his history with Spinne and just what she'd been thinking about playing with their hearts. He wanted to do this peaceably and calmly, most of all.

Instead, his temper got the better of him. As Lehrer had called it, 'the red veil' dropped over his eyes, and the next thing he knew he was pounding at his brother's face with both fists, as hard as he possibly could.

Just before Dunk struck back, he heard Dirk whisper something like, 'I'm sorry.' But it was too late. When Dunk launched himself off the bar and smashed into his brother, the time for words, for apologies, was over.

Dirk raised his arms to fend off Dunk's fists. Frustrated by his inability to hurt his brother, Dunk lowered his shoulder and charged into him instead, sending him hurtling backward through the door by which he'd come. The two dwarf guards tried to stop them, but the one who managed to get a hand on Dirk only got pulled along, leaving the other to gape after them.

Dirk slammed his brother into the long dining table in the centre of the Reavers' private room. Half-empty steins of beer, stacks of dirty dishes, and bits of bones and other less sturdy foods went flying everywhere, splattering every person in the room.

The Reavers sitting at the table scattered as the brothers rolled across the table and through the remains of the meal. The veterans grabbed their beers as they backed away, leaving the rookies without a drink to enjoy during the brawl.

When the brothers finally came to a halt in the remnants of the roast boar, Dirk was somehow on top, and the Reavers let out a great cheer. This distracted Dirk, who glanced around at the others and flashed a sheepish grin.

Dunk flailed about until his hand fell upon a half-eaten haunch. He grabbed the bone by the end and swung it up hard against the side of Dirk's head, knocking him off not only himself but the table too. The crowd booed at this, but a few brave veterans applauded Dunk's resourcefulness.

Dunk leapt off the table to see Dirk scrambling away from him, heading for a shuttered window on the opposite side of the room from where they'd come in. As Dirk reached the window, he turned around just in time for the charging Dunk to hit him with a two-armed tackle.

The two brothers crashed through the window and fell atop a dining table in another underground chamber below. The dwarfs eating there had been in the middle of a toast to the Colleges of Magic for bringing the lucrative Dungeonbowl to their land once again when the two men landed on their table, shattering its legs and crushing it to the floor.

'You're mad!' Dirk said as the two crawled off the table in different directions, the wind momentarily taken from their sails. 'You could have killed us!'

'I don't have what it takes to kill,' Dunk wheezed bitterly as he staggered to his feet. 'Remember?'

'I didn't mean that,' Dirk puffed as he rose just as shakily. 'I was mad.' He gulped for air a moment before continuing. 'Spinne dumped me a few months back. She said she'd found someone else.'

'I didn't know!' Dunk said. 'I thought you were just team-mates.'

Dirk grabbed a stein from one of the stunned dwarfs and drained it as he stumbled toward an empty serving table sitting in front of a large window glazed with gold-tinted glass. 'Then stopped bedding my damned team-mates!' Dirk raged.

From the room above, the Reavers roared their approval. A couple of smaller voices said, 'Awww!'

Dirk smashed the stein on the smooth stone floor. 'Forget it,' he said. 'You can have the whore. I was through with her anyway.'

Dunk had been ready to call the fight done, but Dirk's comment about Spinne stuck like a knife in his ear. He growled with mind-numbing anger and charged at Dirk again. This time, his younger brother was ready.

Dirk grabbed the oncoming Dunk by the shoulders and rolled backward, allowing Dunk's momentum to send him flying toward the tinted window just beyond. Whilst Dunk was surprised at this manoeuvre, he managed to grab hold of Dirk through sheer determination, and refused to let go. As he smashed through the window and cascaded with the shattered glass into the open, sea air beyond, he hauled his brother with him.

A moment after they broke through the window, the two brothers looked around to see where they were.

In the distance, Dunk glimpsed the sun setting over the western side of the gulf, a red-orange orb that suddenly seemed like the entrance to some daemon-infested realm. He felt the wind rushing past his face as he and Dirk fell, and he saw the sunset-mirrored sea reaching up toward them like a sky toppling in the absolute wrong direction. He started to scream, and Dirk joined him in a horrified harmony that lasted until they blasted through the gulf's gleaming surface and into the frigid waters below.

Hitting the sea stunned Dunk for a moment, and the seawater threatened to race into his lungs, but he managed to hold his breath long enough to kick his way to the surface.

As Dunk broke back into the air, the first word from his lips was, 'Dirk!' He whipped his head about, searching for any sign of his brother, even a floating body, but there was nothing there. He panicked for three long seconds before his younger brother burst through the waves in front of him, gasping for air and coughing up the sea.

Dunk swam over to his brother with three painful strokes and grabbed him underneath his arms. He held him there until he was done coughing and could breathe again.

'You all right?' Dirk said when he could finally talk again.

'Yeah,' Dunk said, relieved. 'You?'

'Yeah.'

Dunk let his brother loose and the two of them started to swim toward the docks at the bottom of the cliff, only fifty yards away.

'Let's never do this again,' Dirk said as they headed toward a swarm of dock workers who had seen them cascade into the chilly gulf.

'Deal,' said Dunk.

 # CHAPTER TWENTY-ONE

THE NEXT DAY, Dunk sat in the stands for the first Dungeonbowl game of the tournament, alongside Pegleg and about half of his team-mates. His nose was red and raw from all his sneezing, and every bit of him was sore. Falling into the Black Gulf from a dozen storeys up was better than being tossed over the edge of the *Spike! Magazine* Tournament's stadium, but not by much. And this time, he'd done it to himself.

'Mr. Hoffnung,' Pegleg said from where he sat behind Dunk. 'I understand your brother won't be able to start this game because of your fracas with him last night.'

Dunk hung his head in shame. 'Damn,' he said softly. Then he felt a hook rest gently on his shoulder.

'Well done, Mr. Hoffnung,' the Hackers coach said. 'I have a hundred crowns on the Champions of Death.'

Slick, who was sitting next to Dunk, smothered a cackle.

Dunk sighed and looked around at the large room in which they sat. They sat on hard, stone seats carved out of the rock in a stair-step fashion that allowed the people behind to see over the people in front of them. There was room for at least a thousand people in the room, maybe more, and the seats were rapidly filling up.

The crowd here seemed a bit more polite than the ones in Dunk's last Blood Bowl game. Perhaps that was because the dwarfs charged exorbitant amounts for the few tickets left over after team representatives got their seats. On the way into the observation room, one dwarf had offered Dunk five hundred crowns for his place. Another had made him a far more disturbing proposition involving a pair of young dwarf ladies and a stick of limp celery.

The far wall of the room was smooth and flat, and covered with several images depicting the interior of a well-lit dungeon somewhere in the depths of Barak-Varr. It was a moment before Dunk realised that the images were more than perfectly lucid paintings. When he saw a squad of six Reavers in their blue and white uniforms appear in an image to the left, he realised these were Cabalvision pictures of what was happening in the dungeon at that moment.

Dunk looked up behind him. At the top of the room, a score of dwarfs fiddled with a set of crystal balls through which they somehow shone bright lights. The light passed through the balls and a set of lenses which somehow focused the images on the large wall, allowing all of the spectators to watch and cheer for the players at once.

Six players dressed in the distinctive black uniforms of the Champions of Death appeared in an image on the right of the wall. These included a rotting mummy, a slavering vampire, a nasty wight, a hungry ghoul, a tottering zombie, and a rattling skeleton. As they appeared in the room, seemingly out of thin air, they grouped together into a horrifying huddle, their backs to the camra watching them.

Although Dunk had spent the past three months learning the fundamentals of Blood Bowl until they were second nature to him, he was mystified by what he saw. There was no field, no one had a ball, and the other images on the wall showed a series of rooms and passageways that had six identical chests scattered among them.

'What's going on here?' Dunk asked Slick.

'Do you really want to know?' Slick said. 'You're not going to play. You just have to sit back and enjoy.'

'My brother might end up out there soon,' Dunk said, not mentioning that he'd seen Spinne among the Reavers already in the dungeon.

'The way you two fought yesterday, I'd have thought you wouldn't care about his safety.'

Dunk just glared at the halfling.

Slick cleared his throat and put on his best instructor's voice.

'Seventy-five years ago, the head wizards of the Colleges of Magic decided to resolve a long-running dispute by sponsoring a Blood Bowl tournament. Each of the ten colleges backed a team. The supporters of the winning team won the argument. The wizards liked it so much, they made it a regular event. So, here we are.' Slick smiled broadly.

Dunk stared at him. 'That's it?'

'Ah, so you want the *whole* story? As you wish.' Slick cracked his knuckles before diving in again. He pointed at various images on the wall as he talked.

'Most Dungeonbowl games are just played in the Barak-Varr Bowl, an underground stadium complete with a regular field and stands. This year is a special occasion because we're playing under the classic Dungeonbowl rules, which haven't been used for decades.

'You see where the two teams are right now?' The halfling pointed at the images to the far right and left of the wall, where the representatives from both the Reavers and the Champions of Death milled about. 'Those are the two end zones. Each room has only one way in or out of it, so getting in can be a real battle. The real poser is that the players have to find the ball first.

'You see those chests scattered about the place?' Slick said, pointing them out as he went. 'There are six scattered throughout the dungeon. The ball is in one of them.'

Dunk rubbed his chin. 'What's in the other chests?' he said suspiciously.

Slick clapped Dunk on the shoulder proudly. 'Now you're thinking like a Dungeonbowl player! They're trapped, of course.'

'Trapped?'

Slick nodded. 'Nothing in them but explosives. They make a good, little boom when you lift the lid.'

Dunk shook his head in disbelief. 'So, five times out of six, the chest blows up in your face.'

'See, there's the fun of it!'

Dunk goggled at the halfling. 'If you're sitting here watching, maybe. They must go through dozens of players.'

'Not quite. The first team to score a touchdown wins the game. Also, the dwarfs know their explosives. Some of the players who open the wrong chests don't even have to be carried off the field.' Noticing Dunk's look of disbelief, Slick added, 'Son, it can't be any worse than having an ogre hit you, right?'

Dunk nodded along with that. Even the few times M'Grash had blocked him in practice had been enough for him to pause to rethink his recent career choice.

'How do they pass the ball with those low ceilings?' Dunk asked. As a thrower, he figured this was something he should know.

'They bounce it off the walls, believe it or not. Wait until you see it!'

Dunk looked back at Pegleg for help, but his coach just looked down at him. 'If the game bothers you so much, Mr. Hoffnung, perhaps you should thank Nuffle that we couldn't find a sponsor. The Colleges of Magic each select a team packed with members of certain races. The Grey Wizards favour humans, and they chose the Reikland Reavers this year, just as they usually do.'

Dunk turned back to watch the images moving on the wall. 'So unless we can prove we're better than the Reavers, we'll never get to play in the Dungeonbowl.'

'Or unless something happens to them,' said Slick.

Dunk shot him a dirty look.

'What?' the halfling said guiltlessly. 'It's a hard game. Things happen.'

'That's my brother's team,' Dunk said.

'Weren't you trying to kill him yesterday yourself?'

'Just to beat him *half* to death,' Dunk snapped, letting his irritation with the topic show.

'Ah,' Slick said knowingly, 'much better.'

Mercifully, a whistle blew at that moment, and the game began. 'That's the start of the game, folks,' said Bob's voice. 'The Reavers, led by catcher Spinne Schönheit, charge headlong into the dungeon. The Impaler leaps out in front of the Champions of Death, leaving "Rotting" Rick Bupkiss and Matt "Bones" Klimesh behind to protect the end zone.'

'This is going to be a real bloodletter of a game, Bob,' said Jim's voice, 'at least if the Champs get their way. None of them have blood of their own to spill!'

A flash of light on one of the images caught Dunk's eye, and he saw Spinne appear in the middle of a room.

'What happened there?' he asked Slick. 'With Spinne?'

'She stepped on the teleport pads in the room next to the Reavers' end zone. It's risky – some players who do it don't show up again for a few days – but it can really pay off.' The halfling pointed up at Spinne. 'See, she jumped three rooms ahead of where she was, and she ended up right near a chest.'

'And that's paying off?'

'Wait until she opens the chest to see.'

In the image in the centre of the wall, Spinne leaned over and grabbed the handle on the front of the chest. After taking a deep breath, she flung it wide.

A blast of noise and light knocked Spinne off her feet. For a moment, Dunk held his breath, his heart stopped too. But then Spinne staggered back up, holding her head. After a moment, she snarled and raced straight back toward the glowing circle on the floor that Dunk realised was the teleport pad.

Spinne blinked away, and Dunk snapped his head back to look at the room from which she'd originally come. She wasn't there.

'She disappeared!' Dunk choked.

'No, son,' Slick said, pointing off toward the right. 'There she is.'

Dunk followed Slick's finger to see Spinne appear in the middle of another room. The ghoul and wight playing for the Champions of Death were here, and they immediately charged toward Spinne.

'How?' Dunk asked. 'Ouch!' he said involuntarily as Spinne slammed the wight back into the ground. The ghoul, though, grabbed her and repaid the favour.

'Oh, that's going to leave a mark in the morning!' Bob's voice said.

'If she survives that long,' Jim's voice chipped in. 'Gilda "the Girly Ghoul" Fleshsplitter looks hungry. I hear their coach, the legendary necromancer Tomolandry the Undying, has been starving them for days!'

Spinne got to her knees and ploughed the grey-skinned ghoul back into the teleporter pad. The creature disappeared in a flash of light. With a quick look around to see that there were no chests in this room, Spinne raced off through the door to the east.

'The teleporter pads move people at random,' Slick said. 'They aren't linked in matched pairs. If you step on one, you could end up on any other, or nowhere at all.'

Dunk saw flashes at both ends of the wall. 'What's happening there?' he asked. He saw a new player appear in each end zone.

'That's how the players get into the dungeon,' Slick said. 'Each team's dugout has a teleporter pad too, but this one is matched to a spot in their end zone. The coaches can feed in new players one at a time, as fast as the teleporter will work.'

Dunk shook his head. 'Doesn't that make for a pretty crowded game?'

Slick smiled. 'It makes for mayhem, son. Beautiful mayhem.' The spectators roared as an undead player opened another chest that exploded in his face. Slick gestured all around him. 'You have to give the people what they want!' he shouted.

Suddenly a loud noise erupted from the images on the wall. The players in the dungeon all looked up for a moment. Several of them screamed in terror. There was a sickening rumbling noise. Then the wall went blank and bright, the white light from behind the crystal balls shining through nothing but clear glass.

'This is strange,' said Bob's voice. 'I haven't seen light this bright in three hundred years!'

The crowd buzzed in confusion for a moment. Then, almost as one, all of the dwarfs jumped up and raced toward the exits. This left the visitors, guests, and members of the other teams – those who had bothered to show up to watch this match – milling about and wondering what had happened.

'What happened?' Dunk asked. Slick just shrugged. It was then that Dunk noticed that one of the images was still there on the wall, although it was pitch black.

Before the halfling could open his mouth, Bob's voice rang out again. 'Jim, Nuri Nottmeeson, the Dungeonbowl grounds manager, has just handed me a note. Oh! By all of Chaos's craftiest gods, this is the darkest day in Dungeonbowl history!'

'Bob?' Jim's voice had lost its traditional swagger. 'Bob? What is it?'

'The dungeon the Reavers and Champions of Death were playing in has collapsed. I repeat, *the dungeon has collapsed!*'

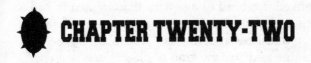

CHAPTER TWENTY-TWO

THAT EVENING, DUNK tried to get into the Trip again, with Slick and M'Grash in tow, but the owner, a dour dwarf on the best of days, wouldn't hear of it. 'Have you not done enough damage around here?' he growled.

Dunk slunk away with his tail between his legs, his two friends behind. The dwarfs who passed them in the massive halls of Barak-Varr stared at the three of them: a halfling (small as a dwarf child), a human (taller than a dwarf, but barely as broad), and an ogre (bigger than the other two put together). With Dunk too depressed to think much, Slick took charge.

'Most of the pubs in this city are built for people only slightly larger than myself. They're large enough to accommodate a few humans, though not in big numbers. I only know of one other establishment in this complex that can seat an ogre at a table,' the halfling said as the trio wound through the labyrinthine passages cut expertly through the cliff face. 'This makes the choice much simpler.'

Slick guided the three friends through the Great Hall of Barak-Varr, a cavernous affair that made even M'Grash seem small by comparison. About halfway down the hall, on the right, they veered off towards a massive set of stone doors, in which was set a smaller set of dwarf-sized doors. A set of glowing dwarf runes blinked overhead in a pattern that seemed to call to Dunk, even though he could not read the Khazalid.

'It translates roughly as "House of Booze",' the halfling said. 'It's my kind of place.'

As the trio approached, the dwarf doorman called to someone inside. By the time they reached the pub's threshold, the stone doors were already rotating back silently on their massive stone hinges. The three then walked under the open archway, which stood at least twice as tall as even M'Grash.

As the giant doors closed behind them, the trio sauntered into the pub. It was a huge place with wide-open aisles running between tables with tops set at all different levels. The upper reaches of the room were filled with smoke rising from the long pipes on which many of the patrons puffed, but this was so high above that it almost seemed like a thick layer of clouds that might open up and rain down on the patrons below at any moment.

Slick led the others to a large table, the top of which stood far over his head. It was perfectly sized for M'Grash, who sat down comfortably at one of the chairs. Slick climbed up a ladder built into the side of one of the chairs, which cunningly had a tiered back.

Slick sat on the highest of the tiers while a pair of dwarf waiters pushed him close enough that he could make use of the table.

Dunk had to climb into his own chair, although he was able to pull himself close to the table on his own. As he made himself comfortable, Slick ordered a round of drinks for them. They arrived only moments later, carried by dwarfs walking on multi-jointed steel stilts. Slick and Dunk received standard-sized steins of Delver's Doppelbock, a local specialty said to be brewed in the deepest of dwarf mines. M'Grash, on the other hand, was brought a barrel-sized stein of his favourite Killer Genuine Draft.

'Thank Nuffle that Dirk will be all right,' Slick said.

'And Spinne too,' Dunk said, raising his glass. It was a bittersweet kind of relief. Of the eight Reavers caught in the dungeon when it collapsed, four had been crushed to death in the disaster. Dirk, hurt though he was, had been the last Reaver to enter the dungeon.

'Have you visited them in the Halls of Mercy yet?' Slick asked.

Dunk shook his head. 'The doctors said they couldn't see anyone until tomorrow.'

'Isn't that convenient?' a voice called up from below. Dunk looked down to see Lästiges standing at the bottom of a chair next to his. She kept talking as she mounted the chair and climbed up to sit next the others, a pair of dwarfs ready to push her close to the tabletop. 'The loss of the great rookie phenom's main rival – his hated brother, who he nearly killed the night before – and the destruction of the team that handed the Hackers' their most recent defeat.'

Dunk glared at the reporter. 'This is a private party,' he said coldly.

'Excellent,' Lästiges smiled at a dwarf with orc's blood on his axe. 'I'm sure you have a lot to celebrate. Either way, I'm sure your employer won't mind if I cover it.'

'We're not here as a Blood Bowl team, miss,' Slick said. 'Just fans of the game.'

'Really?' Lästiges said in a mocking tone. 'Are you sure about that?'

'What's your game?' Dunk asked. He was tired, grumpy, and wanted to be left alone to have a drink with his friends.

'The question is, what's yours? Dungeonbowl is the answer tonight, it seems.'

Dunk opened his mouth to bark at the woman, but Slick silenced him with a wave of his hand. 'Wait,' he said, concern etched on his face. 'What are you saying?' he asked the reporter.

Lästiges smiled, her crimson-painted lips parting to reveal a set of perfectly even, sharp teeth. 'You haven't heard? Instead of dropping out of the tournament, the Grey Wizards have chosen another team to substitute for the Reavers.'

Dunk scowled at the reporter. 'Who?'

'Who else?' she smirked. 'What other human-centric team is right here in Barak-Varr and ready to play? Why the Bad Bay Hackers, of course!'

Slick let out a cheer, and M'Grash joined him, rocking the table with his enthusiasm. Dunk put his hands over his face and sighed.

'As I was saying,' Lästiges said once the cheers faded, 'how much more convenient can you get? This couldn't have worked out better for you if you'd planned it.'

'I didn't plan anything.'

'So it just happened? A kind of spur-of-the-moment sort of a thing? How opportunistic!'

'I had nothing to do with it!' Dunk shouted, standing half out of his seat. As he did, he realised the people at the neighbouring tables were looking at him. Then his eyes settled on two wizards in black robes with red sashes watching him from near the door. They were the same ones from that night in the Bad Water: the tall dwarf and the short elf.

'Ah,' Lästiges said approvingly. 'I see you've finally noticed my friends over there. They make a charming couple, don't they?'

'Are you working for them, miss?' Slick asked, a bit of an edge in his voice.

'I prefer to say I'm working *with* them. They're so clueless on their own. All they understand is *enforcement*, nothing about how to run an *investigation*.'

'And that's your specialty,' Dunk said.

Lästiges reached out and patted Dunk on the cheek. 'And everyone says that Dirk is the brains in the family.'

Dunk looked back over at the Game Wizards and waved at them with a mock smile. They ignored him and went back to muttering at each other over their glasses of dark red wine.

'They really are clueless,' he said. 'One of the biggest threats to the game is standing right behind them, and they haven't even noticed.'

Lästiges turned around to see who Dunk was talking about. She peered hard at the GWs and all around them. 'I think you're the clueless one, rookie,' she said. 'There's nothing there.'

'See that black orc standing at the bar behind your friends?'

Dunk jerked his head in that direction, and Lästiges, Slick, and even M'Grash stared after him.

Lästiges wrinkled her brow for a moment, then said, 'Skragger? You *can't* mean Skragger.'

'That's exactly who I mean,' Dunk said as he raised his stein in a toast to the monstrous orc. Skragger responded in kind with his own stein of Bloodweiser, then arched his eyebrows and jerked a long, sharp-nailed index finger across his throat with a wicked smile.

Dunk gave the black orc a thumbs-up sign and then turned back to Lästiges. 'He's afraid someone's going to break his record for most touchdowns in a season, remember,' he said. 'He says if Dirk tries it, he'll kill us both. He threatened Kur too. You were with me in The Trip when Dirk told me.'

Lästiges laughed. 'Kur doesn't have a chance.'

'You're missing the point,' Dunk said. 'He's trying to keep players from performing at their peak potential, and that can only hurt your friends and your employers at *Spike!*'

Lästiges wrinkled her snowy brow at that. 'How do you figure?'

'How many Cabalvision licenses do you think Wolf Sports could sell if someone was close to breaking Skragger's record. I mean, besides all the great, high-scoring games leading up to that. The few games before, during, and after the breaking of the record? Blood Bowl fans would be tripping over themselves to lay down their crowns.'

'That's an interesting angle,' Lästiges said, nodding her approval. 'Of course, it hasn't occurred to you that he might also have been behind the "accident" today. Or that having the GWs focus on him might take the heat off you for a bit.'

Dunk shook his head. 'I'm not worried about that. I'm innocent. I just want to keep people safe.'

Lästiges reached out and patted Dunk's cheek again. 'Well played,' she said. 'I'd love to think anyone is that altruistic, but, well, this is Blood Bowl we're talking about.'

Dunk smiled, 'Anything I can do to help a good friend like you.'

'Insincerity. Now, *that* I understand. You're serious about the threats though?'

'Slick was there.'

Lästiges grimaced at the halfling. 'I don't think I could cite someone with the name "Slick" as a reliable source.'

'Listen here, miss,' Slick began.

Lästiges cut him off and changed the subject, addressing Dunk again. 'I hear you were seen talking with Gunther the Gobbo in Magritta. That's interesting company you keep.'

'No more so than you.'

'Touché. What did he offer you?'

'Maybe I just wanted to place a bet.'

'That's against most team charters. It's in the fine print of your contract.' Lästiges hesitated. 'You *can* read, can't you?'

'Well enough to know you're not much of a writer.'

'Perhaps you read the exposé I did on the Gobbo last summer? No? That was before your time, I suppose.'

Dunk shrugged.

'I found evidence that the Gobbo is the head of a vast conspiracy of players that runs through nearly all of the top Blood Bowl teams. Together, they work his odds-making racket well enough for him to be able to pay off at least a score of players.'

'I didn't think anyone would care about cheating in Blood Bowl.'

'They do when it's their money on the line. People lay down bets on these teams assuming they're all doing their best to win.'

'And some of the players are professional chokers.'

'Not everyone is good enough to get paid for it.' Lästiges patted Dunk's hand as she said this, and he flashed back to that long fall over the edge of the stadium in Magritta.

'I suppose this conspiracy has a colourful name?'

'The Black Jerseys.'

'Cute. Did you come up with that?'

'I didn't have to. They use it themselves.'

'What's this have to do with the accident yesterday?'

Lästiges leaned forward, every bit serious now. Slick practically climbed on the table to get close enough to hear everything she said, and even M'Grash tilted an ear over her.

'Someone's been killing off Blood Bowl players like snotlings this year,' she said. 'Every time I turn around, I hear about somebody dying under mysterious circumstances. Take the Hackers, for instance.'

'I had nothing to do with those killings in the try-out camp.'

'So I hear, but that's not what I meant. Ever wonder why there were so many openings on the Hackers with such short notice before the first Major of the year?'

Dunk realised he had not, and the fact irritated him. As he finished his beer, the dwarf server was there with another for him in an instant. When he picked it up, he felt a piece of paper wrapped around the grip. As he spoke with Lästiges, he tried to peel it off without her noticing.

Slick filled in the details for Dunk. 'The Hackers lost four players only a month beforehand, son. That's why I was out looking for recruits.'

'What happened to them?'

Slick shrugged. 'No one knows. They just never showed up for practice one day, and no one heard from them again.'

'Odds are they were murdered,' Lästiges said.

M'Grash's elbow slipped off the table, and the ogre bounced his chin off the tabletop, sending all of the other drinks leaping a foot into the air. Dunk was still working at the mysterious paper, so he kept control of his stein. Slick and Lästiges, on the other hand, ended up wearing what was left of their drinks.

'Sorry!' M'Grash rumbled with a sincerity Dunk was sure Lästiges couldn't understand. 'So sorry! Fell asleep!'

As the others – along with a handful of dwarf servers – fussed over the mess, Dunk tore the paper off his stein and unrolled it. On it was written a note. It read:

'My offer stands! Let's do business!'

It was signed 'The Gobbo.'

Dunk scanned the room, still in his chair while the others had dismounted to help the waiters get at the mess. There in the back of the room, directly opposite from the Game Wizards, sat Gunther the Gobbo, raising his stein and favouring Dunk with a greasy grin.

Dunk flipped the Gobbo an obscene gesture that drew gasps from everyone seated on that side of the pub. Then he slid down from his chair and said to Slick and M'Grash, 'Let's get back to our quarters. It seems we have a game tomorrow.'

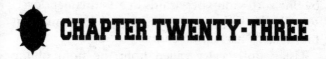

CHAPTER TWENTY-THREE

THE NEXT AFTERNOON, Dunk stood in the visiting team's dugout, outside of a different dungeon, suited up and ready for the game. He'd tried sleeping last night, but wrestling with worrying about his brother and the things Lästiges had told him had ruined much of that. Still, he was ready to get in and play. Frustrated as he was, he felt like breaking something – or someone.

The game was to be a rematch of the game interrupted by the cave-in, with the Hackers taking the Reavers' place. The Champions of Death, being already dead, hadn't lost any players yesterday. A few of them had been flattened, but Coach Tomolandry had managed to patch them back together in time for the game.

Dunk looked around the room. The entire team was on edge. They'd had no time to prepare for this tournament, and Dungeonbowl differed from tradi-tional Blood Bowl so much that there were sure to be mistakes. Plus, there were the teleporter pads, which few of the players trusted.

Dunk sympathised with this. In his experience, magic was something to avoid. The people who worked it were either power-mad wizards who cut deals with unknowable forces or power-mad clerics who cut deals with inconstant gods. Being sponsored by one such group of wizards in a tournament over-seen by the largest and most powerful organisation they had set his hair on end.

'Listen up!' Pegleg called from the front of the room, where he had stood on an empty bench in front of an open locker. 'We have five minutes to game time, and I have something to say.'

The room fell quiet, and all eyes stared at the coach, some glumly, some excitedly, but all intently.

'This game may be more than we bargained for when we came to Barak-Varr, but it's also the chance of a lifetime. If we do well here, we may end up with a long-term sponsorship from the Grey Wizards, and the Dungeonbowl could become a regular stop for us.'

No one cheered at this news.

'To sweeten the pot, the Grey Wizards put up another 50,000 crowns for us. We get half that just for showing up to play today, with 1,000 crowns going to each of you!'

The players whooped it up at the news. M'Grash picked up Dunk in a big hug that threatened to break his ribs.

'And we get the rest if we win the tournament!' The players cheered again, and a knowing smile spread across Pegleg's normally dour face. After giving the noise a moment to die down, the coach put out his hand and hook to signal for silence.

'I want these six players to line up in front of the teleportation pad: Mr. Ritternacht, Mr. Cavre, Miss Mardretti, Mr. K'Thragsh, Mr. Baldurson, and Mr. Otto Waltheim. You're our starters. When you're ready, say a prayer and step on the teleportation pad. With luck, you'll end up in our end zone.'

The six players hustled into position. As Kur strode by Dunk, he shouldered the rookie aside with a satisfied grin. Dunk picked himself up and told himself that three minutes before game time wasn't the right moment to practise his home lobotomy skills on the veteran thrower.

'The rest of you, line up in this order. As soon as the game starts, I'll send you on to the teleporter pad one at a time. Mr. Hoffnung, Mr. Andreas Waltheim, Mr. Klemmer, Mr. Reyes, Mr. Smythe, Mr. Engelhard, Mr. Karlmann, Mr. Hoffstetter, Mr. Albrecht, and Mr. Sherwood.'

The remainder of the team lined up behind Dunk as he stood right behind the starting six. He was thrilled that Pegleg had enough confidence in him to make him the seventh man. If he couldn't be in the starting six, this was literally the next best thing.

'There's no secret to this game,' Pegleg said over the heads of everyone but M'Grash. 'Find the ball and stick it in the end zone. What could be simpler?'

The players all laughed nervously.

'Oh,' Pegleg said, 'and try not to be too surprised if a chest blows up in your face.'

With that, the horn in the dugout sounded, announcing the start of the game. 'Get in there!' Pegleg shouted at the starters. 'And make us some gold!'

The starting six stormed onto the teleporter pad and disappeared in six quick flashes of light. Dunk rubbed his eyes and got ready to follow them. In two minutes, the game would begin, and he wanted to be in it as quick as he could.

These were two of the longest minutes of Dunk's life. He looked over to where Pegleg watched a Cabalvision feed of the match on a large crystal ball. He saw the starting Hackers flexing and stretching in the end zone.

'Mr. Hoffnung,' Pegleg said to him. 'You're my wild card. I want you jumping onto every teleporter pad you can find until you spot a chest. Then open it.'

'Then I take the ball and run.'

Pegleg laughed. 'If there is one. Your job is to eliminate as many chests as you can until you fall over.'

Dunk gulped at that, but he didn't have much time to think about it. The whistle went off, and the game was on.

'Wait,' Pegleg said, holding up his hook for a moment. Then he snapped it down. 'Go!'

Dunk stepped on the pad. For a moment, he was somewhere else, someplace horrible and twisted, both dark and light at the same time. He drew in a breath to scream, but before he could start the Hackers' end zone room appeared around him.

Dunk bit his tongue, then dashed off down the corridor leading out of the room. He could see M'Grash lumbering along in front of him. The ogre's job was to protect the Hackers' end zone, which Dunk thought he might be able to do just by sitting down in the hallway. As the rookie raced past, he clapped the ogre on the leg. This made him feel tiny, which – he realised then – must be how Slick always felt around him.

In the first room after the corridor, Dunk spotted the telltale glow of a teleporter pad. He raced over and stepped on it, closing his eyes as he did. He felt the hot wind of that other place on his skin for a moment, and when the cool dank air of the dungeon replaced it, he opened his eyes. He thought he'd heard screams while in between pads, but he couldn't be sure those hadn't been from somewhere in the dungeon instead.

Dunk found himself standing on a rickety rope bridge strung over a bottomless chasm. His hands lashed out to grab on to the guide ropes and steady himself before he cascaded over the edge and into oblivion. As he did, he looked up and saw the Impaler – a thick-muscled, pale-skinned man dressed in the Champs' black uniform – standing at the bridge's far end, the razor-sharp tips of his spiked gauntlet poised over one of the bridge's four main ropes.

'Velcome,' the vampire said in a Kislevite accent, his eyes glowing red with bloodlust as he bared his fangs in an evil smile. 'And goot-bye.' He brought his fist down, and the spikes slashed through one of the ropes Dunk held.

Dunk felt himself starting to fall, so he released the severed rope and started forward. He had to get to the end of the bridge before the vampire completed its lethal work.

The Impaler swung his other fist at the guide rope, and Dunk was forced to let that loose too or allow it to pull him into the abyss. He realised he would never make it to the end of the bridge before the vampire brought it down, and he glanced around desperately for some other means of escape.

Dunk's eyes fell on the teleporter pad behind him. If he could just reach it, he had a chance. He whipped about and raced back toward the pad. As he did, he heard the Impaler's steel-clad fist fall again and sever one of the bridge's two base ropes with a sickening chop.

Dunk dove for the glowing circle in the middle of the bridge, even as he felt the bridge's wooden planks start to give way beneath him. The toe of his boot found purchase in the gap between two boards, and he launched forward as hard as his legs would push him. Just as the planks spun away beneath him, he stretched out and slapped the pad with his open hand, and he was somewhere else.

Dunk felt himself falling, falling, falling, and when he arrived in another room elsewhere in the dungeon he hit the ground hard. Only his armour prevented him from cracking a rib or worse. He scrambled to his feet and smelled first rather than saw the Champs' mummy – the back of his jersey read Ramen-Tut – opening the chest on the other side of the room.

The scent of ancient must and disease made Dunk's eyes itch, and he flinched involuntarily as the creature flung open the chest. Dunk opened his eyes again when he realised there hadn't been a big boom, and he saw Ramen-Tut triumphantly pulling the ball from the open chest.

Dunk dug in his feet to charge at the mummy, but before he could, Kur raced past him, yelling, 'Get out of the way, punk! He's mine!'

Determined to not let Kur hog all the glory, Dunk chased after the man, straight at the mummy. Ramen-Tut turned, the ball in his spindly, gauze-wrapped arms, and hissed at the two oncoming Hackers. Green gases erupted from the mummy's faceguard, but if Kur wasn't going to back down then neither was Dunk.

The two Hackers slammed into Ramen-Tut at once. Dunk was surprised how light the creature was, but he supposed having all of your internal organs removed would do that to you. He and Kur knocked the mummy back into the chest and piled on him, trying to strip away the ball.

'Urrr!' the mummy groaned as the Hackers laid into him. Then the groan transformed into a desert-dry scream.

One moment Dunk was wrestling with a rotting mummy, trying to keep down his breakfast, and the next he found himself holding a loose bundle of bandages filled with nothing more than dust. Surprised, he inhaled a double lungful of the stuff and got it caked in his eyes.

Dunk stumbled back, hacking up whatever was left of Ramen-Tut from his chest while he wiped the ancient grit from his eyes. As he did, he nearly stepped on the football. Still coughing, he reached down and picked it up, then tucked it into his arms.

'Give me that ball, punk!' Kur snarled.

Dunk spun about to see Kur standing before him with his hands reaching out to him. 'Now!' The starting thrower said.

Dunk hesitated, and the impatient Kur lowered his shoulder and charged at him. More from reflex than anything else, Dunk dodged to the left, and Kur sailed straight past him.

'Nooo!' Kur shouted.

Dunk spun around to see that he was alone. The teleport pad pulsed softly where Kur had once been. The rookie couldn't help but grin as he turned to run from the room.

A moment later, Dunk dashed back into the room with three Champions of Death on his tail: a rattling skeleton and a pair of rotting zombies that smelled worse than a pile of dead skunks. The teleport pads had disoriented him, and he had no idea what direction he was supposed to even be headed in. He decided to take his chance with the teleporter pad again instead of trying to figure it out. They were supposed to toss people around the dungeon at random, so with luck he wouldn't end up wherever Kur had gone.

Dunk kept his eyes open this time as he flashed into the space between spots in his reality. In the spinning, swirling unreality, he thought he saw translucent stretching and moaning at him, and he felt insubstantial fingers tugging softly at the ball. Then the world spun out from under him, and he felt himself falling.

The ball still tucked under one arm, Dunk lashed out with his free hand. His fingers found purchase between two boards in a long series of them hanging strapped between two parallel ropes, nearly wrenching his arm from its socket.

Dunk's legs spun out wildly beneath him as he stared down into an all-too familiar abyss. He looked up and realised he was hanging from planks in the rope bridge the Impaler had cut from under him.

Gritting his teeth, Dunk pulled himself up with his aching arm and reached up high above him with the other, stretching for the teleporter pad glowing from the planks overhead. He slapped the ball into the light, and then he was gone again.

When Dunk snapped back into reality, an ear-splitting roar nearly stopped his heart. It was a moment before he realised someone was shouting his name. 'Dunkel, Dunkel, Dunkel!' it said. 'Dunkel has the ball!'

Dunk leapt to his feet and saw M'Grash standing in one of the room's two doorways, jumping up and down with glee like a schoolgirl spotting a pony. Dunk would have smiled at that were it not for the vampire in the skull-emblazoned armour and helmet darting at him.

'This time, I'll have the ball *and* your life!' The Impaler promised.

With no time to react, Dunk did the first thing that occurred to him after so many hours of practice. He threw the ball.

The ball sailed wide past the oncoming vampire, bounced off the far wall, and landed neatly in M'Grash's outstretched arms. The ogre stared at it for a second as if it was his brain that had suddenly slipped out of his head.

The vampire knocked Dunk flat, then turned and smacked his lips at M'Grash. 'Fantastic!' He said. 'I've just super-sized my next meal.'

The ogre looked up from the ball at the vampire and froze. Still on his back, Dunk shouted at him. 'M'Grash! Throw it back!'

The ogre stomped forward and shoved the Impaler aside. The vampire slammed into a nearby wall and crumpled into a heap. Then M'Grash scooped up Dunk in his free arm and kept moving.

When M'Grash stepped on the teleport pad, the room around them vanished, and the ogre nearly crushed Dunk in terror. After they reappeared in a well-lit hallway, M'Grash set Dunk down with a sheepish, 'Sorry,' and handed him the ball.

Staring ahead, Dunk spotted the Champs' end zone straight before them. Without a word, he charged straight for it, M'Grash hot on his tail. As the emerged into the end zone's room, though, a black armoured ghoul stabbed forth from a hidden corner and grabbed at M'Grash, its flesh-clotted teeth searching for a gap in the ogre's armour. It found it and bit deep.

Only steps from the end zone, Dunk turned around and drove his spiked elbow pad straight into the ghoul's helmet. It punched through with a satisfying pop and stabbed into the cavity where the cannibal's hunger-rotted brain rattled around.

Dunk wrenched his arm free, and the creature fell limp. M'Grash tore the ghoul off his bicep, taking a bit of his muscle with it. 'Thanks, Dunkel,' he said. 'Best friend! Now score!'

M'Grash scooped Dunk up again and carried him into the end zone where he set the rookie down, the ball still cradled in his arms. From somewhere, Dunk heard a whistle blew, and he knew that in the observation theatre the crowd was going wild. He thrust the ball over his head – checking first for angry foes looking to get in a last cheap shot – and grinned.

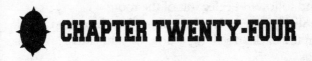

CHAPTER TWENTY-FOUR

'ROOKIE!' KUR SHOUTED as he hurled his helmet at Dunk once they were all back in the Hackers' dugout. 'You're dead!'

M'Grash caught the helmet before it could hit Dunk, then glared at Kur as he crushed it in his bare hand. 'Leave Dunkel alone!' the ogre said.

'That's enough, Mr. Ritternacht,' Pegleg said, his voice filled with more menace than M'Grash could manage with his worst hangover. 'Thanks to Mr. Hoffnung's efforts, we have another mark in our win column.'

'That was *my* score!' Kur said, stabbing his finger at Dunk. 'If you ever take my ball from me again–'

M'Grash stepped between the two men and glowered down at the starting thrower.

'You'll what?' Slick asked in his most innocent voice, which wasn't very.

Kur ignored the halfling and arched his neck around M'Grash's bulk to scowl at Dunk. 'I'll teach you to respect your betters, punk. Your friends won't be able to protect you.'

'Mr. Ritternacht!' Pegleg said. 'Come into the coach's office with me!'

'But coach!'

'Now!'

Kur curled his lip, then spat at M'Grash as he turned and followed Pegleg out of the room.

Slick walked along an empty bench to slap Dunk on the back. 'It's all right, son,' he said. 'Kur's just jealous.'

Dunk hung his head. Moments before, he had been flying high, thrilled at the Hackers' win, but Kur had dragged him back to earth and promised to bury him beneath it. 'It's fine,' he said. 'Let's just go.'

DUNK OPENED THE door to the Reavers' room in the Halls of Mercy, the place where the sick and injured were cared for in Barak-Varr. The healers in charge of the place always opened an extra wing during the Dungeonbowl tournament. The wing had many large private rooms in it so that team members could convalesce with each other while not having to share space with players from other teams.

Dirk and Spinne were alone in the room, each in a bed on opposite sides of the room. Spinne's bed lay near a beautifully carved, wide and open window in the room that looked out over the gulf far below, and the afternoon light spilled in on her, bathing her in its golden glow. When Dunk entered, she turned to see who it was and smiled.

Dirk's bed was tucked back nearer the door, out of the light. He was sleeping when Dunk entered, but as quiet as Dunk strove to be, Dirk awoke as his brother stepped into the room.

'How are you?' Dunk asked, reaching out to put his hand on Dirk's unbandaged shoulder.

Dirk gave Dunk a weak smile. 'I've been better,' he said. 'First some guy knocks me through a window the night before a big game, and then – in the middle of the game – the whole damn mountain drops on my head.'

'Sounds like a rough week.'

'Just part of a rough life.'

'You're a Blood Bowl player,' Dunk said. 'You thought it would be easy?'

Dirk just smiled. Then he looked over at Spinne, who watched them from where she reclined in the sun. 'I think she got the worst of it. They already let out Schembekler and Karr.'

'I'm all right,' Spinne said wanly. She smiled at Dunk as he came over to stand next to her. She reached out and took his hand and held it in her lap.

'I've been thinking,' Dirk called over from his bed. 'You can have her.'

Spinne gasped in horror.

'I mean, look at her,' Dirk continued. 'Talk about damaged goods.'

Spinne tore a pillow from her bed and hurled it at Dirk. It bounced off his upraised arms.

'Hey,' he said, 'I'm an injured man.'

'You'll get a permanent disability if you keep talking like that.'

'Look,' Dunk said. 'Spinne and I, we had a lot of fun, but you're my brother. We can't let a woman come between us.' He carefully avoided looking at Spinne as he spoke, but he braced for a punch at the same time. It never came.

'What?' Spinne said. 'You've let everything else come between you over the years. Why not…?'

'Why not what?' Dunk asked.

'Fine!' Spinne said angrily. 'Have it the way you like. Or not, as the case may be. We can't be together anyhow. You're a player.'

'I was before.'

'You hadn't signed your contract yet.'

'Ah.' Dunk's heart sank. He was torn between what he felt developing between himself and Spinne and his loyalty to his brother. 'Well, I suppose I didn't speak to Dirk for three years. I could go a little longer.'

'Hey!' Dirk said. He reached out for a chamber pot and tossed it over at Dunk. It missed the rookie and skittered under the bed.

'Ow!' someone said.

'I didn't even hit you!' Dirk complained.

'That wasn't me,' Dunk said, his wide, round eyes locked with Spinne's . She shrugged at him, confused, and he dropped to the floor as if Pegleg had screamed for a hundred push-ups.

Staring under the bed, Dunk found himself eye to eye with Schlechter Zauberer. The wizard squeaked in terror and tried to stab the prone rookie with a thin knife that looked to Dunk like an oversized letter opener.

Dunk deflected the feeble attack and grabbed the wizard by the wrist and squeezed until he dropped the knife. He then hauled the pathetic creature bodily out from under the bed, with Zauberer whimpering the entire time.

'I didn't hurt anyone,' the wizard said.

When Spinne saw Zauberer, a short scream escaped her before she could stifle it. Dirk just stared at the thin man in the oversized robes.

'Who is that?' he asked.

Dunk hauled his prisoner to his feet. 'His name is Zauberer, and he's a wizard who trucks with daemons.'

'You *know* him?' Spinne asked, edging away toward the far side of her bed.

'I caught him rummaging through my coach's tent during a game in Magritta. He had a gargoyle with him then.'

Dirk got half out of his bed to peer underneath his mattress. He popped back up immediately and shook his head. 'Nothing there, at least.'

Dunk shook Zauberer by the collar. 'What were you doing under there?'

'Spying on us, I'll bet,' said Spinne. 'Which team are you working for? Did the Chaos All-Stars send you? Or the Dwarf Giants?'

'No!' the wizard protested, his feet barely touching the ground. 'It was nothing like that.'

'So you're just some kind of twisted fan then, hoping to get a good look at Spinne's rack?'

'Hey!' the catcher said.

'No! Really!' Zauberer said. 'I didn't mean to be here this long. I snuck in, and then the woman here woke up, and I was trapped. I thought I'd wait for them to fall asleep before I left.'

'And then I came in, and we found you?' Dunk asked, letting the wizard's heels touch the ground again.

Zauberer nodded as he shrugged his robes back into place. 'And now I'll be going,' he said evenly.

Dunk tightened his grip on the wizard's collar. 'What were you doing here?'

Zauberer pressed his lips together and refused to talk.

'Just throw him out the window,' Dirk said. 'Problem solved.'

Dunk goggled at his brother. 'I'm not going to kill him in cold blood.'

'It's not cold blood. You found him here. He surprised you. He tried to escape.'

Zauberer pulled against Dunk's grasp, but the rookie just hauled the wizard in. 'He's not going anywhere, and he's not much of a threat to us.'

Dirk nodded. 'He is a bit of a scarecrow.'

'Didn't he try to stab you?' Spinne said. 'I thought I heard a knife hit the floor.' She glared at the wizard, 'Did you try to stab him?'

Dunk wasn't sure she wasn't laughing at the man.

Zauberer hung his head. 'Yes, I did,' he said. 'I deserve death.'

Dunk stared at the wizard as if he'd just announced that he wanted to show them his mutant third arm. 'Are you mad?' he asked.

Zauberer shuddered. 'You don't understand. I'm not in the kind of position where I'm allowed to fail. I'd rather die. The alternative is worse.'

Dunk almost relaxed his grip, but he tightened it again when he felt the wizard try to pull away. 'You're out of your mind.'

'Give him what he wants,' Dirk said, sitting up in his bed. 'He's happy, we're happy. What's the harm?'

'He'd be *dead*.'

Dirk stood up and hobbled over to the wizard and his brother. He stretched to his full height when he reached Zauberer, so he could look down at the pathetic man. He glared into the sneak's eyes for a moment then said. 'He's lying.'

'He doesn't want to die?'

Dirk shook his head. 'This guy loves life too much. I can smell the stench of Chaos on him. He's after power, power, and more power. He can't get that if he's dead.' He peered into Zauberer's eyes. 'Let him go.'

'No,' Dunk grimaced. 'He's slippery. Let's call the Game Wizards and turn him over to them.'

'No need,' a voice said from the doorway. 'We're here.'

Dunk looked over his brother's shoulder to see the tall dwarf and the short elf standing next to each other in the doorway like some kind of strange set of salt and pepper shakers. 'Have you been following me?' he asked.

Dunk was so distracted he let go of Zauberer's collar. The wizard turned and bolted toward the window.

'No!' Dunk shouted, dashing after the thin, wizened man, but he was too late.

Zauberer scrambled over Spinne's bed (and her protests) and leapt straight out the window, kicking off from the sill to force himself further away from the cliff wall.

'Damn!' Dunk said as he crawled over Spinne too. She drew her legs out of the way for him, and he peered down toward the gulf far below.

The wizard had vanished.

'Where'd he go?' Dunk asked aloud. As the words left his lips, a gargoyle zoomed past him, nearly cutting him with the tips of its wings.

Zauberer hung from the creature's hands. As he passed by, he cackled, 'One more sacrifice for the Blood God!'

Dunk ducked back into the room, stunned. He saw the two Game Wizards standing stoically in the door. 'What are you waiting for?' he asked. 'Go after him?'

The dwarf turned to the elf and said, 'Do you have a gargoyle waiting outside that window for you, Whyte?'

The elf kept looking straight at Dunk as he shook his head. 'No, I can't say I do, Blaque.'

'Shame that,' the dwarf said, looking back at Dunk. 'Can't help you there.'

Dunk just goggled at the pair in amazement.

'And to answer your earlier question,' Blaque said, 'Yes, we were following you.'

'Why?' Dunk asked.

'I like that,' Blaque nodded as he stroked his short, ebony beard. 'Straight to the point.'

'Don't care for it myself,' Whyte said flatly.

'Are you going to answer his question now or wait for another murderous daemon-conjurer to leap from hiding first?' asked Dirk.

'We've had our eye on Dunk here for a while,' the dwarf said. 'And you're not as funny as you think.'

'What's he done?' asked Spinne, who was now edging away from the window to the nearer side of her bed.

'There's what we think he's done and what he know he's done, right?'

Whyte answered the question. 'There have been a string of murders throughout the Blood Bowl teams this season, far more than usual. They point to a single, bloodthirsty individual methodically killing off any and all who stand in his way.'

'And you think that's Dunk?' Spinne asked, her eyes wide.

'Correct,' said Blaque.

Dirk laughed out loud. 'You're nuts. Dunk, a crazed killer?'

The dwarf fixed his dark eyes on Dirk. 'Didn't he knock you through a window to fall a hundred feet into the gulf?'

Dirk grinned. 'That was more of a mutual thing.'

'There's the matter of the prospects killed in the Hackers' tryout camp,' said Blaque.

'And the Broussard brothers,' added Whyte.

'I couldn't have done that!' Dunk said. 'Lots of people saw me in the Bad Water that night. Gods, *you two were there!*'

'Did I say he was working alone?' asked Blaque.

'I didn't hear you say that,' said Whyte.

'Good,' said the dwarf. 'I'd hate to give the wrong impression. Then there was the collapse of the dungeon yesterday.'

'I was in the theatre!'

'Am I going to have to repeat myself?' Blaque asked.

'I hope not,' Whyte said. 'It's tedious.'

'So I won't,' Blaque said. 'But we're really hear to talk about the killing earlier today.'

'Which one?'

Blaque raised an eyebrow at this but continued on. 'You may remember Ramen-Tut.'

Dunk narrowed his eyes. 'He fell apart in my arms. And it was in the middle of a game.'

'You killed Ramen-Tut?' Dirk said in proud amazement. 'Good job!' When he noticed the GWs glaring at him, he added in a whisper, 'I always hated that guy.'

'We have Cabalvision images of you and Kur Ritternacht attacking Ramen-Tut,' the dwarf said.

'Tackling.'

'Most tackles don't cause their victims to crumble irreversibly to dust.'

Dunk shrugged his shoulders. 'My first time tackling a mummy.'

'During the attack, someone administered a magical charm that caused the victim's dissolution. It had to be either you or Kur.'

'So it was Kur.' Dunk folded his arms across his chest. 'Wait,' he said with a smile, 'You don't know who it was, do you? You can't prove anything?'

'True enough,' Blaque said. 'That's why the Hackers have been banned from the tournament.'

'You can't do that!' Dunk said, stunned. 'Can they do that?' he asked Dirk and Spinne.

'They're not technically in charge of any league,' Spinne said. 'There isn't any league. Each team is in charge of itself.'

'But Wolf Sports broadcasts the tournament,' said Blaque. 'Do you think they know who the vice president of Wolf Sports is?' he asked Whyte.

'I can't say they do,' answered the elf.

'It's Shawbrad-Tut,' Blaque said. 'Father to the deceased.'

Dunk's heart sunk.

'Pack your bags, Dunk,' the dwarf said. 'You're going home; if you survive the trip back with all those angry team-mates, that is.'

'Don't forget Pegleg,' said Whyte.

'True,' Blaque nodded. 'That's one vicious hook.' He shook hands with Dunk, as did the elf.

'If you make it to the Chaos Cup, we'll see you there,' Blaque said. With that, the two Game Wizards left.

Dunk, Dirk, and Spinne stared at the empty doorway for a moment.

Dirk put his arm around his brother. 'Don't worry,' he said. 'It can't get much worse, right?'

Dunk coughed. 'Did I mention a threat on our lives by a black orc named Skragger?'

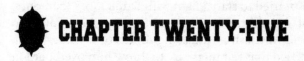# CHAPTER TWENTY-FIVE

THE TRIP BACK to Bad Bay was a long one for Dunk. Pegleg had been furious at what the Game Wizards had done, and he let them know about it. He told Dunk that he didn't blame him in the slightest, but the rookie found it hard to believe that in his heart. Some of the other players, especially Kur, lay all the fault with Dunk, and they expressed their opinion at every opportunity.

Dunk took to sleeping on deck as the *Sea Chariot* made its way along the Old World's long, convoluted coast. M'Grash stayed out there with him every night, and Slick spent many a night up there too, although he enjoyed his comforts too much to make a commitment to it.

As the *Sea Chariot* went north, the weather grew colder and colder. Eventually, about the time the travellers spotted snow on the shore for the first time,

Dunk gave in and went back to sleeping below deck. It was just too cold out in the open air.

'Pegleg had planned to return to the winter training camp for a while after the Dungeonbowl tournament,' Slick told Dunk one night, 'but he was so angry at Wolf Sports he decided to head home right away. He claims it will toughen up the players to get them used to the cold. He's even talking about scheduling some games with a Norse team or two.'

Kur tried to start a fight with Dunk more than once, but the ship wasn't big enough for the thrower to avoid M'Grash at the same time. For a while, Dunk worried that Kur might try to throw him overboard in the middle of the night, but Kur never got up the courage to brave M'Grash's wrath.

'Dunkel hurt, you die,' the ogre told Kur one evening when the thrower had been picking on Dunk.

'I promise not to harm a hair on his head,' Kur said mockingly.

'None of Dunkel's hairs! He hurt, you die.'

'What if someone else hurts him?' Kur said. 'You can't hold me responsible then.'

'Dunkel hurt,' M'Grash said as clearly as he could, 'You die.'

Kur glared at the ogre's massive skull and said just as clearly, 'Understood.'

THE HACKERS SETTLED back into Bad Bay well, but for Dunk it was a bit of an adjustment. Bad Bay was a small farm town on the edge of the River Reik's delta, right where it flowed into the Sea of Claws, in a part of the world north of the Empire, known as the

Wasteland. Its biggest export was beef, which shipped out of the place's small port almost daily, bound for places like Marienburg, L'anguille, and even Altdorf.

This was, in fact, where the Hackers' name came from: the method by which the cattle were traditionally slaughtered in the warehouses next to the port. The water in the bay often ran red with blood, which might also have been how the bay got its name, although Dunk suspected a darker and nastier truth beneath that tale.

There were few places to drink in Bad Bay, and even fewer places to eat. While his salary had made Dunk rich, he had little or nothing on which to spend his money. On off days, he sometimes wandered down to the docks, hoping to find something exciting to buy or even news of Altdorf or other, further lands.

The Hackers practiced five days a week. They played a game once a week. Sometimes, if Pegleg couldn't find an opponent, they just scrimmaged each other, but normally there was a proper team on the schedule. Marienburg had a pair of teams there. The legendary Marauders (once from Middenheim) had settled there a few years back, and just five years ago the Wasteland Wasters had finally mustered enough financial backing to go pro.

Kur had a great season, which meant a lot of time on the bench for Dunk. Once the outcome of the game was determined, Pegleg often substituted Dunk as the team's thrower just to give the rookie some time on the field against real opponents. For a while, the coach had even experimented with a two-thrower line-up, but the fact that Kur and Dunk would never give each other the ball hampered its effectiveness.

Other times, Pegleg put Dunk in as a catcher. 'There is no better training for a thrower, Mr. Hoffnung, than to see how hard it is to catch the ball.'

This meant that Kur had to throw the ball to Dunk, but he almost never did. Kur would rather throw the ball straight out of the opponent's end zone than put it in Dunk's hands.

However, towards the end of a close game against the Wasters, Dunk found himself alone in the end zone. He shouted and yelled for Kur to throw him the ball. By now, the Wasters had figured out that Kur didn't want to do this, so they didn't bother to cover Dunk at all.

'Throw Mr. Hoffnung, the damn ball!' Pegleg roared from the team dugout.

With time ticking down in the final half of the game, Kur had no choice. No one else was open, and running the better part of the field was not an option for him. He hated getting hurt even more than he hated Dunk. So he reared back and hurled the ball at Dunk as hard as he could.

As soon as Dunk saw the pass, he knew it was going to be long. He back-pedalled to the deepest corner of the end zone and leapt straight up into the air for it, but the ball still sailed over his head and landed in the stands. For a moment, he thought about chasing it, but one good look at the Marienburg fans convinced him to call the ball a loss. The fans eventually coughed it up, but it was too late. The clock ran mercilessly out, and the Hackers lost the game.

As the Hackers returned to their dugout, Kur charged Dunk. As he did, he took off his helmet and started beating Dunk with it. 'You missed that throw on purpose!' he raged at the rookie. 'You just cost us that game!'

Although M'Grash had kept Kur from actively hurting him, Kur had made Dunk's life miserable for the past couple months. He took every chance to cause trouble for the rookie. Dunk had had enough. When Kur opened his mouth to berate him again, he reached out and popped the man across the chin.

Kur collapsed like a skeleton turned into a pile of bones. He was out cold before he hit the ground.

'Pick him up,' Pegleg said, 'Him and his stinking glass jaw.'

The Waltheim brothers each got under one of Kur's arms and hauled him off to visit the arena's apothecary.

'You, Mr. Hoffnung,' Pegleg said. 'He had it coming for sure, but this is over. I want the two of you to work this out tonight, or I may have to start talking with the other teams about a trade, and who knows which one of you they'll want.'

WHILE IN BAD BAY, Kur stayed at the best inn within fifty miles, the Hacker Hotel. That night, Dunk walked over there from his decidedly less posh place at the FIB Tavern – which took its name from an obscene variety of Imperial Bastards – to make peace. He suspected he would only get into another fight, particularly because he'd made M'Grash stay back at the tavern, but he had to try. He was embarrassed that he'd lost his temper at a team-mate and actually hurt him, even if that team-mate was Kur. This was something he had to do.

When Dunk reached Kur's private room on the hotel's third floor, he knocked on the door. He knew Kur had to be there. From what Slick had told him, Dunk had broken Kur's jaw, and the medicines the apothecary had given him would ensure he wouldn't be too mobile tonight.

Dunk waited for a moment, and when no one came to the door, he knocked again. There was still no answer.

Dunk listened at the door for a moment and heard voices inside. Perhaps Kur was watching another game on Cabalvision, or maybe some of the other Hackers had come to play him a visit. Either way, Dunk wasn't ready to turn around and go home now. He was afraid he'd lose his resolve if he didn't do this now.

Dunk pushed on the door, and it swung open. In a corner of his mind, he saw that the lock had been shattered, but the sound of someone choking in the other room made him dash right by without inspecting it.

Kur's place featured three rooms: a dining room, a sitting room (complete with a fireplace big enough to stand up in), and a bedchamber. The entrance let into the sitting room, but a quick glance around told Dunk no one was there. The sounds he heard came from the bedroom.

Dunk crept toward the bedroom door and flung it open. There in front of the bed stood two figures. The first was Kur, whose face was both bruised and blue. Next to the Hackers' thrower, his meaty hands wrapped around Kur's throat, stood Skragger.

The black orc turned to see who was interrupting his murdering. When he saw Dunk, he bared his tusk-like teeth and let Kur drop to the floor. The injured man lay there on the ground, gasping for breath.

'Want some of this?' Skragger asked.

Dunk drew his sword. He'd bought himself a fine blade in Marienburg, perhaps the best he'd ever owned, but it had yet to taste blood.

'Put that pigsticker away,' Skragger growled. 'Just talking with yer friend. Sez you didn't give him my message.'

'He's a liar,' Dunk said, still keeping the tip of his blade between himself and the retired record-holder.

'Bad one too.' Skragger looked down at Kur, who was crawling onto his bed, still coughing and hoping for more air. 'Think I made my point.'

With that, Skragger walked straight toward Dunk. 'Leaving now,' he said. 'Move and live.'

Dunk stepped back into the sitting room and gave the black orc a clear path to the exit. Once Skragger was gone, Dunk sheathed his blade and went to check on Kur.

The thrower sat in a pool of vomit on the edge of the bed, still coughing. When Dunk walked in, Kur stood up and charged the rookie. 'You did this!' he said, his voice as hoarse as a stage whisper.

Dunk held up his hands to calm the veteran, but Kur kept straight at him barely able to walk. Dunk caught the man in his arms and carried him bodily back to his bed.

'I had nothing to do with this,' the rookie said as he sat Kur back down, holding his shoulders so the man couldn't leap up and attack him again. 'Pegleg warned you about Skragger. You wouldn't listen.'

Kur sneered at Dunk through his busted lips and broken jaw. 'You little codpiece. You waltz in here and think you can just take my job.' Kur shook his head so softly Dunk wasn't sure the man wasn't just shuddering. 'No one takes my place, in anything, ever. You know why?'

Dunk shook his head. He saw Kur fumbling around with something around his belt buckle, and he feared the man might need to vomit again.

'Because I'm willing to do anything to make sure it never happens.'

With those words, Kur drove the secret punch dagger he'd drawn from his belt buckle straight into the spot above Dunk's heart.

The blade turned on something hard and unyielding. As it did, its honed edge sliced through Dunk's shirt, exposing the breastplate hidden beneath.

'You must not think much of me,' Dunk said as his hand snapped out and knocked the punch dagger away. 'You think I'm dumb enough to come see you alone without some kind of protection. I know you a little too well for that.'

Kur reached up with both of his hands and wrapped them around Dunk's neck. Dunk ignored the feeble attempt to strangle him and drove his fist right into Kur's jaw again. It gave a satisfying pop, and Kur flung himself backward, clutching at his face.

Dunk stared down at the man, struggling to master the rage in his heart. He considered killing Kur – he could honestly say it was in self-defence – but the impulse faded quickly. Instead, he drew his sword and kicked the man in the ribs.

Kur whipped his head around to snap something at Dunk, but he stopped when he came nose to tip with the rookie's blade. He started to say something again, but a jab forward with the sword stopped him.

'Shut up,' Dunk said coldly. 'I've been taking your shit for months now, but that just ended when you tried to kill me. You listen to me now.'

Dunk waited for those words to sink in. When Kur nodded slowly, the rookie continued on.

'I've been letting M'Grash keep you off my back, but that's done too. I don't need him around for that. I'm trained in a half-dozen ways to kill a man, and I'd be happy to try them all out on you.'

Dunk placed the tip of his blade over Kur's heart and leaned forward. 'I want you to think back to earlier today, if you can manage it. I took you down with a single blow. I can do it again any time I like.

'I'm faster than you, stronger than you, and better looking than you. I'm better than you in every way. The only reason you still have your job is that I haven't tried to take it.'

Dunk paused here for a moment and glared into Kur's eyes. 'But I want to make one thing absolutely clear. You shouldn't be afraid of M'Grash. You shouldn't be afraid of Pegleg. You shouldn't even be afraid of Skragger.

'No, you dumb son of a bitch,' Dunk whispered. As he spoke, he sheathed his blade with one smooth move, his eyes never leaving Kur's rattled orbs. Then he leaned forward and pushed Kur back flat on the bed with a single index finger.

Dunk turned to leave then. As he reached the door, he looked back and spat at Kur. 'You should be afraid of *me*.'

CHAPTER TWENTY-SIX

A FEW WEEKS later, Pegleg stormed into the morning chalk talk and made an announcement. 'I just got word that the Chaos Cup is being held in Mousillon in one week. If we get the *Sea Chariot* underway today, we can just make it.'

The players all stared at their coach with blank faced.

'Well?' Pegleg said. 'What are you all waiting for? *Move out!*'

THAT AFTERNOON, AS the tide pulled out, so did the *Sea Chariot*. Dunk and Slick stood at the rail with M'Grash sitting beside them. Most of the other players avoided Dunk these days. After his incident with Kur, Dunk started keeping to himself more and more. He worried that the team captain would try to kill him during a weak moment, so he promised himself not to have any. With the exception of Slick and M'Grash, he didn't know he could trust any of them to not take Kur's side over his. The only exceptions were Cavre and Pegleg, but keeping the Hackers going gave them enough troubles of their own.

'Ever been to Mousillon?' Slick asked.

M'Grash and Dunk looked at each other, then both shook their heads.

'It's an evil place, son, if ever there was one. Some call it "the City of the Damned" and once we get there you'll see why.'

'Full of daemons?' M'Grash asked, a bit of a tremor in his voice. The ogre wasn't afraid of much, but magic, especially dark magic, always set him on edge.

'Nothing so spectacular, I'm afraid, but sometimes more sinister,' Slick said. 'Something went wrong with the city a few generations back. It used to be a wonderful place, nestled there next to the River Grismerie. Then it got hit with something like a dozen earthquakes in the space of a month. It never really did recover.'

'That's it?' Dunk said. 'That doesn't sound so bad.'

'Wait until we get there. When a place like that doesn't come back, there's always a reason.'

THE *SEA CHARIOT* swung through the Middle Sea and sailed north into the Great Western Ocean. Then it made its way into the Bay of Hope and up the River Grismerie until he reached the quay at Mousillon.

Even from the river, Dunk could tell that this was a city with troubles. Not one of the houses or buildings he saw bore a lick of paint. Most of the once-proud roofs were either caving in or had already fallen. A number of towers that once stabbed proudly into the sky now reached up like broken fingers.

In the city, the people were just as dour and colourless as their homes. Many of them wore little more than rags, and even the best-dressed people wore clothes that even M'Grash would have turned up his nose at. Voluminous hoods and cloaks seemed to be the style here. Everyone wore them: men, women, and even children.

Dunk thought this was odd, especially when he saw a mother carrying an infant swaddled in such a garment. As the child began to cry, though, a prehensile tongue at least a foot long slipped out of its hood and snagged a hapless deerfly from the air. It stopped crying then.

'The taint of Chaos is strong here,' Slick said, sticking close to Dunk. Any one of these people could bear mutations from exposure to its unwholesome essence.'

'Any?' M'Grash said, looking at all the hoods around them. 'All!'

'Dirk said he'd be here at Ye Olde Salutation,' said Dunk. 'Any idea where that is?'

Slick pointed to a sign hanging over the door of a run-down inn down a broken street off to the left. It showed a hand making an obscene gesture. 'They may have changed the sign since the earthquakes,' he said. 'I was here before that once, and it was a much friendlier place.

Dunk led the way to the inn, weaving his way through people in hoods of all sizes. Only a few were not wearing the dark garments, but since they were such large people walking around with such beautiful members of their race, Dunk could only guess they were other Blood Bowl players and even cheerleaders.

Inside, the Sal, as Dunk later learned the locals called it, was just as depressing as it looked from the outside. The tables were all warped and crooked, and the stools were just as low and mean and often sported fresh splinters. Black candles illuminated the common room, but just barely. It was the sort of place in which a local could doff his hood and still stay hidden from prying eyes.

After ordering a round of drinks – a local brew called Mutant High Life – from a three-eyed bartender, Dunk asked if he'd seen anyone that looked like Dirk and Spinne. The man pointed him toward the back of the dim and smoky room. As Dunk turned to leave, he noticed the man's thumb was split in two like a devil's fork.

'Have a seat,' Dirk said as Dunk, Slick, and M'Grash walked up and set down their drinks. They all shook hands with him and Spinne, who gave Dunk a hug, friendly, but nothing more. 'Sadly, we're not alone here.'

'Who's the problem?' Dunk said, peering into the surrounding gloom.

'At first, I thought it was Skragger. I think he's been following me around town ever since we arrived. He really has me spooked.' It struck Dunk that for his brother to even admit he was 'spooked' meant he was probably truly terrified.

'Who is it then?'

'I knew you'd show up here eventually,' said Lästiges as she emerged from a nearby booth. 'These two always attract the most interesting sort of garbage, kind of like flies but in reverse.'

'We have to stop meeting like this,' Dunk said.

'Or you'll kill me, just like anyone else who gets in your way?'

Dunk narrowed his eyes at the reporter. 'That means what?'

'I know how the Hoffnungs work. You never let anything or anyone get in the way of what you want. And now I have proof.'

Dunk shook his head. 'You can't. I didn't do it.'

'That doesn't mean she doesn't have proof, son,' said Slick. 'Evidence isn't always honest.'

Lästiges smirked at that. 'I have incontrovertible proof that Dunk here killed most of the other prospects from his recruiting class and that he brought down the roof on the Reavers and even killed Ramen-Tut.'

Dunk waved her off. 'No proof of a plot to kill the Emperor?'

'Give me time.'

'Look,' Dirk said as he stood up to talk with Lästiges, 'this is my brother. I've known him all my life, and he's just not capable of these things.'

Lästiges eyes flashed hot and then icy cold. 'The facts don't lie.'

'But people lie about them all the time,' Dirk said. He looked around the pub. 'Can we all go someplace a bit nicer to talk about it?'

'Is there such a place in town?'

'I have a few ideas.'

'I'm not going anywhere,' Dunk said. 'I don't have anything to prove.'

Dirk rolled his eyes. 'I just think it might help if the lovely young Lästiges got to hear our side of the story.'

'Certainly,' the reporter said, eyeing Dirk. 'It should make for a good laugh.'

'That's just the lack of bias I've come to expect from the media,' Dirk said as he took Lästiges by the arm and led her from the pub.

Slick raised his eyebrows at Dunk as the two left, but Dunk ignored him. He was about to say something to Spinne – he didn't know what – when another repulsive figure shambled out of the gloom.

'I thought she'd never leave,' Gunther the Gobbo said as he oozed onto the stool that Dirk had vacated.

'What is he doing here?' Spinne asked.

'So, kid,' the corpulent Gobbo wheezed at Dunk through his greasy mouth, 'It looks like you're turning into a real up and comer. Killing Ramen-Tut? That was brilliant!'

'That was Kur,' Slick said.

The Gobbo waived the halfling off. 'Whatever. It was a good move, and it shows our little prodigy's ability to be in the right place at the right time.' At this point Gunther's smile grew impossibly wide as he focused his watery eyes on the rookie, and Dunk wondered if maybe Mousillon was the creature's hometown. 'And that's just the kind of service I'm interested in renting from you.'

Spinne threw the contents of her stein at the Gobbo, drenching him. He smiled at her as he strove to lick as much of the beer from his face as he could with his unusually long tong. 'Don't you worry, sweetie,' he said to her, still smiling. 'I'll get around to making you an offer next.'

Spinne's arm lashed out and grabbed the Gobbo around the collar of his hooded cloak. He gurgled as she stood and wrenched him out of his seat. 'Stay away from him,' she said. 'He's not your kind of player, and he never will be.' Then she shoved him so that he fell and skidded off into the gloom again.

Dunk heard the Gobbo scrabbling away, but as the creature left he called out. 'I'll get back to you later, kid, when you have a better selection of company. We'll do lunch!'

Spinne tossed her stein in the direction of the voice. Dunk heard a satisfying cry of pain come from where the stein went. He hoped it was Gunther's voice and not someone else's.

'Thanks,' Dunk said to Spinne in a tone that was anything but grateful. 'I'll be sure to run all of my acquaintances past you for approval.'

'He's scum,' Spinne said. 'You don't want to have anything to do with him.'

'What gives you that right?' Dunk asked. 'Sleeping with me to get under my brother's skin?'

Spinne gasped in anger. Looking down at her hands, she realised she'd already thrown both her beer and her stein, so she just steamed at Dunk instead. It was the kind of look that could peel paint from walls, had there been any left in this town.

'No,' said Dunk, who was feeling meaner all the time. Was it the beer talking already or just the air in this damned town? 'Maybe it's the way you hide behind your contract so you can't repeat your mistake.'

Spinne grabbed Slick's stein and threw the beer in it at Dunk. The rookie dodged out of the way, and before Spinne could follow the beer with the stein, Slick snatched it from her hand.

'Think what you like,' Spinne said. Dunk thought he saw tears welling up in the woman's eyes, but it could just have been from the odd conglomeration of smells in the pub. 'I'll leave you alone from now on.'

With that, Spinne spun on her heel and disappeared into the darkness.

Dunk looked into his beer for a moment, then handed it to Slick and took after the Reavers catcher. 'Spinne!' he said. 'Wait!'

'Thanks, son,' Slick said as Dunk left. 'I like a client who knows how to take care of his agent.'

Outside the Sal, Dunk spotted Spinne marching away up the street. He started after her, calling for her to stop, but she only moved faster. He caught up with her as she raced through a door beneath a sign that read 'The Mousillon Tentacles Hotel'.

'Hold it!' said Dunk as he followed Spinne into the dimly lit lobby. The place was made of crumbling bricks that seemed to be covered with a glowing green mould. 'Please! I want to apologise.'

'For what?' Spinne asked.

Dunk paused a moment, hoping that Spinne would help him out here. He knew he'd behaved badly, but now that she was angry with him, bringing her down was sure to be tricky.

Spinne just glared at him with her blazing blue-grey eyes, daring him to say the wrong thing.

'For being a complete ass,' Dunk said. 'I thought maybe there could be something between us, and well…'

'You decided to make sure that could never be.'

'No,' Dunk said, confused. 'Wait. I thought we were already at that point.'

Spinne frowned at him. 'Only as long as we're both players who play by the rules.'

Dunk smiled nervously. 'What Blood Bowl player ever paid attention to the rules?'

'Exactly!' Spinne said, throwing her hands up in frustration. She spun on her heel again and headed up to her room.

'So, wait!' Dunk said as he chased Spinne up the stairs. 'Are you saying there's a chance for us?'

Spinne stopped in front of a battered door, a tarnished key in her hand. 'Anything can happen, Dunk. It's like Blood Bowl. Sometimes, success is a matter of how much you want it.'

She stuck the key in the lock. 'So,' she said seriously, 'how much do you want it?'

Awash in a mixture of relief and uncertainty, Dunk said the only thing that popped into his head. 'More than anything.'

'That,' Spinne said with a smile as she turned the key and shoved open the door, 'is the first step.'

As the door swung open, Dunk's jaw dropped. Spinne looked at him, confused at his reaction, then turned to see what had stunned him so. As she did, she let out a little scream.

Dirk and Lästiges lay on the bed in the room's far corner, entangled in each other's arms.

AT BREAKFAST THE next morning, Dirk said, 'My roommate was in my room. I knew Spinne's place was empty.' He grinned at Dunk. 'I didn't think you'd drive her out of the pub that quick.'

'Shows how well you know her, I suppose.' Dunk sighed over his meal. Despite ending up alone in his own bed, he'd not slept much that night.

'Look,' Dirk said, 'Spinne and I have had a fling or two before – mostly drunken celebrating after a big win – but there's nothing there. We're team-mates.'

'Thanks,' Dunk said. He wanted to sound depressed and sarcastic, but he was having a hard time pulling it off. Dirk's words sparked just a bit of hope in his heart again. After Spinne had kicked everyone out of her place last night, he had thought his chances with her had been ruined. Now he wasn't so sure. Just how bad do you want it? he thought.

'Think Lästiges is going to get over it?' Dunk asked. After being kicked out of Spinne's room, the reporter had slapped Dirk in the face. 'I think she's under the impression you were just using her to get her off my back.'

'What makes you think that?' Dirk said with a not-so-innocent smile.

'I think it was the part where she slapped you and said, 'You were just *using* me!' But I might have read that wrong.'

'I prefer to think of it as a happy coincidence.' Dirk said, grinning devilishly. 'Sleeping with a beautiful woman will help my brother? Just call me an altruist.'

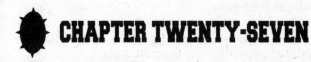

CHAPTER TWENTY-SEVEN

THE HACKERS PLAYED three games over the course of the next week and won two. The loss had been a heartbreaker against the Oldheim Ogres. The creatures had physically outmatched the Hackers, but Kur and Cavre had kept their team in the game until the very end, when Percival Smythe had been crushed in a pile-up after catching a pass near the end zone.

Pegleg had forgone a funeral after seeing Percy's body. 'He went how he would have wanted to,' the coach said, wiping away a single tear with his shining hook. 'Besides,' he pointed down at the ground where the pile of ogres had pressed Percy straight through the turf, 'he's already buried.'

Despite the loss, the Hackers made it into the semi-finals against the heavily favoured Chaos All-Stars. The morning of the game Slick said to Dunk, 'The Gobbo gives them a three-point spread, which is more than I suspected. Are you sure you didn't take him up on his offer?'

'You just want your cut,' Dunk said with a smile.

Slick stuck out his open hand, ready for a bag full of gold to fall into it. 'You're a great player, son, but this *is* business.'

'I know,' Dunk said, 'but I don't do business that way.'

'Bah!' Slick said, but Dunk saw the halfling smiling as he walked away.

As THE GOBBO predicted, the All-Stars pounded the Hackers hard. The All-Stars' captain, Schlitz 'Malty' Likker, a mutant minotaur with six horns on his head, kept M'Grash on his heels the whole first half. Kur threw two interceptions, and a cheap shot from Baron Redd the Damned put Cavre down for the rest of the game with a case of skin rot.

At half-time, the Hackers assembled in their dugout, ready for one of Pegleg's traditional 'you bunch of losers' rants. Instead, their coach told them to turn their attention to the field. 'Orcidas has something going on, and since they're hosting this party, all us guests have to play along.'

'What's happening, coach?' Guillermo Reyes asked, the pockmarks from one of the All-Stars' tentacles still pink and puckered across his face.

'They're milking every last bit they can get out of one of their top endorsement contracts by 'honouring' him with a ceremony during half-time,' Pegleg snarled.

'Who is it?' Kai Albrecht asked, still scratching the rash he'd broken into after getting coated with the green goo that passed for one All-Star beastman's blood.

'Skragger, of course.'

Dunk hadn't been interested before, but the name of the black orc snapped him back to attention. He craned his neck over the lip of the dugout to see the temporary stand a herd of goblins and snotlings had dragged into the centre of the field. 'Anyone notice that the Chaos Cup symbol in the middle of the field looks a lot like a pentacle?' he asked.

'It *is* a pentacle, Mr. Hoffnung,' Pegleg said. 'Strange things happen at the Chaos Cup all the time, and the teams finally insisted on some kind of protection. If you see a daemon, get your tail inside that pentacle's circle, and you'll be safe.'

Dunk eyed the circle carefully. 'Are you sure about that, coach?'

'No,' Pegleg said. 'Ain't magic grand?'

'And now, here to accept the Orcidas Golden Spikes for the third year in a row,' Bob's voice said, 'the greatest black orc player of them all. The Prince of Pain. The Captain of Calamity. The Duke of Dirty Play. Ladies, gentlemen, and creatures of all kinds: Skragger!'

The crowd roared with approval as the black orc stepped up to the front of the makeshift stand that somehow looked much sturdier than anything else in the stadium. Skragger, dressed in a vibrant black Orcidas sweat suit trimmed with blood-red piping, waved at the fans, and they roared back louder.

'He's something, huh?' marvelled Milo Hoffstetter.

'A couple decades of top play and high casualty counts, and you might be there too,' Pegleg said. 'But concentrate on surviving today first.'

Despite his misgivings, Dunk found the event fascinating. This psychopathic orc – a redundant term, Dunk suspected – was the hero of all these fans. And how had he gotten there? Images of Skragger strangling Kur flashed through Dunk's mind. He glanced at Kur and saw the man had turned white as Skragger took the field.

Dunk turned back to the ceremony, where he saw a man in dark robes walking up the steps of the stand in the centre of the pentacle with a pair of golden spikes in his hands. The rookie rubbed his eyes and then looked again, but the image was still the same. 'That's Zauberer out there!' Dunk shouted.

Before anyone could respond, Dunk sprinted out toward the stand. He didn't know what was happening here, but if Zauberer was involved he couldn't let it happen. 'Zauberer!' he shouted at the top of his lungs. 'Stop!'

'Well, Bob,' Jim's voice said, 'it looks like one of the Hackers has decided to join the ceremony.'

'That's number seven, Dunk Hoffnung,' Bob said, 'and he looks excited. Perhaps Coach Pegleg chose him for the traditional human sacrifice.'

'I thought Orcidas gave up on those after last year's summoning of the great daemon Nurgle nearly started another Red Plague.'

'It looks like tradition may have trumped safety concerns once again, Bob. This is the Chaos Cup we're talking about!'

The crowd fell silent with anticipation as Dunk charged the stage. He leapt onto the raised platform and tackled Zauberer just as he was about to present the golden spikes to Skragger.

'Wow, Bob! Hoffnung just waltzed right in there and took that man down. I wish he'd tackle like that during the games!'

'I know what you mean, Jim. I wonder where the defence is at a time like this. Doesn't a player like Skragger rate any bodyguards?'

'Just look at him,' Jim's voice laughed. 'Does he look like he needs them?'

'I don't know what you're up to, wizard,' Dunk snarled at the terrified Zauberer, 'but it ends here!'

The wizard struggled to stab Dunk with the spikes, but the rookie smashed Zauberer in the face first. He was about to follow up with a knockout blow, when someone pulled him bodily off the wizards.

'Gots a death wish, punk?' Skragger growled into Dunk's ear. The crowd screeched with approval.

'Wait!' Dunk shouted. 'This man is an evil wizard! He was going to kill you!'

Skragger just shook his head as he threw Dunk back over the edge of the stage. 'Look around, punk. Game's fulla evil wizards.'

Dunk scrambled to his feet to see Zauberer standing behind Skragger, who was still sneering down at Dunk, the two golden spikes raised high in his fists, poised to stab into the black orc's back.

'No!' Dunk shouted, although he knew it was too late.

Just as Zauberer struck, Schlitz the six-horned minotaur, who'd been up on the stage to help present the award, dove between the wizard and the black orc. When Zauberer brought down the spikes, they drove straight into Schlitz's chest.

Schlitz screeched in horror as the spike plunged into his flesh.

'What?' Skragger said as he turned to see what had happened. 'You bloody bull!' he shouted at Schlitz. 'No one steals my trophies!'

Dunk stood up and craned his neck around Skragger to see what was happening to Schlitz. As he did, he noticed Zauberer skulking away, but he was more concerned about the minotaur than the wizard at the moment.

Sparks of some nameless crimson energy arced between the spikes in Schlitz's chest and quickly grew to cover the creature's entire body. Then a vermilion bolt cracked down from the overcast sky, bathing the clouds and the stadium beneath in a hellish light. The bolt shot straight down through the minotaur and the stage, then flooded through the pentacle, illuminating its every line and edge. There were many gaps in the outer circle.

Dunk reflexively covered his eyes against the flash, and when he drew his hands away he saw Schlitz still standing on the stage, bent down on one knee. The creature's fur and skin glowed an angry orange and red, reminding Dunk of the colour of flowing lava. When the minotaur looked up, Dunk could see that his eyes were a blazing scarlet from rim to rim.

'Who beckons the servant of the Blood God?' Schlitz roared in a voice that carried further than Jim or Bob's. 'Who shall be the first penitent to slake his thirst?'

'Bob,' Jim's voice said. 'I think we're in for a real show here tonight.'

Skragger lowered his shoulder and stomped up to the minotaur, trying to knock him flying from the stage. Schlitz, or whatever daemon rode his flesh, swatted the black orc away like a gnat

Dunk ducked as Skragger went sailing over his head to bounce off the turf behind him. Under most circumstances, this would have brought a smile to the rookie's face. At the moment, though, Skragger's fate was the furthest thing from his mind.

'You!' the blood-eyed minotaur roared as it stabbed a broken-nailed finger at Dunk, red energy still arcing among its six horns. 'You're next!'

Dunk stared up at the minotaur for a moment, then turned and ran.

Schlitz charged after the rookie thrower as he raced down the field.

'It looks like Hoffnung's decided to challenge Khorne's impromptu proxy here to a foot race,' Bob's voice said. 'Jim, do you think he has a chance?'

'Does a zombie smell like roses? Minotaurs are renowned for their hoof speed. I'd say it's only a matter of seconds before the stampeding Schlitz puts an end to a very promising rookie season.'

Dunk knew the announcers were right. He had no hope of out running the minotaur in a fair race. Fortunately, 'fair' didn't enter into his plans.

As Dunk sprinted along the field toward the Hackers' end zone, he heard Schlitz thundering after him, the minotaur's hooves thumping along faster than the rookie's heart. Dunk put everything he had into making the minotaur sweat. The longer the race lasted, the more careless the creature would be.

When Dunk felt the minotaur's hot breath blasting down on his neck and could hear the energy arcing between his horns crackling in his ears, he threw himself to the turf and curled up into a tight ball.

Schlitz's shins ploughed into Dunk's back and knocked the rookie spinning. At the same time, the kneecapped minotaur went sailing over Dunk's armoured form, his momentum sending him soaring into the air.

Schlitz landed headfirst in the Hackers' end zone, his six vicious horns stabbing through and embedding themselves in the turf there. His momentum brought his hooves flying up over his head until they landed hard on the turf in front of him. As this happened, there was a loud and sickening snap.

Bruised but still whole, Dunk scrambled over to where the minotaur lay, his head pointing in one direction and his body in another. Crimson energy arced around Schlitz's body as the orange and red fire under his fur began to flicker and fade. His unholy screech of protest rang throughout all of Mousillon's damned streets and alleys.

Unsure what to do, Dunk reached out and pulled the golden spikes from the minotaur's chest. The unnatural lights blinked out immediately, and the screech dampened to a feeble cry.

Having fallen silent during the possessed minotaur's death scream, the crowd now stared blankly and quietly down at the field to where the minotaur lay.

Still on his knees, Dunk crawled around to where Schlitz's eyes still stared back at his own team's end zone, all the way at the other end of the field. 'Thanks, kid,' the minotaur whispered as the life went out of his soft, brown eyes.

Dunk reached out and closed those eyes, then stood over the minotaur, the golden spikes still in his hands.

'Gimme those, punk!' Skragger said as he came trotting down the field.

Angry, Dunk waited until the black orc was close enough and then flung the spikes at his face. Skragger splayed out his hands and caught them each neatly. Stomping to a halt, he brought the spikes up in front of himself and pointed them at Dunk.

'No one takes my trophies!' With that, he thrust his fists high into the air, the tips of the spikes facing toward the sky, and the crowd erupted.

When the noise came down a bit, Skragger lowered his arms and pointed the tips of the spikes at Dunk's chest. 'Next time I see ya, yer dead!' he snarled.

Unable to hear the black orc's words, the crowd seemed to understand the intent. The people in the stands roared again, and Skragger trotted back to the stage, the spikes held high, basking in the adulation.

As Dunk watched the black orc enjoy his moment, he felt something on his shoulder. He turned to see a snake-headed creature with a trio of tongues standing behind him, dressed in a black-and-white striped shirt. The referee retracted its tentacle as soon as it realised it had Dunk's attention.

'Sssorry, sssir,' the ref said, 'but you're going to have to leave the game. The rulesss againssst killing other playersss during half-time are quite clear.'

Dunk stared at the snakeman, uncomprehending. 'I may have just saved the life of every person in this stadium,' he said, 'and you're worried about the game.'

The snakeman's headed weaved and bobbed nervously as he spoke. 'You may – I'll ssstresss 'may' – have sssaved livesss today, but you alssso killed the captain of the Chaosss All-Ssstarsss. Our sssponsorsss frown on that.'

Dunk glanced back over his shoulder to where the referee was looking. Blaque and Whyte were standing next to a furious Pegleg in the dugout.

'If you leave right now,' the referee said, 'we will let your team continue the game.'

Dunk didn't look back at the snakeman. He just nodded as he began the long walk back toward the Hackers on the sidelines.

'What in Nuffle's name were you doing out there, Mr. Hoffnung?' Pegleg demanded as Dunk stepped down into the dugout. Blaque and Whyte stood silently in a far corner, watching everything.

'Saving us all,' Dunk said, staring dejectedly at the wall before him. The other players didn't say a word.

Pegleg grabbed one of Dunk's spiked shoulder pads with his hook and pulled the rookie about to face him. 'That's not what you're here for, Mr. Hoffnung. That's *not* what I'm paying you for. If you even think about doing something like this again, you will be terminated, and I'm not just talking about your contract.'

Dunk brought his eyes up to look into Pegleg's. 'You can't fire me, coach,' he said flatly. 'I quit.'

CHAPTER TWENTY-EIGHT

THE CHAOS ALL-STARS, energised by the death of their captain – all the surviving players wanted to compete for his spot – thrashed the Hackers in the second half of the game. Dunk was back in his hotel room when Slick brought him the news.

'It's too bad, son,' the halfling said. 'You did the right thing.'

'That's behind me now,' Dunk said, grimacing as he spoke. 'I don't want to have anything to do with that game now.'

'Wait,' Slick said, concern etched on his brow. 'You're not serious about quitting, are you? That was in the heat of the moment. I'm sure Pegleg will let it slide.'

Dunk shook his head. 'That's not going to happen,' he said. 'I'm sick of this game. I'm sick of the death. I'm sick of the threats. I'm sick of the media trying to pin everything on me.' He sat down on the edge of his bed and buried his head in his hands. 'I've had it. No more.'

'Son,' Slick said, his hands spread wide and open, 'that's part of the game, all of it. I thought you knew that going into it.'

Dunk threw himself back on the bed. 'I knew it, yeah, but I had no idea. It's one thing to want gold and glory. It's another to get it.'

Slick climbed up into the chair next to the bed. 'It's all over then, is it?' he said. 'The gold and glory? You've had enough of it?'

Dunk put his hands over his face. He didn't want to hear what Slick was saying to him. He didn't want to think about it at all. The only thing he wanted was to be out of Blood Bowl for good.

'What then?' the halfling said. 'Back to chasing dragons? We know how well that went.'

Dunk didn't say a word.

'You have perhaps a bit too much of the hero in you, son. You certainly proved that today. But where else can you feed that part of yourself?'

'And where else can I get paid so well for it, right?' Dunk said.

'True enough,' Slick said, 'although that wasn't my point.'

Dunk sat up and glared at the halfling. 'Face it, Slick, if it wasn't for my "potential" as a Blood Bowl player, you wouldn't have crossed the street to spit at me.'

Slick stood up on the chair and glared back down at Dunk. 'Think that if you will, but I didn't have to open that door for you that night in Dörfchen, did I?

I didn't have to hand you that spear. That we've since made each other wealthy, well, I'd be lying if I said it wasn't important to me.

'You've never been poor, son. You may have left Altdorf and your family behind, but you never had to scrabble around in the gutter for scraps. You never had to wear rags for clothes. You're so well off now, you don't know how good you have it.'

Slick swung his arms around the place to show Dunk what he meant. As he looked around the grungy, leaky, draughty place, he grimaced and leapt down from the chair. As he headed for the door, he looked back and said, 'There are worse places to be in Mousillon, you know. Playing Blood Bowl – having that kind of gold and glory – lets you make the best of a bad deal. Consider that before you throw it all away.'

THE NEXT MORNING, Dunk climbed aboard the *Sea Chariot* with the rest of the team. He didn't say a word to anyone, and he studiously avoided Pegleg's gaze. But as he walked past the coach, Pegleg simply said, 'Welcome aboard, Mr. Hoffnung.'

The trip back to Bad Bay gave Dunk a lot of time to think. He spent his time above decks, day and night, gazing out into the sky like some mad prophet looking for meaning in the clouds and stars. No one bothered him. Slick brought him his meals, and the halfling and ogre sat with Dunk as they ate, but they seemed content to share each other's company without spoiling the moments with talk.

When the Hackers got to Bad Bay, Dunk was among the last to disembark. He watched the families and friends of the other players greet them at the dock, thrilled to find their loved ones had survived yet another tournament. There would be many a celebration in the tiny town that balmy spring night.

When Dunk finally did leave the ship, he saw Cavre limping up to him on a set of crutches, holding something in his hand. A beautiful woman and a gaggle of children stood at the end of the dock where they'd greeted the man, and they waited for him to return with wide and eager eyes.

'What is it?' Dunk asked as respectfully as he could. For all the problems Dunk had been having with the team, Cavre had always treated him with patience and respect.

'Congratulations, Mr. Hoffnung,' Cavre said, handing him a sheaf of bound papers that featured a colour image on the front. 'You just made your first cover of *Spike! Magazine.*'

Stunned, Dunk flipped the magazine over to look at the cover. There was a picture of him standing over Schlitz's body, the bloodied golden spikes still dripping in his hands. The headline read: 'The Hackers' Hoffnung: The Greatest Killer Ever?'

Dunk narrowed his eyes at Cavre. 'Is this good or bad?' he asked. 'In some circles, this would be a compliment.'

'Look at the by-line on the article,' Slick said, pointing at the cover again. It read: 'Story by Lästiges Weibchen.'

M'Grash put his hand on Dunk's shoulder and said, 'Not good.'

* * *

Dunk thanked Cavre, who went home with his overjoyed family, and strode over to the Hacker Hotel. There, in the Hacker-decorated common room, he sat and read the article. He ignored the number of people staring at him as he did.

'Good on ya,' the bartender said as he brought Dunk and his friends a round of Hackers Stout, a dark and heady brew that was drinking more like bread than water.

Dunk looked up from the magazine, startled. The bartender – a sandy-haired young man named Henrik, with a Hacker logo tattooed on his forearm – smiled at him. 'It's great to see one of ours hit the big time,' he grinned. 'These are on the house.'

'Thanks,' Dunk said, a bit confused. He sipped the beer as he continued to read.

Lästiges had assembled a cadre of 'anonymous sources' who swore to Nuffle that Dunk had been behind a large number of the off-field casualties surrounding the tournaments over the past year. This included the murders of the prospects in the Hackers' training camp before the *Spike! Magazine* tournament, the killing of the Broussard brothers, the collapse of the dungeon in the Reavers-Champions of Death game, and the dissolution of Ramen-Tut, capped off by the slaying of Schlitz 'Malty' Likker in the Chaos Cup semi-finals.

Dunk had to admit that a disturbing number of people had died around him this year, and Lästiges had done a solid job of either lining up liars or fabricating accusations about him. If he hadn't known better, he might have thought he was guilty too. She even tied him to some other killings he hadn't even known had happened. He wondered for a moment if someone was wandering around disguised as him and killing people.

As Dunk kept reading, he became more and more angry. True, he had killed Schlitz, but it was more like the poor, possessed minotaur had killed himself while trying to turn Dunk into paste. He had done nothing to be ashamed of, at least as far as these killings went.

'This is awful,' Dunk said. 'Lästiges is on a crusade for my head here, and if the Game Wizards believe this stuff, she might actually get it.'

'Will they?' M'Grash asked, his boulder of a face filled with concern.

Slick shrugged as Dunk handed him the magazine to read. 'It's possible. First, they've been following you and her around for much of the time she's been "investigating" you. Second, *Spike! Magazine* is the most important magazine in the sport. If the GWs don't make an example out of Dunk, lots of other players might figure they can get away with this kind of stuff. The whole sport could dissolve in a rash of off-field murders.'

Dunk shrugged nonchalantly. 'What can they do to me? Suspend me for a few games? Kick me off the team?'

'Publicly execute you?' said Slick. It wasn't really a question. 'You need to go back and read your contract more thoroughly.'

Dunk sat up straight. 'You said it was a 'standard contract'!' Dunk protested.

'That sort of stuff *is* standard!' Slick said.

'Gah!' Dunk slouched back in his chair and put his hands over his face. 'How did I get wound up in all this?'

While Dunk sulked, Slick read the article, and M'Grash drank his bucket of beer. When the ogre set it down, his hands shook so badly that he nearly knocked it off the table.

'You okay?' Dunk asked. 'This article has really thrown you.' He leaned forward and put his hand on the ogre's massive arm. 'Don't you worry about it, M'Grash.'

'And why should he, Mr. Hoffnung?' Pegleg said as he walked into the hotel's common room. 'You can't buy this kind of publicity!' He grinned from ear to ear.

Dunk goggled at his coach for a moment. 'What?'

'This is the best thing that's happened to us since we founded the team,' Pegleg said as he pulled up a chair and sat down. Dunk had never seen him so excited. 'We're going to have teams lining up to play us after this, and the venues will have to offer us a better cut of the gate to make it worth our while.'

'So, this is good?'

Pegleg put his hand on Dunk's shoulder. 'No, Mr. Hoffnung, it's phenomenal.' Then he leaned in conspiratorially and said, 'So, when do you think you might kill again?'

Dunk froze. He couldn't believe the coach's words.

'You see, the trick is to not do it too often. You need to leave the public wanting more.' Pegleg waved the magazine at Dunk. 'You have to avoid over saturation while still keeping yourself and the team in the public eye. It's a fine line to walk.'

'Coach.'

'Also, if you are open to suggestions, there are some people in the game that might be better dead than others, if you know what I mean. I can provide you with a list and reasons for each if you like.'

'Coach.'

'Or just let your murderous appetites lead you where they may. They've done well by you so far. Perhaps it's best to not mess with a savant's instincts, eh?'

'Coach!' Dunk glared at the startled Pegleg until he was sure the man would be silent. 'I didn't do it. None of it!'

'Come now, Mr. Hoffnung. I saw you kill Schlitz myself, as did thousands of others. Masterfully done, by the way.'

'That was self-defence! I didn't touch any of the others.'

A light went on under Pegleg's yellow tricorn, and he favoured Dunk with a knowing smile. 'I see. If that's the way you like it, Mr. Hoffnung, than so be it. I'm just as pleased either way.'

With that, Pegleg stood and left with a tip of his hat and a sly wink at Dunk.

'Dunkel,' M'Grash said. The rookie looked up at the ogre, who seemed to be near to tears.

'Yes?' Dunk said, putting his hand on M'Grash's monstrous mitt.

'We talk?' The ogre looked as if he might burst if he didn't get to say his piece soon.

'Go ahead,' Dunk said. 'You can tell us anything.'

M'Grash looked sidelong at Slick. 'Talk alone?'

Slick gave the ogre a good-natured smile. 'I can tell when I'm not wanted, big guy. I'll leave the two of you to your chat.'

As Slick rose from the table, he walked behind the ogre and mouthed at Slick, 'Tell me later.'

Dunk stifled a laugh and waved the halfling off. 'Do you want to go somewhere more private?' he asked M'Grash.

The ogre nodded, so Dunk led him from the common room and up into his own quarters. M'Grash had to bend down to get through the door, but once inside he was comfortable enough.

'So,' Dunk asked, a little amused by the sight of the ogre sitting on the floor of his parlour, as none of the chairs were close to large enough. Even the couch would have been crushed under M'Grash's bulk. 'What do you have to say?'

The ogre's faced reddened and screwed up horribly. Dunk braced for an ear-splitting wail, but it never came. Instead, M'Grash whimpered and pointed a trembling finger at the copy of *Spike! Magazine* still in Dunk's hand.

'Me,' the ogre rasped. 'My fault.'

Dunk shook his head. 'Don't be silly, M'Grash,' he said. 'If it's anyone's fault, it's Lästiges for writing such lies.'

'No,' M'Grash said, his voice louder now. He pointed at his chest sombrely. 'Killed them. Me.'

Dunk cocked his head at his monstrous friend as what M'Grash was trying to tell him finally dawned on him. 'You,' he said, collapsing on the couch as he tried to absorb this.

'You killed the other prospects in the camp?'

M'Grash shook his head slowly as he wiped his wet eyes dry. 'Broussards.'

'Luc and Jacques killed all those people?'

M'Grash nodded.

'And then they planted that knife in my tent to make it look like I did it.'

'Uh-huh. Wanted you off team.'

Dunk blew out a long sigh. 'It worked. If they hadn't been killed, I never…' He shot M'Grash a hard look. 'You killed them, didn't you?'

The ogre nodded. 'Wanted Dunk with Hackers.'

Dunk reached out and clapped M'Grash on his massive shoulder. 'You got that, all right.' He wasn't sure how he felt about M'Grash killing the Broussards, but he was sure they'd have been happy to do the same or worse to him. 'Thanks, big guy.'

'Ceiling?' M'Grash said. 'Me.'

Dunk's eyes went wide as he thought of Dirk and Spinne nearly being killed. 'No one actually died there,' he said slowly. 'The Champions of Death got the worst of it, and they just needed to be unburied.' Several of the Reavers had been crushed to death of course, but Dunk was far from certain how capable the big ogre was of comprehending his actions; best not to burden him with distractions like the truth.

Dunk narrowed his eyes at M'Grash. 'You didn't have anything to do with Ramen-Tut, did you?'

'No. Was Kur. Magic knife.' The ogre pointed at his waist.

'Ah. The belt-buckle blade.' Inside, Dunk breathed a sigh of relief. Kur had almost slain him with that same knife.

'Why did you bring down the ceiling?' Dunk asked.

'Coach wanted Dungeonbowl game.'

'So you eliminated the team playing in the one spot that could be open to us.' Dunk marvelled at the ogre for a minute. 'You're not so dumb as people think.'

M'Grash grinned widely, showing all his teeth. 'Thanks!'

'What about Schlitz?'

M'Grash shook his head. 'Saw wizard talk to Gobbo before game.'

'So Gunther was behind it?' Dunk thought about this for a moment. 'He must have wanted our team to lose. If he's working with Zauberer, he probably knew I'd chase out there after the wizard and either get myself killed or kicked out of the game.'

M'Grash nodded along, although Dunk suspected the ogre didn't really understand. Still, he'd underestimated the ogre before, and he was wary of doing so again.

'Anything else?' Dunk asked.

M'Grash nodded. 'Before you came. Killed Hackers.'

Dunk forced himself to breathe slowly. 'That's why the Hackers were looking for so many new players. Why did you kill them, M'Grash?'

The ogre frowned. 'Mean people. Kill mean people.'

Dunk smiled faintly. 'Remind me to never be mean to you.'

M'Grash gathered Dunk in a hug so tight and long that for a moment he feared he was to be the ogre's next victim.

'Dunkel friend!' M'Grash said as he set the gasping rookie down.

'Yes,' Dunk wheezed as he looked up at the gentle killer. 'The question now, though, is what do we do about all this?'

CHAPTER TWENTY-NINE

BEFORE M'GRASH could respond, there was a knock at the door. 'Who is it?' Dunk called.

'Blaque and Whyte,' the dwarf Game Wizard's gruff voice said. 'We'd like to have a few words with you.'

Dunk slipped around M'Grash and opened the door a few inches. He kept the side of his foot braced against the inside of it. The odd-sized elf and dwarf stood there in the hallway in their black robes, the words 'Wolf Sports' embroidered across their chests.

'What's this about?' Dunk asked.

'Aren't you going to invite us in?' Blaque said.

'I just got back from the Chaos Cup,' Dunk said. 'The place is a mess.'

'Have you read the latest issue of *Spike! Magazine* yet?'

Dunk grimaced. 'I'm just getting to it now.'

'I like that cover. It's a good image of you. Don't you like that cover, Whyte?'

'Fantastic,' the elf said. 'Almost like being there.'

Dunk closed his eyes for a moment. When he reopened them, the two GWs were still there. 'I'm beat,' he told them. 'I appreciate you checking in on me, but I'm going to bed.'

'I'm afraid we can't let you do that quite yet,' Blaque said.

Dunk looked down and saw that the dwarf had wedged his foot in the gap in the door.

'Hold on for a moment,' Dunk said as he held up a finger toward the GWs.

Dunk turned toward M'Grash, who'd been watching him with a confused look on his face. He beckoned the ogre over, then pointed at the door and whispered in M'Grash's ear, 'Don't kill them. Just slow them down.'

The ogre grinned down at Dunk as he put his hand against the door.

'My apologies,' Dunk said, poking his nose back through the gap in the door, 'but I have to go.'

'Look here,' Blaque began. Dunk noticed the two wizards now had wands in their hands.

'Wish I could help,' Dunk said. 'While I'm gone, my friend here will take care of you.'

With that, Dunk turned and headed for the window.

As DUNK URGED Pferd to gallop faster on the road that headed south, toward Marienburg, he heard an explosion from the direction of the Hackers Hotel. He looked back toward his still-open window and saw a shower of sparks erupt from it, followed quickly by a medium-sized form in a black robe that went sailing into the bay.

Dunk hoped M'Grash would get through the incident without being turned into a toad. Before the wizard in the water could spot him, he dug in his heels, urging Pferd to move faster than ever.

Once Dunk had left Bad Bay far behind, he began to think what he might do next. Going back to the Hackers was out of the question for now. There were a couple months left until the next of the Majors: the legendary Blood Bowl itself. The team would be all right without him until he figured out what to do about the GWs and his growing reputation as a player-killer.

As he headed south through the Wasteland, alongside the River Reik, his thoughts returned to his childhood and to the one person he always knew he could trust.

The city of Altdorf lay somewhere down the road ahead of him. Lehrer lived in Altdorf. So Altdorf it was.

THE FAMILY KEEP still stood there in the heart of Altdorf's wealthiest district. It was part of a collection of such places piled up on top of each other, each of them built to be more impressive than the last. As the birds darted in and out of the ivy-covered walls, Dunk's thoughts turned to better days.

Dunk had spent his entire childhood in the keep, never venturing any further than the limits of Altdorf itself, with the occasional jaunt a few leagues up or down the Reik. At the time, he'd never known he could ever want anything more. In many ways, Altdorf was the centre of civilisation, and the rest of the world just seemed like the wolves scratching at the door.

Dunk waited outside the keep until dark, which came late in these last days of spring. He saw his target slip out of the place at dusk, dressed in the same grey cloak Dunk still remembered.

Lehrer moved like a panther prowling through the city's undergrowth, constantly on the lookout for other predators. He sauntered past Dunk, keeping to the shadows, and moved silently down the street. Dunk waited for him to pass, then followed him as he ducked into a dark alley.

When Dunk entered the alley, he found it bare but for a few scraps of litter blowing in the breeze shunted down the narrow passage. He drew his sword as he stepped into the darkness and said quietly, 'I only want to talk.'

Dunk parried the blade that cut at him from the darkest part of the shadows. He knew Lehrer would be there, just as he knew he'd be dead if he hadn't been prepared for the blow. His old teacher didn't care to ask questions of people outside of the keep's walls.

'It's been a long time, kid,' Lehrer said as he moved into the half-light of a nearby streetlamp pouring into one corner of the alley. 'I hear you been keeping busy.'

The shorter Lehrer drew back his hood and glared at Dunk, who recognised that look from his long hours in the man's training; slightly impressed, but never enough to really show it. The slight man's silver hair matched the grey of his eyes now and blended in well with his cloak and the drab colours of Altdorf by night.

'Not as busy as some might say,' Dunk answered, sheathing his blade.

'Warmed my heart to see you and your brother in the same line of work,' Lehrer said. He kept his sword out, although he lowered its tip to the ground.

'I doubt my parents would have said the same.'

'Greta would appreciate the gold you're making,' Lehrer said with an ironic smile. 'Lügner would care more about the kills.'

Dunk snorted softly. 'Have you heard from them?' he asked, struggling to keep any taint of hope from his voice.

'Not a peep,' Lehrer said. 'The Guterfeinds are still looking for them, but they've not had a lick of luck yet.' He hesitated for a moment before continuing on. 'They're looking for you too.'

Dunk nodded. 'I,' he started, 'I thought I could make a name for myself as a hero. You know, slaying dragons and all that.'

'Gold and glory.'

'Right.'

'You've been listening to too many stories,' Lehrer said.

Dunk shook his head. 'So it seems. I just wanted to be able to come back here and save everyone, to make things right.'

'It's going to take more than fame and fortune to do that, kid.' When Dunk's face fell, the old teacher added. 'At least it would give you more choices about how to do it.'

'Maybe.' Dunk began to wonder if this was all a mistake.

'Dirk had the right idea,' Lehrer said. 'Leave here and get himself set up in a whole new life. He never looked back.'

'Ironic he got traded to the Reavers then and ended up back here.'

Lehrer laughed. It was a low sound bereft of humour. 'That's fate for you.'

Dunk waited for Lehrer to say something more. When that didn't happen, he realised his old teacher was waiting for him.

'I'm in some serious trouble,' Dunk said.

'So I read.'

'What can I do about it?'

Lehrer stuck out his chin. 'I take it fighting's not an option.'

Dunk shook his head. 'It involves wizards. There's only two of them right now, but there could be more at any moment.'

'Did you do it?'

Dunk's breath caught in his throat. 'What's that?'

'Did you kill all those people?'

Dunk frowned. 'Does it matter?'

'Not to me,' the old man said, shifting his weight.

'I need to make this go away,' Dunk said. 'Otherwise, I won't be able to settle in a major city for the rest of my life.'

'If the Game Wizards put a bounty on your head, you can expect more hassles than that.'

'So what do I do?'

'Well,' Lehrer said, 'if there's anything my time with the Guterfeinds has taught me, it's that no job is complete until you pin the blame on someone else.'

Dunk grunted. 'After so many years with our family, how can you work for those people?'

Lehrer eyes Dunk carefully. 'They're not all bad. Your family wasn't all good either.'

'We had nothing to be ashamed of.' Dunk surprised himself with how angry he sounded.

Lehrer shook his head. 'You still see your family through the eyes of a child. It's time to grow up, kid.' With that, he turned and slinked back into the shadows. 'Good luck.'

Dunk thought about following the old man, but if Lehrer wanted to leave he wasn't sure how he could stop him.

'Just know one thing,' Lehrer's voice called back through the darkness from somewhere further down the alley. 'It wasn't your fault, kid. Not all of it.'

# CHAPTER THIRTY

THAT NIGHT IN the Skinned Cat, Dunk just wanted to be left alone with his thoughts. This was the kind of place where hard people drank hard drinks and gave each other plenty of space, which suited Dunk just fine. In his younger days, he'd heard many a tale about the place, most of which seemed too fantastic to believe. The only thing that he'd been sure of was that he never wanted to set foot in the place, yet here he was.

As Dunk finished off what he'd promised himself was his last stein of the horribly potent dwarf draught Bugman's XXXXXX, the only thing he was closer to was leaving his dinner in the gutter outside the pub. He'd turned Lehrer's advice over and over in his mind, but he couldn't figure out a way to make it work.

'Pin the blame on someone else.' It sounded like a fine notion, but Dunk couldn't think of where to begin. The only obvious people to shift the blame to were either his friend (M'Grash) or dead (the Broussards).

There was Kur, of course. Not only had he let Dunk share the blame for Ramen-Tut's death but he'd tried to kill the rookie too. Dunk didn't think he'd shed a tear for the veteran thrower if he were to take the fall for all those murders. Still, it wouldn't be simple to make that happen.

The easy way to handle it would be to give up M'Grash. The ogre had been responsible for enough of the mayhem that it wouldn't be hard to make the rest stick to him. Dunk didn't want to try that quite yet though. The ogre had been a friend to him when he needed one and had saved him from Kur more than once. He even owed his spot with the Hackers to M'Grash.

Dunk wished he could leave the blame with the Broussards. How he'd explain their own deaths and all those who came after though, he didn't know. Sure, the dead sometimes walked, and even played Blood Bowl, as he'd seen with the Champions of Death, but this would be a long stretch.

Dunk had given up and was motioning for the bartender to bring him another pint of the Bugman's when the last person he'd expected to see slipped into the other side of his booth.

Gunther the Gobbo smiled across the dagger-scarred table at Dunk. 'I've been looking for you everywhere, kid,' he said. 'I never thought I'd find you in a dive like this.'

Dunk fought an urge to shove the table into the Gobbo's greasy, overfilled gut and crush him with it. 'How did you find me at all?'

The Gobbo grinned as wide as an alligator. 'I read, kid, and I know a little bit about you.' He leaned over the table and nearly drooled on the wood. 'Don't be so surprised. The kind of business I'm in, it's my job to know as much as I can about hot new talent like you.' He winked at the bartender. 'And to know as many different kinds of people as I can. You never know where the next star player's going to crop up.'

'What do you want?' Dunk said, glancing around the place nervously. He didn't see any sign of Blaque and Whyte, but he was ready to flee at the first sign of them.

The Gobbo slapped his clammy, wart-covered hand on the table, and Dunk nearly leapt from his skin. The bookie laughed. 'A little jumpy there, aren't you, kid? No need for that. I'm here to help you.'

'Like you did at the Chaos Cup?' Dunk said.

The Gobbo chuckled at that. 'You're not going to hold that one against me, are you? How was I to know you'd chase out there after Zauberer? That little madman told me he'd be wearing a disguise.'

'Then what was he doing out there?' Dunk asked suspiciously.

'He was going to kill Skragger, of course,' the Gobbo said. 'I thought you were smarter than that kid.'

'But why?' Dunk hated even talking with the Gobbo, but his curiosity had to be satisfied. This just didn't seem to add up.

The Gobbo folded his hands in front of him on the table. A pint of Bugman's appeared in front of Dunk, while the barmaid slid a massive stein of Bloodweiser in front of the bookie.

'Ever heard of a dead pool, kid?' The way the Gobbo leered at Dunk, he was sure it was something horrible, but he had to shake his head.

'It's a kind of bet based on a list of famous names, a pool in which the gamblers wager on which of the names will die next. With the right crowd, you can end up with a lot of money on the line.'

'And Skragger's name was on that list?'

The Gobbo nodded. 'This is a list for Blood Bowl players only, and he's been on it forever. I put a ton of money on the guy back when he was a rookie, and I've just been letting it ride ever since. Can you imagine how he managed to survive all those years?

'Do you know how many Blood Bowl players make it to retirement? About one in ten. It's even harder for the better players. They set themselves up as targets, and everyone wants to take them down. Skragger was the biggest target there was.'

The Gobbo stopped for a moment to throw back the entire stein of Bloodweiser in one gulp. 'Another Blood for me!' he shouted at the bartender, who pointed at the barmaid already coming their way with a refill.

'By his last year, Skragger was at the top of most dead pools. A lot of people lost money on him. They pulled theirs out when he made it to the end of the season, but not me. I just let it ride. In fact, I doubled what I had down.

'Most people just thought it was a long-term investment. After all, he's got to die sometime, right? Probably in a violent way, knowing him.'

'And now you stand to gain a lot if he dies.'

The Gobbo shook his head. 'Not anymore. Now that everyone knows someone's gunning for the guy, they all leaped on his name too. If he dies this year, the take will be split so many ways I'll lose my shirt.'

'Sorry to have ruined your year,' Dunk said deadpan.

The Gobbo cocked his head at the rookie. 'Don't worry about it, kid. There are more bets where that one came from. In fact, that's where you come in.'

'Here it comes.'

The Gobbo grinned wide enough for Dunk to wonder if the bookie ever cleaned his teeth. 'I need someone like you to work for me.'

'I don't know if I'll ever play Blood Bowl again.'

'You leave that to me. With enough gold to grease the way, anything can happen.'

Dunk goggled at the man. 'You could buy off the GWs?'

The Gobbo winced. 'Maybe, maybe not. Everyone has his price. Besides, there are lots of ways for a resourceful fellow to get what he wants.'

'Does this have anything to do with the Black Jerseys?'

'Shhh!' The Gobbo put a fat finger in front of his mouth, then leaned forward again and said, 'Let's just say I think you'd look good with a black shirt under your Hacker green.'

'What's in it for me?' Dunk asked.

'Besides getting the GWs off your tail?' The Gobbo stared at Dunk incredulously. It didn't suit him. There was so little about him that was credible in the first place.

Dunk shook his head. 'How do I know you're not just setting it up so you can turn me in? Is there a bounty on me already?'

'Five hundred stinking crowns,' the Gobbo said with a snigger. 'You don't have to worry about me, kid. Adding another name to my little metateam's roster is worth far more than that.'

'Metateam?'

'Zauberer came up with it. You know how wizards are with words. Or maybe you don't. Anyhow, it's a team made up of parts of other teams that covers them all like a blanket.'

'Which is you make sure the games come out the way you need them to in order to give you the most profit.'

The Gobbo nodded. 'You're not as slow as you look, kid.' He leaned forward again, whispering this time. His breath smelled of verdigris.

'Let's quit dickering around here, kid, and get down to business. The Black Jerseys make a lot of money for me and from me. If you don't end up working for us, then you'll be against us.'

Dunk held up a hand. 'Are you saying there are Black Jerseys already on the Hackers?'

The Gobbo gave Dunk a sardonic grin. 'What do you think, kid?'

'Then what do you need me for?'

'Insurance, kid. I always like to have a backup plan or three. After all, that guy gets hurt, then where am I with the Hackers?'

Dunk sat back. 'I don't know. I'm thinking of washing my hands of all this and leaving the game behind. There's always Albion, or the New World.'

The Gobbo shook his head. 'Don't do that, kid. You got one hell of a career here. You'd be throwing it away.'

'It looks to me like it's already gone.'

'I can fix that. Let me outline a deal for you.'

Dunk nodded to show he was listening.

'Smart money – okay, *my* money – is on your Hackers making it into the Blood Bowl finals this year.'

'Are you serious?'

'As a Chaos cultist. The trick is that the Hackers will then lose the game. I need you in there to help make sure that happens.'

'But I can't play in the game. If I show up in the stadium, the GWs will grab me for sure.'

'If you manage to pull it off, I'll make that problem disappear. Plus, you'll be on my salary from there on out. That game alone could make you fifty thousand crowns.'

The number nearly took Dunk's breath away, but he focused on the GW problem instead. 'That money won't do me any good if I can't spend it.'

'I have the perfect patsy for you. I'll even provide the evidence for Blaque and Whyte to nail him to the stadium wall.'

'Who is it?' Dunk asked.

'Zauberer, of course.'

Dunk smiled despite himself. Then he heard his voice say, 'All right, I'll do it.'

DUNK SPENT THE next month holed up in a number of different inns. He kept changing his address every few days, just in case someone recognised him. Luckily, in a city the size of Altdorf there were plenty of places to stay and thousands of other transients for him to hide among.

While he waited for the Blood Bowl to roll along, Dunk did his best to stay in training. Although he couldn't get in any practice time without raising suspicions, he spent much of his days working out in whatever room he was staying in at the time. He wanted to be ready for the big game when it came along, and the grunts and growls he made tended to convince the others staying in the inn that it wasn't worth bothering the lunatic down the hall.

Every now and then, Dunk wandered down to the Altdorf Oldbowl, the home stadium of the Reikland Reavers. Eventually, he saw what he wanted: a home game coming up the next week.

THE CEILING OF the halfling inn known as Slag End was so low that Dunk had to enter on his knees. In a city as cosmopolitan as Altdorf, there were many places like this, but Slag End was the closest to the Oldbowl. Dunk suspected he'd find who he was looking for there, the night before the Reavers' home game.

Slick sat in a dark corner in the main parlour, smoking a pipe that was nearly as long as he was and sipping at a mug of Teinekin Beer. When he saw Dunk walking over to him on his knees, the halfling let the pipe drop from his mouth and said, 'Esmerelda's sacred pots, son. Is that you?'

Without waiting for a reply, Slick leapt to his feet and charged into Dunk's outstretched arms. The two embraced for a moment, then Slick pulled back to look at Dunk. 'How have you been? *Where* have you been? You look good – great even! Sit, sit, and tell me everything!'

Dunk squeezed himself into the corner next to Slick's chair, refusing a seat himself, as they were all too small to hold him. 'My apologies, son. It's the reason I come here, most big folk won't, but it makes it hard to entertain such guests. Come, let's go someplace else.'

Dunk refused. 'This is fine, Slick. I need to talk, and I can't stay long.' With that, he told Slick everything that M'Grash had told him and what he'd been doing since, including the offer that Gunther the Gobbo had made to him and the fact that he'd accepted it. Throughout it all, Slick sat and puffed on his pipe, blowing the occasional ring but mostly just listening and taking it all in. Later, Dunk would realise that this was the longest he'd ever seen the halfling stay quiet when there was a conversation to be had, but that fact made it clear that Slick was giving his words his full attention.

'I knew it,' Slick said when Dunk was done. 'That ogre always worried me. He's a good one to have on your side, to be sure, but he's trouble too. Ogres don't have any sense of morals, no way to tell right and wrong. M'Grash's childhood may have "humanised" him a bit, but he's still an ogre beneath it all.'

The halfling looked over at Dunk. 'You did the right thing by coming here, though. Those GWs were ready to hang you from gates of the nearest stadium. They need to make an example out of someone, and you're at the top of their list.'

It was here that Slick became grave. 'You should consider handing them M'Grash,' he said. 'It's the simplest way out of this. Everything else involves too much risk.'

'I can't do that,' Dunk said. 'That ogre did everything out of loyalty to me and the team. The only people he killed were the Broussards, and that couldn't have happened to a better pair of bastards.'

'Son, this isn't about loyalty. It's about two of the most important things in life: money and breathing. Blood Bowl has made us both wealthy, but you can't enjoy money without breathing, and you can reverse that, and it's just as true!'

Dunk shook his head. 'I won't allow it. Loyalty, friendship, has to count for something. I won't sell out M'Grash to save my own skin. Money's not that important to me.'

Slick gasped at this. 'Spoken like someone heady with the possibilities of youth!' He waved his hands at himself. 'Look at me. I'm not a young halfling anymore. I don't have much in the way of talents, and my only skills centre around smoking, drinking, and the gentle art of conversation, particularly in convincing coaches to hire players for a bit more than they're really worth.'

'Is that more important than a friend's life?' Dunk asked. He wasn't really sure he wanted to hear Slick's answer.

'You should ask M'Grash that. He seems happy to let you take the blame for what he did.'

'And if he came forward? The GWs would still pin all the other killings on me. Then we'd both be in for it.'

'You might be able to pin it all on him.'

'Or not. I'd rather try that with someone else. That way if I blow it, at least I'm not hurting a friend too.'

Slick shook his head as he stood up and approached Dunk. In the cramped quarters, the move made Dunk more than a little claustrophobic.

'He's your friend, not mine. As your agent, I feel compelled to inform the GWs about all of this and establish your innocence. For your career, it's the right thing to do.'

'Keeping me and M'Grash away from the GWs is good for the Hackers over the long term. That's good for my contract too. It makes it a good investment for you.'

'I don't know, son,' Slick said. 'It sounds like a good theory, but I'm more worried about the short-term. If the GWs catch up with you, what's going to happen to *you*?'

Dunk smiled softly. It wasn't the money that Slick was worried about after all.

'Well.' Dunk sensed that Slick wanted to do the right thing but needed a good excuse for it. 'What if M'Grash was your client too?'

Slick furrowed his brow for a moment, then sat down. 'That's a mighty good question, son, but it's moot, isn't it? Why would he make me his agent?'

'He doesn't have one now, and I'll bet Pegleg screwed him on his contract,' Dunk said, warming to the idea. 'Just think of the gains you could make for M'Grash, and your percentage.'

'Of course,' Slick said, instantly warming to the idea. 'Do you think you could get him to do that?'

'Hey, he's my friend, right?' said Dunk. 'Besides, I'd say he owes me a favour or two.'

# CHAPTER THIRTY-ONE

A FEW WEEKS later, Blood Bowl fever hit Altdorf hard. Throughout his years of living here, this was the season that Dunk had hated most. Hundreds of thousands of 'people' of all races descended on the city, swelling it nearly to bursting and straining its normally bountiful resources to the limit.

Most years, Dunk would simply hole up in the family keep and avoid the craziness around the big event as much as he could. After all, even walking across town could turn from a simple jaunt into an epic quest. It just wasn't worth going outside.

In those days, the roar of the crowd and the chants of the fans roaming through the streets terrified the young Dunk and annoyed his teenage self. For weeks after, he'd hear, 'Here we go, here we go, here we go,' echoing in his dreams.

This year was entirely different.

Dunk couldn't wait for the Blood Bowl tournament to begin. It would be three weeks of open games arranged by the team coaches, followed by a semi-final round and then a final round for the big prize: the Blood Bowl trophy and the lion's share of the half-million-crown purse. It was also Dunk's chance to redeem himself if everything went to plan. It was an insane, risky plan, of course, but it was all he had, so he clung to it like a rabid fan to a stray football.

At Slick's advice, Dunk had shaved his head bald and painted it so it looked like a Hacker's helmet. 'You're hiding in plain sight,' the halfling said. 'Who would think the fugitive thrower from the Bad Bay Hackers would walk around dressed up as one of its biggest fans?'

Dunk had to admit that he looked very little like himself. People did stare at him as he walked down the street, but it seemed they were looking at the decorations on his head rather than him. He even went out and bought himself a replica jersey that had his number, ten, on it and his name emblazoned across the back.

In the pubs, Blood Bowl fans hailed Dunk and slapped him on the back. 'Go, Deadly!' they shouted at him, thinking he was emulating the 'Deadly' Dunk Hoffnung mythologized in the pages of *Spike! Magazine*.

Lästiges had followed up her 'exposé' of Dunk's killing spree with another feature article detailing Dunk's short career and his links to Dirk, Spinne, Slick, and anyone else Dunk had ever met. According to the report, Dunk had killed half a dozen Game Wizards while making his escape and then dared the world to find him.

Accordingly, although they had to know the story wasn't true, the GWs had raised the bounty on Dunk's head to five thousand crowns. That was more than most people in Altdorf made in their entire lives, and it was enough to grab the attention of more than a few bounty hunters. Fortunately, no one was able to penetrate Dunk's disguise.

Rumours placed Dunk all over the place. Some said he'd escaped to the New World. Others claimed he'd struck a deal with the gods of Chaos and would be the new starter taking the place of Schlitz for the Chaos All-Stars. One local rag even claimed that Dunk was an illegitimate grandson of the Emperor himself and had been secreted away in the Imperial Palace.

While all this insanity swirled around him, Dunk got Slick to find a ticket for him to the Hackers' games. 'Where else would someone dressed like me be on game day?' he asked.

'I don't know, son,' Slick said. 'The Game Wizards will be there in force. Do you think they'll be as easy to fool as everyone else?'

'I'll be standing in a crowd of over a hundred thousand raving fans, dressed like this. If they can pick me out of that, they deserve to catch me. As part of my contract I get seats to all games in which we play. Get me one of those.'

'You're not still playing for the Hackers, son.'

'Has Pegleg torn up my contract?'

'No,' Slick smiled, 'he hasn't. He'd have to spend a fortune to fire you. Besides which, he's milking the publicity of you being a Hacker for all it's worth.'

'How'd you negotiate a severance clause like that?'

'It was easy, son. Pegleg figured you'd be dead long before he thought about firing you. Most bad Blood Bowl players end their career on the field. It's rare that they live long enough to refuse to play.'

IN THEIR FIRST game, the Hackers were set to take on the Moot Mighties, a halfling team from Mootland. 'The "halfling reserve" as some like to put it,' Slick said as he gave Dunk his ticket.

'Does a halfling team stand a chance against the Hackers?' Dunk asked. 'I don't mean to offend, but it sounds like a mismatch.'

Slick shook his head. 'You really need to start following the sport more.' He drew a deep breath, then spoke. 'In most circumstances, you'd be right. Most of the halfling Blood Bowl teams only ever play each other in their own stadium, known as the Batter Bowl, named after former Mootland League Commissioner Balbo "Beery" Batterman, of course.'

'That's fine, but the Hackers will murder them. Literally. M'Grash could probably take on the lot of them alone.'

Slick winced. 'It's been done before. The Mighties got tired of all the grief they got for being so small. The legendary ogre player Morg'th N'hthrog boasted he could take them all on at once, and they dared him to prove it.'

'What happened?'

Slick pursed his lips. 'Let's just say the next season was a rebuilding year for the Mighties.'

'And they won't meet the same fate against the Hackers? It sounds like M'Grash could trash everyone on the field and then use the scrubs to pick his teeth.'

'On any given day, any team can beat any other team.'

'That sounds like something the Gobbo would say. I smell the Black Jerseys at work here. Why give the Hackers such a creampuff of a team to play though? Who's going to bet on the Mighties?'

'All they have to do is beat the spread.'

'What's the spread?'

'Six touchdowns.'

Dunk frowned. 'That's all?'

'The Gobbo's giving even odds the Mighties won't survive the game long enough for the Hackers to score seven times.'

Dunk nodded. 'The Black Jerseys could make sure the Hackers lose somehow, and the Gobbo would rake in a dragon's hoard.'

'But you said the Hackers have to lose in the finals for the Gobbo to make his big score. So the Hackers play the Mighties and get an easy win and rack up a bunch of points. I heard the Mighties coach actually challenged the Hackers. I'll bet the Gobbo set that up.'

'I'm surprised the players don't refuse to take the field. They'll get creamed.'

'Maybe,' Slick said. 'The Moot Mighties, though, aren't just any halfling squad. They have a treeman on their team by the name of, well, his real name is unpronounceable. The Mighties call him Thicktrunk Strongbranch.'

Dunk goggled at his agent. 'A treeman player? What position does he play?'

Slick grinned. 'Thrower, of course.'

Dunk shook his head. 'This, I have to see.'

COME GAME TIME, Dunk sat in the stands, surrounded by thousands of newly minted Hackers fans. Scores of them wore replicas of his jersey, and a few even had their heads painted like him. They seemed uniformly drunk and rowdy, but Dunk found their unbridled enthusiasm contagious. He was soon cheering along with the rest of the fans, screaming and chanting until he was sure he'd never be able to talk again.

When the Hackers took the field, they charged out there like champions. Dunk wasn't sure what Pegleg had said to the players in the locker room ahead of time, but they came out ready to play. He watched them down there with a pang of regret. He surprised himself by how much he wanted to be out there playing alongside them.

A quick head count told Dunk that the Hackers had yet to replace him. They only had fifteen players on the field. In some strange way, that gave him hope that everything would somehow all work out for the best.

When the Mighties rolled out onto the field, the crowd erupted into laughter, all except for a sizeable halfling cheering section in along the eastern end of the field. The little fans rooted at the top of their lungs for their homeland heroes and were just as rowdy as any of the other spectators. Dunk noticed there were more beer vendors walking the aisles in the halfling section, selling Bloodweiser draughts in commemorative steins to all the thirsty fans there, who seemed able to drink twice their weight in cheap, watery beer.

The halflings went mad as the treeman strode onto the field. Thicktrunk Strongbranch towered over the field, dwarfing even M'Grash. He waved his leafy boughs at the crowd, greeting the fans of Mighties and taunting the Hacker Backers, as a blood-streaked banner a crew of battle-scarred rowdies standing well behind Dunk proclaimed the Bad Bay fans.

The Hacker Backers started to chant right away. 'The tree! The tree! The tree is on fire! We don't need no water! Let the bugger burn! Burn, bugger, burn!'

Strongbranch just smiled at them all as he sauntered out to the Mighties' end of the field.

The coin toss went to the Mighties, but that was the only thing that did. They elected to receive the ball. Gigia Mardretti kicked it deep into the Mighties territory, and one of the halflings pitched it to the treeman.

M'Grash was the first Hacker down the field. He lowered his shoulder and slammed into Strongbranch with all his incredible might.

The treeman struggled to stay upright, but it was a futile effort. The towering oak of a player toppled over backward, slowly at first and then accelerating to bone-crushing speed.

'Tiiiiiiim-beeeerrrrr!' the Hacker Backers sang in unison as the treeman was laid low.

Strongbranch dropped the ball as he fell, and Kur was there to scoop it up. An instant later, he was in the end zone, celebrating the Hackers' first touchdown.

Two of the Mighties had been standing in the wrong place when Strongbranch fell. A well-experienced crew of halfling litter bearers raced on to the field and carried them off. Two more players bravely took their place to the hooting of the Mighties' fans.

'Wow, Jim,' Bob's voice said as the teams set up for the Hackers to kick the ball again. 'That was a quick score. Isn't that some kind of record?'

'You'd think so, wouldn't you, Bob? The fastest score ever though was made in literally no time at all, since the clock doesn't start until someone touches the ball.'

'I think I remember that. Wasn't that Old Golden-hooves?'

'You got it, Bob! The centaur player was so fast that he reached the Elfheim Eagles' end zone before the kick-off hit the ground and caught it in the end zone!'

Dunk looked up towards the top of the stadium above the north end zone. There he saw a live Cabalvision broadcast of the game displayed on a massive white wall. The images of Jim and Bob chatting with each other flashed up for a moment, along with a grainy replay of that long-ago centaur score.

'The Mighties have only taken two casualties so far, Jim, so you owe me a crown!'

'Those little guys are tougher than they look, Bob. Let's go to our new sideline correspondent, the lovely Lästiges Weibchen, to get a report on how they're doing.'

Dunk stared in disbelief as Lästiges's face splashed onto the wall, her head alone taller than M'Grash.

'Thanks, Jim!' Lästiges said with a winning smile. 'It's not looking too good for Perry and Mippin down here. The Mighties' team apothecary tells me they won't be back on the field today. More stunning, they might even miss dinner tonight!'

The rising noise of the crowd drew Dunk's eyes away from the monstrous image to watch the next kick-off. As he scanned the sidelines he spotted Lästiges down there near the Mighties' bench, a fist-sized golden ball floating near her head, watching her and broadcasting the image via Cabalvision to the Wolf Sports team.

One of the halflings near Strongbranch caught the ball again. This time, instead of tossing the treeman the ball, the stubby player dashed into Strongbranch's arms.

'Throw him! Throw him! Throw him!' the crowd chanted as the treeman raised the halfling over his head. Dunk couldn't believe what he was seeing, but neither could he look away. Strongbranch reared back an arm, the one with the ball-carrying halfling in it, then hurled it down the field over the heads of everyone, including M'Grash who leaped up to try to knock the little guy down.

The halfling, who had rolled himself up into a well-armoured ball, went sailing down the field and hit the turf just shy of the end zone. From there, he bounced once and spun out flat, just on the other side of the goal line. The little guy stood up and stabbed a fat-fingered hand into the air. The ball was in it.

The crowd went nuts. Even the Hacker Backers cheered. Dunk found himself screaming his heart out for the little guy.

It was the last time the Mighties would score. Now wise to the treeman's strategy, the Hackers put two receivers back in their own end zone. They camped there until Strongbranch decided to try his halfling-hurling trick again.

When the halfling zoomed toward the end zone, Cavre stepped up and caught the flyer before he could land. Then he tucked the hapless halfling and the ball he was carrying under his arm and raced him all the way back down the field to the other end zone, scoring a touchdown for the Hackers instead.

Cavre was so excited by the strategy's success, he spiked the halfling along with the ball. The halfling litter bearers were already waiting in the end zone for this and toted the little guy off in seconds.

The rest of the game was a rout. The Hackers pounded the Mighties into the dirt, sometimes literally. After only six scores, the Mighties no longer had enough players left to field a whole team and had to concede the game.

The crowd rushed the field as the referees announced victory for the Hackers, and Dunk went down with them. He was careful to avoid the Hackers, though, for fear that his disguise wouldn't be enough to fool any of them. He knew that some of them, Kur in particular, wouldn't hesitate to turn him in for the bounty on his head.

As Dunk watched, a battalion of Hacker Backers upended Strongbranch, who toppled into the crowd to another rousing round of 'Tiiiiiiim-beeeerrrrr!' It was then that he felt a hook snag his shoulder. He turned to see Pegleg staring at him.

'That's quite a getup you have there, sir!' the coach shouted over the noise of the crowd to Dunk, his sea-grey eyes piercing right through the rookie. 'We hope to one day see our friend, Mr. Hoffnung, back among us!'

'I don't think it will be too much longer!' Dunk shouted back.

'Let's hope not!' Pegleg shouted. 'This team needs him more than he might know!'

'Tell us, coach!' Lästiges's voice shouted at Pegleg over Dunk's shoulder. 'How does it feel to be one step closer to the Blood Bowl?'

Pegleg shot a knowing glare at Dunk for a moment before devoting his attention to the reporter. 'Like coming home!' he shouted as Dunk slipped back into the crowd, not once looking back. 'Like coming home!'

 **CHAPTER THIRTY-TWO**

THE HACKERS PLAYED two more games in the playoffs. In the first, they faced off against the Underworld Creepers, a team made up of skaven and goblins who normally scrimmaged in the sewers of the largest cities in the Empire. The final score was 7 to 2, in favour of the Hackers. It wasn't much of a game after a pivotal moment in the first half.

As Dunk watched the game, he saw that one of the Creepers was smoking – and not tobacco. Smoke and sparks poured out of a black, round shell the lanky, green goblin had tucked under its arm as it raced down the field.

'Look, Jim,' said Bob's voice. 'Number fifty-eight, Gakdup Goremaker, seems to have a bomb!'

'He sure does, Bob! And look at him go! He's trying to get rid of that deep in Hacker territory.'

'For the folks at home, Jim, can you tell us if this sort of thing is legal?'

Jim's voice laughed. 'As in "within the proper rules of the game"? Of course not. But I can't remember a game featuring goblins that didn't feature some kind of cockamamie scheme. Do you remember the Pogo Stick of Doom?'

'Remember it? I think I'm still cleaning the turf out of my teeth after the last jump of the pogo stick's inventor Pogo Doomspider. Attaching a rocket to it in a game versus the Dwarf Warhammerers just wasn't too wise!'

Goremaker scrambled down the field, carrying his deadly cargo straight to Kur and tossing it into the surprised thrower's arms. Kur was no fool though. Even from Dunk's spot in the stands, he could see the thrower recognise the bomb for what it was instantly. He brought back his arm and fired it into the Creepers' dugout.

Dunk had been prepared for a loud blast, but the ear-splitting boom that followed almost deafened everyone in the Emperor's Bowl. From the large number of skaven and goblins that vacated the dugout as the bomb came in, Dunk could only guess that the Creepers had had a whole stockpile of explosives stored away there.

Despite the blast, play on the field didn't pause until M'Grash brought the ball into the end zone a full minute later. He'd have been there quicker if he hadn't stopped to kick every deafened goblin out of his way.

As the Hackers were setting up for the next kick-off, Wolf Sports cut down to Lästiges again. 'The Underworld

Creepers suffered a staggering ten casualties from that self-inflicted explosion,' she told the camra. 'Despite this and the restriction keeping the total number of players on a team to sixteen, the Creepers still have eleven eligible players ready to take the field.'

'That's goblin maths for you, Lästiges!' Jim's voice said.

'What happened with the referee this time?' Bob's voice said. 'Where was the penalty call?'

'The Creepers are old hands at this sort of mayhem, Bob,' Lästiges said. 'Apparently one of their cheerleaders slipped a small bomb down the referee's pants before Goremaker made his ill-fated dash for glory. I'm being told that he will not return to the game, leaving only one referee to cover the entire match.'

'No other referees are willing to step up?' asked Jim's voice.

'As you know, the high casualty rate among referees has crippled recruiting efforts. Besides this, most referees consider it horrible luck to take over in a game during which another zebra has already been slaughtered.'

THE NEXT GAME, the Hackers took on the fabled Elfheim Eagles, a team composed entirely of high elves, the most sophisticated, long-lived, and flat-out haughty people on the planet. Dunk wondered how the Gobbo would have allowed such a match-up. The honour of the high elves was legendary, and Dunk doubted there could be a Black Jersey among their number.

The captain and coach of the Eagles, Legless Warwren, spent much of the game raging at the referees, who'd clearly been bought. Dunk couldn't be sure whether the money had come from the Hackers' coffers or those of the Gobbos, but when he saw Kur kneecap an Eagles blitzer right in front of the end zone, and in full view of the orc ref standing there, he knew what had happened.

As honourable as they were, the Eagles refused to lower themselves to the Hackers' level and cheat, whether blatantly or not. They managed to complete the game, which was more than could be said for the Moot Mighties or the Underworld Creepers, but the outcome was never really in doubt.

ONCE THE PLAYOFFS were over and the tallies were in, the Hackers were the top-rated seed of the four teams to move on to the semi-finals, the others being the Reavers (of course); Da Deff Skwadd, a team of orcs hailing from the Badlands far to the Empire's south; the Dwarf Giants, a team of dwarfs from Karaz-a-Karak in the Worlds Edge Mountains.

As Da Deff Skwadd had barely squeaked into the semi-finals, their seeding pitted them against the Hackers, while the Reavers faced off against the Giants. Dunk hadn't heard much about the orcs, other than that they had a troll on their team and were all terrible at spelling. In the end, Dunk thought, it probably didn't matter much. If the Gobbo couldn't figure out a way to pay off a bunch of orcs to throw a game, he wasn't really trying.

Dunk almost hoped the Hackers would lose to Da Deff Skwadd. Then he wouldn't have to go through with his plans for the final game. Of course, he'd then be on the run with a huge bounty on his head for whatever might be left of his miserable life.

When the game came around, Dunk sat in the same spot as always. The other fans around him were just as rabid as he was about the game at this point, and they suited him fine. When the Hackers took the field at the start of the game, the Hacker Backers almost knocked each other out by cheering too hard. They were so worked up they all spent the entire game standing on their seats, screaming for more touchdowns and orc blood – not necessarily in that order.

It wasn't too far into the game when Dunk felt something tugging at his leg. He looked down to see Slick standing there in front of his seat, desperately beckoning him to sit.

Dunk slipped to his seat immediately. He knew that something horrible must be wrong if Slick had risked coming into this section of the stands. 'What is it?' he asked.

'Blaque and Whyte are here, son,' the halfling said.

'I figured they would be,' Dunk said. 'But how are they going to find me up here?'

'They were down in the dugout at the start of the game, questioning people. Kur wanted to give you up so badly I thought he'd start making up stuff in the hopes it would be true. The GWs were too sharp for him though and ignored him right away. Then I heard them say they'd start scouring the stands today. Blaque mentioned the Hacker Backers, and I knew I had to warn you.'

Dunk closed his eyes in frustration and then opened them. 'Did it ever occur to you,' he asked the halfling, 'that they might have known you were listening?'

Slick gasped. 'They said that so I would hear them? And then…' The halfling's face threatened to turn Hacker green. 'Oh, dear.'

Dunk popped up from his seat to peer around the stadium like a prairie dog in a sea of drunk, violent, and over-decorated people. As he craned his neck around, he saw the tall dwarf Blaque stomping down the aisle to his left. He glanced the other way and saw the short elf Whyte prancing down the aisle to his right. The two were matching time perfectly, and they would converge on his seat in mere seconds.

Dunk dunked back down and hissed at Slick. 'Let's scatter! They can't follow us both at once.'

'They only want you, son,' Slick said as he slapped a thick hand over his face, miserable with grief. 'I'm worthless.'

'If I do manage to get away, and I'm going to go for it right now, they'll go after you next. Now that you've shown that you're in contact with me, you're not safe either.'

A look of horror dawned on Slick's shamed face as the truth of Dunk's words hit him.

'Someone your size shouldn't have too much trouble hiding here for a few minutes. They're going to chase me out of here. When that happens, that's your chance.'

'What *are* you going to do, son?' Slick said, putting his hand on Dunk's arm.

'I'm making this up as I go,' Dunk confessed.

Blaque appeared at the end of the aisle, over Slick's shoulder. Dunk looked back and saw Whyte completing the pincer move from the other side. With the vast sea of people crowded around them, there was nowhere for the rookie to run.

Dunk jumped up and smacked the man next to him, a barely standing brute who'd tottered his way through every game so far, loyally screaming his lungs out for the Hackers. The man glared back at Dunk, who suddenly realised the man hadn't just had the Hackers' logo painted on the side of his shaved head. It was tattooed.

'What do *you* want?' the man screamed in Dunk's face, spittle flying as he spoke.

Dunk raised one knee and shouted. 'Give me a boost, pal! I'm going over!'

The drunk fan smiled and laced his fingers together in front of him. 'About time someone round here finally showed some bloody team spirit!' He shouted with a grin.

Dunk put his boot in the man's hands and then jumped up. As he did, the man pulled upward, shoving Dunk high into the air. 'Body pass!' The drunk shouted as his hands came over his head.

The people all around turned their heads in time for them to toss up their hands and catch Dunk. The rookie breathed a sigh of relief as he felt a dozen hands cradle him for a moment. He'd seen crowds that were just too drunk or mean to care drop people instead of grabbing them, and the last thing he needed was to land headfirst on the stone steps right in front of Blaque and Whyte.

The crowd beneath him started to pass him up toward the top of the stadium, just as they had during Dunk's first game. Visions of hurtling over the top of the Emperor Stadium flashed through his head as he spotted the GWs turn tail and head back toward their aisles. If they couldn't catch him now, they'd just follow him until it was safe.

Dunk reached down and grabbed one of the fans holding him. It was a tall burly man with a blood-red mohawk and a set of piercings that followed cheek-bones sharp enough to cut diamonds.

'Leggo, deader!' the man shouted. 'You're going over!'

'No!' Dunk insisted. 'I got up here for one reason only. I want to kiss a Hackette before I die!'

The Hackettes were the Hackers' squad of professional cheerleaders. They were uniformly gorgeous in the kind of way that Dunk couldn't really fathom but from a distance. He'd never even stood close to them, for two reasons. First, they only showed up at real games, and Dunk was either in the dugout, on the field, or nursing a possible concussion at those times. Second, Pegleg absolutely forbade even a conversation with these ebullient young beauties for fear it would distract the players from the task at hand; winning the game.

The fans all around Dunk roared with approval at his choice of how to end his life. They all suspected that the security guards that protected the ladies would tear Dunk into tiny bits. The burly guards, often washouts from one Blood Bowl team or another, or a former player who'd taken one too many blows to the head, were rumoured to be testy because they supposedly had to be castrated to take the job, although Dunk had no proof that this was true. He hoped that whatever the reason, the guards would be in a less-than-murderous mood when he landed before them.

Being passed down toward the field went faster than being pushed toward the top. As Dunk slid along the raised hands of the people in front of him, he looked back to see Blaque and Whyte turn around and then race down after him. As they got closer to the bottom rows, they had to fight their way through the rowdiest of the spectators, people who had left their seats to stand at the bottom of the aisle and were strong and tough enough to maintain their positions against all rivals.

Dunk grinned, but as he reached the restraining wall that supposedly kept the fans from the field, he braced himself. The last of the fans, the ones who were standing in the front row, right in front of the lovely Hackettes, gave him the kind of heave-ho that only comes with lots of practice and tossed him straight over the heads of the guards.

Two of the ladies linked their arms together and caught Dunk as he hurtled into their midst. He smiled at them as they set him down gently. They returned the favour with dazzling grins.

'My undying thanks,' Dunk managed to say.

'It happens all the time,' one of the women said, a stunning blonde with bright blue eyes. 'Someone isn't paying attention and his friends decide to send him for a ride.'

'We used to beat the guys senseless,' a ravishing brunette with an amazing tan said. 'Then one of them managed to tell us it wasn't his fault.'

A mind-blowing redhead stepped up and said, 'Since then, we've been a bit gentler with the guys. After all, who can blame them for wanting to get a closer look?'

The rest of the women giggled. Dunk wondered if the stadium had suddenly gotten a lot warmer or if it was just him.

'Of course, we're not really the ones you should be worried about,' the blonde said. 'It's them.'

Dunk turned to see a pair of guards charging toward him. They looked like they'd been castrated that morning and were looking to take out their aggravations on someone.

'Hey, ladies,' Dunk said, pointing up towards Blaque and Whyte, who had just managed to finally fight their way through the fans on the other side of the restraining wall. 'You see those two guys with the Wolf Sports robes? Network executives.'

The cheerleaders squealed with delight and charged toward the two Game Wizards, sweeping the guards back with them. The two men were charged with protecting the women, so they went along with them rather than chasing down Dunk.

The rookie smiled to himself as he raced toward the tunnel that led to the team locker rooms. In less than a minute, he lost himself in the maze of passageways that riddled the underside of the stadium and left Blaque and Whyte and the rigged semi-final game far behind.

CHAPTER THIRTY-THREE

DUNK WATCHED THE rest of the game in a sports pub he picked out at random, a place known as the Spiked Ball, and then stuck around for the second game too. The Reavers handed the Giants their heads – sometimes literally. This means the Hackers would end up playing the Reavers in the finals, just as Dunk had hoped.

Dunk wanted to meet with Slick somewhere, but he didn't dare go to Slag End or to Slick's hotel. The GWs would follow the halfling around if they could find him, and Dunk just couldn't take that risk. He thought about going to the Skinned Cat to see some familiar faces, but he feared the Gobbo might show up there. He didn't want to see Gunther until the final match.

Dunk had a week until the next game, and he spent most of that time working out and moving around a lot. Since the GWs had seen him in his fan costume, he had to change his look again. He washed his head clean and got rid of his replica jersey. Soon he hoped to be wearing the real thing again.

In Beggars Square, Dunk picked up a new outfit: the simple brown robes of a monk and a fist-sized football carved from wood and spiked with blackened nails, Nuffle's holy symbol, hanging from a rough length of jute around his neck. Dunk pulled the hood low over his head as many of the penitents did during these wild days in Altdorf to serve as an example of restraint. They stood out like bears in a beehive, but everyone in town considered them sacrosanct and left them alone. No one ever bothered one of Nuffle's own, especially during the Blood Bowl tournament, for fear of jinxing both themselves and their favourite teams. As long as Dunk didn't run into some other monks who tried to drag him along to services in one of the churches that spotted the town, he would be just fine.

THE NIGHT BEFORE the big game, Dunk set his plan into motion. To guarantee a loss for the Hackers, he'd have to play for them, and that meant getting back on the team. It wasn't going to be easy to arrange, but Dunk didn't see how he had a choice.

Still dressed as one of Nuffle's monks, Dunk strolled into the Jaeger Inn, one of the handful of first-class hotels located near Emperor Stadium. The teams who played in the Blood Bowl tournament stayed in these places, so much so it was almost impossible for anyone else in the area to take a room here.

Dunk walked straight to the Jaeger's private dining hall and let himself in. The doors were guarded, but when he pulled back his hood for an instant to reveal his face, the sentries were so stunned they let him in. He was still a part of the Hackers after all.

Inside the dining hall, Pegleg was just finishing a toast when Dunk walked in and stood at the foot of the table. Every eye in the room turned to look at the man in the monk's robes, unable to see who he really was under his hood. The murmur of voices in the room fell silent.

It was Pegleg, standing at the head of the table, who broke the silence. 'To what do we owe this honour, good brother?' he asked. 'Are you here to tell us that Nuffle himself has blessed our efforts and that we can expect him in our dugout tomorrow afternoon?'

The rest of the Hackers laughed nervously at this. Then all fell silent again.

Dunk reached up and drew back his hood, exposing his face and head. The collective gasp almost sucked every bit of air from the room.

'Mr. Hoffnung,' Pegleg said, 'welcome back.'

No one else said a word. Down at the far end of the table, next to Pegleg, Slick gave Dunk a hearty smile and wave.

'It's good to be back,' Dunk said.

'It's a pity you can't stay long,' Kur said as he stood up from his spot halfway down the table. 'We have no place for murderers here.'

The rest of the team burst into peals of nervous laughter at this. When they were finished, Dunk spoke.

'I heard you might need another thrower for the final game.'

Kur sneered at the rookie. 'We've gotten this far without you, punk. We don't need anyone's help, especially not yours.'

Dunk smiled knowingly. 'That's not what the papers are saying, especially after those three interceptions you threw against the Da Deff Skwadd. Those orcs picked you off more often than they picked their noses.'

'That was all part of my plan,' Kur said, although Dunk was sure no one in the room, Kur included, believed it. 'I just put the ball deep into their territory so we could take it from them there. Those moronic orcs never stood a chance. I could have taken on the whole lot myself.'

Dunk had seen Kur say the same thing on Cabalvision in an on-field interview with Lästiges after the game. 'I think the orcs would love to see you try that,' he said.

Kur stepped away from the table. 'Isn't there a fat bounty on your head?'

'Better that than to have a bountiful, fat head like yours.'

Kur strode toward Dunk and stood in the rookie's face. Their eyes met and locked. They were still the same height, but Dunk had filled out over the course of the last year and was just as broad across the chest as the veteran. The week's worth of stubble on his head made him look harder than his shaggy locks ever had. He was more than ready to stand toe to toe with Kur.

'I'm claiming you for your bounty,' Kur said. Dunk thought he detected a hint of desperation behind the veterans' bravado, and he smiled.

'Sorry, *old* man,' Dunk said. 'You have to catch me first.'

Kur's hands snaked out and caught Dunk by the collar of his robe and held him fast. 'That's easily enough – ow!'

Dunk smashed his forehead into Kur's sharp nose, smashing it flat. Despite the shock and pain, Kur refused to let go of Dunk's robes, even as the blood poured from his face.

Dunk threw up his arm and bent over, letting his robes slip right over his head. Kur, who'd been trying to hold Dunk in place, staggered backwards and fell into the end of the table, striking the back of his head on its edge.

Kur grabbed the back of his head and brought his hand around to his face. It was coated with blood. On his knee now, he glared up at Dunk and snarled. 'I'll skin your skull!'

All eyes in the room went to Dunk, who stood framed in the doorway, wearing a Deff Skwadd jersey. 'Give it a try,' he said with a cocky smile. Then he turned and fled.

Dunk raced down the hall and out the front door of the Jaeger Inn. As he ran down the brightly lit boulevard, dodging back and forth through the people milling about the crowded streets, he could hear Kur stomping after him.

Dunk charged around the next corner and then another, each time far enough head of Kur that the rookie could still be seen but not caught. As Kur got closer, Dunk ducked through a rough door, over which hung a sign that depicted an elf's decapitated head.

A pair of hands grabbed at Dunk as he raced through the dimly lit place, but he spun away from them, just as he'd been trained to shake a tackle. Dunk smiled at that, knowing that Pegleg would have been proud.

Dunk raced down a corridor and stopped dead in front of a pair of double doors that barely hung on their hinges. In the room beyond, he could hear plates and steins clanging, accompanied by rough words and off-key songs. For a moment, he worried that he'd lost Kur at the door, that he'd not been able to shake the bouncer as Dunk had. Then he saw the starting thrower appear at the end of the hallway.

'Nowhere to run?' Kur said, venom dripping from his voice. Dunk saw that the man had the punch-dagger from his belt in his fist. Fresh blood dripped from its blade.

Dunk stepped back until he had both hands on the doors behind him. He pressed back against them and felt them give.

'You're as dumb as you are weak,' Kur said as he stalked down the hallway. 'First, you take the fall for all those killings, including some that I committed. Then, you show up at our dinner to ask for your job back when there's a 20,000-crown bounty on your head.'

'I didn't realised they'd upped it,' Dunk said.

'They made an even better change too,' Kur said as he came within striking distance and brought his blade high. This was it, Dunk knew as he leaned back into the doors behind him and braced for the attack.

'Now,' Kur said, 'it's "dead or alive".'

Kur roared as he charged at Dunk and drove his bloodied blade home. Dunk grabbed Kur's arms as he stepped back into the room beyond. Then he spun and used Kur's momentum to throw the man behind him with all his might.

Kur sailed through the air for a moment before he came crashing down into a battered dining table. He landed in the remnants of a platter of roasted boar and skidded along the length of the table until he came to rest near the head.

Kur looked up to see more than a dozen gruesome, green-skinned creatures with rough, tusk-filled mouths gaping wide at him as they glared down through wide, yellow eyes. The room had fallen silent, except for one slurred voice in a corner somewhere rasping out the last refrain of a drinking song.

'Kur Ritternacht, starting thrower for the Bad Bay Hackers,' Dunk announced brightly to the orcs assembled around the room, who stared first at Kur, who was still lying on their banquet table, and then him. Dunk pointed to the red Deff Skwadd jersey he wore. Then, before he backed out of the room and closed the doors behind him, he called out, 'Consider him a gift from a fan!'

The screams and pleas for pity that emanated from Da Deff Skwadd's year-end dinner followed Dunk all the way out to the street. He tried to stop himself from smiling but failed utterly.

THE NEXT MORNING, Slick and Dunk reported for the game at the Hackers' locker room as if nothing had happened. Dunk wore another set of monk's robes to the stadium, and Slick used his personal pass to walk him straight past the tight security.

Once inside the locker room, Dunk held back near the exit and Slick walked straight up to Pegleg. The coach didn't wait for the halfling to speak before laying into him. He snagged Slick's shoulder with his hand and said, 'What kind of stunt was that your boy pulled last night, Mr. Fullbelly? It's less than an hour before the biggest game in this team's history, and I don't have a single thrower to show for it!'

Pegleg held up his hook, which had a deflated football impaled on the end of it. 'I even thought of playing the position myself,' he said, 'but I'm just not equipped for it!'

'Calm yourself, Pegleg,' Slick said smoothly. 'Don't fear. I have the solution for you right here.'

The halfling motioned to Dunk, who drew back his hood again and strode up to Pegleg. 'Ready and reporting for duty, coach,' he said.

'Dunkel!' M'Grash cheered. Everyone else in the room simply gaped at the rookie as if he were some sort of ghost.

Pegleg frowned and narrowed his eyes at the thrower. 'You had this in mind all along, didn't you, Mr. Hoffnung?'

Dunk started to nod proudly, but Pegleg cut him short, brandishing his football-blunted hook at him. 'I should gut you right here!' he shouted.

M'Grash stepped forward and covered Pegleg's hook and ball with a monstrous hand. 'Don't!' he growled. Then he grinned broadly at Dunk. 'My friend!'

Dunk winked at the ogre then stared coldly back at his coach. 'If you'd rather I leave,' he started.

At that moment, the door to the locker room slammed open, and Blaque and Whyte stormed in, their wands out and crackling. 'Hold it right there!' Blaque shouted at Dunk.

'It's the Game Wizards,' Slick said in a not terribly convincing tone. 'Thank Nuffle you're here!'

The halfling walked over to Dunk and took him by the hand. 'Come with me, son,' he said as he led Dunk over to stand in front of the two GWs, who stood there panting for breath.

'You've led us on a merry chase,' Blaque said to Dunk between deep breaths. 'But it ends here.'

'That it does, my friends,' Slick said as he presented Dunk to the pair. 'I'm pleased to finally hand over this dangerous threat to you.'

Blaque shot Slick a curious look. 'The Game Wizards thank you,' he said slowly. 'Now, what's your game?'

'No game,' Slick said. 'I just want to make sure that you know that it was Slick Fullbelly who placed Dunk Hoffnung in your hands, right in front of all these wonderful witnesses.'

'You sawed-off bastard,' Dunk growled. 'I thought I could count on you!'

'You can mull that over all you like, son,' Slick said with a self-satisfied grin, 'while I count every crown in that bounty.'

Blaque looked to Whyte. The elf just shrugged at him and put his hand on Dunk's shoulder.

'Now wait just a minute,' Pegleg said, his voice coated with menace. 'Where do you two think you're going with my thrower?'

'We're taking him back to headquarters for now. We'll schedule a disciplinary hearing after that,'

Blaque said. 'You'll be invited to testify on his behalf.'

'Once you get him to wherever you're taking him,' Pegleg said, 'he'll only be good for playing for the Champions of Death, I'm sure. I need him now!'

Whyte stopped binding Dunk's hands behind his back with a length of thin rope.

'What happened to Kur?' Blaque said, glancing around the locker room for the veteran.

Pegleg glared at Dunk for an instant before answering. 'He took a wrong turn somewhere last night and fell into the wrong hands. He won't be playing for some time, maybe months, and I need a thrower today!'

'Let me play,' Dunk said to the GWs. 'Let me play one last time before you take me away.'

Unsure about all this, Blaque turned to Whyte. 'Now that we finally have our hands on this fugitive, does it make sense at all to let him go?'

The elf shook his head slowly. 'I just can't see it.'

'I'll turn myself back over to you right after the game,' Dunk said. 'You have my word on it.'

Blaque burst into laughter at that. Whyte just stood there stoically until his partner finished.

'You want us to take the word of a Blood Bowl player?' Blaque finally said. 'You *are* a rookie.'

'A rookie who's been bringing in some top ratings!' a voice thundered from the locker room's entrance. All heads turned to see an angular man in the bright blue robes of a Wolf Sports wizard stroll in through the doorway, his close-cropped white hair swept back in a tight widow's peak. The smug look on his face told people he thought he owned the place. The phalanx of weapon-bristling bodyguards who surrounded him only emphasised the attitude.

'Ruprect Murdark!' Slick blurted as everyone else in the locker room gasped. 'My, what a coincidence that the owner of the Wolf Sports network would grace us with a visit right now.'

The wizard favoured Slick with an arrogant wink. 'A true mystery that,' he said, 'but that will have to wait for later! Right now, I'm more concerned with that young man's fate!'

Blaque and Whyte lined up on either side of Dirk and grabbed him by his elbows. 'We were just bringing him in, Mr. Murdark,' Blaque said eagerly.

'You're not taking him anywhere!' the wizard pronounced. His spotless and stylish robes swirled about him as he spoke. 'Think of the ratings!'

'I'm sorry, sir,' Blaque said. 'I don't believe I understand your meaning.'

'I said, "think of the ratings". Dunk Hoffnung, player on the run, returns to the game for one last match, in the Blood Bowl itself!' Murdark held up his fingers in a wide circle, as if framing a crystal ball.

'The ratings will go through the roof! I only wish I had more time to publicise it! This is high drama! Blood Bowl at its best!'

'But sir…' Dunk felt the Game Wizards' grips tighten on him as if he might be torn from their grasp at any moment.

'No "buts"' Murdark said. 'That man plays today! Let him go, or I'll fire you both on the spot!' Sparks of energy crackled between the wizard's fingers as he spoke, the electric arcs dancing wildly in his eyes. 'And that will be the least of your troubles!'

Blaque turned as pale as Whyte. The dwarf gaped at Murdark for a moment, then glanced over at the elf, his eyes pleading for some kind of advice. Whyte had none to give.

The dwarf grimaced as he looked up at Dunk and said, 'All right. One last game.'

'Don't get your robes in a bunch!' Murdark said with a smug smile. 'You can arrest him again right after the game! No better way to cap a Blood Bowl tournament than a public execution!'

Dunk shot a frightened look at Slick. The halfling shrugged at him with a nervous smile. 'That's entertainment,' he said.

CHAPTER THIRTY-FOUR

'BLOOD BOWL FANS of all ages,' Bob's voice said, ringing out over Emperor Stadium, 'welcome to the ninety-eighth Blood Bowl!'

The roar shook the stadium to its roots and gave Dunk reason to wonder if a sufficiently loud noise could actually stop a beating heart. Standing in the dugout, he stared out at the stands before him and held his breath. This was the sort of adulation and attention reserved only for kings and emperors, and only rarely then. Dragon slayers never rated this.

To start the game, Jim and Bob announced the names of each of the players on both teams as they trotted out to the centre of the freshly re-laid Astro-granite field, waving at the crowd and absorbing the raw power of all that intense, nearly tangible emotion focused on them. The announcers got through all of the names on both of the team lists, and Dunk found himself standing his the Hackers' dugout alone. For a moment, he feared that Blaque and Whyte had changed their minds and would snatch up him there on the spot. Then he heard Bob's voice again.

'Last, but certainly not least, we have the Hacker's starting thrower: Kuuuuurrr–'

'Hold it, Bob,' Jim's voice said. 'We have a last-minute substitution here. It's – Nuffle's spiked balls! In as the Hacker's starting thrower: Dunkel Hoffnung!'

The crowd went insane. Dunk kept his head down and trotted out to the middle of the field where the rest of his team was waiting for him. As he did, he saw Dirk and Spinne standing with the Reavers on the other side of the referee holding the game coin in the middle of the field. They stared at him with open mouths.

'Talk about the comeback of the year!' Bob's voice said.

Dunk raised his hand to acknowledge the crowd's exultant roar of approval. As he did, he knew that he'd play this game until the day he died. There was simply no better place for him to be.

The Hackers won the coin toss, and Cavre informed the ref that the team would receive the ball. When the two teams met to shake hands before heading to their own ends of the field, Dirk and Spinne grabbed Dunk.

'What are you doing here?' Dirk demanded. 'The GWs will haul you in for sure.'

'They already have,' Dunk said. 'I'm just here to do a job.'

'What could that possibly be?' Spinne asked.

Dunk discovered that he enjoyed the note of concern in her voice. 'If I help the Hackers lose the game, the Gobbo will pin all the killings on Zauberer instead. I'll be a free man.'

Dirk and Spinne glanced at each other, looks of horror painted on their faces.

'Can I count on your help?' Dunk asked.

Dirk grimaced. 'Normally, sure, but…'

'What is it?'

Spinne spoke up. 'Skragger has promised to kill you, Dirk, and everyone else in your family if the Reavers win, especially if Dirk scores three more touchdowns and breaks Skragger's record.'

Dunk grabbed Dirk by his shoulder pad. 'He knows where the rest of our family is?'

'He claims to,' Dirk said. 'I'm not willing to risk it.'

The whistle blew to start the game. 'What's the worse fate?' Dunk asked. 'Death or prison?'

Dirk frowned before he answered. 'You brought it on yourself, Dunk.'

Dirk turned and trotted down to the Reavers' end of the field. Spinne looked after him in shock for a moment, then turned and gave Dunk a quick kiss. 'I'll talk to him,' she said. 'Wish me luck.'

Dunk nodded at her as she took off running. 'I hope you kick our asses.'

'Did you see that, Bob?' Jim's voice said.

'I sure did, Jim! It looks like the rivalry between two of the players down there might be more than just friendly! Let's see that again!'

Dunk looked up at the massive image displayed on the wall over the end zone and saw Spinne kiss him. The crowed hooted like mad as Dunk strapped on his helmet to hide how much he was blushing.

Moments later, the kick-off sailed down the field toward the Hackers. Cavre fielded the ball and then pitched it over to Dunk.

Dunk fell in step behind M'Grash, who bowled over a pair of Reavers trying to get past him. Then Dunk stepped back and hurled the ball downfield.

The throw sailed wide over the head of Gigia Mardretti and landed in Spinne's outstretched hands instead.

'Wow!' Bob's voice said. 'It looks like Hoffnung has just given his girlfriend an early birthday present! You don't see turnovers that clean every day!'

Before Jim's voice could respond, Gigia charged into Spinne and knocked her flat. The ball rolled from her grasp, and the Hackers' catcher scooped it up. Another Reaver hit her before she could go another step and the ball game rolled on.

Within minutes the Hackers had scored their first touchdown as Andreas Waltheim ran the ball into the end zone. Dirk should have been able to bring him down, but he seemed to have tripped when trying to tackle the Hacker blitzer.

After the next kick-off, Dirk got the ball and hurled it down the field straight toward Dunk. He caught the ball and ran towards M'Grash again. This time, he flipped the ball to the ogre and shouted, 'Cavre's open. Throw it!'

To Dunk's knowledge, the ogre had never thrown the ball before in his life. Dunk was sure that M'Grash had plenty of strength for the job, but that wasn't all there was to throwing the football. He watched as the ogre slung back his arm and then fired it down the field toward the distant Cavre.

A Reaver blitzer dashed over and got in front of the ball. It hit him like a warhammer and knocked him flat, but he kept a hold of it, perhaps because of how it had dented his armour. A nearby Reaver lineman gathered the ball up from his fallen friend and raced it back toward the end zone.

Dunk saw M'Grash heading for the lineman and waved the ogre off. 'I got him!' he shouted as he ran toward the ball carrier. The lineman hung out a stiff arm which Dunk promptly collided with and moments later the Reavers' had their own first touchdown.

By HALF-TIME, THE Reavers had a 3 to 2 lead over the Hackers. As Dunk and the rest of the players filed into their locker room, Pegleg grabbed the thrower with his hook and pulled him aside.

Out of earshot of the rest of the team, alone in the tunnel, Pegleg shoved his hook into Dunk's face and said, 'What in Nuffle's sacred rules are you doing out there?'

Dunk decided to play dumb. 'I don't know, coach. I guess I'm still a bit slow from so many weeks off. It's coming back to me though. I'll make it up in the second half.'

'That's not what I'm talking about, and you know it, Mr. Hoffnung,' Pegleg hissed. 'You're moving around just fine out there. Too well, in fact, for how rotten you're playing. Answer me this,' he said. 'Are you trying to lose this game?'

Dunk hesitated. He wanted to come clean about what he was doing. Maybe the coach could even help him out. He knew that Pegleg wanted to win the game, but perhaps he could see that a loss would be in the Hackers' long-term interests. After all, it would ensure that both Dunk and M'Grash would be able to keep playing for the team. Otherwise, the Hackers would be gutted.

Dunk looked Pegleg straight in the eye and said, 'Yes.'

Pegleg backhanded Dunk with the blunt side of his hook, knocking the thrower to the ground. 'Are you out of your damned mind?' he raged at the rookie.

'But coach!' Dunk said, cowering before the man's wrath. 'Let me explain.'

'There is *nothing* to explain!' Pegleg roared. 'You have betrayed the trust of *every* member of this team.'

'But–' Dunk ducked under another swipe from the coach's hook, this time with the sharpened end.

'But nothing! I can only assume, Mr. Hoffnung, that someone got to you somehow. This is *not* the man I've watched develop into one of the most promising Blood Bowl players I've ever seen. This is *not* the man who's gone from a dilettante to a dedicated leader.'

Pegleg leaned over Dunk and shook his hook at him. 'I don't know what they promised you, Mr. Hoffnung. Money, women. Maybe they threatened your life. *None* of that matters now because you're life ends *here!*'

Before Pegleg could slash Dunk's neck open with his hook, Dunk lashed out and knocked the coach's legs from under him.

'This is about my life, M'Grash's life, and the fate of this team,' Dunk grunted as he leapt on top of the coach and pinned him to the ground. 'If we lose this game, Gunther the Gobbo will provide us with a patsy to pin all those murders on.'

'If you really killed all those people, Mr. Hoffnung, then good riddance to you!' Pegleg snarled as he struggled to pry his hook free from Dunk's grasp.

'I didn't do it,' Dunk said. 'It was M'Grash!'

Pegleg stopped wrestling against Dunk for a moment. The look in his eyes was tired but still defiant. 'So,' he said, 'you're telling me that Mr. Gobbo will provide you and M'Grash, two of my best players, with a clean slate should you lose the game for him?'

Dunk nodded. 'It's all part of Black Jerseys conspiracy of his. He sets the odds the way he likes and then forces the game to go the way that earns him the most money.'

'Of course he does, Mr. Hoffnung.'

Dunk nearly let go of the coach, but he remembered the man's vicious hook just in time to keep from being gutted. 'You know about this?'

'I read, Mr. Hoffnung, and I've been coaching this team for a long time.' Pegleg squinted up at Dunk. 'You know what the most stunning thing about this year has been?'

'Getting to play in the Blood Bowl.'

'Certainly, but more than that. It's that I know this isn't our year. We didn't get here on our own. Someone arranged for it.'

'The Gobbo,' Dunk said, exasperated that Pegleg wasn't getting it.

'No, Mr. Hoffnung,' Pegleg said softly. 'It was me.'

This time Dunk did let go of the coach. He leapt backward before Pegleg could renew his attack, but

the coach's hook didn't twitch as he scrambled up
against the wall.

'I am part of the Black Jerseys, Mr. Hoffnung,' Pegleg said as he sat up and placed his back against the
tunnel 's opposite wall. 'I persuaded Mr. Gobbo to
make us the champions this year. I promised him half
of our purses all the way through the tournament in
exchange for his help.'

'You... you were behind it?' Dunk couldn't even
believe the words as they left his lips.

Pegleg nodded slowly. 'And now you tell me that
I've been double-crossed.' He doffed his yellow tricorn. The wig attached to it came off too, and he sat
there with his grey stubble showing.

'I knew it would happen eventually,' Pegleg said. 'I
just didn't know when. I'd hoped...' He fell silent for
a moment, and Dunk wondered if he was about to
cry.

'I'd hoped it would be next season, sometime, *any-
time*, after this game.' Pegleg crumpled up the hat and
wig in his hands. 'Just once,' he said, staring dully into
Dunk's eyes. 'Just once, I wanted to be a *champion*.'

Dunk reached out and put his hand on Pegleg's
knee. 'Coach,' he said, 'I think there's still a chance
that could happen.'

CHAPTER THIRTY-FIVE

As Dunk charged back out through the tunnel after the rest of the team for the game's second half, Slick reached up and caught his arm. 'Hold on a moment, son,' he said. 'I have someone who wants to have a chat with you.'

Fearing it was the Gobbo, Dunk tried to pull away. 'Not now, Slick,' he said, 'I have a game to play.'

Slick grabbed on with both hands, though, and insisted. 'Trust me, son,' he said. 'I set up a quick interview with you on live Cabalvision. Think what it'll do for your career!'

'Look,' Dunk stopped and said, 'you should get out of here, distance yourself from me.'

Slick narrowed his eyes at Dunk. 'Now why would I do something like that, son?'

Dunk grimaced and checked to make sure no one else was listening. The tunnel was empty again. 'I'm going to double-cross the Gobbo. From here on out, I'm playing to win.'

Slick grinned. 'You don't know how pleased I am to hear that.' Then he grew concerned again. 'But what about the GWs? The only reason I turned you in there was I figured you'd go free at the end of the game. If that was so, then why let all that lovely reward money go to waste.'

Slick reached down and tousled the halfling's curly hair. 'I figured,' he said. Then he sighed. 'I'm not sure what I'm going to do about them. Right now, I'm just going to play the best game I can and let the dragon's scales fall where they may.'

Slick grinned. 'In that case, you really should do this interview.'

Dunk let out a good-natured groan and let his agent lead him by the hand out of the tunnel. When he emerged into the sunlight, the crowd roared its approval. Before he could turn to acknowledge it, he found Lästiges stepping right into his face.

'Thanks, Jim!' the reporter said to someone Dunk couldn't see as she turned to him. He noticed a small golden ball hovering next to them, a small, eye-sized hole pointing first and her and then him, flickering back and forth between the two.

'I'm down here on the field with Dunk Hoffnung, the rookie sensation slash mass murderer, whose story seems to have taken Blood Bowl fans every-where by storm.' Dunk heard Lästiges voice booming above him like that of some sharp-tongued goddess. The crowd cheered in response to her words.

'Tell me, Dunk,' Lästiges said as the eye in the golden ball pointed toward the thrower, 'how does it feel to be playing in what we're told will be your last game with the Hackers?'

Dunk grinned. 'Don't tell me they're talking about trading me already.' His voice boomed alongside Lästiges's – or so it seemed. He was sure he couldn't really sound so confident as that voice did.

Lästiges smiled like a crocodile at Dunk's response. 'I'm referring to the bounty placed on your head, which the Game Wizards tell me was claimed by your former agent. Tell me how it must have felt to be betrayed like that.'

Dunk just smiled again. 'My *current* agent, you mean,' he said, gesturing down to Slick standing beside him. The floating camra pointed down at the halfling, who watched himself waving at the crowd, his face almost fifty feet high. 'Anyone who can get that kind of money out of Wolf Sports is a keeper! My only question is whether I get the standard ten percent!'

Lästiges smiled wider, and this time it almost seemed real. 'Rumour has it you tricked Da Deff Skwadd into nearly beating to death Kur Ritternacht last night, opening the way to your start in today's game. Can you comment on that?'

Dunk opened his mouth but then slammed it shut again when he saw someone hobbling up behind Lästiges on a new set of crutches. 'Here comes Kur right now,' he said, pointing at the veteran thrower who was stamping his way along the sidelines toward Dunk. 'Why don't you ask him yourself? I've got a championship to win!'

With that, Dunk trotted on to the field, leaving Lästiges and Kur behind. As he went, he heard Slick say, 'That's an amazing rig you have there, miss. Do you mind if I have a look at it?'

The second half of the game was much different than the first. Before the two teams lined up for the kick-off, Dunk met Dirk and Spinne in the centre of the field again.

'New game plan,' Dunk announced with a grin. 'We're going to whoop your ass.'

Spinne was stunned. 'You're not worried about the Game Wizards?'

'It's a trick,' Dirk said, measuring his brother's reaction.

Dunk shook his head. 'I'm not worried about any of that anymore. Just look around you. See where we are.' He flung his arms wide as if he could throw then around the entire stadium. 'This is the Blood Bowl. *The Blood Bowl*. We may never have a chance to play in a game like this again. I don't know about you, but I'm not going to waste it on someone like Skragger or Gunther the Gobbo.'

Dirk frowned. 'Nothing's changed. You just want us to try to beat you.'

'No,' Spinne said, intrigued. 'I think he's serious.'

'You can *try* to beat us,' Dunk said, 'but you're going to have to play your best to do it.'

'If you want to win so badly, why tell us?' Spinne asked.

Dunk smiled at her and then chucked his brother on the side of his helmet. 'I'd love to win, but I came here to *play!*'

The whistle blew, and Dunk trotted into his position at the far end of the field, so excited to finally play for real that he practically bounced along the

Astrogranite. When the ball came sailing through the air, he made a running dive and came up with it. Directing Kai, Henrik, Lars, and Karsten to form a line for him, he made some good yardage forward while Cavre and Simon blasted downfield to get open for a pass.

Meanwhile, Dunk motioned for M'Grash to get in front of him and charge forward. Dunk pumped his arm downfield, faking a pass to Carve, then blasted right through the hole the ogre had opened for him. He was halfway to the end zone before any of the Reavers came close to touching him, and he raced straight past them.

Only Dirk stood between Dunk and the goal line now. As Dunk sprinted closer to where his brother waited for him, he could see that the younger Hoff-nung still hadn't made up his mind about whether or not Dunk was really here to play, and he smiled to himself.

Dirk had the angle on Dunk and came at him just shy of the end zone. Rather than trying to juke around his brother, Dunk lowered his shoulder and drove into him as hard as he could, his legs pumping like a stallion at full gallop.

Dunk smashed into Dirk's chest and knocked his brother back into the end zone. He followed after him, holding the ball into the air as he crossed the goal line, soaking up the crowd's rabid cheers.

As he passed by Dirk, Dunk spiked the ball right into his brother's helmet. It bounced high off Dirk's head and landed in the stands. The fans there went wild, screaming, 'Dunk! Dunk! Dunk!'

Dirk stood up and beckoned for his older brother to come over to him. When Dunk complied, the two butted their helmets against each other like rutting rams.

'All right,' Dirk said. 'You wanna play? Let's go!'

With the score now tied, it was a real game once again. The Hackers and Reavers faced off against each other like two punch-drunk boxers, throwing everything they had into every punch, hoping for a knockout blow.

The Reavers scored next. Dirk connected with Spinne for a long bomb that put her in the end zone. Dunk raced up behind Spinne, hoping to intercept the ball, but it was just out of his reach. He then tried to tackle her, but she put on a burst of speed and left him in her dust.

As Spinne danced around the end zone, celebrating her victory, Dunk had the chance to take a cheap shot at her and knock her into the stands. Instead, he crept up behind her, tapped her on the shoulder, and said, 'Boo!'

Spinne nearly jumped out of her armour, and Dunk dashed away before she could take her revenge. The crowd exploded into laughter and shouted for more.

When the next kick-off came to the Hackers, M'Grash somehow ended up with the ball and managed not to drop it. Confused, the ogre glanced around for some sort of direction. He was used to hitting people carrying the ball, not handling it himself.

'Go, go, go!' Dunk shouted. 'I'm right behind you!'

With a wild, ear-shattering howl, M'Grash launched himself straight down the field like a mad bull, only much more dangerous and bigger. Reaver after Reaver stepped up to take him on, only to find themselves face down in the Astrogranite. Eventually they brought him down, only yards from the end zone, but it took six of them to do it, one on each limb another on his head, and the last, Dirk, stripping the ball.

Dirk landed hard and rolled away from M'Grash before the ogre toppled over onto him but held on to the ball and scrambled to his feet. Looking downfield, he didn't have anyone open. Most of his team was still prying themselves loose from M'Grash. So he tucked the ball under his arm and sprinted ahead.

Dunk knew that he had to stop his brother or it would be another Reaver touchdown for sure. He looked up at the clock and saw that time was running out. If the Reavers scored again here, the game would be over. There would be no catching them.

Dunk charged straight at Dirk, who corrected his course to avoid his brother's path, angling toward the far sideline. Dunk changed his route as well, putting the two of them on a collision course well shy of the end zone.

When the two brothers reached each other, Dirk juked left, then right, in a vain attempt to throw off Dunk's tackle. Dunk, though, remembered his training. He kept his eyes on Dirk's waist, not his shoulders or feet, and he threw his arms wide to wrap them around his brother and bring him down.

Dunk hit Dirk hard enough to dent both armours. Dirk grunted and started to topple, but as he did he managed to get rid of the ball.

Dunk crushed Dirk to the ground. He smiled as he heard the air whoosh from his brother's lungs. He'd done his job well. He was a good Blood Bowl player, maybe even a great one, and he knew it.

The crowd erupted into a mind-numbing cheer, and Dunk wondered what had happened. He rolled off of Dirk and looked back toward the end zone to see Spinne standing there alone, holding the ball triumphantly over her head.

Dunk looked up at the Cabalvision images playing on the wall high over the end zone. On the replay, he saw Dirk's pass wobble along like a wounded duck until Spinne plucked it from the air and carried it the last few steps into the end zone.

The Reavers now had a two-touchdown lead. The game was over. The Hackers had lost.

'Sorry, Dunk,' Dirk said as he stood up and offered his brother a hand. 'The best team won.'

'Hey,' Dunk said wistfully, 'it's not all bad. We actually got to *play*. And at least now I can get the Gobbo to hand over Zauberer to take the blame for those killings.'

Spinne charged over and grabbed Dirk in a victorious embrace. 'We did it!' she screamed. 'Reavers win!' The crowd echoed her over and over as the rest of the Reavers rushed over to them and grabbed them up as they exulted over their triumph.

A large hand fell on Dunk's shoulder as he took off his helmet. 'Tried Dunk,' the ogre said as Dunk turned toward him. A tear as large as an apple fell from the creature's eye.

'It's all right, big guy,' Dunk said, patting M'Grash's arm. 'We did the best we could.' He blew out a big sigh. 'I guess there's always next year.'

As Dunk spoke, he looked over to the sidelines to see Blaque and Whyte waiting for him there. He flipped them a quick salute. 'Or, maybe not.'

Dunk started to make the long walk back to the Hackers dugout when someone grabbed his arm and whipped him around. It was Spinne. She wrapped her arms around him and planted the most incredible kiss Dunk had ever experienced square on his lips.

After a stunned moment, Dunk brought his arms up around Spinne and returned the kiss, his passion matching her own. The crowd bellowed its approval.

'Hi,' Dunk said as they broke their embrace. 'I think they like it.'

'Nothing like a little sex to spice up the violence,' Spinne said. Then, with a wink, she was gone, back to celebrate the Reavers' victory with her team.

'Wait!' Dunk said. 'Sex?' But she was too far away already to hear.

While Dunk stared after Spinne, Dirk came up and chucked him on the shoulder. 'Good game,' Dirk said. He stuck out his hand, and Dunk took it and pulled his brother into a back-thumping hug.

'By my count,' Dunk said, 'that last pass of yours broke Skragger's record.'

Dirk smirked. 'You know,' he said, slinging an arm around Dunk, 'I think you're right.'

'So,' Dunk said, 'what are we going to do about him?'

'Skragger?' Dirk said with a swagger. 'Against the Brothers Hoffnung? He doesn't stand a chance.'

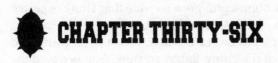 # CHAPTER THIRTY-SIX

DUNK STOOD ON the sidelines and looked up at the stage a horde of halflings had hauled into the centre of the field for the presentation of the Blood Bowl cup to the Reavers. The cup itself, a travelling trophy that stayed with the winning team for only a year at a time, was a mithril and gold cup covered with skulls and spikes. Dunk could have sworn that he saw the eye sockets of one of the skulls glowing with red malevolence, but he was too far away to be sure.

'Good work, kid,' a voice behind Dunk said. He turned to see Gunther the Gobbo standing there, a greasy, gap-toothed grin on his face, a furry bit of rat-on-a-stick still caught between his incisors. 'You just made me a fortune.'

'I'm sure,' Dunk said with a frown. He'd gotten what he thought he'd wanted, but it left him feeling hollow inside.

'No, kid, really,' the Gobbo said in a low voice.
'Didn't you ever wonder why the Reavers were trying
to lose so hard?' His eyes gleamed with daemonic
delight.

'Skragger threatened my brother,' Dunk said.

'Sure, sure,' the Gobbo said, grinning. 'Skragger's
been a Black Jersey from way back.'

Dunk blinked at that. 'You mean you wanted the
Reavers to lose?'

The Gobbo's grin grew so wide that Dunk expected
the top of his head to flip backward.

'You played both sides here, didn't you?' Dunk said
gaping at the grimy, flabby creature. 'You betrayed the
Black Jerseys to line your own pockets.'

'Think whatever you want to, kid,' the Gobbo said.
'I'll just say one thing: nothing pays like treachery.' He
patted Dunk on the arm and turned to leave. Before
he did, he said one last thing.

'By the way, as far as the GWs go, you're on your
own. Pleasure doing business with you, kid.'

Dunk's heart sank as he watched the bookie stroll
down the field to chat with Skragger, who stood fum-
ing in one of the end zones.

In the centre of the field, the Reavers accepted
the Blood Bowl cup. Dirk raised it high above his
head, and the crowd erupted with nearly insane
applause.

To Dunk, it seemed like a Cabalvision broadcast
from someplace far, far away. He felt a tiny hand
reach up and grab one of his. He looked down and
saw Slick smiling up at him. The halfling's happiness
tore at Dunk's misery, and he felt the corners of his
own mouth tugging upward.

'Give me some good news, Slick,' Dunk said. 'I could use some right now.'

'Well, since you asked so nicely, son, I'd be happy to.' The halfling rubbed his chin as he spoke, a sure sign he'd been up to something. 'While you were playing your heart out, I had a long conversation with Lästiges.'

'Selling the rights to my execution?'

'Of course not,' Slick said in mock horror. 'For those, I'd hold an auction with the Cabalvision networks. Something like that's too big for a sidelines deal.

'However, I did strike a deal with her. She gets the exclusive rights to your story, for this past season, that is. In exchange, she does me a small but vital favour that will help us all.'

Dunk squinted at the halfling. 'I have no idea what you're talking about, Slick, but I'm glad you're on my side.' He smiled as Slick trotted off to talk with Blaque and Whyte, who were standing at the entrance to the tunnel that led to the Hackers' locker room.

It was then that Dunk felt the tip of a knife prick his side. 'You little bastard,' a voice said in Dunk's ear. 'You ruined everything.'

Dunk's breath caught in his throat, and he said softly, 'Hi, Kur.'

The Hackers' injured thrower pulled the tip of his knife slowly from Dunk's kidney toward his spine. The rookie felt his blood well up under the blade's razor-sharp caress.

'Make a move, and I'll kill you where you stand,' Kur said.

'Had a rough day?' Dunk said with false concern.

'I'm with a group called the Black Jerseys,' Kur said. 'We run things around here. No one wins a Blood Bowl without our say so. And you've messed that up.'

'My deepest apologies,' Dunk said. As he finished, he felt the knife jab into his skin, just a little, enough to make him want to jump. Instead he gritted his teeth.

'Don't you dare mock me,' Kur said. 'You think you're so damned clever. Well, this is the end of the road, smart guy. The Hackers were supposed to win today. I was supposed to lead us to victory. And you bollocksed it all up.'

'So now you'll kill me with that little knife of yours, just like Ramen-Tut?'

'Just like I've killed dozens of players. Scores, maybe, you high-bred moron. You're just another notch on the crest of my helmet. I don't spend my nights out drinking with 'friends' like that post of an ogre of yours. I'm out there carving out my future, my legacy, in blood.

'The best part of it,' Kur said in Dunk's ear, 'the very best part, is that I know you had nothing to do with all those murders.' He started to snigger. 'Did you, "killer"?'

It was then that Dunk realised that the entire stadium had gone dead quiet. He looked out at the Reavers and saw Dirk and Spinne staring back at him, their jaws gone slack. Everyone else on the stage was gaping at something above the end zone.

Dunk glanced in that direction and breathed a smile. 'Care to repeat that for me again?' he said to Kur. 'I don't think the people in the cheap seats quite heard you.'

Dunk felt Kur turn his head to see what the rookie meant. Dunk knew that the sight of the two of them displayed on the jumbo wall looming over the end zone would stun the injured thrower for a moment. That was when he made his move.

Dunk took a half step away from Kur and then spun back, slamming a spiked elbow pad into the man's face. The unarmoured Kur never had a chance. The spike took him right between the eyes and plunged straight into his brain. He was dead before Dunk could shake his wide-eyed corpse off his arm.

The crowd went nuts.

Dunk looked up and saw a floating golden ball looking straight at him. He smiled at it as Lästiges stepped up toward him.

'That's quite a revelation, Dunk,' the reporter said to him, a broad smile on her crimson-painted lips. 'I suppose this puts the facts about your case in a new light.'

Dunk glanced behind him and saw Blaque and Whyte hauling Kur's body away.

'I hope so, Lästiges,' Dunk said breathing a massive sigh of relief. 'I just want to say thanks to everyone, to my coach Pegleg, to my agent Slick, to the rest of the Hackers, and to all the fans for all their support. It's been a hell of a year.'

'Is this a retirement speech?' Lästiges asked, mock concern marring her smooth brow.

Dunk shook his head. 'Pretty much the opposite, actually. Dunk Hoffnung is here to stay!' he roared up at the crowd, and the crowed roared back. *'I love this game!'*

* * *

LATER, IN THE Hackers' locker room, after everyone else had left, Dunk gave Slick a massive hug that threatened to squish the halfling. 'You,' he said, 'are the best agent ever!'

Slick gave a little bow after he extricated himself from Dunk's grasp. 'What have I been telling you since we met?'

'All those interviews kept us here forever,' Dunk said as he slammed his locker shut. 'We need to hustle if we're going to make the team dinner.'

'You don't think they'll all want to hang you for losing the game?' Slick asked.

'We played the best we could,' Dunk said. 'We shouldn't have even been in that game. We wouldn't have been without the Black Jerseys rigging it. The Reavers were the better team.'

'And there's always next year,' Slick added.

'There's always next year,' Dunk agreed, smiling in spite of himself. 'I tell you, losing never felt so good.'

'It palls pretty quickly, kid. Take it from me.'

Dunk and Slick turned to see the Gobbo slither in from the tunnel to the Hackers' dugout. The creature wore a murderous frown.

'You cost me today, kid,' the Gobbo said, waving a fat finger at Dunk.

'I thought you got what you wanted,' Dunk said evenly. 'The Hackers lost.'

'Sure,' the Gobbo said, throwing his hands in the air. 'Today was a good day for me, but with Kur blabbing on Cabalvision about the Black Jerseys, I'm ruined! I'll never be able to use them again!'

'You double-crossed me,' Dunk said. 'Suck it up.'

'Come on, kid,' the Gobbo said, 'you don't think I was serious about that, do you? A little joke among friends.'

'Not funny.'

'Well, if we're not friends anymore, I suppose it's only fair that I tell the GWs all about your ogre friend's killings. Or I could tell the Colleges of Magic about how he destroyed their dungeon. Wizards don't appreciate things like that the way you and I do.' The stunted creature stood staring defiantly at Dunk and Slick, confident he'd played the last, winning card.

Dunk stalked toward the Gobbo and thrust a thick finger into the creature's soft chest. 'You breathe a word about M'Grash to anyone, try to destroy me or any of my friends, including my brother and I'll cru-cify you.'

The Gobbo sneered up at the Blood Bowl player. 'How do you think you're going to do that?'

'There are still a lot of Black Jerseys out there,' Dunk said as he leaned over to growl into the Gobbo's pit-ted face. 'If they learn you rigged the Blood Bowl to cut them out of the winnings, there won't be a place in the Old World you can hide.'

'You wouldn't,' the Gobbo started, then caught him-self mid-sentence. He snorted angrily as he glared into Dunk's unforgiving eyes. 'Yes. Yes, you would.'

'Get out of here,' Dunk said. 'If I so much as smell you again, I'll beat you into a puddle.'

The Gobbo gasped, offended by the threat, but he turned and skulked off towards the tunnel again. As he reached the exit, he looked back and said, 'You owe me, kid. You owe me big. And Gunther the Gobbo always collects his debts!'

CHAPTER THIRTY-SEVEN

'DID YOU SEE the look on his face?' Dirk asked. 'Just before you killed him? When he looked up at the Cabalvision and saw what everyone else in the stadium was watching. Priceless!'

Dunk shook his head and smiled sidelong at Spinne, who sat there at a private table in the Skinned Cat with them and Slick as they held their own celebration of the day's events. 'I'll have to look for it on the commemorative recording,' he said wistfully.

'Be sure you get it on Daemonic Visual Display,' Dirk said. 'I picked up a player this year, and the DVDs are just amazing.'

Spinne put her arm around Dunk and gave him a hug. 'You did great today,' she said. 'I was impressed.'

'Look who's talking,' Dunk said. 'That catch you made to finish off the game? Incredible. I'll watch that part of the recording over and over.'

'You should watch how I got rid of the ball,' Dirk said, waving a half-eaten turkey leg at his brother. 'You might finally learn something about how the game is played.'

'Next year, Dirk,' Dunk said between hearty swallows of his Killer Genuine Draft. 'Next year. Assuming the Hackers are willing to take me back.'

'And why wouldn't they?' Slick asked, his concern exaggerated by the vast quantities of Teinekin Beer he'd already consumed. 'We have a contract, for one.'

'In case you hadn't noticed,' Dunk said, 'I missed about a quarter of the season. On top of that, Coach nearly killed me during half-time for trying to throw the game.'

'Tish-tosh,' Slick said. 'Pegleg saw how you played your heart out in the second half. That quick score you made when you got back onto the field had the entire team cheering for you, even the scrubs.'

'Really?' Dunk said, slightly amazed. He raised his stein for a quick toast. 'I guess there's hope.'

'Besides which, aside from any meetings in the Majors, of course, I think I can help Pegleg arrange for a few grudge matches between Hackers and Reavers next year,' Slick said. 'But they'll only really work if you two Hoffnungs are on the teams. We'll negotiate the Cabalvision rights separately and rake in a fortune. Who wouldn't want to see it?'

The laughter from the four friends ended abruptly as the door to their private room smashed inward off its hinges. They spun about in their chairs to see Skragger framed there in the doorway, crushing the throat of the hapless serving girl who'd tried to stop him. He dropped the girl's lifeless body to the floor and stepped into the room.

'Blew deal,' the black orc growled as he pointed a crooked finger at Dirk. 'Broke record. Gotta pay.'

Dunk, Dirk, and Spinne leapt up from the table while Slick scooted under it. Dunk glanced around the room and saw that it was a dead end but for a single window that looked down over a forty-foot drop. He wasn't quite ready to try that, yet.

Dunk flipped over the table, placing it between Skragger and the rest. Slick squeaked like a mouse as he found himself exposed. He scrambled around to one edge of the overturned table to get a better view.

'There are three of us,' Dirk said nervously. 'We can take him, right?'

Skragger strode forward and kicked the table into splinters with a single blow. Slick skittered back against a wall and then made a dive for the now-open door.

'Maybe not,' Spinne said, 'but we'll go down fighting.' As she spoke, she stepped up and levelled a bone-crushing roundhouse kick to Skragger's chest.

Skragger took two steps back from the force of the blow and smiled, showing all his tusks and broken, rotten, vicious teeth. Spinne grabbed her broken toes and hopped around, yelling, 'Ow! Ow! Ow!'

Dunk stepped up, ready to take on the black orc, but his brother breezed by him and slammed into Skragger like a blitzer taking down a thrower who'd held on to the ball too long. Skragger grunted as Dirk's pumping legs drove him backward into the wall next to the door.

Once they'd come to a stop, Skragger balled his fists together and brought them down on Dirk's back like a warhammer on an anvil. Dirk collapsed at Skragger's feet, and the black orc kicked him aside with a steel-booted toe to the ribs.

Dunk glanced back at the window and gauged his chances. A fall from the window would likely mean a broken leg at least, probably worse. At the moment, though, it seemed like staying in the room with Skragger would be certain death. Though if he jumped, he'd be abandoning Dirk and Spinne to the black orc's non-existent mercies. Looking at his brother and then at Spinne as she hobbled over next to him, he realised he couldn't do it.

'Your turn,' Spinne said to him.

'Can I pass on that?' Dunk said as he watched Skragger crack his neck and knuckles to prepare for his next challenger.

'It's you or me,' Spinne said, looking at her damaged foot.

'Since you put it that way,' Dunk said. He leaned over and gave Spinne a tender kiss on her soft, sweet lips. 'Wish me luck.'

'Awwww,' Skragger said. 'Saying goodbye? Don't. All be in hell tonight!'

Dunk strode up to Skragger and feinted left. The black orc went for it, and Dunk pulled back and levelled his best right hook into the creature's jaw, putting everything he had into it.

Dunk felt a tusk break against his fist, but before Skragger could spit it out, he hit him again, this time a hammering blow to the belly. The black orc bent over double, and Dunk smashed his right into him once again.

Dunk pounded at Skragger mercilessly, keeping the black orc on defence the entire time. As he rained blow after blow into the murderous veteran, Spinne cheered him on. Her voice put new energy into his arms, and he brutalised the orc until the skin peeled from his bloodied knuckles and he felt like he might never be able to raise his arms again.

Dunk staggered backwards, exhausted, straight into Spinne's arms. She propped him up as best she could with her injured foot.

'How'm I doing?' Dunk panted.

'Looked good from here,' Spinne said. Then she gasped as the blood-covered Skragger stretched himself back up to his full height and favoured her with an evil smile.

'Finished?' Skragger asked Dunk. It was all Dunk could do to just goggle at the creature. The black orc growled as he stepped forward. 'Will be, soon.'

Spinne let Dunk slide to the ground, then stepped between him and the black orc. 'Come get some,' she said to him.

Skragger growled and lashed out at the catcher. She ducked beneath his blow and then came up and popped him in the throat. He stumbled back, coughing hard and clutching at his throat.

Spinne stepped in for the kill, and the black orc's clawed hand reached out and snagged her around the neck. Keeping her at arm's length, he pulled her up off her feet and began to squeeze the life from her. She tried desperately to pull his fingers from her throat as her legs kicked feebly beneath her, but it was like trying to pull apart an iron band.

Dunk knew he had to do something or Spinne would be dead in seconds. He glanced over at Dirk and saw that his brother was rousing but would be far too late. Throwing caution to the wind, he vaulted up onto his haunches and charged straight at Skragger's legs.

Dunk hit the black orc right in the knees and heard one of the joints crack. Skragger howled in pain and hurled Spinne against the far wall, where she narrowly avoided spilling out through the high window.

The black orc's leg gave way, and he slammed down atop Dunk, crushing the air from him. With another howl no less bloodthirsty than the last, Skragger pulled Dunk from under him and wrapped both hands around the rookies' throat.

'Dead!' the orc snarled. 'Now!'

The world around Dunk seemed to pull away from him as if he was looking at it down a long, dark tunnel. He knew that in a moment the light at its end would flicker and go out forever.

'Put that man down!' a voice demanded from the doorway.

Dunk felt the grip on his throat slacken, and the world became bright again. He gulped for air as he turned to see who had come to his rescue.

There, framed in the doorway, stood Slick, backed up by Pegleg and Cavre. Dunk could see the rest of his team-mates peering over their coach's shoulder as he levelled his legendary hook at the black orc.

'You have two choices, Mr. Skragger,' Pegleg snarled as he stepped into the room, the rest of the Hackers following him into the cramped space. 'You can try to take us all on, in which case I'll gut you with my hook while the others hold you down.'

'Or?' Skragger said as he let Dunk slip to the ground and stood to face the wrath of a full Blood Bowl team.

'You can take the easy way out,' Pegleg said, nodding at the window.

Skragger nodded as he considered the scowling faces of the players facing him. Then he noticed Dunk tapping him on the leg.

'Take them on,' Dunk croaked as he glared into the black orc's shaking eyes. 'I want to see you get torn apart.'

'Not today,' Skragger sneered. He turned and sprinted three long steps toward the window. He dove through it as if he was stretching out to reach his last end zone and then disappeared over the edge. He didn't scream, but a moment after he left the room there was a sickening splat.

Cavre came over to help Dunk to his feet while Pegleg did the same for Spinne. Slick directed Karsten and Henrik in getting Dirk steady again. M'Grash watched the whole thing from the doorway, too large to join the others in the smallish room.

'I thought we might have lost you there, Dunk,' Cavre said. 'When Slick told us Skragger was trying to kill you, I thought we'd never get here in time.'

'Yes,' Pegleg said, a hint of admiration colouring his voice. 'You did well in keeping the orc busy until we could get here. Many would have given up before then.'

'I... I didn't know you were coming at all,' Dunk said.

'Come now, son,' Slick said, 'you didn't think I'd just run off to let you die.'

'The thought crossed *my* mind,' Spinne said, now sitting on a chair that Gigia had shoved under her.

'You were the last people I expected to see come through that door,' Dirk said, stretching his back as Guillermo checked him for a concussion.

'And why would that be, Mr. Hoffnung?' Pegleg said. 'You're a Hacker, and the Hackers back their own.'

'Really?' Dunk said to the coach. 'I wasn't sure you'd want me any more.'

Pegleg smiled warmly. 'We can always use someone with your talents and love of the game. Besides which, we only have just over two months before the start of the *Spike! Magazine* tournament.'

Dunk shook his head as he came over to put his arm around Spinne. He smiled at Slick and Dirk and then up at Pegleg as he said, 'It never ends, does it?'

'It never does, Dunk.' Pegleg flashed the rookie a broad, gold-toothed grin under his yellow tricorn hat. 'And that's the best part.'

A GUIDE TO BLOOD BOWL

Being a volume of instruction for rookies and beginners of Nuffle's sacred game.

(Translated by Andreas Halle of Middenheim)

NUFFLE'S SACRED NUMBER

Let's start with the basics. To play Blood Bowl you need two warrior sects each led by a priest. In the more commonly used Blood Bowl terminology this means you need two teams of fearless psychotics (we also call them 'players') led by a coach, who is quite often a hoary old ex-player more psychotic than all of his players put together.

The teams face each other on a ritualised battle-field known as a pitch or field. The field is marked out in white chalk lines into several different areas. One line separates the pitch in two through the middle dividing the field into each team's 'half'. The line itself is known as the 'line of scrimmage' and is often the scene of some brutal fighting, especially at the beginning and halfway points of the game. At the back of each team's half of the field is a further dividing line that separates the backfield from the end zone. The end zone is where an opposing team can score a 'touchdown' - more on that later.

Teams generally consist of between twelve to sixteen players. However, as first extolled by Roze-el, Nuffle's sacred number is eleven, which means only a maximum of eleven players from each team may be on the field at the same time. It's worth noting that many teams have tried to break this sacred convention in the past, particularly goblin teams (orcs too, but that's usually because they can't count rather than any malevolent intent), but Nuffle has always seen fit to punish those who do.

TOUCHDOWNS AND ALL THAT MALARKEY

The aim of the game is to carry, throw, kick and generally move an inflated animal bladder coated in leather and - quite often - spikes, across the field into the opposing team's end zone. Of course, the other team is trying to do the same thing. Once the inflated bladder, also known as the ball, has been carried or caught in the opposing team's end zone, a 'touchdown' has been scored. Traditionally the crowd then goes wild, though the reactions of the fans vary from celebration if it was their team that just scored to anger if their team have conceded. The player who has scored will also have his moment of jubilation and much celebratory hugging with fellow team mates will ensue, although a bear hug from an Ogre, even if his intention is that of mutual happiness, is best avoided! The team that scores the most touchdowns within the allotted timeframe is deemed the winner.

The game lasts about two hours and is split into two segments unsurprisingly called 'the first half' and 'the second half'. The first half starts after both teams have walked onto the pitch and taken their positions, usually accompanied by much fanfare and cheering from the fans. The team captains meet in the centre of the pitch with the 'ref' (more on him later) to perform the start-of-the-game ritual known as 'the toss'. A coin is flipped in the air and one of the captains will call 'orcs' or 'eagles'. Whoever wins the toss gets the choice of 'kicking' or 'receiving'. Kicking teams will kick the ball to the receiving teams. Once the ball has been kicked the whistle is blown and the first half will begin. The second half begins in much the same way except that the kicking team at the beginning of the first half will now become the receiving team and vice-versa.

Violence is encouraged to gain possession, keep and move the ball, although different races and teams will try different methods and varying degrees of hostility. The fey elves, for instance, will often try pure speed to collect the ball and avoid the other team's players. Orc and Chaos teams will take a more direct route of overpowering the opposing team and trundling down the centre of the field almost daring their opponents to stop them.

Rookies reading this maybe confused as to why I haven't mentioned the use of weapons yet. This is because in Blood Bowl Nuffle decreed that one's own body is the only weapon one needs to play the game. Over the years this hasn't stopped teams using this admittedly rather loose wording to maximum effect and is the reason why a player's armour is more likely than not covered in sharp protruding spikes with blades and large knuckle-dusters attached to gauntlets. Other races and teams often 'forget' about this basic principle and just ignore Roze-el's teachings on the matter. Dwarfs and goblins (yes, them again) are the usual suspects, although this is not exclusively their domain. The history of Blood Bowl is littered with the illegal use of weapons and the many devious contraptions bought forward by the dwarfs and goblins, ranging from monstrous machines such as the dwarf death-roller to the no-less-dangerous chainsaw.

THE PSYCHOS... I MEAN PLAYERS

As I've already mentioned, there are many ways to get the ball from one end of the field to the other. Equally, there are as many ways to stop the ball from moving towards a team's end zone. A Blood Bowl player, to an extent, needs to be a jack-of-all-trades – as equally quick on the offensive as well as being able to defend. This doesn't mean that there aren't any specialists in the sport, far from it – a Blood Bowl player needs to specialise in one of the many positions if he wishes to rise above the humble lineman. Let's look at the more common positions:

Blitzers: These highly-skilled players are usually the stars of the game, combining strength and skill with great speed and flexibility. All the most glamorous Blood Bowl players are blitzers, since they are always at the heart of the action and doing very impressive things! Their usual job is to burst a hole through their opponents' lines, and then run with the ball to score. Team captains are usually blitzers, and all of them, without exception, have egos the size of a halfling's appetite.

Throwers: There is more to Blood Bowl than just grabbing the ball and charging full tilt at the other side (though this has worked for most teams at one time or another). If you can get a player on the other side of your opponents' line, why not simply toss the ball to him and cut out all that unnecessary bloodshed? This, of course, is where the special thrower comes in! These guys are usually lightly armoured (preferring to dodge a tackle rather than be flattened by it).

Throwers of certain races have also been known to launch other things than just the ball. For decades now, an accepted tactic of orc, goblin and even halfling teams is to throw their team-mates downfield. This is usually done by the larger members of said teams such as ogres, trolls and in the case of the halflings, treemen. Of course this tactic is not without risk. Whilst the bigger players are strong it doesn't necessarily mean they are accurate. As regular fans know, goblins make a reassuring 'splat' sound as they hit the ground or stadium wall head-first – much to the joy of the crowd! Trolls are notoriously stupid with memory spans that would shame a goldfish. So a goblin or snotling about to be hurtled across the pitch by his trollish team mate will often find itself heading for the troll's gaping maw instead as the monster forgets what he's holding and decides to have a snack!

Catchers: And of course if you are throwing the ball, it would be nice if there was someone at the other end to catch it! This is where the specialist catcher comes in. Lightly armoured for speed, they are adept at dodging around slower opponents and heading for the open field ready for a long pass to arrive. The best catcher of all time is generally reckoned to be the legendary Tarsh Surehands of the otherwise fairly repulsive skaven team, the Skaven Scramblers. With his two heads and four arms, the mutant ratman plainly had something of an advantage.

Blockers: If one side is trying to bash its way through the opposing team's lines, you will often see the latter's blockers come into action to stop them. These lumbering giants are often slow and dim-witted, but they have the size and power to stop show-off blitzers from getting any further up the field! Black orcs, ogres and trolls make especially good blockers, but this fact has hampered the chances of teams like the Oldheim Ogres, who, with nothing but blockers and linemen in their team, have great trouble actually scoring a touchdown!

Linemen: While a good deal of attention is paid to the various specialist players, every true Blood Bowl fan would agree that the players who do most of the hard work are the ordinary linemen. These are the guys who get bashed out of the way while trying to stop a hulking great ogre from sacking their thrower, who are pushed out of the way when their flashy blitzer sets his sights on the end zone, or who get beaten and bruised by the linemen of the opposite side while the more gifted players skip about scoring touchdowns. 'Moaning like a lineman' is a common phrase in Blood Bowl circles for a bad complainer, but if it wasn't for the linemen whingeing about their flashier team-mates, the newspapers would often have nothing to fill their sports pages with!

DA REFS

Blood Bowl has often been described, as 'nearly-organised chaos' by its many critics. Blood Bowl's admirers emphatically agree with the critics then again they don't like to play up the 'nearly-organised' bit, in fact some quite happily just describe it as 'chaos'. However, it is widely accepted that you do need someone in charge of the game's proceedings and to enforce the games rules or else it wouldn't be Blood Bowl at all. Again, this point is often lost on some fans who would quite happily just come and spectate/participate in a big fight. In any case, the person and/or creature in charge of a game is known as 'the ref'. The ref, in his traditional kit of zebra furs, has a very difficult job to do. You have to ask yourself what kind mind accepts this kind of responsibility especially when the general Blood Bowl viewing public rate refs far below tax collectors, traffic wardens and sewer inspectors in their estimation.

Of course some refs revile in the notoriety and are as psychopathic as the players themselves. Max 'Kneecap' Mittleman would never issue a yellow or red card but simply disembowel the offending player. It is also fair to say that most (if not all) refs are not the bastions of honesty and independence they would have you believe. In fact the Referees and Allied Rulekeepers Guild has strict bribery procedures and union established rates. Although teams may not always want to bribe a ref – especially when sheer intimidation can be far cheaper.

THAT'S THE BASICS
Now I've covered the rudimentary points of how to play Blood Bowl it's worth going over some of the basic plays you'll see in most games of one variation

or another. Remember, it's not just about the fighting; you have to score at some point as well!

The Cage: Probably the most basic play in the game yet it's the one halfling teams still can't get right. This involves surrounding the ball carrier with bodyguards and then moving the whole possession up field. Once within yards of the team's end zone the ball carrier will explode from his protective cocoon and sprint across the line. Not always good against elf teams who have an annoying knack of dodging into the cage and stealing the ball away, still you should see the crowd's rapture when an elf does misstep and he's close-lined to the floor by a sneering orc.

The Chuck: The second most basic play, although it does require the use of a semi-competent thrower, does rule a large proportion of teams out from the start. Blockers on the 'line of scrimmage' will open a gap for the team's receivers to run through, and once they are in the opposing team's back field the thrower will lob the ball to them. Provided one of the catchers can catch it, all that remains is a short run into the opposing end zone for a touchdown. The survival rate of a lone catcher in the enemy's half is obviously not great so it's important to get as many catchers up field as possible. The more catchers a team employs, the more chances at least one of them will remain standing to complete the pass.

The Chain: A particular favourite of blitzers everywhere. Players position themselves at different stages up field. The ball is then quickly passed from player to player in a series of short passes until the blitzer on the end of the chain can wave to the crowd and gallop into the end zone. A broken link in the chain can balls this up (excuse the pun), giving the opposing team an opportunity to intercept the ball.

The Kill-em-all!: Favoured by dwarf teams and those that lack a certain finesse. It works on the principle that if there isn't anyone left in the opposing team, then who's going to stop you from scoring? The receiving team simply hides the ball in its half and proceeds to maul, break and kill the opposition. Chaos teams are particularly good at this. When there is less than a third of the opposing team left, the ball will slowly make its way up field. The downside is that some teams can get so engrossed in the maiming they simply run out of time to score. Nevertheless it's a fan favourite and is here to stay.

ABOUT THE AUTHOR

Matt Forbeck has worked full-time in the adventure game industry for over 15 years. He has designed collectible card games, roleplaying games, miniatures games, and board games, and has written short fiction, comic books, and novels. His previous novel is the critically acclaimed *Secret of the Spiritkeeper* for Wizards of the Coast.

Blood Bowl is his first novel for the Black Library; its sequel, *Dead Ball* will be along soon.

READ TILL YOU BLEED
DO YOU HAVE THEM ALL?

WWW.BLACKLIBRARY.COM